Do:

... take the wheel as often as you can

... develop a system for keeping your lies straight

... hold out for a happy ending

...KILL THE COMPETITION!

L A

Out of the Ordinary

Belinda opened her mouth to scream, but she couldn't draw enough air into her lungs. Gasping, she slammed down the trunk lid. She sobbed into her hand, looking around wildly to see if anyone else had seen what was in the trunk of her car.

But no, it was a lovely, quiet day in the Atlanta suburbs—birds sang and, in a yard across the street, children jumped on a trampoline and screamed with laughter. Blood rushed to her head and she felt a faint coming on. She couldn't faint, she told herself. She had to summon help. She bent at the waist until the tingling in her brain subsided enough to stand. Walk. *Run* to her house.

She skidded into the foyer. Her mind raced, the people she knew spinning like a roulette wheel. Who to call? The wheel slowed and the ball settled on Wade Alexander.

Her hands shook as she punched in his number. The phone rang once, twice.

"Alexander."

"Wade, this is Belinda Hennessey." Her heart pounded in her ears.

"What's wrong?"

"You t-told me to call you if anything unusual happened."

"Right."

"S-something unusual happened."

Books by
Stephanie Bond

KILL THE COMPETITION
I THINK I LOVE YOU
GOT YOUR NUMBER
OUR HUSBAND

STEPHANIE BOND

Kill the Competition

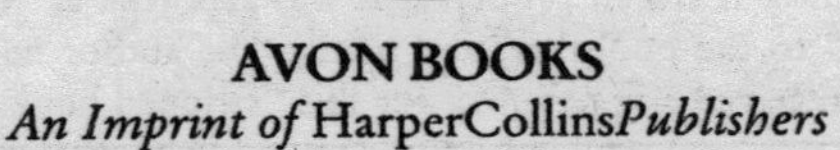

AVON BOOKS
An Imprint of HarperCollins*Publishers*

This is a work of fiction. Names, characters, places, and incidents are products of the author's imagination or are used fictitiously and are not to be construed as real. Any resemblance to actual events, locales, organizations, or persons, living or dead, is entirely coincidental.

AVON BOOKS
An Imprint of HarperCollins*Publishers*
10 East 53rd Street
New York, New York 10022-5299

ISBN: 0-06-053983-6
www.avonromance.com

First Avon Books paperback printing: November 2003

Printed in the U.S.A.

10 9 8 7 6 5 4 3 2 1

Chapter 1

Belinda Hennessey opened the shower door and leaned out, hair dripping, her soapy ear piqued for the voice of the predominant man in her life—although granted, the fact that she'd never even met the guy was a tad on the pathetic side.

From the clock radio on the crowded vanity, a sexy, Southern-bred accent reeled into the room over the whir of helicopter blades. "Traffic is jammin' up on I-85 southbound below the I-285 junction due to a three-car accident in the rightmost lane. Southbound Peachtree Industrial and Buford Highway are feelin' the effect, so my advice is to hop over to Georgia 400 while it's still a speed limit ride, which won't be for long." He whistled low. "If you're comin' into Atlanta from the northeast this mornin', I hope you're not runnin' late. I'm Talkin' Tom Trainer for the MIXX 100 FM traffic report."

Oh, that voice. Belinda shivered, then glanced at the time and swore softly. She yanked a towel around her, made wet tracks to the bedroom, and let the ho-hum carpet soak up most of the water dripping down her legs. With one hand she ran the towel over the rest of her while flipping through hangers in her closet. Her shoulder muscles still twinged from an "iron arms" session in the gym—a degrading experience she had allowed herself to be talked into in lieu of lunch a couple of days ago. According to a fitness report on the radio, now that she had entered her thirties, she was losing muscle mass at an alarming rate.

Yes indeed, it was a fine time to be single again.

When her fingers touched a knee-length gray jersey dress, she pulled out the garment and tossed it onto the unmade bed. An indignant yowl sounded from beneath the leopard print comforter, and Downey's black head appeared.

"Sorry," Belinda offered. "I'm running late."

Downey blinked. The feline's morning disposition reminded her of the man who'd given her the cat, her ex, Vince Whittaker. She hesitated to refer to Vince as her ex-*husband*, since their marriage had lasted a mere six hours. Downey was the best thing to come out of that train wreck, despite her current slit-eyed disdain.

"I know—I shouldn't be late on my first day driving the car pool."

The shower was her downfall. This town house was the first place she'd ever lived in that had an adequate hot water heater, so she leaned under the spray every morning until her skin was just short of a good scald. The indulgence was heavenly, but the trade-off was hell.

With the agility of a hurdler, she leapt into underwear, panty hose, dress, jacket, and pumps, then gave her unremarkable auburn hair a one-minute blast from a blow dryer. A touch of translucent powder, mascara, and lipstick would have to pass for makeup; her cheeks were still pink enough from the shower to skip the blush. There wasn't time to make the bed, although she knew she'd be plagued with thoughts of dropping dead before the day ended and her mother's *tsk, tsk* when her parents came to gather her personal effects. *"I knew this move to Atlanta so soon after the you-know-what was too much for her, Franklin."* (Her mother refused to make direct references to the reneged wedding.) *"Look, she didn't even make her bed—I heard on the* Today *show that untidiness is a sure sign of depression."*

Little did her mother know, she didn't have time to indulge in a good cathartic bout of depression. Her new job was consuming every waking hour, and for that, she was eternally grateful . . . because the urge to wallow was so close to the surface. Especially today. Since opening her eyes to stare at the white fluted globe covering the lightbulb in her bedroom ceiling (over the past two months she'd grown to hate that globe), she hadn't been able to shake the sense of impending doom. The last time she'd felt this out of sorts had been on her wedding day.

Yilk.

She dropped an earring twice, poked it in as she jogged down the stairs to the foyer, then dashed into the kitchen to grab an instant breakfast drink from the fridge. Her briefcase sat open on the table, surrounded by accounting spreadsheets. She shoved the papers inside and slammed down the lid, catching her thumb and bruising the nail.

Gritting back a foul word, she checked Downey's water, knuckled the cat's regal pouting head, and managed to slide behind the wheel of her clover green Honda Civic just after 6:30 A.M., only five minutes late. But getting started a measly five minutes late in the Atlanta commute could mean the difference between arriving in time to prepare for her 8:30 A.M. meeting, and tearing into the meeting already in progress with murmured apologies to her scowling boss, Margo. And "tardy" wasn't the opinion she wanted the woman to take into her first performance evaluation, which was mere days away. She'd worked long hours for the Archer Furniture Company in the hopes of getting a raise that would put her on the same earning level of her previous financial position in Cincinnati.

She thought of the sliding balance in her savings account and sighed. Everything in Atlanta was more expensive than it was in Cincinnati. Carpooling was only one of the cost-saving measures she'd adopted since her impromptu move. If she could've gotten a refund on a gently worn wedding gown, she would own a couch—not to mention a television that worked more often than only when it rained. But seating for one was adequate for the time being, and since it was June and perennially sunny, she'd grown accustomed to listening to the radio. Besides, one of the girls in the car pool kept everyone abreast of television shows to help pass the long-suffering ride from suburbia into the city and the reverse trek at the end of the day. Living vicariously through the amorous women on *The Single Files* was a safe substitute for an actual social life—Belinda prayed the show would be renewed for the next decade or so.

As she backed out of the one-car garage in the early morning dusk, a horn blared. Her neighbor, Perry Ponytail, grinned and waved from his late model SUV in the driveway two doors down. The man's last name was actually a long word with few vowels that started with a P, but his distinctive hairstyle—a prematurely slick-bald crown combined with a sparse six-inch ponytail—conjured up a more memorable surname. The toothy construction worker had been trying to get her to go out with him since the day she'd moved in, but so far she had managed to outmaneuver him. Even if the man had been more appealing, to say that Vince had left a bad taste in her mouth would be an understatement of gigantic proportions.

Men were . . . unnecessary.

She gave her neighbor a three-finger wave, then backed out onto the street and zipped past him before he could flag her down.

Meadow Gate subdivision (strangely, no meadow and no gate) was a pleasing blend of tasteful vinyl-siding homes, modern synthetic stucco town houses, and cheery faux-stone-patio homes. The agreeable landscape, however, was negated by the fact that residents were forced to turn left at the mouth of the entrance onto Peachtree Parkway, a zoomily busy north-south thoroughfare, without the benefit of a traffic light.

Stifling a groan, she chained onto the line of cars whose occupants waited for either a break in the traffic, a kind driver to yield, or the nerve to gun their way across three lanes of traffic. All of them, she knew, were cursing their real estate brokers and landlords for not warning them of this dangerous little aggravation. There seemed to be no good solution to the vehicle snarls created by the population explosion in Atlanta. Belinda herself had considered horseback before one of the women from the office had asked her last week to join their car pool.

And while she was grateful for the chance to get to know three of her female coworkers, and for their company to make the interminable commute more bearable, driving the car pool for the first time on the day she needed to arrive early for her boss's meeting smacked of poor planning. She blew her bangs in the air. Hormones? Nerves? Fear? Insecurity? For some reason her body was on heightened alert. Prickly, clumsy, jittery, susceptible. She stuck her throbbing thumb in her mouth and considered leaving it there for a good, comforting suck. With her life in such a state of disarray, she wasn't feeling very grown-up these days.

Perry Ponytail pulled in behind her and honked cheerfully. Belinda flashed a tight smile in the rearview mirror, then locked her doors and turned up the radio, hoping for another dose of the sexy-throated traffic reporter. It was a mild case of celebrity worship, she knew, but his voice on the radio had been the first friendly sound she'd heard when she'd driven into the engorged, alien city, and she . . . *appreciated* him.

"Whew-we, folks, forget what I said about Georgia 400 southbound! Somebody dropped a *commode* in the road at the Northridge exit and caused a twelve-car pileup across all lanes. No one behind this clogged-up mess is goin' anywhere for a loooong while. This is Talkin' Tom Trainer for the MIXX 100 FM traffic report."

She cringed for the unfortunate commuters trapped in the mishap, but the incident was forgotten when a sympathetic driver on the parkway stopped and allowed the entire queue of cars to merge while the northbound lanes were clear. She would've kissed the man full on the lips if she could have, but she settled for an enthusiastic wave of thanks before assuming her spot in the creeping line of cars that extended as far as she could see.

Anxiety coated the inside of her stomach as she anticipated the next sixty-plus minutes of bumper-to-bumper traffic. She checked the security of her seat belt and planted her hands on the steering wheel at ten o'clock and two o'clock, Driver's Ed style. Visibility would be better once the sun had risen fully, but for now, a couple of seconds of distraction equaled an insurance deductible she couldn't afford.

She flipped on her right signal and began edging over to the rightmost lane. Perry Ponytail disappeared into the sea of hoods and headlights behind her. After counting three stoplights and verifying the name of the street, she turned into Libby Janes's subdivision. Stalwart brick-on-basement homes, sloping yards, palladium windows, attached two-and-a-half-car garages—the kind of home she and Vince had aspired to own. They'd spent Sunday afternoons going to open houses while Vince had amassed a filing cabinet full of house plans and names of mortgage companies. Since he was saving for their down payment, she'd volunteered to foot the wedding expenses. As it turned out, chicken kiev hadn't been the wisest investment for her nest egg. And if there was a God, Vince's spanking-new ranch home was parked on a starving termite colony.

Libby's house was a two-story, taupe-colored monstrosity with an unkempt yard and lights blazing in every window. Belinda pulled into the driveway, dimmed her headlights, and lightly tapped the horn. After a minute, she cracked open her canned breakfast and yielded to the dread building in her stomach.

Margo would expect her to have completed the valuation for the mom-and-pop furniture manufacturer being championed for acquisition, even though her boss hadn't e-mailed the final figures she needed until 10:30 last night. If she were a suspicious person, she might suspect that Margo was setting her up to fail in front of Juneau

Archer, the elusive owner who was supposed to put in an appearance at this morning's meeting. Her boss had a reputation for being competitive—and unpredictable. Around the watercooler, people called her Manic Margo—and worse. Belinda hadn't exactly clicked with the woman, but she was willing to accommodate the mood swings in return for that handy little paycheck every two weeks. So it wasn't the world's most exciting job—she still wasn't about to fail. She really needed this starting-over thing to pan out.

Belinda puffed out her cheeks and checked her watch. Perhaps she should knock on the door? She hadn't yet mastered car pool protocol.

Suddenly the front door burst open and Libby appeared, pleasingly plump in a brown stretch skirt, her bottle-blond hair a helmet of pink sponge rollers. Libby always did her hair in the car, even if she was driving. Libby's cubicle was near Belinda's at Archer, and she had extended the invitation to join the car pool. Belinda hadn't formed an opinion of the woman beyond "vigorous." If Libby were a drink, she'd be carbonated.

A red-faced man stood behind her, in hot pursuit of an end to their conversation, shaking a piece of paper. Belinda squirmed at witnessing the domestic drama, but Libby glossed over his concerns with a smile and a peck on the cheek. Then a girl appeared for a good-bye kiss. She was a shorter version of Libby, stuffed into preteen clothes. Libby gave the girl's crop-top an ineffective tug, then turned and tottered toward the car, juggling purse, laptop bag, and insulated coffee mug. She opened the front passenger door and fell inside, ushering in a cloud of cologne and the jangle of enough gold jewelry to melt down into a brick.

"Lordy, Belinda, *tell* me this is Friday." Her voice trilled like a bird's.

"It's, um, Monday."

"Good gravy, I was afraid so."

Chapter 2

Libby's gaze bounced around the beige interior. "Cute car."

"Thanks. I—"

"Don't ever have children, Belinda." Libby sighed and rearranged herself. "They'll turn you into an old, grouchy woman."

Belinda checked the rearview mirror for people, dogs, and cars, then backed out onto the street. "You're not old, what—thirty-five?"

"Bless you. I'm thirty-nine. And it's not the model year, honey, it's the mileage. I think my odometer is on the verge of rolling over." She fanned her cleavage with one hand and sipped from her coffee mug.

Belinda turned on the air conditioner. "How many children do you have?"

"Well, there's Glenda—her daddy, Glen, is my second husband. Then there's Glen, Jr., my husband's son by his first marriage. He's a freshman in high school, second time around. And I have a son, Billy, by my first husband, who lives with his daddy, Big Bill. Billy's a senior in high school. His truck was broken into at school, so he borrowed my SUV this week until the window is replaced, else I wouldn't have asked you to drive the car pool right off the bat like this."

"I don't mind."

"Kids. Most days I wouldn't throw them back, but if I had it to do over again, I might opt for the road you've taken."

One corner of Belinda's mouth lifted. Her "road" was more like a footpath, and she had no idea where it might lead. Fairly terrifying, considering a few months ago she'd had her life mapped out well into menopause.

Libby looked up and squeezed each curler, apparently checking for "doneness." "I know you don't like to talk about your ex—what was his name? Vic?"

"Vince."

"Well, I know you don't like to talk about Vince, but you're lucky the marriage ended before you had little ones."

Belinda bit the inside of her cheek. When she'd joined the car pool last Thursday, Libby had remarked on the thin stripe of white skin on Belinda's left ring finger. (Who knew that two years of fluorescent office lighting could produce a tan line around her engagement ring?) *"A brief, unsuccessful marriage,"* she'd told the women. A half-truth. But pawning herself off as a divorced woman would elicit fewer questions than admitting she was—*dum dum dum dum*—acutely single.

Libby clucked. "I changed my mind—the children are fine. It's the men I would throw back."

Belinda slowed for a stop sign, then realized she'd missed the woman's cue. "Did you and your husband have an argument?" Not that she really wanted to get involved. . . .

"Not *an* argument—*the* argument. The same uninterrupted argument Glen and I have had since the day after we got married: money. Do you believe he threatened to cut up my Bloomingdale's card?"

Belinda hid her smile as she watched for an opening in the oncoming traffic. Allegedly the president of the department store chain had sent Libby a thank-you card last year. "Isn't Glen an accountant? We're all frugal." These days, by necessity.

"You might be frugal, but Glen is cheap. For Valentine's Day, he actually suggested that we go to a card shop, exchange cards in the aisle, then put them back because he didn't see the use in spending the money!"

"Okay, that's cheap."

Libby huffed. "I swear, if he cuts up my Bloomingdale's card, I'll cut off his pecker."

Belinda choked on her breakfast drink. "You don't mean that."

"Yes, I do. I have a mean streak. Want a homemade bear claw?" She opened a sack, and the scent of cinnamon sugar rode the air.

"No, thanks. I'm having—" She squinted at the can. "Berry Bonanza with extra calcium."

Libby made a face, then bit into a lump of fried dough. "Sugar and caffeine, girl, that's the way we get our engines started in the South. You're going to have to get with the program."

"I'm trying to lose a few pounds." More like twelve, which had climbed onto her hips from a steady diet of comfort food after the wedding and now refused to dismount.

"You look nice and curvy," Libby insisted, cheeks full. "What size cup do you wear, D?"

"Um, a C." And not even her mother knew that about her.

"Did you have a fun weekend?" Libby asked.

Belinda checked the street signs and turned right into the entrance of the upscale apartment complex where the two other carpoolers lived. "I wouldn't go that far."

"Don't tell me you worked."

"A little."

Libby began unwinding curlers, leaving corkscrews of yellow hair hanging around her ears. "Doesn't the Mistress of the Dark get enough blood during the week?"

Belinda had concluded that Libby wasn't Margo's biggest fan—something about Margo once taking credit for a document that had come out of Libby's technical writing group. But there were two sides to every story, and Belinda had vowed not to gossip about her boss with the women, all of whom were veteran employees of the Archer Furniture Company. "I was preparing for a meeting this morning with Mr. Archer."

"Mr. Archer is coming in? Must be some meeting."

"A potential acquisition—Payton Manufacturing?"

"Oh, yeah, I saw the memo. Don't they make sleeper sofas?"

"Right. And Murphy beds."

"Don't tell me Margo's actually going to let you sit in on the meeting?"

Belinda stopped in front of the clubhouse, where Carole and Rosemary stood, then waved. She glanced at the clock and willed them to run. "That was my understanding."

"I wouldn't be so sure." Libby snorted. "When Mr. Archer is around, Margo likes to be the only female within a hundred yards. She has the hots for him, you know."

Carole Marchand, twenty-something mail room employee with short, barrette-studded black hair, slid into the backseat behind Libby and slammed the door. "Who has the hots for whom? Cute car." The metal braces gave her a slight lisp.

"Thanks."

"Margo, Mr. Archer," Libby tossed over her shoulder.

Rosemary Burchett, immaculate in her gray Donna Karan suit and dark pageboy, placed a lumbar pillow in the seat behind Belinda, then slid in place and caught her gaze in the rearview mirror. "You haven't heard? Margo turns positively giddy when Juneau is in the vicinity."

The woman said Margo's name with veiled loathing, and the owner's name with the familiarity of a loyal executive assistant. From what Belinda could gather, Rosemary handled correspondence and generally fronted for the absentee owner. Belinda found the unruffle-able older woman a tad intimidating, and it seemed that she wasn't alone—even Margo stepped aside when she met Rosemary in the hallway.

"Mr. Archer is coming in today?" Carole asked, shifting her gaze sideways. "So that explains why Rosemary is dressed to the nines."

Rosemary returned a bland smile. "Even if he puts in an appearance, Margo shouldn't get her hopes up. As if Juneau would be interested in the likes of her."

"Well, we all secretly lust after the man," Carole said, clicking her seat belt home. "But Margo is positively shameless. I actually heard her *giggle* once when she was in his office. I think the earth stalled for a second or two."

"Isn't she supposed to be leaving for Hawaii soon?" Rosemary asked.

"This evening," Belinda verified. Her boss had talked about little else. "She'll be gone for two weeks."

"Hallelujah," Libby said. "That's like a two-week vacation for the rest of us."

Belinda didn't say anything, although she had to admit she was looking forward to the independence, however brief.

Carole sniffed. "Something smells brilliant."

Libby offered them a bear claw. Carole, who was a veritable bag of bones, took two. Rosemary looked tempted but declined. She was the one who had talked Belinda into pumping iron Friday. Apparently Rosemary had slid past forty without acknowledging the milestone and now approached fifty with a similar disregard. The woman smoothed a hand over her hair and fastened her seat belt, seemingly lost in thought. Her cheeks were pinker, her eyes evasive. Either Rosemary was nervous at the prospect of seeing her long-lost boss, or she, too, had a crush on the man.

Belinda steered back toward the parkway. The good news—it was daylight, so she could see where she was going. The bad news—it was daylight, so she could see just how many cars were trying to get where she was going. "Is Mr. Archer single?"

"Widower," Rosemary said. "His wife died two years

ago, but she was sick a long time before that. Like Stanley."

"Rosemary's last husband," Libby murmured behind a paper napkin. "Cancer. Took a while."

Belinda glanced at Rosemary, but the woman was staring out the window. Belinda swallowed a swell of emotion. The previous generation knew the true meaning of loyalty. No six-hour marriages for them, no ma'am.

"Wow, traffic looks even worse than usual," Libby said to change the subject as they approached the bulging lanes.

"There's a crash on Georgia 400, so we're the detour." Belinda put on her signal.

"Smile, girls," Libby said. "We don't want Belinda to be late for her meeting."

Belinda's three passengers pressed pleading faces to the window, and a few seconds later, a man in a late model BMW slowed and yielded magnanimously. She eased into the opening. "So that's the secret, huh?"

"Yeah," Carole said. "We prostitute ourselves every day to get a break in traffic."

Libby flipped down the visor mirror and began teasing her hair with a fine-toothed comb. "Shoot—we made that man's day."

Carole laughed. "You're probably right, men are such suckers. Guess what Gustav said over the weekend?" She smacked the back of the seat. "No, you'll never guess, so I'll tell you. He said that after he gets his green card, maybe we should just stay married." She scoffed. "As if he's in love with me or something. And as if I'm going to walk away from that twenty thousand sitting in escrow."

Belinda kept her eyes on the brake lights of the car in front of her. The girl had entered a green card marriage for money? Belinda knew there were people out there who did things like that, i.e., *criminals*. But she'd never met one.

Carole licked each finger. "Stay married, what a joke. I've got my eye on a brand-new Thunderbird, and then—no offense, girls—I won't need to carpool."

"Yeah, right," Libby said. "Then who on earth would you talk to?"

Rosemary laughed her agreement, and Carole leaned forward. "Oh, that reminds me! Did anyone watch *The Single Files* last night?"

"I watched a movie on the other channel," Rosemary said, covering a yawn.

"My set is on the blink," Belinda said.

Libby sighed. "We found pot in Glen, Jr.'s backpack, so we had a marathon family conference. What did I miss?"

"Oh, it was *so* good," Carole said, bouncing up and down. "Remember last week Tandy and Nicholas broke up? Well, this week they both had dates at the same restaurant—it was hysterical! Meanwhile, Indigo tried to be the last person leaving the gym so she could flirt with the hunky personal trainer."

"The guy with the codpiece?" Libby asked.

"Right. But instead, Indigo got locked inside the gym, and had to call Jill to come and get her out."

"Jill?" Rosemary asked, apparently interested after all. "What could she do?"

"Remember the cute locksmith from a few episodes back?"

"The one who got Jill out of the car trunk she accidentally locked herself into?"

"Right. Jill's been trying to think of a reason to call him, so this was her chance."

Rosemary frowned. "What could a man possibly find attractive about a woman who wants him to commit breaking and entering?"

"It was for a good cause," Carole insisted.

"I forget I'm talking to the woman who earns spending money by marrying immigrants."

Carole stuck out her tongue, and Belinda observed, with no small amount of curiosity, the playful push-pull of the motherless young woman and the daughterless older woman. While she had always enjoyed pleasant female acquaintances, the mystique of true female solidarity had always eluded her. Perhaps estrogenic compatibility had something to do with sharing a childhood bathroom with sisters, an experience she had missed out on as an only child.

"Incoming spray," Libby announced.

Slow to recognize the signal, Belinda zoomed her window down a few seconds behind everyone else, just as a cloud of Aqua Net filled the car. Libby wielded the can like a graffiti artist, shellacking each teased hank of hair.

Rosemary's tongue darted out, and she grimaced. "Christ, Libby, you make a case for flavored hairspray."

Libby ignored her and commenced round two of her coiffure—coaxing the shoulder-length strands downward while preserving the "lift." "So how did the show end, Carole?"

"I was hoping you could tell *me*. My psychic, Ricky, called, so I missed the last ten minutes."

"Oh, not Ricky again," Rosemary muttered.

Libby angled the visor mirror so she could smirk at Carole. "Why didn't you ask your psychic what was going to happen on the show?"

"Very funny. He and I had more important things to discuss. Ricky had a vision about my future as a single woman."

She paused for effect, but the women were apparently used to her drama, and they waited her out. Belinda glanced from woman to woman, wondering who would give in first. At least their teasing camaraderie kept her mind off the crawling traffic, which seemed to be reproducing.

Carole emitted an exasperated sigh. "Ricky says the love of my life is right under my nose—I think he means at the office!"

Libby cackled. "At Archer? Is it one of the gay designers, or one of the gay salesmen?"

"They're not *all* gay."

"Other than Mr. Archer, name one straight, single male at the office."

"Martin Derlinger," Rosemary offered.

Carole winced. "Ewww, the copy machine guy? He sniffs his fingers."

Rosemary made a rueful noise. "You can't fight destiny."

Belinda laughed under her breath, while making impossible promises to God in exchange for green lights.

Libby turned around in her seat. "If Ricky is such a powerful psychic, why didn't he tell you the guy's name?"

"Because," Rosemary said, "if he told her everything at once, he wouldn't be able to collect a hundred bucks every week."

"He only gets so many visions at a time," Carole said in a huff.

"Yeah, well next time ask him for the winning Lotto South numbers," Libby said. She played the lotto religiously.

"Ricky won't use his powers for financial gain."

Libby and Rosemary hooted, then proclaimed the psychic a scam artist and Carole a fool with her money, but Belinda only half-listened, nervously drumming her fingers on the steering wheel. She pressed the gas pedal in preparation for merging onto Peachtree Industrial Boulevard, a larger highway with fewer stoplights. Cars surged forward en masse, zooming from forty to sixty miles an hour in one elevated heartbeat. The fact that people weren't killed every day in this enormous, throbbing network of machines and asphalt was a miracle to her. And the meeting . . .

Her boss was not going to like what she had to say about Payton Manufacturing. In the bleary hours after midnight, she'd begun to suspect Payton of inflating its profits by underreporting debt. She needed more proof, but since Margo had made it clear that Archer had to beef up its manufacturing segment before their company could be taken public, she would not be happy about a delay in acquiring Payton, good reason or no. In fact, Margo's e-mail message last night had hinted that "raises would abound" if Belinda "impressed the CEO in the meeting" and "facilitated the decision to proceed with the acquisition." But was her boss trying to rally an ally, or set up a scapegoat?

"Shouldn't we, Belinda?"

She turned her head toward Libby. "Hm?"

"I was saying that since we've all been married at least once, we should be writing down all this stuff."

"What stuff?"

"Men stuff. Sex stuff. Marriage stuff."

The Berry Bonanza with calcium had a metallic aftertaste. "Why?"

"To pass on to our daughters, and to women everywhere." She tucked a curl in place. "Incoming."

Belinda groped for the button in the armrest and zoomed down her window. At least the aerosol fog dispersed quickly at seventy miles an hour. When they zoomed up the windows, Belinda pushed her scattered bangs out of her eyes. Libby would arrive looking great, and she would arrive looking like a haystack.

"You mean, like, us write a sex book?" Carole asked.

"Why not?" Libby flipped up the visor mirror. "A book of advice on men and marriage from women who've been around the block."

Rosemary's laugh was sandpapery. "Relationship advice for grown-up women? That would certainly be a departure from everything else on the market. If I see another book on 'how to please your man,' I'm going to be violently ill."

"Exactly," Libby said, shoving the hairspray into her bag and whipping out a legal pad. "Ladies, we can do this. Tentative title—" She scribbled furiously. "A Postscript to Nine Marriages. How does that sound?"

"Immoral," Rosemary said.

"Wow," Carole said. "We really have nine marriages between us?"

Libby counted on her beringed fingers. "I'm on my second, you're on your third, Rosemary was married three times, and Belinda—you were married just once, right?"

Belinda's neck grew warm. "Um . . . right. But I don't think I'll be able to contribute much to this project. I . . . wouldn't feel comfortable giving relationship advice to other women."

"How long were you married?" Carole asked.

"Not long."

"Is he why you moved to Atlanta?"

"Leave Belinda alone," Rosemary chided. "She's not used to us yet."

"Right," Libby said. "We don't want to scare her out of the car pool. If she wants us to know whether the man broke her heart, she'll tell us."

She felt their curious gazes latch on. Belinda wet her lips and tasted Aqua Net. She barely knew these women—she couldn't divulge the extent of that day's profound humiliation. Hadn't she left Cincinnati to escape the pitying air?

Yet these women were inviting her to unburden her misery. Was that how sisterhood worked—women bonded by having emotional "goods" on each other? The urge to wallow tugged at her again. The women would almost certainly shower her with sympathy and call Vince vile names . . . at first. But how long before the sympathy gave way to the suspicion that she must be unlovable for a man to behave so abominably?

The flush climbed Belinda's face in the ensuing silence. She wavered. *He didn't break my heart, he drained it. Left it intact, only smaller.* She inhaled deeply, visualizing her lungs expanding into the relative emptiness of her chest. When her brain began to tingle, she exhaled. "I'd rather not talk about it."

She could almost hear them bristle. "Okay," Libby chirped in a voice that said they really didn't want to know anyway.

Stinging from the awkward turn of events, Belinda cast about for a diversion. "So no one ever said what happened to your last fourth in the car pool. Did she move on to a better job, or simply move to a better location?"

In a blink, the mood went from taut to tense. Gazes met, then averted.

Libby toyed with her pen. "Her name was Jeanie Lawford. She died."

Belinda's throat constricted. "I'm so sorry. What happened?"

"She fell down an elevator shaft at work," Carole said. "The one that's sealed."

"About six months ago," Rosemary added quietly.

Belinda's mouth opened and closed as she tried to absorb the awfulness of such an abrupt, unnecessary death. "No one told me."

"We'd rather not talk about it," Libby murmured, then looked away.

A finger of disquiet traced Belinda's spine. A retaliatory cold shoulder notwithstanding, why wouldn't the women want to talk about the death of a close friend? Had the woman committed suicide? A blaring horn behind her brought her back to the traffic and to the fact that she had inadvertently decreased her speed. She swallowed and pressed the gas pedal. Maybe this carpooling thing wasn't such a good idea after all. Belinda leaned forward and turned up the radio volume.

"Good news for folks on I-85 southbound—the accident blockin' the right lane below the I-285 junction has been cleared. You folks on 285 eastbound, stay with me, and I'll get you where you're goin'. This is Talkin' Tom Trainer."

"Thank you, Tom," she breathed, feeling as if he were speaking to her. The man with the anesthetic voice would never know what a comfort he was to a new driver like her, who was still trying to sort out Peachtree Street, Peachtree Court, Peachtree Lane, Peachtree Circle, Peachtree Way, Peachtree Place, Peachtree Trace, Peachtree Avenue, Peachtree Corners, Peachtree Commons, Peachtree Run, West Peachtree and Old Peachtree. She was beginning to think Atlanta's population surge could be explained by the fact that once people were lured into the city, no one could find their way out.

"I see you discovered Tom," Libby said, gesturing to the radio. Her tone was tentative, as if she were offering an olive branch.

"Yeah." Belinda smiled, softening toward the woman. It was nice of them to try to include her, and it wasn't their fault she was barely holding herself together. She wracked her brain for something girly to say. "I think his voice is kind of sexy."

Libby laughed. "You and every other she-type in Atlanta." She pronounced it *uh-lan-uh*, the sign of a true native.

Alternating between gas and brake, Belinda eked into the engorged lanes of I-285, locally known as The Perimeter, since its eight lanes girdled the city. One grueling mile until the spaghetti intersection of I-85 southbound, which would deliver them into Midtown. She might make the meeting after all. Perhaps she could have a private moment with Margo before the meeting to explain her concerns about Payton's financials. Her boss might have noticed the discrepancies herself and had already secured an explanation.

So why couldn't she shake this prickly feeling of impending doom?

"Speak of the devil," Carole said, pointing out the window. "There's the traffic chopper with Mr. Sexy Voice."

Belinda leaned forward. "Where?"

The reply was drowned out by the sickening crunch of metal against metal as her car hit something bigger and more solid than itself. Her seat belt brought her up short, then whipped her back against the seat. She inhaled sharply and experienced a flash of gratitude that the impact hadn't been fierce enough to trigger the airbags. Her mind reeled, registering a sparkle of pain in her neck. "Is everyone okay?"

Breathless yesses chorused around her, but her initial

relief was replaced with a stone of dread when she looked up to see what she'd collided with. *Yilk.*

"Good gravy," Libby murmured.

Belinda closed her eyes and imagined the dollars draining from her savings account, just as a breaking traffic report boomed over the radio.

"Oh, no! Folks, just when things were clearin' up on I-85 southbound, now there's a crash on I-285 eastbound. I saw this one happen—some poor driver in a Honda Civic rammed a police car!"

Chapter 3

The police cruiser's blue light came on, bathing Belinda's cheeks with condemning heat each time it passed over her face. The officer was male, that she could tell from the span of his shoulders. And he wasn't happy, that she could tell from the way he banged his hand against the steering wheel. Since the cruiser sat at an angle, and since her left bumper was imbedded in his right rear fender, and since his right signal light still blinked, he apparently had been attempting to change lanes when she'd nailed him.

The officer gestured for her to pull over to the right. When traffic yielded, he pulled away first, eliciting another sickening scrape as their cars disengaged. She followed like a disobedient child, and despite the odd skew of her car and an ominous noise that sounded like *potato potato potato* (probably because she was hungry), she managed to pull onto the narrow shoulder behind him. The driver side door of the squad car swung open, and long uniform-clad legs emerged. Belinda swallowed hard.

"Whip up some tears," Libby said.

"What?"

"Hurry, before he gets back here."

"I can't—owww!" She rubbed her fingers over the tender skin on the back of her arm where Libby had pinched the heck out of her. Tears sprang to her eyes, partly from the pain and partly from the awfulness of the situation. She tried to blink away the moisture but wound up overflowing. She was wiping at her eyes when a sharp rap sounded on her window.

"Uh-oh," Carole whispered. "He looks pissed."

An understatement. The officer was scowling, his dark hair hand-ruffled, his shadowed jaw clenched. Belinda zoomed down the window and waited.

"Is everyone okay?" he barked. Bloodshot eyes—maybe gray, maybe blue—blazed from a rocky face.

"Y-yes."

"Then save the tears."

She blinked. "I beg your pardon?"

Libby leaned forward. "My friend is late for an important meeting, Officer."

He eyed Belinda without sympathy. "That makes two of us. I need your driver's license, registration, and proof of insurance, ma'am."

Belinda reached for her purse, which had landed at her feet. "I'm sorry, Officer, I didn't see you."

"Yes, ma'am, these big white cars with sirens really blend."

Libby harrumphed, but Belinda shot her a warning glance and handed over the documents he requested.

He glanced at her license, then back at her.

"It's me," she mumbled. The worst driver's license photograph in history: She'd been suffering from the flu, and for some reason, wearing a Mickey Mouse sweatshirt had seemed like a good idea. She was relatively certain that a copy of the humiliating photograph was posted on bulletin boards in DMV break rooms across the state of Ohio.

"I'll be right back."

He circled around to record the numbers on her license plate, then returned to his car, every footfall proclaiming his frustration for inexperienced, un-photogenic female drivers. He used his radio, presumably to report her vitals. She'd never been in trouble in her life, but her gut clenched with the absurd notion that some computer glitch might finger her as a lawless fugitive—kidnapper, forger, murderer. Her new friends wouldn't be able to vouch for her, except to say that she maintained a neat desk.

"He's kind of cute with that whole bad-boy unshaven look," Libby muttered. "But he doesn't have much of a roadside manner."

"Well, I did hit his car."

"It isn't *his* car—it belongs to the taxpayers. You hit your own car, really."

Belinda closed her eyes and focused on the sensation of vehicles passing with enough speed and proximity to send vibrations through her crippled Honda. The vacuum pulled at her hair, and the tang of asphalt stung her nostrils. A symphony of car horns sounded around her. Everything in Atlanta was faster than she was accustomed to. She couldn't imagine ever feeling as if she belonged to this teeming city, couldn't conjure up the hopeful romanticism that had shot through her when she'd sat in her Cincinnati apartment hunched over her computer, scanning the Archer employment ad.

> Wanted: Finance specialist for privately owned firm in Atlanta.

In hindsight, she'd been at a low point—3:00 A.M., on the verge of returning to work after two weeks of vacation that were supposed to have been spent standing in line at the Louvre and instead had been spent standing in line at the post office, returning wedding gifts. To her emotionally scraped self, Atlanta had beckoned like a big-bosomed matron. Warm, perfumed, comforting. Now she was thinking she'd watched *Gone With the Wind* one too many times.

The crunch of gravel signaled the officer's approach.

She opened her eyes, but the flat line of his mouth caused the Berry Bonanza with calcium to roil in her stomach.

"Do you live in Cincinnati, Ms. Hennessey?"

"No, I moved here two months ago."

A muscle worked in his jaw as he scribbled on a ticket pad. "I need your address, please."

She recited it as he wrote.

"You were supposed to obtain a Georgia driver's license within thirty days of moving here."

His tone pushed her pulse higher. "I didn't know."

He tore off one, two, three tickets, then thrust them into her hand. "Now you do." He unbuttoned his cuff and began rolling up his sleeve. "I need for you ladies to move to my car, please."

Belinda gaped. "You're hauling us in?"

The officer looked heavenward, then back. "No, ma'am. You have a flat tire and at this time of day, it'll take forever for your road service to get here."

She pressed her lips together, thinking this probably wasn't the best time to say she didn't have a road service. Or a cell phone to *call* a road service.

He nodded toward the cruiser. "You'll be safer in my car than standing on the side of the road."

"I . . . thank you."

He didn't look up. "Yes, ma'am. Will you pop the trunk?"

While the women scrambled out of the car, Belinda released the trunk latch, but the resulting click didn't sound right. She opened her door a few inches, then slid out, bracing herself against the traffic wind that threatened to suck her into the path of oncoming cars. The toes of her shoes brushed the uneven edge of the blacktop, and she almost tripped. Her dress clung to her thighs, and her hair whipped her cheeks. The rush of danger was strangely exhilarating, strangely . . . *alluring.*

Then a large hand clamped onto her shoulder, guiding her to the back of the car and comparative safety. "That's a good way to become a statistic," he shouted over the road noise.

She tilted her head to look into reproachful eyes, and pain flickered in the back of her neck. Tomorrow she'd be stiff. "This is very nice of you," she yelled, gesturing as if she were playing charades.

He simply shrugged, as if to say he would've done the same for anyone. Dark stubble stained his jaw, and for the first time she noticed his navy uniform was a bit rumpled. He frowned and jerked a thumb toward the cruiser. "You should join your friends, ma'am."

At best, he probably thought she was an airhead. At worst, a flirt. She pointed. "The trunk release didn't sound right."

He wedged his fingers into the seam that outlined the trunk lid and gave a tug. "I think it's just stuck." Indeed, on the next tug, the lid sprang open. He twisted to inspect the latch as he worked the mechanism with his fingers. "The latch is bent, but fixable." He raised the trunk lid and winced. "I assume the spare tire is underneath all this stuff."

A sheepish flush crawled over her as she surveyed the brimming contents. "I'll empty it."

He checked his watch. "I'll help. Anything personal in here?"

She shook her head in defeat. Nothing that she could think of, and what did it matter, anyway?

But her degradation climbed as he removed item after item that, in his hands, seemed mundane to the point of intimate—a ten-pound bag of kitty litter, a twelve-pack of Diet Pepsi, a pair of old running shoes with curled toes, an orange Frisbee, a grungy Cincinnati Reds windbreaker, a *Love Songs of the 90s* CD, two empty Pringles Potato Chips canisters (she'd heard a person could do all kinds of crafty things with them), and two gray plastic crates of reference books she'd been conveying to her cubicle one armload at a time.

Her gaze landed on a tiny blue pillow wedged between the crates, and she cringed. Unwilling to share that particular souvenir of her life, she reached in while he was bent away from her and stuffed the pillow into her shoulder bag.

"I'll get the rest of it," he said.

She nodded and scooted out of the way. "Can I help with—"

"No." He looked up at her, then massaged the bridge of his nose. "No, ma'am. Please."

Glad for the escape, Belinda retreated to the cruiser, picking her way through gravel and mud, steeling herself against the gusts of wind. The girls had crowded into the backseat, so she opened the front passenger door and slid inside, then shut the door behind her. The console of the police car was guy-heaven—buttons and lights and gizmos galore. The radio emitted bursts of static. No one said anything for a full thirty seconds.

"Your hair looks like crap," Libby offered.

Belinda sighed and dug in her bag for a brush, displacing sunglasses, wallet, lipstick holder, compact, and electronic address book. At least now she had an excuse to end the driving arrangement. "I'll understand if you want me out of the car pool."

"Nonsense," Rosemary said, although she sounded a little less than sincere.

"Honey," Libby cooed through the metal screen partition, "Atlanta traffic is like life—sooner or later, you're going to hit or be hit."

"You're staying," Carole said. "The odds of you being in another accident now are, like, really low."

Belinda tried to smile. The accident seemed to have broken the ice, along with her budget. "Does anyone have a cell phone? I should call Margo to tell her I'm going to be late."

"I left mine at home," Rosemary said.

"My battery's dead," Carole said.

Libby cringed. "My service was temporarily disconnected."

And Belinda hadn't reactivated her own wireless phone service since she'd moved. She glanced at her watch with one eye closed and pulled the brush through her tangled hair. She'd never make the meeting, and Margo would be irate. The only upside was that she had longer to contemplate what she was going to say about Payton Manufacturing. Assuming her boss would still want her input. Assuming her boss would still want her employed.

"I hope no one sees us," Rosemary said, holding her hand over the side of her face.

Carole laughed. "Haven't you ever been in the backseat of a police car?"

"No."

"It's no big deal, you know. Being arrested."

"No one is under arrest," Libby said.

"And if you don't mind," Rosemary said coolly, "I'd rather not hear the sordid details of your trips to the hoosegow."

Carole made a face, then twisted and looked out the rear window. "I've never seen a cop change a tire before."

"It was the tears, I'm telling you," Libby said. "Otherwise, we'd be standing out there with our thumbs in the air."

Rosemary scoffed. "He would've called the Department of Transportation or a HERO unit."

Libby sighed. "But this is so much more chivalrous. I loooove big Southern men. Did he make a pass at you, Belinda?"

Belinda stopped working at the rat's tail in her hair. "Um, *no*."

"I'll bet you're the cutest woman who ever rammed his car."

"As dubious a distinction as that might be, he's only changing my tire so he can get the heck out of here."

"He got your address—I bet he'll call you at home."

"He got my address so he could write me three big fat tickets."

"How much are the fines?" Carole asked.

She gave up on her hopeless hair and pulled out the three citations signed by—she squinted at the scrawl—

Lt. W. Alexander. After adding the numbers in her head, she laid her head back on the headrest. "Two hundred and twenty-five dollars."

"Oooh," they chorused.

Oooh was right. No telling what the car repairs would cost, and her insurance premium would probably go up. So much for having her TV fixed. And a couch was definitely being pushed farther onto the horizon unless that raise materialized.

Worse, the slips of neon-colored carbon paper in her hand seemed to scream, "You're bad, Bad, BAD." She'd been driving for fifteen years and had never once violated a traffic law. In fact, in thirty-one years, she couldn't remember breaking *any* rules, written or otherwise. She'd been born innately good, her mother had once said. Every child's friend, every teacher's pet. Valedictorian, Most Likely to Succeed, Who's Who Among American College Students. Devoted daughter, employee, and fiancée.

By all accounts, her life should be a raging success. Instead, she was sitting in a police car on the side of a festering interstate, miserable, poorer even than a mere hour ago, decidedly indecisive and significantly insignificant. She pressed her fist to her mouth. She needed a better reason to be here, a better reason to stay here, than simply because it wasn't Cincy.

"One of the tickets will be canceled when you get your Georgia driver's license," Libby soothed.

"And Gustav's cousin has an auto body shop," Carole said. "He'll give you a discount on your car repairs."

In the rearview mirror, Belinda saw Libby elbow Rosemary.

Rosemary sighed. "And no one is going to die if you miss one lousy meeting."

Belinda smiled at their attempt to cheer her up, but her appreciation was cut short by the sight of the officer striding back, wiping his hands on his handkerchief. She stuffed everything back into her bag, opened the door, and stepped outside.

"All done," he shouted. Black grease streaked his temple.

"Thanks," she said, but her voice was lost in the wake of a bellowing eighteen-wheeler flying by. The wind nearly knocked her out of her muddy shoes.

The officer reached out to steady her. "Are you sure you're okay? You don't look well."

Nice. "I'm fine."

He cleared his throat. "Your headlight is broken, and you need to have the trunk latch looked at. And that spare tire isn't meant for heavy-duty wear."

She nodded, then signaled the women. They climbed out of the cruiser and expressed their appreciation to the officer as they filed by.

"Yes, thank you," Belinda said, and extended her hand. "Again, I'm sorry to have made you late, too."

He hesitated, then gave her hand one quick pump. "You'd better get on the road."

"Yes." She turned and walked toward her car.

"Ma'am?"

She turned back, then touched her neck where it twinged.

"This is Coca-Cola territory," he shouted.

"Excuse me?"

He nodded toward her car. "The Diet Pepsi will have to go. It's all Coke around here."

She brushed her hair out of her eyes and squinted into the morning sun. "I've never acquired a taste for Coke."

He gave her the first semblance of a smile. "You will."

It was a small gesture, an offhand remark from a virtual stranger. But spoken with the certainty that she'd be staying long enough to absorb the local culture. He couldn't have known how much it meant to her to know that despite being obviously ill-suited for this dynamic city, she was still welcome to *try* to fit in.

She climbed behind the wheel, ridiculously cheered. The officer turned on his lights and edged out into the traffic, waiting until she nosed in behind him before pulling ahead. A few seconds later, his siren sounded, and traffic parted like the Red Sea to allow him by. He weaved through the maze of taillights and soon disappeared from her vision.

"You gotta love a man with a siren," Carole said.

Libby hummed her agreement.

Belinda mulled over his casual words, then was drawn back into the honking, irritated soup around her. While the officer had leapfrogged through the jam-packed lanes, she and the cars around her had progressed all of twenty feet. The two lanes of traffic merging onto I-85 southbound were at a complete standstill. She turned up the radio volume, hoping for a spot of good news. A few commercials later, her favorite traffic reporter came on.

"Well, folks, it's officially rush hour! I-85 southbound is a parkin' lot all the way down to the I-75 connector. We're talkin' fifty minutes, at least, to make your way through that mess. I hope the driver who rammed the police car got a note for his or her boss, because they're gonna be L-A-T-E."

Belinda squeezed her eyes shut. The day had to get better . . . didn't it?

Chapter 4

Despite their protests, Belinda stopped to let the women disembark before looking for a parking place. "I'm sorry I made everyone so late."

Libby dismissed her concern with a wave. "We could be late every morning for a month and Archer Freaking Furniture would still owe us hours."

"Those chumps in the mailroom probably haven't even missed me," Carole said.

Rosemary flashed a sympathetic look in the rearview mirror. "If I see Margo, I'll try to run interference for you."

"Thanks," Belinda murmured, experiencing a surge of warmth toward the aloof older woman. She wasn't used to accepting help from others—it never occurred to her to ask. In the aftermath of their non-wedding, Vince had remarked that she was "arrogantly independent," that she made people, including him, feel unnecessary. She had dismissed his words as those of a man looking for a way to blame her for his change of heart. But was a woman in need simply more attractive to others?

The last door slammed, and her new comrades moved toward the elevators, Libby and Carole chatting, Rosemary lagging behind. Belinda pressed the gas pedal, her heart suddenly racing at the prospect of facing her unpredictable boss. The numbers from the spreadsheets she'd built ran through her head—if she was late, at least she could be prepared. She still didn't know, though, what she could say about Payton Manufacturing that would satisfy Margo and her own conscience.

By the time she found a parking place at the tip-top of the garage, which had been erected for all the employees located in the twenty-story Stratford Plaza building on Peachtree Street, her bladder nagged and her watch read 9:25. She hefted her briefcase and purse, then scrambled to the bay of elevators and stabbed all five buttons. The Out of Service sign on the sixth one gave her pause—and the willies. Poor Jeanie Lawford.

Belinda shivered. If some horrible accident were to befall her, what would her epitaph read? *Here lies Belinda Hennessey. She was lacking.*

Thankfully, her disheartening train of thought was derailed by the arrival of an elevator. After a glance to ensure the floor of the car was intact, she rushed forward, only to collide with a tall blond man exiting with equal momentum. She ricocheted off his leather bomber jacket but, with improvised acrobatics, managed to stay on her feet.

The man reached forward to clasp her arm in an iron grip. She shrank back, overcome by the sensation of the stranger invading her personal space in such an isolated spot. At the sight of his large hand clamped around her forearm, panic blipped in her chest.

"Ma'am?" He relaxed his hold on her, and his voice sounded as if he were speaking to a child. "I said are you all right?"

She gave herself a mental shake at her paranoia, uncharacteristically close to tears at the sum of everything that had happened this morning. "I'm fine."

"Are you sure?" He smiled, producing one deep dimple and a flicker of gold in his green, green eyes. A strange sense of déjà vu hit her, yet she'd bet her life that she'd never met the man.

"Yes, I'm fine."

"Okay." He flashed another smile. "Have a great day."

She'd probably passed him in the halls of the building, she concluded as she watched him walk away. The sound of the elevator door closing brought her back to the matter at hand—she was *so* late. The elevator car went on its merry way before the call button could retrieve it. She inhaled, fighting for control, then eyed the door to the stairs. She could probably jog down to the eighth floor just as quickly as taking the elevator, and heaven knew she could use the exercise.

Besides, there was less chance of stairs falling out from under a person, plunging that person to her death before she had time to prove to the world and to herself that she had made the right choice in leaving behind everything she knew and starting over.

She arrived at the eighth floor winded, and she race-walked through the lobby of Archer Furniture, nodding to a secretary who gave her a sympathetic stare. By the time she wound through the maze of cubicles to the boardroom, her watch read 9:37.

Belinda stood in front of the closed double doors and breathed deeply to calm her pounding heart. She smoothed her hair, hoping she looked more put together than she felt—doubtful, considering the fact that she'd managed to acquire a three-inch-wide run in her panty hose from ankle to knee and her best pumps were covered with mud and flecks of gravel. Turning the knob with an unsteady hand, she pushed open the doors.

Empty.

Empty black swivel chairs around the table flanked by empty Payton Manufacturing couches sent over to foster the merger. Her stomach bottomed out.

A noise caught her attention. Clancy Edmunds, Archer's receptionist-slash-host-slash-hall monitor, was clearing paper cups and crumpled napkins. Belinda hadn't been able to get a read on the meticulous, stocky man who had a penchant for bright-colored clothing, but he seemed nice enough. He glanced up and smiled, revealing square, wide-spaced teeth. "Hi, Belinda."

"Good morning, Clancy. Did the meeting end?"

"About twenty minutes ago." Then he winced apologetically. "Margo was a tad miffed you weren't here."

She closed her eyes briefly. "I was in an accident on I-285."

"Everyone okay?"

She nodded.

"Well, traffic happens. Margo will have to understand that not everyone flies to work on their broomstick."

Another fan. "Do you know where I can find her?"

"I saw her walk Mr. Archer to the lobby. Actually, she was trotting after him. Then she said, um . . . that she was looking for you."

Great.

"Want a Krispy Kreme?" he asked, holding up a jelly-filled doughnut. "I picked them off the conveyer belt myself less than an hour ago."

Doughnuts were apparently a Southern panacea. She smiled at his attempt to cheer her, but shook her head. "I might as well face the firing squad."

"Literally—Margo lives to fire people, you know."

She swallowed. "Oh?"

He leaned forward. "But you're probably okay because"—he craned to look over her shoulder and seemed satisfied they were alone—"the last guy she fired, Jim Newberry, filed a big, whopping lawsuit against the company."

She wasn't sure how to respond, so she didn't.

At her silence, Clancy looked nervous. "Of course, that's not public knowledge, and I'm only telling you because it seems relevant and I know you won't repeat it."

"Of course." Belinda pointed with her thumb. "I'd better get going." She backed out of the meeting room, pivoted, and practically ran to Margo's spacious corner office.

Empty.

Margo's executive assistant, Brita, a slender giant, glanced up from her computer keyboard, where she sat behind a half-wall. "She's looking for you."

"Um . . . thank you." With dread building in her chest and pressure building in her bladder, Belinda put one foot in front of the other and followed the path of teal indoor-outdoor carpet toward the five-feet-high, eight-feet-square cubicle where she spent the majority of her time these days. Along the way, she passed two dozen or so replica cubicles alive with music and chatter transcending the shared walls insulated with gray woven fabric that Downey would love to sharpen her claws on.

The modular mini-offices were situated in clusters of four, and the foursomes populated the entire floor—only Juneau Archer and Margo merited true offices with real furniture. A third office sat empty. Jeanie Lawford's? Jim Newberry's? For everyone else, the pecking order seemed to be determined by one's chairs, with top distinction going to those whose main chair and visitor chair matched and were upholstered in a desirable color (cobalt blue), all the way down to those whose two chairs *didn't* match and were upholstered in undesirable colors (pea green and/or burnt orange).

When Belinda rounded the corner, she passed Libby's cube. Her carpooling mate made a face and a chopping motion with her hands. Belinda realized what her friend was trying to warn her of when she walked into her own cubicle to find Margo perched in the pea green visitor's chair dressed in designer black, slim leg crossed over knee, pointy-toed shoe swinging. The woman's foot stopped, and so did Belinda's pulse.

"*Where* have you been?"

She had considered herself lucky that the opening to her cubicle faced a window—okay, a beam and a *slice* of window—and now she was especially grateful that no one sat opposite her to ogle this encounter. Still, all surrounding chatter stopped, and radio volumes were cut. Meanwhile, a hot flush consumed Belinda, and the smooth, professional apology she had memorized evaporated on her tongue. "I . . ."

"Well?" Margo shot up, appearing taller than her four-foot-ten-inch stature. Her body was tanning-salon orange and compactly muscled. Her tight black French twist and emerald green eyes (a la tinted contact lenses, Belinda suspected) made her seem even more severe—and unstable. "Tell me—*what* was more important than this morning's meeting? Did you oversleep? Have a fight with your boyfriend?"

Belinda was struck dumb at the woman's scathing tone. No one had ever talked to her like that. People in Ohio were passive (although Cleveland had a reputation).

The woman crossed her arms. "Because you weren't here with the numbers, I had to postpone the meeting with the board of directors. And Mr. Archer wasn't too happy about coming in to the office for nothing."

The thought crossed Belinda's mind that if the man was CEO, surely he could find something at the office that needed his attention, but she decided against voicing that observation, especially since everyone in the department was listening. "I'm sorry I'm late. I was in a car accident."

"Was anyone injured?"

"No. But my car—"

"You could have called."

"I didn't have access to a cell phone . . . that worked."

"If you're going to live OTP, you're going to have to be more responsible."

Belinda sorted through the stored acronyms in her memory bank and came up empty. "OTP?"

The woman's mouth tightened. "*Outside. The. Perimeter.*"

Translation: Uncool people who live in the boonies and schlep into the city daily to work for *I*TP people. Belinda's body sang with humiliation. "Again, I apologize—"

"I was planning to leave for Hawaii this evening."

"Yes, I remem—"

"*Was* being the operative word." Margo's little foot tapped. "Mr. Archer isn't available the rest of the day, so it looks like I'll have to postpone my vacation to get this meeting taken care of."

Low groans sounded around them.

"*So*. If I can reschedule the meeting for tomorrow morning, do you *think* you can manage to get here on *time*?"

The quiet around them intensified. Belinda's neck tickled with the promise of pain. Whiplash? Aneurysm? She bit down on the inside of her cheek. "Yes."

Margo pursed her mouth, a little knot of flesh covered with black cherry lipstick. "Good." She turned to go. "But this had *better* not happen again."

And she sniffed.

Later, when the girls would ask Belinda what exactly had made her snap, she would say it was that sniff. Dry. Disdainful. Deliberate.

In the fraction of the split second it took for Belinda's aching brain to process the sound and for her overworked sensibilities to perceive its meaning, she experienced her first true epiphany in thirty-one years:

All her life she had followed the rules governing good behavior, and if she fell down an elevator shaft today, what did she have to show for her clean living? She was a jilted, broke, glorified calculator living in an alien city, driving a nightmare commute to a job for which she was overqualified, working for a short, unpleasant woman.

A cool sensation enveloped her, akin to the thrilling numbness of standing next to the interstate with massive vehicles speeding by. A reckless person would step into the path of disaster for the sheer exhilaration of the rush before the splat. And right now, she felt reckless.

Belinda wet her lips and tasted Aqua Net. "If you're going to belittle me in front of my coworkers," she said to Margo's retreating back, "I'll need a raise."

Margo stopped. Someone on the other side of the cubicle gasped—probably Libby. The air itself seemed to flee, leaving an ear-clogging vacuum in its wake. In slow motion, the diminutive woman turned and narrowed her eyes. "Ex*cuse* me?"

Belinda dropped her briefcase on the tidy work surface of her cubicle and offered her boss the bland smile of a person whose morning—and life—had nowhere to go but up. "I said you don't pay me enough to patronize me, Margo."

In her peripheral vision, Belinda saw the tops of heads pop up over cubicle walls all over the floor. Margo's eyes went from slits to protruding organs. She took two slow steps back to the cubicle opening and swept her blazing gaze over Belinda. Belinda identified her need to exhale, but her lungs wouldn't budge.

"Unless you apologize for that remark," Margo said through clenched teeth, "I can arrange for you to be paid *nothing*."

Fired? Belinda swallowed as she mulled whether her body could back up her newly liberated mouth. Breaking rules meant facing consequences. Could she draw unemployment if she was fired? She had enough Slim-Fast to last a week or so. Her childhood coin collection would yield about three hundred bucks—just enough to rent a U-Haul and hightail it back to Cincinnati. Downey would be overjoyed to return to the cooler climate and to the fish-scented air.

"I'm waiting," Margo said, foot still tapping.

The woman's shoes probably cost as much as a decent couch, Belinda thought wildly, light-headed now from lack of oxygen and a swimming bladder. "I . . ."

"Yes?"

Hoping the woman couldn't see she was shaking in her muddy Aerosoles ($29.95, on clearance), Belinda exhaled. "I . . . I have apologized enough." She punctuated the statement with a tight smile that belied her state of mind. "And now . . . I'm going to the ladies' room."

Before exiting the cubicle, her feet driven by a rush of adrenaline, Belinda caught a glimpse of Margo's shocked expression. She felt the eyes of her coworkers on her as she passed their cubes. Her skin tingled with the absurd expectation that Margo would chase her down and jump on her back, but when she closed the lounge door behind her, she was alone. Alone with her sudden, ballooning remorse.

She rushed into the first stall to relieve some of her physical burden, but as she peeled off her ruined panty hose, the weight of what she'd just done started to sink in. Margo was probably calling security at this very moment to have her removed from the building. With the sagging economy and a discharge on her record, she'd be hard-pressed to find another job with such good benefits—including the discount on furniture she'd been looking forward to when she was finally able to set aside a few extra dollars.

She emerged from the stall and caught sight of herself in the mirror—Midwestern pale, helter-skelter hair, serious brown eyes, not a rule-breaking bone in her body. She practiced an apology while she washed her hands. "I wasn't myself," she murmured. "I had a really dreadful morning and—"

The door to the lounge swung open, and Margo marched in with a thundercloud on her forehead. Belinda busied herself drying her hands, rehearsing in her head.

"Belinda—" Margo began.

The door opened, and a woman Belinda recognized as a software developer walked in.

"Leave," Margo barked.

The woman bolted, and Belinda's pulse spiked. She glanced around the small room and judged the distance to the door. Her legs were longer—she could make a run for it if she had to.

Margo cleared her throat. "Belinda," she repeated, her expression softening, her voice . . . *contrite*? "I want to apologize for losing my temper." She lifted both hands and almost smiled. "I was upset about postponing my vacation, and I overreacted."

Belinda blinked. "Oh . . . kay."

"I shouldn't have said what I did."

"Oh . . . kay."

"The truth is, I admire the way you stood up to me out there." Margo angled her head. "The credentials on your résumé are very impressive, but when I met you, I couldn't reconcile the two. I underestimated you."

Belinda pushed her bangs out of her eyes.

"In fact, I've been looking for someone around here with a little backbone, someone I can groom for senior management. Someone who isn't afraid to go after the competition."

The woman actually did smile this time.

"What do you say, Belinda? How would you like to help me take Archer public?"

Belinda squeezed her bare toes inside her shoes. "Sure. I mean—yes, if it's good for the long-term health of the company."

Margo made a humming sound in her throat. "Life is short. Right now, I'm more worried about the *immediate* health of this company. I'll reschedule the meeting with Mr. Archer and the board of directors for tomorrow—midmorning, just in case you encounter difficulties again. I suppose the traffic does take some getting used to."

"Er . . . yes." Belinda swallowed. "Margo, I found some irregularities with the Payton P&L statements, and I was hoping we could discuss them before the meeting."

Margo looked pained. "I'm going to be running full speed."

"I'll e-mail you."

Her boss lifted her hands, stop-sign fashion. "No e-mail. My computer is being upgraded. Whatever you think you saw, I'm sure it's nothing—Payton is a solid company."

"But—"

"Belinda, I don't want unnecessary last-minute questions to postpone the transaction. All the players are primed—Juneau, the Payton family, the board of directors, the venture capitalists. An endorsement from Archer's chief financial officer will help seal the deal."

"But . . . Archer doesn't have a chief financial officer."

"The former CFO had some personal problems, and

we had to let him go. Juneau and I have been conducting a quiet search for a CFO, but we haven't found someone with the right mix, someone who can be trusted."

Her boss flashed another smile—teeth and everything. "I think maybe you're the right person, Belinda."

She blinked. "Me?"

"Mr. Archer will defer to my judgment if he likes what he sees tomorrow in the meeting." Margo examined her black cherry manicure. "And you're right—I don't pay you enough. Compensation for the CFO position is 80K."

Eighty thousand dollars? Belinda couldn't help it—she laughed.

Margo looked up. "All right, 90K, but that's my final offer."

Belinda nearly swallowed her tongue. A new couch. In leather.

"Then, of course, there's the executive benefits package—stock options, bonuses, expense account."

Belinda didn't know what to say. "I don't know what to say."

"Say yes."

One of the sink faucets had developed a leisurely drip. *Go. For. It. Go. For. It.* "Yes."

This smile included gums. "Good. It'll take a couple of weeks for the paperwork to be processed, assuming there aren't any . . . *snags*." A persuasive smile diluted Margo's pointed gaze.

Belinda's neck started to itch. Assuming she didn't do anything to stall the acquisition. *Here lies Belinda Hennessey. She was Chief Financial Officer.* "I'll . . . take another look at those numbers."

"Atta girl," Margo said with a wink.

A *wink*.

"Welcome to the top, Belinda. We're going to make a killing."

Margo extended her hand and Belinda shook it, half expecting her to have one of those shock buzzers in her little palm. She didn't, and her grip was iron-woman strong. "Thank you, M-Margo."

Margo released her hand just short of the point of pain. Her designer heels clicking on the tile, she turned and left.

Yilk. Belinda turned and stared at her wide-eyed reflection, then sank into the faux marble counter, weak with relief. Apparently, she had more to get used to down here than Coke.

Chapter 5

"All I can say," Libby sang as she swung into the passenger seat, "is that you, Belinda Dawn Hennessey, are my hero."

Belinda winced. "How do you know my middle name?"

Libby looked sheepish. "Friend in HR. Must have come up in conversation."

Carole slammed the back door. "Well, I can't believe I missed it. Rosemary, why didn't you call me? I could have whipped up an urgent delivery for the eighth floor."

Rosemary closed her door. "By the time Libby called me, the encounter had reached the level of urban legend."

Belinda fought the smile that pushed at the corners of her mouth. Was this what gloating felt like?

"Well, I had a front row seat," Libby said. "And Belinda put Margo in her place like a pro."

"About time someone did," Rosemary said.

When the other women chorused agreement, a pang of guilt struck Belinda—she owed Margo her allegiance, more so now than ever. She drove out of the parking garage and poked her damaged bumper into a crack in the solid traffic on Peachtree Street. Thanks to their collective face-press, a driver let her merge.

"You know," she said as she slid in behind a behemoth SUV, "Margo did have to postpone her vacation."

"Big deal," Libby said. "Margo is always gallivanting off somewhere exotic with one of her tadpoles."

"Tadpoles?"

"She likes younger men."

"And older men," Rosemary added dryly.

Carole leaned forward. "Hush! I want to hear all about the showdown. What happened?"

Libby turned in her seat and retold the story with gusto, gesturing wildly, and embellishing at will. "And then Belinda just up and says, 'Excuse me, I'm going to the john.' "

Belinda squinted. "Well—"

"And then off she went," Libby finished with a flourish.

Carole gasped. "Just like that?"

"Just like that," Libby declared, having taken ownership of the story. "She marched off, calm as you please. Margo stood there for a while with smoke coming out of her pointy little ears, and then she followed Belinda."

"Into the bathroom?"

"Yeah."

"No way."

"Yes way, yes ma'am."

Carole gaped at Libby. "What happened in the bathroom?"

Libby's shoulders fell. "You'll have to ask Belinda."

Carole's head pivoted. "Well?"

Belinda shrugged carefully. "We . . . talked."

"About?"

"About the misunderstanding."

They waited for more details.

"And . . . we agreed we needed to work together on this acquisition."

Carole frowned. "That's all?"

Belinda nodded. All day she'd pondered the unspoken

deal she'd struck with Margo in the ladies' room, along with her revelation that the people who get ahead in life were rule breakers. Ruthless competitors. She didn't need a psychology primer to know that social rule breakers reached higher levels of success and recognition—the incredible promotion offer aside, more people had spoken to her today in the halls than in the two months she'd worked at Archer. Because she'd dared to defy her pushy boss, everyone knew her name. One moment of insanity had given her a higher profile than a decade of do-gooding.

"You'd better watch your back," Rosemary said. "If Margo swallowed her pride, she's probably planning to swallow you as a chaser. She doesn't like competition."

Belinda contemplated the warning as she gunned and braked her way through Midtown traffic. For a moderately sized company, Archer certainly resonated with drama.

The temperature sat on the high side of ninety, and the sun hung at a merciless slant. She turned up the radio, wondering if the traffic reporter would reference her morning mishap—it was, admittedly, a thin connection to the man with the velvety voice, but she would take it. However, the eye in the sky had more pressing situations to report than her long-forgotten fender bender with the police officer.

"Folks, it's a mixed bag for drivers on I-85 northbound. Two construction delays before you hit Spaghetti Junction, but stay in the left lanes, and you'll be okay. HOV lanes are definitely the fastest route home tonight! This is Talkin' Tom Trainer for MIXX 100 FM traffic."

With a pleasant start she realized she'd actually understood what he'd said—spaghetti junction, where I-85 and The Perimeter came together, was the most fierce tangle of overpasses and ramps the city had to offer, and the HOV lane was for "high-occupancy vehicles," aka carpoolers. She was getting the hang of the lingo, but the traffic was still a two-handed, white-knuckle stress fest.

The homebound commuters were a hot, sweaty, lead-footed, hungry bunch of people who communicated with their horns and their hands.

Libby made a rueful noise. "As if the cars and buses and eighteen-wheelers going eighty miles an hour aren't dangerous enough, a body has to worry about some fool freaking out with road rage."

"Yeah," Carole said from the back. "Belinda, do you have a weapon?"

Belinda frowned. "You're kidding, right?"

"No. You really should put something under the seat to protect yourself when you're on the road. I have a tire iron."

"I have a lead pipe," Libby said.

"Stun gun," Rosemary added.

"Is that legal?"

"Good gravy, yes," Libby said. "While I was going to night school, I packed a .25 automatic."

Belinda coughed. "A gun?"

"Sure. But after I started carpooling, I relaxed a little. A tire iron has a nice balanced feel to it, like a cast-iron skillet."

"Ah."

Carole's head jutted forward. "A few months ago we took self-defense courses after work. We got to beat up on a big guy with lots of padding, and learned how to send a man's nose bone into his brain."

A finger of suspicion nudged Belinda. "What made you decide to take self-defense classes?"

"It was Jeanie's idea," Carole said, her tone rueful. "And she talked us into it. Rosemary got the best marks in the class."

"Wow."

Rosemary smirked. "It wasn't quite as ferocious as Carole makes it sound."

Belinda laughed. "Still, I feel safe with you guys."

The sudden silence in the car resonated with deeper significance, and Belinda realized that the women did make her feel safe—literally and figuratively. Something had changed between this morning and this afternoon. . . .

She had changed. Had taken a risk. Lowered her guard. It felt, well . . . *good.*

Libby leaned toward her. *"Y'all."*

"Hm?"

"You guys is Yankee-speak. You're in Atlanta now, girl, so it's *y'all."*

Belinda tested the words on her tongue. "You. All."

Libby laughed. "We'll work on it." She pulled the yellow legal pad from her bag. "Now, back to our book."

"Not this again," Rosemary said.

"I thought of a better title—do you want to hear it?"

Rosemary sighed. "Do we have a choice?"

Libby made a face.

"I want to hear it," Carole said.

"Thank you. How about *I Think I Love You*?"

Belinda took her eyes off the road just long enough to glance over. "Isn't that a song?"

"The Osmonds," Carole said, nodding.

"No, not the Osmonds, you child," Libby said. "It was the Partridge Family. Keith Partridge, feathered hair, jumpsuit."

"I don't get it," Carole said. "The title, I mean."

Libby sighed. "Don't you see? It's perfect. I Think I Love You—we all thought we were in love with these men when we married them."

Belinda pursed her mouth. True enough.

"Speak for yourself," Rosemary said. "I *was* in love with each one of my husbands."

"Okay. The subtitle is just for you."

"Christ, there's a subtitle."

"Relationship DOs and DON'Ts for Grown Women. And I'm going to let Rosemary come up with our very first DO or DON'T."

Belinda bit back a smile.

"This is nonsense," Rosemary said.

"But it passes the time," Libby said. "And you should

have the best advice of all of us. Come on, give us a DO or a DON'T."

Rosemary rolled her eyes. "Okay. DON'T sleep with a man until you're married."

Silence exploded into the car.

"That's archaic," Carole finally said.

"Yeah," Libby seconded.

"The old rules are the best ones," Rosemary chirped. "Every generation of women has tried to change the rules, yet there are more unmarried and more unhappily married women than ever."

Belinda bit into her lower lip. She'd had good-girl values drilled into her brain since birth. She'd tried casual sex in college and hadn't cared for it. When she'd met Vince, she'd recognized a potential life mate. During the two years they'd dated, they'd engaged in some heavy petting, but she'd refused to have sex with him—until the night before the wedding. Vince had said they would be too tired after the ceremony and festivities to truly enjoy their wedding night. *"Tonight we can be spontaneous,"* he'd whispered. Champagne and sheer curiosity had worn her down. Twenty-four hours later, she was single again. Coincidence? She thought not.

"What do you think, Belinda? Should a woman hold out for a ceremony?"

"I . . . don't have an opinion."

"Well, I think it's irresponsible *not* to sleep with a guy before you get serious," Carole said. "That's like buying a house without going inside."

When Belinda pulled up to the clubhouse in the apartment complex, the women were still debating the validity of Rosemary's DON'T.

Rosemary opened the door and stuck one leg out. "If you want me to contribute to this so-called book, then it's going to have some old-fashioned rules."

Libby worked her mouth back and forth, then heaved a bosom-bouncing sigh. "Okay."

Belinda turned around in her seat. "Girls, I'll be on time in the morning, I promise."

"Are you sure you want to drive?" Rosemary asked.

"The car seems to be running fine, as long as you don't mind riding in an eyesore." Depending on the estimates, she might not be able to pay for the repairs right away.

Rosemary shrugged. "I don't mind. But bring your gym bag and we'll tackle the weight machines at lunch. Legs tomorrow, arms on Thursday."

Belinda's smile froze. "Okay."

"I'll bring you the name of Gustav's cousin, the auto body guy," Carole said.

"Thanks."

They closed their doors, waved to each other, and moved off in opposite directions.

Libby returned the legal pad to her bag. "At this rate, I'll be ready to retire by the time we finish this book."

Belinda laughed and steered back toward the entrance. "It's a cute idea, though—a multigenerational approach to men."

"*Men*—you can't live with 'em and you can't just shoot 'em." Libby sighed. "I think I'll make pork chops for dinner."

"Uh-hm." Since that hefty raise Margo promised her wouldn't kick in for a while, she was thinking pork 'n beans for dinner.

"Glen likes pork chops." Libby patted a Bloomingdale's bag near her knee. "And if I butter him up with a little fried food, maybe I can smuggle in my new wind sock."

"When did you buy that?"

"At lunch—my friend in HR was going to the downtown location and asked me to ride along." Libby made a rueful noise. "Jeanie got me into wind socks."

Belinda remembered her earlier thought of whether the woman had committed suicide. On the other hand, Carole had mentioned it was Jeanie's idea to take self-defense classes—had she been afraid of something . . . or someone? Belinda affected a light tone.

"Libby, was your friend's death really an accident?"

Libby looked up. "Did you hear something different?"

Belinda pulled the car into Libby's driveway. "No, I . . . no."

Libby's suspicious expression turned to distress. "Oh, Lordy, there's Glen. See you tomorrow." The woman catapulted out of the car and practically ran past her husband, who was talking to a neighbor. Her husband smiled, then caught sight of the Bloomingdale's bag. His expression changed, and when Belinda pulled out, he was striding after Libby, his face a tomato. Hopefully those fried pork chops would calm him down.

Libby's reaction to the question about Jeanie Lawford's death nagged at Belinda as she rejoined the heavy traffic, but she tried to put the unfortunate woman out of her mind.

The ping of pain from the accident had flowered into a persistent ache. "Mmmm, what a day," she murmured, then smiled in spite of her discomfort. What was a little stitch compared to the opportunity her tardiness had inadvertently led to? Chief. Financial. Officer. Could most successful people trace their achievements back to one pivotal action? One decision to take a chance, to break a rule?

The car behind her blasted her with its horn. She smiled in the rearview mirror and pulled ahead. She was still smiling as she turned into her subdivision.

Perry Ponytail was in his driveway, shirtless and washing his king-cab truck. Feeling generous, Belinda waved as she drove by. She pulled into her driveway and shifted into park in front of her garage door—she needed to unload her car trunk and take pictures of the damage for her insurance company. She hauled her purse and briefcase out of the floorboard, then walked to the end of the short driveway to check her mailbox.

Junk mail, junk mail, card from Vince, junk mail.

Her heart squeezed. A card from Vince?

Chapter 6

Some men were leg men and some were breast men. Vince Whittaker was a Hallmark man. He gave cards for every obscure holiday on the calendar, and for no reason at all. Somewhere in her remaining unpacked moving cartons was a hatbox full of cards he'd given her. While they'd been dating, she had considered his card-giving thoughtful. Since the wedding, however, she had come to believe that he liked the efficiency of the little colorful squares of paper: If one gave cards that expressed a sentiment, one didn't have to verbally express said sentiment.

Because she hadn't talked to him since moving to Atlanta, she mused over the numerous card options at his disposal: miss you, thinking of you, I'm sorry, congratulations, sympathy, get well (if he was presumptuous enough to think she had a broken heart), and thank you (if he was uncouth enough to gloat over his freedom).

She pushed her thumb underneath the envelope flap.

"Hey, Belinda!"

She shielded her eyes to see Perry walking toward her, his white, wiry torso gleaming from sweat and suds. "Hi, Perry."

"Sure is hot, ain't it?"

He zeroed in on her boobs, and she wished she hadn't removed her jacket. "Yes, it's hot, all right."

"How's the furniture business?"

"Fine."

"I'm in the market for a new recliner."

"Ah. I can't help you there because I work in the home office."

"Where's that?"

"The Stratford Plaza building on Peachtree."

He nodded. "My company has the electrical maintenance contract on that building. Swanky place."

"Yes."

He smashed a fly that landed on his stomach, then yanked his thumb toward his shiny truck. "While I got the hose and bucket out, I was thinking we could wash your car."

"Oh, no, thank you, Perry."

"I'll do most of the work. I can pull your car down while you change into cutoffs and a T-shirt."

And if her T-shirt just happened to get wet during the car-washing, he wouldn't object. These Southern men were a crafty breed.

"Thanks, Perry, but I had a fender bender this morning, so there's no use washing my car until I have it repaired."

He tore his gaze from her chest to walk around the car and inspect the damage. He whistled low. "Yep, looks like you'll need a headlight and maybe a bumper. Where's your tire?"

"In the trunk."

He circled the car and squinted at her trunk lid, which sat decidedly askew.

"I think the trunk latch was damaged, too."

He ran his fingers along the wide part of the seam, gave a couple of tugs and popped it open. Her deflated tire sat on top of the miscellaneous mess. He shook his head as he examined the ragged tear in the rubber. "Definitely gonna need a new tire." Then he fingered the latch mechanism and made a clicking sound with his cheek. "Yeah, it's broken."

"Leave it open, I'm going to empty the trunk later."

He lowered the lid partially and wiped his hand on his splattered jeans. "What did you hit?"

"A police car."

"No shit?"

"Er, no."

"Damn. Want to go get some barbecue?"

"Thank you, no." She patted her briefcase. "I brought work home with me. Busy, busy, busy."

"Okay. Maybe some other time."

"Maybe."

She waved good-bye and hurried across the patch of grass between the curb and her front door. Inside she heaved a sigh of relief, stepped out of her shoes in the foyer, then walked through the first floor to park her purse and briefcase on the breakfast bar.

"Downey, I'm home."

Belinda didn't expect the cat to come running, and she didn't. Downey was still pouting over the move to Atlanta, away from Vince. She had reminded the little fur ball more than once that if Vince had wanted her, he would have kept her (the voice of experience), but Downey refused to let go.

After grabbing a Diet Pepsi from the refrigerator, Belinda sat at the small glass table tucked into a niche in her kitchen and contemplated the envelope from Vince. How had he gotten her address—from her mother? Not that she would be difficult to track down using a public records source. Regardless, a sovereign woman would write Return to Sender on the front and send it winging back to Cincinnati.

She opened the can of soda, took a sip, and held the envelope up to the window.

But what if the contents of his card offered some explanation to his behavior—he was gay, he was stupid, he was dying—that could give her closure?

It was a nice envelope, buff-colored, substantial in pound and gently textured. Square and oversized, extra postage—Birds of the Audubon Society. Fancy packaging for a deep message, or fancy packaging to compensate for lack of one?

The envelope was thick—maybe it contained a tell-all letter? Pictures? Cash?

Yilk—a wedding invitation?

He'd sworn no other woman was involved, but he was the same man who'd sworn to love and honor her until death parted them and then changed his mind three hundred and sixty minutes later.

She closed her eyes and willed away the melancholy that threatened to descend. Why had the card arrived today of all days, when she'd gotten possibly the biggest break of her career and was starting to feel good about her move to Atlanta?

A touch against her shin made her jump. Downey blinked up at her and yawned.

"Oh, *now* you want my attention," Belinda teased. With one hand she lifted the cat to her lap and with the other waved the unopened envelope. "A mysterious message from your precious master."

Downey swatted at the envelope, then decided that her paw needed grooming. Belinda propped the envelope against a yellow fruit bowl and studied it while she stroked Downey's neck. For now, she'd leave it. And think.

The phone rang, sending Downey springing to the floor. Belinda rose and flipped on lights as she walked back to the front of the town house and into the room that would serve as a sitting room when she could afford something to sit on. For now, it housed two unopened moving cartons, one blue upholstered swivel chair, one temperamental television, and one end table that served as magazine rack and telephone stand. She picked up the portable handset, thinking she'd someday splurge on caller ID. For now, so few people knew her number that it didn't matter.

"Hello?"

"Hello, dear, it's Mother."

She smiled. "Yes, Mother, I recognized your voice."

"Did I catch you at a bad time?"

Belinda glanced around her quiet, empty rooms. "No. Have you finished packing?" In a few days her parents were embarking on the cross-country trip to the Grand Canyon they had planned for years. They were supposed to have left after the wedding, but her mother hadn't wanted to leave her in Cincinnati by herself at such a vulnerable time. After she'd moved to Atlanta, her mother hadn't wanted to leave her on the East Coast by herself at such a vulnerable time. Belinda had at last convinced her to go.

"Almost dear, almost. I hate to bother you with this pesky detail, but Mr. Finn, the mailman, brought me a package that you had returned to Suzanne Rickman before you left—you know, the silver-plated candlesticks? Well, a corner of the address label somehow got torn off, and by the time it was sent back to you, you'd moved. Mr. Finn thought rather than forwarding it on to you in Atlanta, that maybe I'd know Suzanne's address. But the only address I have for Suzanne is when she still lived at home. I called her parents, but their machine says they're on vacation and—"

"Hang on, Mom," Belinda cut in, knowing the story would go on and on otherwise. "I have Suzanne's address in my organizer." She walked back to the breakfast bar to empty her purse. "How are you and Dad?"

Her mother emitted a musical sigh. "Worried about you."

Motherhood was guilt on a slow drip.

"Well, you shouldn't be. I'm making new friends, and my job is going well." She wedged the phone between ear and shoulder and transferred items from her purse to the countertop. "In fact, today my boss hinted at a promotion." She told herself the seed of doubt that sprouted in her stomach as soon as the words left her tongue was due to the fact she didn't want to count her chickens before they were hatched, not because she was having doubts about her role in the matter.

"A promotion, isn't that nice. Have you met any young men?"

Priorities, priorities. Perry's face popped into her head—skip for obvious reasons. Then the dark-eyed policeman from this morning—skip for obvious reasons. "Um, no. In fact, there are no men in Atlanta, Mom, just women."

"Oh, Belinda, stop teasing me."

She frowned at her empty purse and picked through the items she'd removed. "Mom, my address book is probably in the car. Can I call you later?"

"Of course. Your father says hello and have you checked the oil lately."

Her father was a retired mechanic and lived in abject fear of her car engine locking up from lack of lubrication. If Frank Hennessey knew the hardships that Atlanta traffic was inflicting upon her car, he'd stroke out. "Tell Dad I'm taking the car in for a complete tune-up this week." True. Sort of.

"He'll be so happy to hear that."

"Give him my love."

"Bye, dear."

She hung up the phone and jogged upstairs to change clothes—might as well empty the trunk while she was outside. After dragging on shorts and T-shirt (*with* a bra, just in case Perry and his hose were still in the vicinity), she gave in to the guilt and bent to straighten her bed even though she'd be mussing the covers again in a few hours.

The leopard-print bed-in-a-bag had been an impulse buy after the move, and she still wasn't entirely comfortable with the choice, despite the fact that she was now a born-again bad girl. But she hadn't been able to stomach the thought of using sheets that she and Vince had shared, even though their activity had been largely innocuous. So, out with the Waverly plaid and in with the wild animal print.

Grrrrr.

A quick plump to the solitary goose-down pillow—

she'd gotten rid of the one permeated with Vince's cologne.

His too-sweet, too-trendy, too-memorable cologne.

Her thoughts landed on the envelope sitting downstairs. If Vince had met someone, or was—heaven forbid—getting married, wouldn't her mother know about it?

Certainly. But Barbara Hennessey would never drop that kind of bombshell on what she perceived to be her wounded daughter. If she knew something, she would go out of her way not to mention Vince's name.

Belinda chewed on her lip. Come to think of it, her mother *hadn't* mentioned Vince's name.

She shook herself mentally, situated the shammed pillow in the center of the bed, and thumped it with satisfaction. Men were unnecessary, so one pillow would suffice.

Belinda retraced her steps to the front door, exited barefoot, and allowed Downey to follow. The sun-resistant Bermuda grass was a soft, tickly rug for her toes, and a haven for enough insects to tempt even cranky Downey from her malaise. Thank goodness Perry and his truck were nowhere in sight—off to the barbecue place, she assumed. A few children played in the yards of the larger homes across the street. The *ship, ship, ship* of a sprinkler that she couldn't see filled the cooling air, and the sun was beginning its slide.

She used a disposable camera to record her beloved car's injuries and told herself this was why one had auto insurance. She then resigned herself to the trunk. She removed the violated tire and leaned it against the bumper, then divided the nonessential items between the garbage and the garage. Back into the trunk went the tire and the two crates of reference material that she vowed to carry to her cubicle tomorrow. After all, soon she might have a bigger office.

She discounted the sudden pain in her stomach as hunger pangs.

When she opened the car door, Downey promptly jumped inside and made a nuisance of herself while Belinda rummaged under the seats for the waylaid organizer.

"I know you're hungry," she muttered to the yowling cat. "So am I."

Hungry, and minus an organizer, she admitted a few minutes later. She didn't recall having used it at the office, although as preoccupied as she'd been the rest of the day, she might have. Hopefully it was in her cubicle somewhere, because it contained not only her address book but her personal and business schedule as well.

She pulled the car into the garage and shooed Downey through the door leading inside. "Let's eat, my friend." But she had no sooner poured kibbles into a bowl than the phone rang again—her mother, no doubt. Obsessing over Suzanne's package and conveying a checklist from her father for the car tune-up.

"Hello?"

"Is this Belinda Hennessey?"

She tensed for a telemarketing spiel. "Yes."

"This is Lieutenant Wade Alexander of the Atlanta PD."

Her mind froze.

"We were involved in an accident this morning, ma'am."

Recognition slammed into her. "Oh. Of course." Libby's remark clanged in her memory. *He got your address—I bet he'll call you at home.* "What can I do for you, Lieutenant?"

"I believe you left something in my cruiser."

Her organizer. She winced. "Yes. What a relief, I thought I'd lost it." She recalled removing items from her purse to find a hairbrush while sitting in his car—how careless. "How can I arrange to get it back that would be convenient for your schedule?"

"My schedule is pretty erratic the next couple of days." Fatigue weighted his voice. "How about I drop it by your office?"

"That's very kind of you."

"Just doing my job, ma'am. Where do you work?"

"At the Stratford Plaza building on Peachtree, Archer Furniture, eighth floor."

Silence resounded on the other end.

Belinda frowned. "Hello?"

"I'm familiar with the place," he said slowly. "I'll get it to you as soon as possible."

"Thank you." She pressed her lips together. "Lieutenant Alexander . . . I hope you made your meeting this morning."

More silence, then, "Yes, ma'am. Goodnight."

Belinda replaced the handset and groaned. If the man didn't think she was an idiot before, he certainly did now. Hopefully he would leave her organizer with a receptionist, and she wouldn't even have to see him.

Well, until traffic court, that is.

From across the room, her briefcase loomed large. *"I'll take another look at those numbers."* Easy to say when she'd been alone today with Margo—so why did she suddenly feel the need to procrastinate?

She downed two Advil tablets for her sore neck and ran her hands through her overlong, flattened hair. Another to-do item: find a hairstylist. As if finding a new doctor, dentist, ob/gyn, and insurance agent wasn't bad enough. She'd have to ask the girls to recommend someone convenient and not outrageously priced. Meanwhile, a scrunchie might be in order.

The weather was too clear for the television to pick up anything but fuzz—a new set was definitely second on her shopping list behind a couch—so she found an R&B station on the radio. (Talkin' Tom had flown home hours ago.) A can of clam chowder, a handful of crackers, and an apple sufficed for dinner. She ate at the glass table, staring at the envelope Vince had sent, and gleefully fantasized about running into him when she went home for the holidays.

"Oh, you saw me on CNN? Yes, I was honored that Archer made me their CFO so quickly. And who knew we'd become the darling of the analysts after the company went public?" (Hearty laugh). "Our breaking up was the best thing for both of us, Vince."

It could happen.

She switched on her computer so it could boot up

while she washed the dishes. For the next hour, she pored over the Payton financial statements, reading the small print and referencing every footnote. The capital expenditures seemed suspiciously high, especially in light of the rash of corporations that'd been caught dumping expenses on the wrong side of the balance sheet to prop up their bottom line.

Belinda sighed and steepled her hands. Payton used a reputable accounting firm, and legally, disclosure had been satisfied. Still, the numbers weren't transparent enough to suit her.

"I don't want unnecessary questions to stall the acquisition."

Margo couldn't have been more clear, but Belinda didn't want to greenlight a transaction that would come back to haunt Archer; surely Margo didn't want that kind of headache.

On the other hand, people at the top were paid to deal with headaches. She sat back in her chair. What seemed risky to her was probably rote to Margo and other senior executives. And if she was going to fit in at the top, she needed to be more assertive, to take on the competition.

With a confident appearance, a few buzzwords, and a practiced pitch, she might be able to pull this off.

Belinda pushed to her feet and cleared her throat loudly enough to pull Downey's attention away from grooming her hindquarters.

"Felines and gentlemen, based on the financial statements of Payton Manufacturing, it is my opinion . . .

. . . that the acquisition of Payton would indeed give Archer the fiscal synergy it needs in preparation for going public."

Belinda swept a level gaze around the board room table, stopping long enough to make eye contact with Juneau Archer (a striking but gently befuddled man), two venture capitalists who served on Archer's board of directors (short, dubious-looking men), Monica Tanner, VP of design (slim, nail-biting forty-ish Archer veteran), and

Tal Archer, VP of sales and marketing (disinterested mid-thirties gay heir apparent), and finally, Margo. Of the team assembled, she was the last person to contribute to the pitch, and if she had to say so herself, she'd wowed them with her charts and spreadsheets.

One of the board members leaned forward. "Ms. Hennessey, Archer has been formulating this acquisition for nearly a year. You're by far the newest member of the team—"

"Gentlemen," Margo cut in. "Belinda came to us from Visher-Floyd Insurance in Cincinnati. She was on the team that coordinated the acquisition of Three Signs and Limpkin, resulting in one of the largest insurance companies on the eastern seaboard. She has spent countless hours combing Payton's financial statements." She flashed Belinda a charming smile. "I trust her judgment."

Belinda smoothed back a strand of hair that had escaped her chignon and concentrated on looking competent.

The director who had appeared to be on the verge of questioning Belinda's credentials looked at his partner, then splayed his hands. "If you trust Ms. Hennessey's judgment, Margo, that's good enough for us. The board will vote on the matter tomorrow morning, but since our two votes plus Juneau's constitute a majority, I believe congratulations are in order."

Exclamations and handshakes traveled around the table. Margo looked at Belinda and mouthed, "You killed them."

Belinda returned a calm, professional nod, but inside she basked in her boss's praise. She just might give this risk-taking philosophy an earnest go.

Chapter 7

"So, I heard the board of directors approved the acquisition," Rosemary said.

Belinda labored to bench-press a lousy twenty-five pounds. At the top of the extension, she glanced up at the older, firmer woman who was spotting her. "Yep," was all she could manage. She lowered the bar to her chest, and her pecs groaned in relief.

"Juneau seemed pleased," Rosemary said. "And Margo is in rare form."

Belinda followed Rosemary's gaze across the noisy gym, where Margo was receiving one-on-one attention from the gym's buff trainer on a mysterious-looking machine that appeared to work the crotch muscles.

Anxiety needled Belinda—walking the line between loyalty to Margo and loyalty to her friends was proving to be a high-wire act. "Am I finished? I think I heard something pop."

Rosemary dragged her gaze from Margo. "One more set, then we'll hit the showers."

Belinda grunted her way through the repetitions, hoping she'd be able to lift her jelly arms to wash her hair. Her legs still throbbed from yesterday's punishment.

(Rosemary called it "lunges." Tomato, tomoto.) Between her sore muscles and mild whiplash, Advil was becoming her between-meals snack. She glanced at the dry sauna longingly—maybe another day.

The locker room experience was another one of those unfamiliar girly situations; call her old-fashioned, but the sight of bare-breasted and-butted women walking around chatting about the best plastic surgeons made her pull her towel just a little tighter around her own ta-tas.

Rosemary, too, was refreshingly modest, but when Belinda emerged from the curtained dressing room, fully clothed and coiffed, she practically stepped on Margo—naked. (Okay, the little woman was wearing flip-flops. And lipstick.)

"Hello," her boss said, just as if she weren't full-frontal with a subordinate.

"Hi," Belinda said, keeping her eye contact high while sliding past.

"Belinda."

She closed her eyes briefly, then turned back. The woman's nipples were as big as saucers. "Yes?"

"I meant to tell you how nice you looked at the meeting yesterday, and today."

Belinda knew the brown wool-blend flattered her auburn hair, so the compliment was probably sincere, but it was weird coming from an unclothed woman. She tried to imagine Margo in her underwear. "Thank you."

"And your hair—well, I think all professional women should wear their hair up."

So it was a good thing that the coin had landed heads for bun, versus tails for stretchy headband. "Thanks." Her eyes were watering from the strain of keeping them fixed. She blinked and pointed over her shoulder. "I should go—Rosemary is waiting."

A little wrinkle appeared between Margo's eyebrows. "Someone mentioned that you've become friends with Rosemary." From the tone of her voice, there was no love lost between the women.

"I carpool with Rosemary, Libby, and Carole from the mailroom."

"A word of caution, Belinda. A member of senior management has to be careful of the company she keeps."

Belinda blinked. "Jeanie Lawford was a member of senior management, wasn't she?"

Margo's eyes narrowed. "What do you know about Jeanie Lawford?"

Belinda swallowed. "Just that she died . . . suddenly."

Her boss's face melted into a mournful expression. "Yes, so sad. I had big plans for Jeanie, and yes, I gave her the same advice about her carpool buddies. She told me she was trying to find a way to bow out gracefully. I hope you do the same."

Belinda held her gaze. "I believe I'm a good judge of character."

Margo's black-cherry-colored mouth curled, but the warmth didn't reach her eyes. "So am I." Then she glided away, leaving Belinda with an eyeful of steely buns.

Rosemary was checking her watch when Belinda emerged from the locker room. "Sorry. I ran into Margo. Nude."

Rosemary rolled her eyes as she shouldered her gym bag. "That woman is unbearable. I don't understand how she has the wool pulled over Juneau's eyes."

They exited the gym into the busy first floor of the Stratford Plaza that housed service businesses, a food court, and the entrance to a high-rise hotel.

Belinda shrugged. "Maybe Mr. Archer overlooks her . . . *personality* . . . because she's good at her job. And you have to admit he's rarely at the office."

"I know. I wish you could've met him before his wife became ill—he was so full of vigor and ambition. Her struggle completely drained him, and he hasn't recovered."

As they threaded through the lunch crowd, Belinda thought ahead to the food court. Rosemary would hit the salad bar, while *she* was thinking more along the lines of a *candy* bar. "The son isn't interested in taking over the family business?"

"Tal?" Rosemary sighed. "Tal Archer isn't interested in anything he can't snort up his nose. He couldn't care less about the business, but he couldn't get a job making his salary anywhere else in this town."

Belinda swallowed the urge to ask for more details before the discussion spun into full-fledged gossip. Margo was right about one thing—if she was going to be CFO, she needed to maintain a professional distance from the watercooler talk.

"I'm going to the salad bar," Rosemary said.

"I think I'll browse. I'll see you upstairs."

She waited until Rosemary was out of sight, then contemplated blowing her diet on a burrito. She bit into her tongue, wavering. A sudden jostle to her right shoulder forced her teeth down so hard that she tasted blood. An eye-needling pain ricocheted through her mouth and jaws, stealing her breath.

"I'm so sorry," a man said.

Her eyes were closed, but his voice sounded familiar—and she associated it with pain. As her mouth sang, she opened one eye, then the other. Tall, blond, bomber jacket. The guy from the elevator.

"You again," he said, green eyes laughing. "I don't believe it."

She swallowed blood. "Believe it."

"Are you all right?"

"Haven't we had this conversation before?"

He looked sheepish, then reached into the back pocket of his chinos and pulled out a folded white handkerchief. "You're bleeding."

Vince didn't own a handkerchief. Southern men apparently bought them by the gross—perhaps so they could instigate accidents. She accepted the cloth and dabbed at her lip until the red disappeared.

He leaned forward for a better look. "Are you going to need stitches?"

"No. But a smoothie is sounding good for lunch."

"My treat."

"That's not necessary."

He extended his hand. "Julian Hardeman."

She hesitated, but he wasn't giving off serial killer vibes. "Belinda Hennessey." It was a nice hand.

"What kind of smoothies do you like, Belinda Hennessey?"

And he had great eyes. "Strawberry kiwi lime."

"One strawberry kiwi lime smoothie coming up." He veered away, heading toward a crowded counter. His clean-cut good looks turned a few heads. He had an open, honest-looking face, with a light sunburn on his cheeks and nose. A generous, ready smile and a pleasing profile. And no wedding ring.

Not that any of it mattered in lieu of her resolution that men were unnecessary.

She looked away, back, and away again, realizing with a jolt that Julian Hardeman was the first man she'd *studied* since Vince. ("Since Vince" had somehow become a time marker.) She had grown so accustomed to behaving like an engaged woman that she was going to have to ease back into the idea of openly looking at men again.

"One strawberry kiwi lime smoothie."

Belinda looked openly, and her pulse tripped. "Thank you."

He lifted another tall cup. "Thought I'd try one, too. Care to join me?"

"I should get back to work."

"Come on, give me five minutes to prove that I'm a nice guy." He smiled. "If I fail, then you can avoid me from now on."

He was appealing, she had to give him that. And she needed to make an effort to meet new people—it wasn't his fault that he had a penis. "Okay. Five minutes."

Through the swarming mass of hurrying bodies, he led the way to a tall café table. When she set down her gym bag, he said, "I see you work out."

"In the loosest sense." He laughed, revealing perfect teeth, and she was struck by the sense that she knew him from somewhere other than the elevator.

"Do you work in this building?" he asked.

She nodded. "I'm a finance specialist for Archer Furniture Company."

The smoothie cup stopped halfway to his mouth. "Archer?"

"You're familiar with the company?"

"A friend of mine used to work there. Jeanie Lawford."

The icy fruit blend stung her tongue, then soothing numbness settled in. The woman's name kept turning up, like the corner of a rug. "I'm new to the company, so I didn't know her. But I did hear about the terrible accident. I'm sorry for your loss."

He nodded appreciatively, his eyes somber. "Jeanie was a great girl. That kind of stuff keeps you awake at night."

"So her death was an accident?"

"Hm? Oh, yes. Tragic." He stared at the contents of his cup.

She wondered briefly if he and Jeanie had been more than friends, then cast about for a safer topic. "So you work in the building, too?"

"No, my office is in the Blake building across the street, but parking is better here, and I belong to the gym. And my stockbroker is on the ninth floor." He smirked. "The way the market's been bucking lately, I've been spending a lot of time in his office."

"What do you do for a living?"

He hesitated, then pulled at his chin. "I'm a news reporter."

"That sounds interesting." And explained his well-modulated voice.

"It has its days." He angled his head. "I can't place your accent."

"Cincinnati. I moved here to take the job with Archer."

"How do you like it so far? The city, I mean."

"Fine. Except for the nightmare traffic."

He laughed heartily. "One person's nightmare is another person's job security."

She nodded, but her attention was drawn to a tall uniformed man bearing down on her table. Lieutenant Wade Alexander, carrying a small brown paper bag. He didn't look much happier than when she'd last seen him, but what had she expected? "Excuse me," she said to Julian as she slid down from the chair. "I really do need to get back to work. Thank you for the smoothie."

He stood with her. "Maybe I'll see you in the gym."

She smiled. "I'll be on my guard."

He turned and, to her surprise, did a double take at the officer striding her way. "Lieutenant Alexander."

The other man nodded curtly. "Hardeman."

Belinda's surprise gave way to the realization that it wasn't so unusual for a police officer and a reporter to be acquainted. From the body language, though, she inferred that the men weren't exactly chums.

"I hope you're not here to see me," Julian said with a little laugh.

"Not this time." Officer Alexander held up the bag. "Ms. Hennessey left something in my cruiser."

Julian looked back and forth between them, and Belinda's neck warmed. "Lieutenant Alexander and I were involved in a little accident yesterday morning."

Julian grinned at the other man. "Don't tell me that was you on I-85 southbound?"

Great—every reporter in town had heard about the incident.

The officer didn't smile back. "Yes."

Julian chortled, then cast an apologetic look in her direction. "I understand now why you're so apprehensive about the traffic."

A flush climbed her neck. "It was my fault. Lieutenant Alexander was very gracious."

"Gracious?" Julian grinned again. "I've never heard anyone accuse you of that before, Alexander."

The officer gave him a pointed gaze. "Don't let us keep you, Hardeman."

The comment hung in the air for five stretchy seconds. Belinda had the uneasy sensation that she was standing between two bucks, and on the verge of being marked.

Julian's smile faded, then he recovered quickly. "Yeah, I need to be going. Take care, Alexander. I'll see you around, Belinda."

She gave him a little smile, then turned her attention back to the officer, who arrowed his dark gaze at Julian's retreating back. The men had history.

She coughed politely. "You're quite the detective to find me in the food court."

When he glanced back, she noticed that his jaw was clean-shaven today, and his eyes were clear—clear and not blue, but gray. His expression eased as he nodded toward the entrance. "I passed your friend, and she thought you might still be here. I didn't mean to intrude on your lunch."

"You didn't. Julian and I just met."

One side of his mouth slid back. "Hardeman works fast." He extended the paper bag.

She frowned at his presumption but took the package, registering that it didn't seem heavy enough to hold her electronic organizer. A peek inside nearly caused her to pee her pants—the tiny blue pillow she'd removed from her trunk and stuffed into her purse because she was too embarrassed to let him, or anyone, see the message a well-meaning aunt had cross-stitched onto its surface:

Belinda and Vince
xoxoxoxo
Married April 5, 2003

She closed the bag with a crunch.

"Is something wrong?"

"This isn't what I thought I left in your car."

The cop pursed his mouth. "It looked personal. I thought you'd want it back."

"I don't—" She pressed her hand to her mouth and took a deep breath. "I mean, I didn't realize this was . . . missing. I thought I lost my electronic organizer."

"I'll take another look when I leave."

"Thank you. Again." Her mind raced for a way to salvage her pride, but it came up empty. "I should get back to work."

Officer Alexander started to go, then turned back, hands on lean hips. "Ms. Hennessey, this is really none of my business, but . . ."

"But what?"

He shifted from foot to foot. "Are you still driving on that spare tire?"

Her dad would love this guy. "I'm getting the tire replaced today."

"Good." He straightened. "Julian Hardeman has a reputation for playing games."

She blinked. "Excuse me?"

He held up both hands, stop-sign fashion. "I realize you're married, and I'm not saying that you'd be interested, but since you just met him, I thought I should warn you."

First Margo telling her with whom she could "associate," and now him? Belinda held up a hand, trying to absorb the whole Southern macho protect-the-little-woman syndrome. The man had only changed her tire—proprietary behavior required at least a ceiling-fan install. "Okay, first, I'm not married."

He looked at the bag holding the effusive pillow, and she realized his confusion.

"The marriage didn't . . . work." She lifted her chin. "And second, I'm sure your advice is well-intended, Lieutenant, but I prefer to form my own opinions."

He nodded, but a muscle in his jaw moved, as if he wanted to say more. His gaze was so encompassing and so . . . *protective* that she had the crazy urge to walk closer. To compensate, she backed away. Men were unnecessary. And a woman with a new philosophy of breaking rules did not foster a pop-up attraction to a man of the law.

"I have to go. Thank you again for . . . this." She held up the crumpled bag, then turned and fled.

Chapter 8

"I've got one," Carole said from the backseat. ' "DO be concerned when he wants to talk.' "

"Good one," Libby said, then brushed doughnut sugar off the legal pad before scribbling down the line.

"I have a feeling this DO comes with a story," Rosemary said with a sigh.

Belinda hoped so—conversation took the pressure off her to come up with a "rule" to contribute to the manuscript. Concentrating on the rabid morning traffic was taxing enough, although the upshot of driving a car with a few dents was that other commuters assumed you were a bad driver and gave you breathing room.

"It's Gustav," Carole said. "He's trying to talk me into sleeping with him."

"Too much information," Rosemary said, waving her hands.

Libby turned around. "Good gravy, I figured you'd already slept with him—his feet are the size of breadboxes."

Carole sucked at her braces. "I've seen him in the shower—that whole feet-penis size thing is a total myth."

"Really?" Libby asked. "How about hands? I always

heard a man's hands were a good indication of the size of his manhood."

"I heard thumbs," Carole added.

Rosemary coughed. "I always regarded a man's nose as a good indication."

They all stared.

"Miss Priss speaks," Libby said. "See, Rosemary, I knew you'd be able to contribute to this book."

Rosemary glared. "Don't you dare write that down."

Belinda caught Carole's eye in the rearview mirror. "I thought that consummating the relationship was required for a green card."

Carole shrugged. "We've developed a system to keep our lies straight. And we put on a good show—share the same bed and same bathroom. The INS people ask you all kinds of personal information."

Libby licked glaze off her thumb. "Aren't you physically attracted to Gustav?"

"He's okay, I guess."

"So, how do you all share a bed and not fool around?"

"We put one of those full-body pillows between us," Carole said matter-of-factly. "You know, the pillows for women who sleep alone."

Belinda opened her mouth to ask where she could buy one.

Rosemary scoffed. "Another example of society trying to convince women that their beds should never be empty."

Belinda changed her mind.

Libby clicked the end of her ink pen. "Carole, what was that you said about keeping your lies straight?"

"I said we've developed a system."

"That's it." Libby wrote furiously. "Another good one. 'DO develop a system for keeping your lies straight.' "

"There's no room in relationships for lies," Rosemary declared.

Libby harrumphed. "Are you kidding? Lies are the glue that holds relationships together. We lie to our spouses, to our kids, to our ministers, and to ourselves. It keeps the peace. What do you think, Belinda?"

She thought the conversation was cutting a little close to the bone, that's what she thought. She'd spent a sleepless night with her one skimpy pillow thinking about the fibs she'd told since arriving in Atlanta—about Vince, about Payton Manufacturing. "I suppose avoiding the truth is okay as long as no one gets hurt."

Rosemary winced and shifted the lumbar cushion at her back. Perhaps that explained her surly mood. "Someone always gets hurt, even if you aren't aware. You should always be honest, because sooner or later, your past will catch up with you."

Libby raised her eyebrows. "Okay, to balance out the DO about lying, I'll add a DO about being honest. Happy?"

"Not today," Rosemary murmured.

Libby shot a quizzical look at Belinda, then set aside the pad to work on her hair. "So, Carole, are you going to nail Gustav or not?"

"I'm going to talk to my psychic about it."

"Christ, I'm out of this conversation," Rosemary said, twisting lower in the seat.

Carole shot a frown at the older woman, then stuck her head between the front seats. "The truth is, Gustav just isn't my type."

"Now there's a question," Libby said, unrolling her curlers. "Why does everyone believe they have a 'type'?"

"I don't know if it's so much a type, as it is holding out for that connection that you feel when you find Mr. Right." Carole sighed. "You know what I'm talking about?"

"No," Libby said flatly. "I don't have a type, and the only man I ever felt connected to is the doorman at Bloomingdale's. How about you, Belinda? Do you have a type?"

"Tall, dark, and uniformed," Carole teased. "I think that cop has a thing for you."

Belinda rolled her eyes. "I told you he came by yesterday only to return something I left in his car."

"He could have mailed it."

"It was . . . personal. But unimportant," she added. Belinda chewed on her thumbnail, rethinking her decision not to tell the girls about the "other" man at the risk of bringing up the sensitive subject of their coworker. She was suddenly overcome by the unfamiliar urge to share. "By the way, yesterday at the food court I ran into a guy named Julian Hardeman. Do you know him?"

Libby's eyes were shrouded with banana curls, but she shook her head. "Carole?"

"Doesn't ring a bell. Is he cute?"

Belinda squirmed. "I suppose so." Panic blipped that she'd be barraged with girly questions she wouldn't know how to answer, so she blurted, "He said he knew Jeanie Lawford."

They were silent for a few seconds, then Carole murmured, "I believe she was seeing someone, but Jeanie was so closemouthed about everything, I couldn't be sure."

"Closemouthed?" Libby snorted. "Try paranoid."

"Yeah, she was a little weird about her privacy and security stuff. Always locking things up and looking over her shoulder."

"Was she afraid of something? Is that why she took the self-defense class?" Belinda asked.

Libby shrugged. "Not that I know of."

"If you ask me," Carole said, "she was a little loopy there toward the end."

"She did seem preoccupied," Libby muttered behind a wall of hair. "But I chalked it up to getting a lot dumped into her lap when Jim Newberry was let go."

"How long did Jeanie work for Archer?"

Libby peeked through her hair and squinted. "Eight months?"

"Sounds right," Carole said.

"And what did she do?"

"Computer nerd," Libby said. "She came in as manager of the technology group. When Jim left, Jeanie was promoted to chief information officer."

Belinda mulled the similarities between herself and Jeanie—both had worked for Archer for a short period of time and both had benefited from someone else's misfortune. If she were the superstitious type, she might be . . . concerned.

"How did the accident happen?"

Libby shrugged. "Nobody knows. That elevator had been acting up, stopping on floors with the car a couple of feet too high or too low. It was a big joke around the office, people saying who they did and didn't want to get stuck on the elevator with."

"A few people were stuck once, weren't they?" Carole asked.

Libby nodded. "Jeanie was in that group, with Martin Derlinger and Clancy."

Carole made a face. "Yuck and yuckier."

"I think Clancy's nice," Belinda said with a laugh.

"He and Carole have mail control issues," Libby said out of the side of her mouth.

"Clancy's issues are way deeper than my mail bag," Carol insisted. "I walked into his cube last week and he was looking at porn on his computer screen."

Libby gasped. "Gay porn?"

"He zapped it before I could get a good look."

"Margo would have his head—she's the only person allowed to download porn at work."

The girls laughed, and Belinda joined in halfheartedly, once again torn by the desire to blend with her coworkers, and loyalty toward Margo. Maybe the woman wasn't a candidate for boss of the year, but she hadn't reached the position of chief operations officer by waging a popularity contest.

Libby sighed. "That reminds me. Performance evaluations start Friday."

"Oh, God," Carole said. "Already?"

Libby turned her head. "Margo was going to wait until she got back from Hawaii, but since her trip was postponed, she decided to do them now."

"Let the sucking up begin," Rosemary offered from the back.

"Have you rejoined the conversation?" Carole asked dryly.

"Does Margo have final approval on everyone's evaluation?" Belinda asked to divert an argument.

Rosemary nodded. "Juneau used to. But he handed that responsibility over to Margo as well."

"She's in her glory when she's putting people down," Carole said. "I dread it."

"Me, too," Libby said. "A performance evaluation with Margo is a one-hour spanking." She twisted her mouth to mimic the woman. "You make *too* many phone calls, you take lunch *every* day, and you wear too much *pink*."

Belinda laughed.

"I'm not exaggerating—I got cited for pink last year."

"Me, too," Carole said.

Belinda stopped laughing, incredulous.

"You want to kill her," Libby said. "But you sit there and take it because you know you have to."

"One of these days," Rosemary said, "Margo's going to go too far."

"Yeah, why couldn't she have been the one to fall down the elevator shaft?" Carole asked.

"Right."

"You said it."

Belinda swallowed at the vicious turn of the conversation. A little resentment toward one's boss was one thing, but to want her dead? *Yilk.*

Her dismay must have shown, because Libby laughed. "Talk to me after your crucifixion." Then she angled her head. "Unless you're expecting a big raise?"

Belinda's pulse picked up, but she affected a careless smile. "I'd just like to be able to buy a new couch and television."

"They're offering the sofa beds that Payton sent over to

employees at a discount," Rosemary said. "I've got my eye on that nice brown plaid sleeper. If you're interested, talk to Clancy."

"Thanks, I'll look into it."

"*If* you get a big raise?" Carole asked with a smile.

Belinda conjured up a mild shrug. "No matter what, sooner or later I'm going to have to buy a couch. My mother is threatening to ship my aunt's seventies sofa that's sitting in my parents' garage."

"I need a raise for more dental work," Carole said, running her finger over her braces. "But I doubt if I get one, not in this economy."

"Well, I'd better get a good raise," Libby said. "Because it's the only way I'm going to get Glen off my back about my credit cards."

Belinda was distracted from Libby's grim expression by an Atlanta PD cruiser passing her Civic in the left lane. Strangely, her pulse quickened until she determined the occupant wasn't Lieutenant Alexander. She pressed her shoulders back, irritated with herself. Her skin still prickled with embarrassment when she imagined the moment he had pulled her hoaky little pillow from beneath the seat of his cruiser. So not only did he know her marriage hadn't broken any longevity records but he also probably thought she was clinging to the past. That pillow would have been long gone if not for her guilt over the hours her Aunt Edie had spent making those tiny stitches. And as far as other mementos of her relationship with Vince—well, she'd left Cincinnati so abruptly that it had seemed easier to pack everything to sort later.

She bit into her lip, reminding herself she shouldn't care what Lt. Alexander thought of her. Or what he thought of Julian Hardeman, for that matter. The tension she'd sensed between the two men could probably be traced back to some classic scenario of the press and the cops being on opposite sides of a story.

Fortunately, the telltale intro to a radio traffic report halted her train of thought.

"Traffic is movin' fine on the Top End and all around

The Perimeter. Once you pass Spaghetti Junction, you're lookin' at a speed limit ride to the connector and into downtown. But you folks headin' into the city on I-20, you're in stop-and-go traffic because of a burst water main around the Villa Rica exit. Roll down your window and get those tempers cooled off when you drive by, you hear? This is Talkin' Tom Trainer for MIXX 100 FM traffic."

A little shiver raced over her shoulders—that man's voice was utter magic.

"The car is riding smoother," Libby said.

"I got the tire replaced last night," Belinda said. Ninety-five smackeroos. "And Carole, I drove by your husband's cousin's auto repair place afterward, and he's going to call me with a quote. Thanks again for the referral." She didn't add that the man had hinted he knew someone who could arrange for her car to "disappear" if she needed quick cash.

"You're welcome." Carole sighed. "That's my quandary—I can't get a new car until I get rid of Gustav, but when I do, I'll lose my connection to a good mechanic."

"But if you stay married," Libby pointed out, "you'll get to keep the money *and* the connection."

"Yeah, but Gustav would probably want to use the money to buy a house or something." She sounded glum.

"And you'd rather have a car?" Belinda asked with a smile.

"Oh, yeah. A house ties you down. And heck, people in this town practically live in their cars anyway."

True enough.

"Incoming," Libby warned. They all zoomed down their windows, except for Rosemary, who was either dozing now or faking it. Regardless, her face would be slick with hairspray by the time they arrived at the office.

"Have the acquisition papers been signed yet?" Carole asked. "I delivered a package from Payton Manufacturing to Mr. Archer yesterday, and one to Margo."

Belinda squirmed, relatively sure that Carole shouldn't

be talking about the mail even if she thought they all knew about the impending correspondence. "I could be wrong, but I suspect the contracts will come from Payton's attorneys by courier or guaranteed service."

"Woo-woo," Carole said. "Hunky Hank."

"Who?" Belinda asked.

"The APS delivery guy," Libby said, teasing the dark roots of her yellow hair with a tiny comb. "All the girls got it bad for him."

"Most of the guys, too," Carole added. "He really fills out those little shorts—oooh! Maybe he's the man Ricky said was right under my nose. Maybe Hunky Hank is my destiny."

"That's supposed to be the top female fantasy in America," Libby said. "Doing it with the APS guy in the back of his truck."

Belinda frowned. Did she have a fantasy? Besides the poor unsuspecting guy on the radio?

Libby patted and picked at her hair, preparing for the last coat of varnish. "I fantasize about a man who will mow the lawn."

Carole laughed. "Belinda, while you and Rosemary work out during lunch, Libby and I shop and ogle the landscapers."

"I don't ogle," Libby declared. "I . . . monitor. It might give me some material for the book."

"You are so full of crap," Carole said, poking the woman in the shoulder.

Belinda smiled at the interplay and took advantage of the opportunity to zone into her own thoughts. She was being fast-tracked at her new job, she was making friends, and that glint in Julian Hardeman's eye yesterday hadn't been a contact lens. She had every reason to be happy, to sleep like a newborn at night.

So why couldn't she put her finger on what was bothering her? Was her self-esteem so battered that she couldn't accept good fortune at face value? That she was suspicious of a man's interest in her? Of course, she might not have been suspicious at all if Lieutenant

Alexander hadn't been compelled to issue a "warning" about Julian. As if she should trust *his* advice simply because he'd changed her tire, returned her pillow, and had that I'll-take-care-of-the-world chip on his big shoulder.

She pushed her cheek out with her tongue. For all he knew, she might be *looking* for a man with a "reputation." Not only had the abstinence route gotten her nowhere but it had also taken a long time to get there. Maybe she'd give the casual sex thing another try—maybe the logistics had improved since she was a coed.

Belinda was still nursing the idea midmorning when her phone rang. She shuffled papers until she found the phone, then jammed the receiver between her ear and shoulder. "Belinda Hennessey."

"Hi, Belinda, this is Julian Hardeman."

Her stomach flipped. "Hello."

"I was hoping we could have lunch today—something that requires utensils." His voice rumbled deep and full of promise. "What do you say?"

Desire struck her midsection—a nice surprise, since she was afraid she'd lost the ability to summon that particular response. Should she take a chance? Especially since she had the distinct feeling that his lunch invitation would lead to more than just a free meal.

Belinda crossed her legs and smiled. "I say yes."

Chapter 9

"Isn't this better than the food court?" Julian asked as they were seated at a Thai eatery a couple of blocks down Peachtree Street.

Belinda agreed, while wondering what on the flammable menu she'd be able to ingest on her jumpy stomach. Julian wore gray chinos and a plum-colored shirt that flattered his fair coloring. Carole would say he looked "hot," and Belinda would concur.

His gaze roamed over her white V-necked blouse and pale blue jacket with an appreciative gleam. "You look . . . great."

Had Vince ever looked at her like that? "Thanks."

"I'm sorry I took you away from your workout," he said with eye contact that belied his casual tone.

The man's green eyes were mesmerizing, but she made her tongue move. "My friend Rosemary says this is our day to rest and allow our muscles to recover, so I'm off the hook."

"I typically go to the gym in the evening." He leaned forward, sending the barest hint of musky cologne her way. "But if you're going to be there every day during lunch, maybe I'll change my schedule."

He lifted his eyebrow, waiting for her response. This was her cue—was she interested? A thrill zipped over her thighs. There was something very sexy about a man who made his intentions known right up front. He was attracted to her.

"Don't you want to see how lunch goes?" she asked mildly.

"I already know it's going to go well." His voice held no hint of cockiness, just quiet confidence. It suited him. And it made her feel daring.

The waitress brought ice water and said she'd be back to take their order. Belinda sipped the water gratefully to douse the sudden hike in her temperature. "Any suggestions?" she asked as she scanned the menu.

Julian grinned. "How adventurous are you?"

His playful mood was contagious. "I'm feeling rather brave today."

"Then let's share an order of spicy basil leaves and shrimp."

"That's not exactly Southern comfort food."

His knee bumped hers. "Comfort is highly overrated."

A very grown-up feeling traveled her spine. He wanted to have an affair. It was surreal, this mundane conversation resonating with sensuality. A hum of awareness traveled over her nerve endings. So this was how people did it—made the leap from acquaintance to lover without the bother of small talk and small encounters in between. What sounded lewd in the pages of women's magazines now seemed like a perfectly natural occurrence unfolding between two consenting adults.

"Or," he said lightly, "we could always play it safe and order chicken fried rice."

The waitress returned with her pad in hand. "Are you ready to order?"

One side of his mouth crept up as his gaze bore into hers. "Belinda?"

Her mouth watered, and it wasn't from the talk of food. She'd broken the rules once this week, and she was getting a promotion out of it. If she broke her "men are unnecessary" rule, who knew what exciting things might happen?

She spoke to the waitress but didn't take her eyes off Julian. "We're going to split the spicy basil leaves and shrimp."

"That's a very hot dish," the waitress warned.

"Yes, we know," Julian said, his smoldering gaze locked with Belinda's.

The waitress walked away, and he leaned forward on his elbows. "I'm pleased that you agreed to meet me. I was afraid that Lieutenant Alexander would talk about me behind my back."

She tried not to register surprise. "Why would you think that?"

He shrugged. "Alexander and I aren't the best of friends."

"How do you know each other?"

"Through our jobs. I've been involved in a couple of police matters. He and I clashed."

"I thought maybe that's what had happened. You'll have to forgive me—I'm too new in town to connect your name with a particular newspaper or television station."

His smile returned. "I work for a television station and a radio station, but I'm behind the scenes at the TV station."

"And on the radio?" She wracked her brains for the call letters to the all-news stations so she could sound halfway informed.

"Well, even if you heard me on the radio, you wouldn't connect my name—I use a different on-air name."

"What is it?"

"I'm a traffic reporter, Talkin' Tom Trainer on MIXX 100 FM."

She went completely still. "No."

He grinned. "Yes."

"I don't believe this—I know you!"

"No kidding?"

She nodded, her mouth half-open. "I listen to you

every day." She laughed, unable to believe the coincidence. "But your accent . . . it sounds different."

His cheeks turned pink. "The on-air voice goes with the good-ole-boy on-air persona."

She nodded, noting the resemblance in his voice and the voice she was accustomed to hearing on the radio. No wonder when she'd first met him she'd had the feeling that she'd known him from somewhere—it wasn't his face she'd recognized but his voice. "This is amazing." She brought her hand to her mouth. "Oh, my God. No wonder you knew about my accident with Lieutenant Alexander—you watched it. I heard you announce it!"

He nodded, smiling. "I couldn't resist ribbing him, he's such a smug SOB. Unfortunately, he can't take a joke."

"He does seem a bit grim, although I can understand why he'd be angry with me."

"Don't take it personally. I hear he's going through a bad divorce."

Her heart dipped in empathy for the lieutenant.

"So," Julian said, brushing her hand with his. "Now that you know who I am, are you going to change your order?"

Under his pointed stare, her body strained toward him, her fantasy man from the radio. She wet her lips, gratified when he unconsciously mimicked her movement.

"Yes," she said, then flagged down the waitress. "Would you please bring us a side of Thai chili sauce for dipping?"

When she looked back to Julian, he had pushed out his cheek with his tongue and was nodding in approval.

Belinda wadded up a paper towel, stuffed it in her mouth, and dropped into her burnt orange office chair for a few seconds of blessed relief. She should have known she was in trouble when the food the waitress sat in front of her singed her nose hair. The first couple of bites of spicy basil leaves and shrimp hadn't been bad. And then the afterburn had set in.

The only way she could describe the experience was

swallowing trick birthday candles that wouldn't go out. After the first couple of layers of skin had dissolved from her tongue, she had lost all sensation, including the ability to speak in full sentences. Thankfully, Julian was a practiced talker and had required little more than positive body language to keep him chatting about his unusual job. Just when she'd thought she might combust, he'd been called to cover a chemical spill on Georgia 400. He'd tossed money on the table, and they'd practically sprinted back to the Stratford building parking garage.

"Tomorrow," he'd said with a rakish smile. "Meet me in the gym, in front of the dry sauna at noon."

She'd nodded (because she couldn't speak). Watching him jog away, her chest had gotten this weird, welled-up feeling that he was dashing off to risk his life so that the rest of Atlanta could arrive home safely.

Or at least get home in time to watch the Braves play.

She sucked on the paper towel, trying to absorb some of the pepper oils lingering on her tongue. What did Julian have in mind—working out together? And eventually working *in and out* together? She closed her eyes and squeezed her knees tight. How amazing that their paths had actually crossed. It was fate, wasn't it?

Her phone rang. She yanked up the receiver, then too late remembered she couldn't talk. Carefully she pulled the moist paper towel out of her mouth. As soon as the air hit her raw tongue, her mouth exploded with pain. Involuntarily, she moaned into the phone.

"Hello?" a male voice asked.

"Mm-hm." She clenched her teeth until the worst of the pain passed.

"Is this Belinda Hennessey?"

She tried to concentrate on breathing only through her nose. "Mm-hm."

"This is Lieutenant Wade Alexander."

"Oh. Heh-wo." She winced.

"Did I call at a bad time?"

"Um. No. Whaz up?"

After a few seconds of silence, he said, "I was calling

to let you know that I searched the cruiser, but I didn't find your address book."

"Oh. Thanz anyway."

"You're welcome. Are you all right?"

"Fine."

"Okay. Well . . . are you still driving on that spare?"

She smirked. "No."

"Okay. Well . . . good-bye then."

"Guh-bye."

She frowned at the phone when she set it down. At least he'd stopped calling her "ma'am." Then she remembered that Julian had said the man was going through a divorce, and she regretted her unkind thoughts. She wondered if he'd gotten his big heart broken, or if he'd been the one doing the damage.

"Belinda."

She jumped, then turned to see Clancy Edmunds standing at the opening to her cubicle. "Heh-wo, Cwancy."

"Is that an Elmer Fudd impersonation, or did you have lunch at the Thai place?"

"Thai."

He grimaced. "Your lips look like Melanie Griffith's."

"Thanz."

"Okay, I won't make you talk. Just come to the boardroom and point to whichever sofa bed you want. They're going fast."

She smiled—at least she meant to—and followed him in the direction of the boardroom, gingerly touching her lips and testing her tongue against the roof of her mouth. It all felt like a big, pulpy mass. En route, Clancy made an appreciative sound in his throat. She looked up to see a sandy-haired uniformed APS deliveryman coming their way, and she assumed it was the same guy that the girls had been salivating over. From the look of the young man's gear—back support harness, padded gloves, and thick-soled shoes—he was prepared for just about any maneuver, although she rather doubted that delivering packages in Midtown was all that dogged. Still, the accessories were . . . *effective.*

He gave her a friendly nod, then turned his attention to Clancy. "Ms. Campbell isn't in her office, and her secretary isn't around, either. Will you sign for this?"

"Gladly," Clancy purred.

Belinda pressed her lips together to hide a smile, but that hurt, so she just stood there and looked at the ceiling.

"Hello."

She looked back to find the well-equipped deliveryman smiling at her.

Clancy glanced up and frowned. "Oh. Hank Baxter, this is Belinda Hennessey."

"Hi," she managed to vocalize on an expelled breath.

"Are you new here?"

She touched her mouth and looked to Clancy for help.

He sighed. "Belinda had a skirmish with Thai food today. She's been here a couple of months, but Margo keeps all the pretty ones hidden away."

"Too bad," Hunky Hank said with a grin.

"Here." Clancy slapped the guy's clipboard against his chest and snatched the envelope out of his hand. "I'll make sure Margo gets the package."

Hank nodded. "Nice to meet you, Belinda."

Clancy stared openly at the man's ass as he walked away, then turned back and made a rueful noise. "Why are all the good ones straight?"

She barely heard him because she was trying to steal a look at the return address on the overnight letter packet. When Clancy caught her, she blushed. He shrugged and held up the brightly colored envelope. "Looks like something from Payton—this could be the big day."

The food in her stomach seemed to reignite. The big day. The big deal. The big promotion. The big lie.

"I'll drop this on Margo's desk later. Come on, let's tag you a sofa. Mr. Archer wants these things out of the boardroom pronto. Apparently he caught someone taking a nap in here."

She frowned. "Weally?"

He leaned close. "I heard it was Tal. Must be tough on Mr. Archer having such a loser for a son."

She was glad they had reached the boardroom, because she didn't want to get caught up in the melodrama of the grapevine. She had enough on her mind, struggling with the decision of spending her ill-gotten raise before she even ill-got it.

"They're all nice sofas," he said, sweeping his arm wide. "Nicer than anything Archer makes, that's for damn sure. I bought the gray striped one for my den, and the brown plaid is already spoken for."

"Rosemary?"

"Uh-huh."

That left a cream overstuffed model with high arms, a cobalt blue contemporary couch with lime green pillows, a sleek black armless model, and, Belinda's pie-in-the-sky favorite, a red leather beauty, with deep seating and flared arms. A sound of longing escaped her throat.

"Isn't it decadent?" Clancy breathed.

"Mm."

"Let's unfold it," he suggested. They removed the sumptuous red leather cushions, and Belinda was amazed at how easily the queen bed opened.

"Give it a bounce," Clancy said.

She did, and found that the firmness rivaled her own bed. She lay back and closed her eyes, giving in to the fantasy of entertaining a lover on her pull-out red leather couch. God help her, she wanted it. Badly.

"How muth?" she asked, wishing she could feel her teeth.

"Fifteen hundred."

She winced and sat up.

"It's a four-thousand-dollar couch, sweetie."

She didn't doubt that it was a good deal, but at this discount, she'd have to pay cash, and she still didn't know how much the car repairs were going to cost. "I'll fink about it."

He clucked. "Monica Tanner called this morning and asked a hundred questions about this piece—you'd better snap it up before she does."

She wavered. Her living room *was* balefully empty. Her mother would be thrilled that she'd finally bought a couch, although Barbara Hennessey would think her daughter had "turned wild" when Belinda described it. Julian's wink sprang to her mind. Little did her mother know, buying a red leather couch was the tamest of her contemplations today.

"Free delivery if you can wait a few days," Clancy encouraged.

"Otay."

Chapter 10

"Except for a little sunshine slowdown in the east-bound lanes on the Top End of The Perimeter, all is runnin' smooth on the freeways this mornin'! Folks, it's a beautiful Friday in Hotlanta. Drive safe! This is Talkin' Tom Trainer for MIXX 100 FM traffic."

"And you didn't know it was him?" Carole asked.

"Not a clue," Belinda said. Just hearing his voice sent her pulse jumping. When she'd driven home yesterday, he'd still been covering the chemical spill cleanup. It gave her a quiet little thrill knowing he was soaring overhead, and she wondered if he'd thought about her as much as she'd thought about him. Any time that Lt. Alexander's words about Julian had worked their way into her thoughts, she had discounted them as well-meaning but misguided. Hadn't she decided to form her own opinion? Perhaps the officer assumed she was looking for some kind of permanent solution to her single state, but she wasn't. And while she still considered men unnecessary, she had developed a new appreciation for their . . . *usefulness*.

When she'd woken this morning to Julian's voice on the radio, her entire body had been in a state of heightened awareness that had rivaled her tender mouth. She'd felt every nubby loop on the terry washcloth as she'd showered, had felt her eyelashes brush her cheeks when she'd blinked, had sensed the nerve endings dance in the pads of her fingers. And the man hadn't even touched her. Yet.

"I see your speech has returned," Libby said sarcastically.

Belinda squinted. Libby wasn't her normal cheery self this morning. "Thanks to Rosemary letting me know that bread would get rid of the sting."

"My pleasure," Rosemary said, but a little pinch appeared between her eyebrows. Enduring back pain was the single outward concession she had made to aging.

Warmth crept into Belinda's cheeks. "Rosemary, I'm sorry. I forgot to mention that I told Julian I'd meet him in the gym today."

Libby huffed. "I've got one for the book: DON'T dump your girlfriends when you meet a new guy."

Belinda's flush deepened—another bonding faux pas. "I didn't mean—"

"It's okay," Rosemary cut in. "My back is so tight, I think I'll skip my workout."

"I knew that good old Southern boy radio bit was an act," Libby exclaimed. "Men are natural born liars and were put on earth to make our lives a living hell."

Silence crackled in the car.

"Someone woke up on the wrong side of the curling iron," Carole murmured.

Libby's mouth tightened, and she burst into tears.

Belinda swerved onto the shoulder, then corrected.

"What's wrong?" Carole asked, leaning forward.

"We're broke," Libby sobbed. "My SUV, you know I was letting Glen, Jr. drive it until he got his truck fixed? Well, the bank repossessed it yesterday while he was in Algebra, which he's failing. Oh, hell, there goes my mascara." She dabbed at her eyes with a paper napkin, spreading the black mess. "Glen is being just awful. He cut up all my credit cards—both of my Visas, all of my

MasterCards, plus Discover, American Express, Diner's Club, Best Buy, Sears—"

"We get the idea," Carole cut in, patting her shoulder.

"And worst of all—"

"Your Bloomingdale's card," they all said in unison.

She nodded miserably and sprang a new gusher. "Glen is barely talking to me, said I'd better get that raise." She sniffled. "Rosemary, do you mind driving the car pool next week? Glen's trying to get the SUV back, but I don't know how long that'll take."

"No problem," Rosemary said with a flat little smile. She looked as if she was going to say something else—I told you so?—but didn't.

Carole made soothing sounds as Libby repaired her makeup. Belinda bit into her lip, assuming that Libby hadn't made good on her promise to lop off her husband's pecker if he yanked her Bloomingdale's card. She was starting to feel connected to these women, and it did concern her that one of them was in trouble and she might be able to help. Plus she was having second thoughts about buying the wicked couch.

"Libby," she said carefully, "I have cash in my purse to pay Clancy for the sofa bed, but if you need to borrow—"

"Oh, Belinda," Libby breathed, tearing up again. "That's so sweet of you, but no, I'd never borrow money from a friend." She sighed. "I'm sorry, girls, for being a downer this morning. But don't worry, I'll think of something. Always have a plan B."

"That's a good DO for the book," Belinda said quietly.

Libby smiled through her tears. "I'll write that one down."

"Was Atlanta your plan B, Belinda?" Carole asked.

She pursed her mouth. "Yes, I suppose it was."

"What was he like? Your husband, I mean."

Husband. It was one of those words that if you said over and over, it sounded nonsensical. "He was . . ." She conjured up Vince's pleasant face—mild blue eyes, fresh-scrubbed skin, nondescript hair, average build. "Vince was . . ." Her tongue faltered as mixed emotions flooded her. What *was* Vince like? What about him had convinced her that he was the man she'd wanted to spend the rest of her life with? Proximity? Timing? Expectations? Maybe the answers lay in the unopened envelope sitting on her kitchen table at home. Or maybe the answers lay in the fact that she hadn't yet opened the envelope.

"Belinda?"

She pushed aside the jumble of thoughts. "Ask me another day, okay, Carole?"

Carole nodded. "Guess you don't want to think about him now that you've met someone new."

Belinda's defenses reared. "Julian isn't 'someone new.' He's just someone . . ."

"To sleep with?"

She squirmed. "I didn't say that."

"It's really no big deal," Libby said. "Sometimes a torrid affair is exactly what a woman needs to get her bearings after a divorce."

Except Belinda wasn't divorced. In hindsight, maybe official papers would have given her breakup with Vince a sense of closure, instead of leaving their relationship hanging out there in limbo with a big question mark behind it. WHY?

"In fact," Libby said, "maybe I'll add that one to the book, too. 'DO engage in retaliatory sex.' "

"Don't." In the backseat, Rosemary shook her head. "Women who buy into equal opportunity affairs only wind up hurting themselves."

Libby scoffed. "You and your rules, Rosemary."

"Rules make your life less complicated," she replied.

"You mean less interesting," Carole said with a laugh.

Rosemary dismissed them with a wave, shaking her head.

They all had a point, Belinda conceded. Up until now, her life had been fairly uncomplicated, but fairly uninteresting. She sank into her own thoughts as the girls debated the wisdom and sacrifices of obeying written and unwritten rules. She chewed on her ragged thumbnail. For the first time in her life she'd begun to take chances, and as a result, her life was definitely moving and shaking.

But was this all-over, quaky, nail-biting consciousness a sustainable condition? Would she acclimate to the keen awareness of a daredevil or eventually implode?

Implode, Belinda decided as she nervously made her way toward the sauna. She tried to tell herself she was overreacting, that Julian probably wanted a jogging partner, or something equally innocuous. Determined to look breezy, she'd worn basic pull-on navy shorts and a faded white Adidas T-shirt. Her hair, she'd skimmed back into a ponytail. Her pulse kicked even higher when she didn't see Julian near the sauna door that was located along a hallway, between the men's and women's locker rooms.

Maybe he'd gotten held up at work, she thought, nodding to someone passing by. Maybe he'd forgotten about meeting her. Or maybe he'd simply changed his mind. She noted the Out of Order sign on the sauna door, then turned her back to wait with her face fixed in as offhand an expression as she could manage.

Maybe this was her chance to bail, she thought, her thumbnail between her teeth. Julian had made no secret of the fact that he desired her, but was she ready to enter into a physical relationship so soon after Vince had trampled on her heart and her femininity? He'd left her within twenty-four hours of leaving her bed—he couldn't have expressed the fact that she hadn't satisfied him any larger if he'd rented a billboard.

A touch to the back of her arm stole her thoughts and her breath. She whirled around to see Julian standing in the open door of the sauna, his mouth curved in a mischievous smile, his finger beckoning. Realization dawned with a thrill, and her feet moved forward. He clasped her hand and pulled her into the twelve-feet-square wood-lined room. A slatted bench ran along three walls. Small puck lights in each corner, combined with the light coming in the small window in the door, cast a warm glow over his smiling face. Lean, long arms and legs extended from pale running shorts and sleeveless tee, and a white towel was draped around his neck. Crisp heat enveloped her, a few degrees shy of uncomfortable. Obviously the sauna was in good working order.

She angled her head up at him, breathless at his proximity in the semidarkness. "Did you put that sign on the door?"

"Guilty," he said, then lifted a towel over her head and settled it around her shoulders. "I thought a private sauna would be fun."

Despite the languid pull of her body, her brain was firing off warning signals. SLOW! PROCEED WITH CAUTION. "What if someone comes in?"

"We'll throw them out," he said, nuzzling her ear. "You smell amazing."

His voice was guttural, sending barbs of need to long-neglected parts of her body. She reasoned that proximity to the hallway would keep things from getting out of control.

"I looked up your number and called you last night, but no one answered."

She gave him a sheepish smile. "I went a little overboard on the Thai food yesterday. I'm afraid my mouth was out of commission all evening."

He made a sorrowful noise in his throat and lowered his mouth to within a whisper of hers. "How is it today?"

Somehow the darkness made everything . . . easier. She moved her lips, and for the first time in over two years, Belinda kissed a man other than Vince Whittaker.

Her senses were jarred by the unfamiliarity of the way Julian tasted, the way he slid his lips and tongue against hers, but she acclimated quickly to his gentle coaxing. She closed her eyes and lifted her hands to his shoulders. His skin was warm and firm beneath her trembling fingers—new textures, new contours. The veteran good girl in her kept thinking the door would burst open any minute and someone would walk in on them. But the newer, younger bad girl in her conceded the thrill of the clandestine kiss a few feet away from where people were walking and talking.

He moaned into her mouth, then broke the kiss. "Let's relax."

She followed him to the bench and sat next to him, her heart pumping double time. He bent over to remove his shoes and socks, and she did the same, self-consciously. Revealing one's feet struck her as an intimate act. Thank goodness her do-it-yourself pink pedicure was up to snuff. When he removed his T-shirt, her bare toes curled under on the wood plank floor. *Nice.*

Lean shoulders, smooth chest, flat stomach, all covered with a sheen of perspiration. To her disappointment, he put the towel around his shoulders again and leaned against the wall of the sauna, his long legs stretched out in front of him. He shot her a sideways smile, then closed his eyes. "I won't peek if you want to do the same."

Belinda blinked. Remove her shirt? A naughty jolt passed over her at the possibility. She shot a glance toward the door. Occasionally, glimpses of passersby appeared in the small window, but the hum of the dry heater overrode any outside noise. They were wrapped in their own warm little cocoon. If someone stumbled in, she'd be covered with a towel.

Moving on impulse, she set aside the towel and pulled the hem of her T-shirt over her head. The gods had smiled on her in the bust department, although she had to rely on industrial bras to keep everything in place. After a quick look to make sure his eyes were still closed, she draped the towel over her shoulders and reached around to unhook her bra. As soon as the air hit her bare breasts, they peaked against the coarse fabric of the towel. She set aside her clothing and leaned back carefully, feeling very liberated and yes, pretty darn sexy.

"Can I look now?" he asked.

"I suppose," she said, holding on to the ends of the towel.

He surveyed the expanse of skin between the towel,

from collarbone to navel, then closed his eyes tight again with a groan. "Quick, let's talk."

She laughed, feeling a rush of feminine satisfaction. "Okay. You sounded chipper on the radio this morning."

"It's Friday, traffic was light, and no one was killed on my watch. That's a good day. Plus I was looking forward to seeing you again."

In the dark vacuum, she could fully absorb the resonance of his voice. "I'll bet you've seen a lot of things from your helicopter."

"Yeah. I love flying, but sometimes it's depressing, seeing the masses of cars and houses. It can make a person feel . . . *small*."

Her skin was inundated with the vibration of his voice and the therapeutic heat rolling over the room. She turned her head and studied his striking profile in the low lighting. "But you connect with those masses of people every day." She wet her lips. "Yours was the first voice I heard when I drove into Atlanta on I-75 two months ago."

He opened his eyes and turned his head. "Really?"

She nodded. "I arrived on a Wednesday afternoon, smack in the middle of rush hour, and I thought, 'What have I gotten myself into?' I was flipping through the radio channels and heard your voice. You put me at ease, made me feel not so alone." She bit into her lip, then smiled. "I've had a crush on your voice ever since."

His white teeth flashed. "How about the rest of me?"

She caught his light, playful mood. "I like what I've seen so far."

In an instant the atmosphere went from hot to sizzling. He leaned toward her and she met him for a slow, exploratory kiss that quickly surged in intensity. Together they shifted to a reclining position, with his body angled above hers. Her towel fell away, baring her breasts to his hooded gaze.

"Magnificent," he murmured, thumbing a peak.

Once again she was assailed by a split second of wrongness in his unfamiliarity. But his fingers were persistent and deft, and soon longing pooled between her thighs.

"Do you like this?" he whispered.

"Mm-hm."

"How about this?" He lowered his head and took one of the nipples in his teeth, flicking his tongue against it.

Belinda's head moved side to side. "Mm-hm."

He alternately treated both peaks to tiny bites, bringing her alive with pleasure-pain. She held his head against her breasts, aware of his erection searing into her thigh through their clothes. His body slid against hers, both of them slick with perspiration. He shifted until he was on his side, shielding her body from any would-be intruders. He slid his right hand down her rib cage, over the indention of her navel, and slowly, slowly, into the waistband of her shorts. She inhaled sharply and covered his hand with hers. Maybe this was too much, too soon . . . too risky.

"You're on fire, I can feel it through your clothes," he said near her ear. "I want to touch you, to make you feel good."

Belinda swallowed, willing her pulse to slow and her erogenous zones to decelerate, but her body refused to cooperate with her brain. Frankly, what he was doing felt very, very good, and it was nice to be appreciated by an attractive man. So she removed her hand and found another place to put it that made his breath rush out.

His fingers dove into her slippery curls, and her hips undulated against his hand. A groan escaped her throat, but he covered her mouth with a deep kiss. He strummed her like an instrument until she felt an orgasm surfacing. Her breathing became more shallow, and she buried her head in his shoulder as she came against his fingers. Her climax was too powerful for longevity, she reasoned when she descended more quickly than she expected.

And it wasn't as if they had all day.

All the while she had been stroking his arousal through his thin shorts. With a ragged breath, Julian pushed down his waistband and freed it into her hands. Long and lean, like his nose—hm—and slick with need. He dipped his head to her ear again.

"I want to make love to your breasts."

His request came with a tweak and a thrill—Vince hadn't been the adventurous type and had never known quite what to do with her breasts. "Yes," she murmured, and trusted that this man knew what he was doing. He leveraged himself up and rubbed his lubrication over her cleavage. Moving on instinct, she squeezed her breasts together around his erection and was rewarded with an appreciative groan.

He pumped his hips fast and furious for a couple of long minutes. She tried to relax and enjoy the new sensation, really she did, but she was distracted by the thought of the silhouette that someone would see if the door opened.

At last his body jerked, and his fluid spilled over her chest and neck. Warm and sticky, like everything else in the room. He pushed himself up, still breathing hard, and used his towel to gently wipe up the mess.

"Wow," he said, smiling down at her.

"Yes, wow," she murmured, still a little dazed by what she'd done. Julian, on the other hand, seemed less affected.

"Listen, I know this is short notice, but I'm flying to Raleigh in the morning for a promo gig, coming back Sunday evening." He reached out with a finger and caressed her cheek. "I'd love some company."

Flying away for the weekend with a hot, sexy man—she'd had worse offers. But she'd already promised the girls she'd spend tomorrow afternoon with them at a spa to take advantage of free-service coupons that Carole had won on a radio call-in contest. And she didn't want to be the kind of woman who dumped her friends when a new man appeared on the scene. Besides, she was looking forward to a girls' afternoon in the . . . suburbs. "Thank you, Julian, but I've already made plans for tomorrow."

He made a rueful noise. "Guess I'll have to ask you sooner next time."

At least he planned to see her again. And she wanted to see him again, too.

Didn't she?

Belinda reached for her bra, leaned forward to put it on, and was surprised when he moved behind her to fasten it. He took his time, then gave her spine a quick pressure massage with his thumbs and dropped a kiss on the back of her neck. His laugh rumbled in her ear. "I don't believe I have enough energy left to work out."

She rolled her shoulders and murmured agreement.

"Let's take a quick nap," he said, stretching out on the bench. He placed one hand beneath his head and extended his other hand to touch her waist. His eyes fluttered shut, and his breathing immediately settled into a deep rhythm.

She might have dozed earlier, but now she was wide awake, waiting for remorse to hit her. When it didn't, she was left feeling even more confused. She found her T-shirt and pulled it over her head, then gathered her socks and shoes and managed to slip out the door without making any noise. In the empty hallway she released a pent-up breath and padded toward the women's locker room. If remorse was going to hit her in the next few minutes, she might as well be standing under a showerhead getting clean.

Footsteps sounded behind her—*tiny* footsteps.

"Is that you, Belinda?"

Margo. Belinda closed her eyes briefly, then turned and manufactured a smile for her boss, whose microscopic white leotard was sweat-drenched. "Hi, Margo."

"I didn't see you in the gym." Her gaze dropped to Belinda's bare feet. "Taking a sauna?"

"Well—"

"Isn't it out of order?" Margo indicated the sign on the door.

To her abject horror, the sauna door opened, and a shirtless Julian, looking like he'd been ridden hard and put up wet, stuck out his handsome head. "You forgot something." He held up a white sock.

Mortification bled over her. Belinda stepped forward to block Margo's view, retrieved the sock from his hand, and tucked it into her shoe with as much dignity as she could muster. "Thanks."

"I didn't run you off, did I?" he murmured, an irresistible twinkle in his eye.

"Er, no. I need to get back to work."

"Okay. Be listening for me on the radio."

She nodded, thinking perhaps she could pass him off as a mere acquaintance, someone who had happened to be in the sauna. Or at least pretend as if nothing of naughty consequence had occurred.

Then he leaned out farther and waved. "Hey, Margo."

Margo lifted her hand. "Hey, Julian."

He disappeared into the sauna, and Belinda's mind raced at the implication of Margo and Julian knowing each other. Despite a nauseous stomach, Belinda conjured up what she hoped was a casual expression for her boss. "You know Julian?"

"Well, not in the Biblical sense," Margo said with a dry smile. "How was it?"

"Excuse me?"

"The sauna—how was it?"

Remembering the advice of her wedding director, Belinda bent her knees slightly to avoid fainting. "Um, fine. Hot." She waved her hand over her neck. "Actually, that's probably why the sign is on the door—the sauna is overheating. I think."

Margo nodded. "And that would explain why your shirt is inside out."

Belinda looked down. Sure enough, her T-shirt read "sabibA," the serged seams exposed, and the fabric content tag in plain view.

"It's okay," Margo said with a shrug. "There was a time when I wouldn't have minded hooking up with Julian myself, but I guess he prefers redheads." She angled her head. "Come to think of it, he had a thing for Jeanie Lawford, and she was a freckly little thing."

The mounting similarities between herself and Jeanie

Lawford were too numerous for easy digestion. She managed a small laugh. "It's a little unsettling to be compared to a dead woman."

"You're much too smart to wind up like Jeanie."

At the odd timbre in Margo's voice, Belinda's throat constricted. "What do you mean, 'wind up like Jeanie'?"

Margo gave her a rueful smile. "I mean you watch your step."

Innocent (if tactless) remark, or veiled warning? Belinda stood, knees bent, holding her socks and shoes, and watched her boss disappear into the locker room.

Chapter 11

By the time Belinda got back to her desk, she was a nervous wreck. Fooling around in the workplace—what was she thinking? *Here lies Belinda Hennessey. She was indiscreet.* The enormity of her lapse was outweighed only by her relief at not having been caught in the act, although it was clear that Margo had a good idea of what had transpired.

And that bizarre comment about Jeanie. . . .

"Hey."

She turned at the sound of Libby's voice. The woman's blond hair was a mess, and her pink mouth drooped. "Hey, Libby. What's going on?"

Libby dropped into the visitor's chair. "I'm suffering withdrawal. Bloomingdale's is having a white sale."

Belinda bit back a smile. "Oh."

"I can't stand the thought of all those goodies over there twenty, thirty, even forty percent off. Think of all the money I could be saving."

"But think of all the money you'll save by not shopping at all."

"I know, I know. But you know that thrill of buying something new?"

Belinda thought of her naughty red couch and flushed. "Of course. But needing that kind of high to the point of risking your financial security isn't healthy."

Libby pointed to her brain. "Here, I know that. But here"— she rubbed her thumb against her fingers in the universal "money" symbol—"I just keep thinking four hundred thread-count white Egyptian sheets on *clearance*." She moaned. "I need to win the lottery. Life isn't fair."

"True enough."

Carole appeared in the cubicle opening, her arms full of padded envelopes. "Are you all having a party without me?"

"Pity party for me," Libby said.

"Bloomingdale's sale?"

Libby nodded miserably. "I ate at my desk and cried over the sale circular. What are you doing up here looking so chipper?"

Carole grinned. "I rode up the elevator with Hunky Hank—we were stuck between the fourth and fifth floor for ten whole minutes." She gave Belinda an accusing look. "You're holding out on us. He said he carried up something for you yesterday."

Belinda pointed to a gray crate sitting under her desk. "My collection of exciting reference books."

"Still, I think he digs you." Carole jerked her thumb toward Belinda's slice of window. "Speaking of digging, I wanted to take a look at the, um, bushes."

One side of Libby's mouth slid back. "Yeah, right."

They all headed over and looked down. Eight floors down, a half-dozen shirtless men were stacking stone around the bases of newly planted trees. Blonds, brunettes, tall, stocky—it was a veritable smorgasbord of bronzed man-meat. Belinda wondered how many women were standing at their office windows ogling the unsuspecting laborers—not that it kept her from getting an eyeful for herself.

Carole emitted a hungry noise. "Maybe one of those guys is my destiny. Ricky said he was right under my nose."

"See the tall blond?" Libby asked. "Word is, that's one of Margo's boy-toys."

Belinda looked again—stringy hair, dirty hat. "He looks a little . . ."

"Skanky? I'll say. Must be a power thing."

She shook herself. Here she stood gossiping about her boss's supposed conquests when her body still sang from the application of Julian's hands.

Carole turned her back to the window. "So, how was helicopter man?"

Belinda blinked. "Hm?"

"Didn't you meet him at the gym?"

"Oh. Julian's . . . fine. He asked me to go to Raleigh with him this weekend."

Libby's eyes narrowed. "So, are you dumping us?"

"No." Belinda smiled, then moved back toward her cubicle. "I'm looking forward to being pampered at the spa for a few hours."

"Good girl." Libby snapped her fingers. "Hey, I need to look up something in that policy and procedures manual I loaned you."

"Do you need it back?" Belinda asked, reaching for the thick three-ring binder. "I can take out the pages I'm using."

"No, I want to double-check something in case I'm summoned for my evaluation with Margo this afternoon."

"Summoned? You mean the interviews aren't scheduled?"

"Heck, no—she likes to catch people off guard. Some people will get their comeuppance today, and the rest of us will have to sweat it out over the weekend."

Belinda's stomach clenched. She made a mental note to see if there was a section in the manual on employee hanky-panky. She hefted the bulky binder from the corner of her desk and stared down at the object that had been sufficiently hidden beneath—her electronic address book. One mystery solved.

Libby ran a finger down a page in the manual, read for

a few seconds, then slammed the book closed. "Too many rules," she muttered.

Belinda and Carole exchanged a perplexed glance, then Clancy came around the corner, carrying a zippered cash bag. "Is this a hen party, or can I join?"

"Hens only," Libby said. "So you're fine."

He stuck his tongue out at her. "I came to see Belinda." He shook the money bag. "Time to pay for your delicious couch."

"We'll see you later," Libby said and walked away with Carole.

Belinda pulled a key from her jacket pocket to unlock the drawer where she'd placed the envelope of cash. "I'm already having buyer's remorse."

"Honey, are you Catholic?"

"Baptist."

"Worse. You know you'll probably go to hell for buying a red leather couch."

She handed over fifteen one-hundred-dollar bills. "That's what I'm afraid of."

"Oh, don't worry—Margo says it isn't such a bad place."

She shook her finger at him. "Stop it. Are all the couches sold?"

He nodded. "You, me, Rosemary, Monica Tanner—she settled for the black one—a lady in HR and a friend of Carole's from the mail room bought the other two." He held her wad of money under his nose and inhaled before tucking it into his cash bag. "I haven't had this much money since managing the Who Will Margo Fire Next? pool."

Rather than responding, Belinda thought it was safer to change the subject. "So when can I expect my yummy couch to be delivered?"

"Next Wednesday was the earliest I could arrange to get yours and Rosemary's on a truck. I need your address, and I have to write on the order if the delivery guys will have to carry the sofa up any stairs."

She reached for a notepad. "It's a town house, and they won't have to maneuver stairs. My living room is level with my yard."

"That'll make the boys happy. Do you need for them to haul away your old couch? They can drop it at Goodwill."

"Thanks, but I don't have a couch right now."

"Ah. Did your ex-husband get all the furniture?"

She blinked. "Well . . ."

He brushed off her embarrassment. "Honey, there are no secrets around here."

She so hoped that wasn't true. "We, um, divided up everything. He got the couch, and I got the cat."

He grinned. "You're a cat lover?"

"I wouldn't go that far. Downey and I sort of tolerate each other, I guess. She misses my . . . ex."

"Yeah, cats can sulk, just like people. Have you tried warming up her food?"

"No."

"Trust me—a few seconds in the microwave, and she'll be your friend for life." He checked his watch. "Gotta run. I have a feeling that Margo's going to call me for my evaluation so she can ruin my weekend. I've heard that raises this year are more scarce than a Gay Pride flag in Cobb County."

There was that stomach twinge again. "Good luck."

After he walked away, she massaged her temples. She and her friends were experiencing individual dramas that would rival anything on *The Single Files*—Libby with her finances, Carole with her marriage-for-hire, Rosemary with her body's limitations, and she with her sudden . . . truth issues.

She smoothed her hand over the sleek surface of the address book. At least she'd be able to call her mother later with Suzanne's address. It was one of the reasons her mother had postponed the cross-country trip for so long, because she had obsessed over every little loose end of the non-wedding. Her poor mother would probably collapse when everything was finally over and done with.

Belinda stopped—*when* everything was over and done with? She and Vince *were* over and done with. Hadn't she proved that by moving three states away? By not tearing open the envelope he'd sent her? By having an . . . *encounter* with another man?

Maybe she'd jot a quick note on the back of Vince's envelope before sending it back: *Having too much fun in the dry sauna with my new helicopter pilot lover.*

She lifted her chin. And she had a good mind to let Lt. Alexander know that she could darn well take care of herself where Julian Hardeman was concerned. She put her hand on the phone and picked it up in defiance. She could at least call the man and let him know she'd found her address book. She looked up the phone number for the Atlanta PD, asked for him, and was transferred to the Midtown precinct.

"Alexander," he barked.

Her tongue was suddenly glued to the roof of her mouth from the frivolity of her phone call. The man was probably dealing with a triage of serious crimes, and she was taking up his time with this trifling matter. "Lieutenant Alexander, this is Belinda Hennessey."

"Hello." His voice eased a tad.

She wet her lips. "I just called to let you know that I found my address book." She wondered if she sounded as stupid as she felt.

"Oh. Good."

Apparently so. "But I appreciate you taking the time to look for it."

"Sure thing."

"And for taking the time to stop by my building to return my, um, pillow."

"No problem."

She smiled into the phone. "Just doing your job, right?"

"I guess so, ma'am."

So they were back to the ma'aming. "Okay, well, I'm sure you're busy, so I'll let you get back to work."

"Ms. Hennessey?"

"Yes?"

"Be careful."

"I wouldn't expect you to agree, Lieutenant, but I'm actually a good driver."

"I mean be careful at your office. There was a terrible incident in your building a few months back."

Apprehension settled on her shoulders, and she chose her words carefully. "You mean the woman who fell down the elevator shaft?"

"So you heard about it."

"Yes, but . . . how does something like that happen these days?"

"The Stratford Plaza building is over twenty-five years old—its infrastructure isn't the best, but regardless, the incident shouldn't have occurred."

"Sounds like a maintenance problem."

He didn't respond for a few seconds, then said, "Just watch your step."

She frowned—two similar warnings in the same day? This was starting to get creepy. "Don't worry about me, Lieutenant," she said lightly. "I always take the stairs."

"Well, in case anything unusual happens, I want you to have my cell phone number."

She entered the number into her electronic organizer as he rattled it off. Warning bells sounded in her ears—was he truly concerned about her safety, or was he trying to . . . no, of course the man wasn't *interested*. He was going through a divorce, for heaven's sake. "Lieutenant, what do you mean by 'unusual'?"

"Nothing specific," he replied, his voice casual. "Just keep your eyes open."

"I will."

"Okay."

"Okay." She wet her lips, overcome with the urge to say she'd heard about his divorce and just wanted to say that things would be fine. But she didn't know him well enough, and she didn't know that things would be fine—for her *or* him. "So . . . good-bye then."

"Good-bye."

She returned the receiver to its cradle and pursed her mouth. Cop-speak notwithstanding, she found it curious that he'd referred to Jeanie Lawford's fall as an "incident" rather than an "accident." She was probably reading too much into the conversation, she told herself, because of this affinity she was feeling toward the dead woman. It was eerie enough to know that she'd taken Jeanie's place in the car pool, but had she also taken the woman's place in Julian's . . . *lunch hour*?

"Guess we all dodged a bullet today," Libby said as they piled into the Honda.

"A reprieve from evaluations," Carole said.

"At least we're employed through the weekend," Rosemary said.

Belinda fastened her seat belt. "Are you worried about your job, Rosemary?"

The woman shrugged. "My primary duty is to front for Juneau, keep him apprised of what's going on in the office. Margo sees me as an obstacle." She shook her head. "I've been with the company for thirty years, started when Tal was in preschool, but loyalty doesn't mean anything these days."

"Not to Margo," Carole said.

"Surely Mr. Archer will protect your job," Belinda said.

"He's all but turned the company over to her," Rosemary murmured.

Libby clicked her belt into place. "Margo won't be happy until she's CEO, president, and queen of the universe."

Belinda turned over the engine, backed out, and began winding her way down from the eighth floor of the parking garage. Now she understood what had been causing the pucker in Rosemary's brow. At Rosemary's age, reemployment at such a high administrative level might be difficult to secure. Belinda tightened her grip on the steering wheel—they were going to be a somber bunch for the ride home.

And she dreaded the Friday rush hour traffic, which was triple the mess of any other day of the week. Then, after an interminable drive, she'd spend the evening watching a fuzzy television while Downey ignored her. Maybe she'd go through the remaining packing boxes and clear more space for the impending couch. Maybe she'd finish the book she'd been reading. Maybe Julian would call, and she'd have another chance to figure out how she felt about what they'd done.

She was forced to stop on the sixth floor of the parking garage behind a solid line of cars. "What's going on?" Libby asked.

Belinda heard the telltale chopper blades on the radio and turned up the volume. "Folks, this is a red alert—due to a gas main break, the Georgia D.O.T. just closed down I-85 at the Druid Hills exit. If you haven't left downtown, your options are limited."

The girls all moaned and flopped back in their seats. Belinda winced, glad that Downey didn't have to be walked.

"Peachtree northbound is already a parkin' lot," Julian continued, his speech stretched around exaggerated vowels. "Roswell Road is jammed, ditto Buford Highway. If you're just now leavin' your office in Midtown, my advice is to pull that little Honda over at the next waterin' hole and wait this one out!"

"Belinda, he was talking to you!" Carole said, bouncing in her seat.

Belinda's face suffused with heat. Their encounter must have meant something to him if he singled her out of three million people.

"I don't know about the rest of you," Libby said, "but I could go for a martini."

"The man had a point," Rosemary said. "We might as well go someplace cool and wait until the traffic thins."

"Gypsy Joe's is just a couple of blocks over," Carole said. "I haven't been there in ages. Not since—" She pressed her lips together.

"Jeanie liked it there," Libby said with a sad smile. "Let's go raise one for her."

Belinda hesitated—Jeanie again.

Rosemary pointed. "Pull into that parking space. We'll never get out on Peachtree in this mess, and it's faster to walk anyway."

Outnumbered, Belinda did as she was told. Anything was better than sitting in traffic. And the mood in the car had improved considerably.

"Can I lock my laptop in your trunk?" Libby asked.

Belinda sighed. "Sorry, the latch is still broken. Can you slide it under the seat?"

"Speaking of under the seat," Carole said, "did you ever get a weapon?"

"Not yet," Belinda said with a wry smile.

"I'm bringing my legal pad," Libby declared. "We can work on our book."

"Getting a book published would solve your money problems," Carole offered.

Rosemary scoffed. "We'll probably have to pay to have it published."

Feeling as if she were still standing on the periphery of the women's friendships, Belinda listened to their banter as they walked to the elevator bay.

"I think I'll take the stairs," she announced.

Libby frowned. "The elevator's here. Ride with us."

Fit in with us. Belinda wavered, but the repulsion of the elevator was stronger, as if Jeanie's spirit lingered there. "No, thanks. I need the exercise."

Libby shrugged. "Suit yourself." Before the doors closed, the three women were engrossed in conversation.

Belinda turned toward the door to the stairs, wondering if she was wired to always choose the solitary way.

Chapter 12

Belinda met up with the women at the entrance to the parking garage, and Carole pointed down the side-walk in front of the Stratford Building. "This way."

"Looks like we made the right choice," Rosemary murmured, surveying the gridlock of cars.

Belinda agreed. Peachtree Street and side streets were jammed with cars, SUVs, delivery trucks, and minivans. The only movement came from bicycles and scooters weaving through traffic, and pedestrians on the sidewalks.

Her ears buzzed from the lively noise of horns honk-ing, music blasting out of lowered windows, and the hum of engines. Hazy heat rose from the sea of metal, blurring the mid-rises and high-rises on the horizon. Belinda's feet slowed as a change came over her—excitement buoyed in her chest, and she somehow knew that she wanted to be part of this dynamic city.

In front of her, Libby tossed over her shoulder, "All this ruckus is crazy, isn't it?"

Inspired, Belinda stopped and lifted her arms, as if she could embrace the atmosphere. "I love the energy." She lifted her face to the sun, but her smile faded at the sight of a large dark object hurtling toward the ground—and her. A body? She opened her mouth to scream, but her voice was paralyzed. Thank goodness her feet had a mind of their own, carrying her backward just as the object plowed into the sidewalk. The crowd around her shrank with a collective gasp and stopped to stare at the splattered mess. Her heart stuttered back into rhythm when she realized the matter on her shoes wasn't blood but dirt. A pulverized plant lay at her feet in a heap of broken pottery.

Libby, Rosemary, and Carole ran back to her, eyes and mouths wide.

"Good gravy, Belinda, are you all right?"

"Barely," she whispered, realizing how close she'd come to buying the farm. She leaned her head back to scan the twenty stories of the Stratford building for the origin of the falling plant, but the sun blinded her.

"You could have been killed," Rosemary exclaimed.

"Where did it come from?" Carole asked.

Belinda shielded her eyes, but none of the windows provided a clue—no openings, no movement. "I don't know." She turned and addressed the crowd. "Did anyone see anything?" The spectators shook their heads, then began to disperse.

A uniformed city ambassador appeared, wearing a rueful expression. "A cleaning crew or one of those watering services probably knocked a plant off a windowsill, then got scared when they realized what they'd done," he said. "I'll inform the building security, and get this mess cleaned up. I'm sorry this happened, ma'am."

Belinda nodded, but her limbs remained leaden.

"Do you still feel like getting a drink?" Rosemary asked, her eyes clouded.

Belinda puffed out her cheeks in an exhale. "More than ever."

The women crowded around, cooing and fretting. She waved off their concern, manufactured a smile, and forced her feet to move, grateful to be alive.

At the corner, Carole said, "Let's cross the street here,"

then stepped out to pick a path between cars jammed in the intersection. "In case more plants start raining down."

Rosemary followed but said, "You picked a bad intersection—this is where Margaret Mitchell was run down by a car in 1949."

As she walked, Belinda surveyed the nondescript corner of Peachtree and 13th Street. "Really?"

"She was crossing with her husband, and a speeding taxi came around the curve."

"Maybe this area is cursed," Carole declared, looking heavenward.

"Kind of prophetic, huh?" Libby asked as they threaded their way through traffic. "That one of Atlanta's national treasures would be run down by a car, and now the city is famous for traffic."

Despite the blazing sun, a shiver passed over Belinda. It was as if the city had claimed the famous writer in every way, influencing her life *and* her death. When she reached the other side of the street, she turned and looked back, promising herself she'd bring flowers to this spot. Then she lifted her gaze to the Stratford Building and silently counted up eight floors to the Archer office windows, which looked as innocuous as the other panes of glass. Had the plant originated from an eighth-floor window, and if so, had it been pushed . . . or dropped?

She started at a touch to her arm.

"Ready?" Rosemary asked softly.

Belinda nodded, then turned to follow the women a half block to Crescent Street, popular for its trendy bars. Belinda had heard about the strip, but until now, she'd had no occasion to go there. Even in her younger days, she hadn't favored the bar scene, hadn't cared for the sense of being "on" all the time—on alert, on the prowl, on display.

"Inside or outside?" Carole asked as they approached Gypsy Joe's. The place was packed with merry patrons, and John Mayer's "Why Georgia" played over the speakers. Smartly dressed young men and women stood chatting with friends while scanning the crowd for possibilities. Fitness abounded, as well as palpable sexual energy. Belinda felt frumpy in her conservative blue pantsuit and dirt-spattered pumps.

"Inside," Libby said. "Where it's air-conditioned."

Out of element in the social setting, Belinda was happy to follow their lead. Inside, the music was louder, as was the general noise level. Behind the long blond-wood bar, televisions were tuned to news and sports programs. She was momentarily struck by how much she missed the company of television, and she wasn't sure if that was more motivation to get hers repaired, or motivation to get rid of it completely. The bar, engulfed by customers, extended the length of the main room. Tall round tables studded the remainder of the room and another step-down area, most of them already filled.

"There's a table," Carole said, pointing. She hurried to it, and when they caught up, she had rounded up enough chairs for all of them. A breathless waitress came by and took their orders for martinis, the house special.

"Are you sure you're okay?" Libby asked Belinda. "That was a close call."

"I'm fine," she said, now feeling as if she'd overreacted. If the street ambassador had a ready explanation, he must have seen it happen before. She changed the subject, and by the time their drinks arrived, everyone seemed to have put the incident behind them.

"To Jeanie," Libby said and lifted her glass.

They clinked glasses, and Belinda had that weird "replacement" feeling again, as if she were the substitute player who'd only made it into the game because one of the starters had, well . . . died.

Belinda took a healthy drink from her glass. "Tell me about Jeanie."

The three women looked at each other, and Libby shrugged. "She was petite, strawberry blond, lots of freckles, outdoorsy. Cute and quiet."

Rosemary sighed. "Jeanie had her whole life in front of her."

"She wanted to travel," Carole said. "She hardly ever talked during the car pool because she was always listening to foreign language tapes."

Belinda wondered if the headphones were Jeanie's way of slowly extricating herself from the car pool, as Margo had suggested. "How did she and Margo get along?"

"Fine at first," Libby said. "But when Jim Newberry was fired, Margo expected Jeanie to pick up the slack, and there was tension."

"Although when Jeanie's body was found, Margo seemed pretty devastated," Rosemary said. "Personally, I always thought Margo didn't attend the memorial service because she couldn't face the fact that Jeanie was gone."

"Was anyone with Jeanie when she fell?" Belinda asked.

Carole shook her head. "Martin Derlinger found her body when he came in that night for a copy emergency, whatever that is. When the elevator door opened, the car was hanging low, and there was Jeanie, lying on top."

Belinda winced.

Libby leaned in. "My friend in HR said Archer had to pay for him to see a head doctor because he was so traumatized." She flushed. "Of course, that's confidential."

Belinda drank and tried to sound casual. "You said that Jeanie was acting strange before her accident. Did you ever get the feeling that she might be in trouble?"

Libby frowned. "You mean like someone was stalking her? She never said anything to me." The other women shook their heads.

"Jeanie was a small-town girl," Rosemary said, "and she was afraid in the city. She didn't mind the extra workload when Jim was fired, but she hated working late and leaving in the dark. I think that's why she took the self-defense class."

"*I* think that's why she joined the car pool," Libby said. "It gave her an excuse to take work home instead of staying late at the office like Margo preferred."

"So she wasn't in the car pool the day she fell?"

The three women looked at each other, then Rosemary

nodded. "Actually, she was. We waited for Jeanie that day, but we assumed she'd decided to work late."

Carole's eyes were glassy. "If we'd gone back to look for her—"

"It wouldn't have made a difference," Rosemary chided. "Her neck was broken."

Belinda took another drink from her glass. So the women didn't want to discuss her death because they felt guilty. "Margo said that Jeanie was involved with Julian."

Libby's eyes narrowed. "How on earth did that come up in conversation?"

A flush overtook Belinda. "Margo saw me at the gym today with Julian. She, um, hinted that Jeanie and I had similar coloring."

"I take it she thought she was being snide?" Libby asked.

"Well . . ."

"I don't see a resemblance," Carole said, squinting.

"Me neither," Libby said. "Jeanie had that elfin Opie Taylor look, and you've got that whole Julianne Moore thing going on."

"You're really pretty," Carole declared. "Once a person gets a good look at you."

"Thanks. I think."

"Quiet beauty," Libby clarified to Carole. "It's a Northern thing." Then Libby looked back. "But have you ever considered doing something different with your hair?"

Belinda fingered a limp hank. "Actually, I was going to ask for the name of a good, cheap stylist."

"You should always change hairstyles after a breakup," Carole offered. "After my last divorce, I went blond."

"It was white," Rosemary corrected.

"And hideous," Libby added. "But Carole has a point—and that's a good one for the book." She whipped out the legal pad and wrote furiously. "After a breakup, DO try a new hairstyle."

"What the hell does hair have to do with relationships?" Rosemary asked, signaling the waitress for another round. Since she'd been doing less talking, more drinking, her glass was nearly empty.

"A new hairstyle is symbolic," Carole insisted. "It marks a new beginning."

"I'm in," Belinda said, finishing her drink, too. "Can you recommend a stylist?"

Libby snapped her fingers. "I know the perfect stylist. *Me*."

Carole's eyes bulged. "You?"

"I grew up working in my aunt Cherry's beauty salon. I still cut my own hair."

Rosemary's gaze cut to Libby's bouffant. "That's an endorsement?"

"Oh, bwah-hah-hah." Libby leaned forward. "Belinda, I'll come over in the morning before we go to the spa—it'll be so fun!"

Rosemary and Carole were shaking their heads and mouthing, "Don't do it." And while Belinda was hesitant, she was intrigued about the prospect of doing something so girly. Besides—her hair wasn't that great to start with, so she didn't have much to lose. And hats were back in style. Somewhere.

"Okay."

Libby clapped her hands. "Oh, this will be great." She took a big swallow of her drink, then sighed. "I should call and let Glen know I'm going to be late, but frankly, I just don't give a good damn."

Rosemary made a rueful noise. "Libby, don't be so hard on Glen. You know you're a shopaholic. You need help."

"I need a raise. And another drink."

On cue, the second round of drinks arrived. Belinda eyed hers warily.

Carole pulled a cigarette from her purse. "Does anyone mind?" No one did. In fact, Rosemary borrowed one for herself, and they lit the tips with a Bic lighter.

Carole inhaled, then turned her head to exhale a plume of pale smoke. "Maybe Margo will get laid over the weekend, and she'll be in a good mood Monday."

"Good gravy," Libby said. "If that were the only requirement, she'd be Pollyanna every day. Her legs open more often than the doors at the all-night Go-Mart."

Considering where her own legs had been today, Belinda felt compelled to defend the woman. "Come on, girls—I report directly to Margo. Keep it clean, okay?"

"You can't honestly say that you respect the woman," Libby said.

"I respect the position," Belinda said carefully. "Maybe she isn't the easiest boss, but she has plans to grow the company, which will mean more money to employee stockholders." She chased the mouthful of propaganda with a swallow of martini.

The women exchanged glances and raised eyebrows. Carole pursed her mouth. "Guess we'll have to watch what we say when you're around."

"Don't worry, Belinda," Libby said with a dry laugh. "If we put a hit out on Margo, we won't ask you to contribute."

"You're assuming the worst. Maybe Margo will approve raises across the board."

"Spoken like someone who expects a raise," Libby said lightly. "Maybe even a promotion?"

Suddenly the room seemed unbearably warm. "I don't expect anything."

"But what do you think?" Rosemary pressed.

"I think that Margo is pleased with the progress on the Payton project."

"And?" Libby prodded.

"And I trust her to reward the entire team."

Libby snorted. "This is the same woman who threatened to fire you four days ago."

Belinda splayed her non-drinking hand. "She was stressed about Payton. We were able to reach an understanding."

Rosemary's mouth curved in a sly smile. "You mean a deal?"

Belinda's skin prickled, but she tried to maintain a casual tone as she changed tack. "If working with Margo is so bad, why haven't all of you quit?"

"Because," Rosemary said, "we keep hoping Juneau will see the light and come back to run the firm."

Belinda pursed her mouth. "Maybe that's why Margo is hostile. Maybe she perceives that resistance." She wet her lips. "Are you sure that the way you feel about Margo has nothing to do with her being . . . female?"

"Absolutely not," Libby said.

"No way," Carole added.

Rosemary was quiet and took a deep drink from her glass. "Actually, Margo and I used to be friends."

"What?" Libby and Carole chorused.

"It was before either one of you came to work for Archer," Rosemary said, pointing to Libby and Carole with her pinkie. "She and I were neighbors when my husband was still alive." Rosemary drew shallowly on the cigarette, then exhaled. "Margo moved in two doors down, and said she was looking for a job. She seemed nice, and I helped her to get on at Archer. She started as a secretary, like me, but she was more ambitious. Then she got power hungry. I didn't approve of the way she tried to manipulate Juneau, especially when he became so distracted by his wife's illness." She flicked ash. "Margo and I had words, and she's had it in for me ever since." Rosemary shrugged. "But I have an idea—no more talk about Margo this evening. Let's have a good time."

"I'll drink to that," Belinda said, lifting her glass. Libby and Carole followed suit.

Libby insisted they work on the book over dinner. Dinner sounded like a good idea to Belinda, since the vodka was doing strange things to her. They ordered salads and, contemplating the drive home, she switched to iced tea. But everyone's tongues had loosened, and by the time the food arrived, Libby was writing as fast as she could, jotting down everything the girls said.

"DON'T expect copulation and conversation at the same time," Carole offered.

"DON'T underestimate the extent to which men underestimate women," Rosemary added.

"DON'T trust a man whose most long-term relationship is with his dog," Libby said.

"DO prepare for inevitable setbacks in your relationship," Belinda said, "like sex."

They all stared.

"I think she said a naughty word," Libby whispered.

"Are you talking about Vince?" Carole demanded. "Or Julian?"

"No one else had to explain their advice," Belinda objected with a laugh.

"She's right," Rosemary said, digging into her salad. "Give the woman a break."

"Okay," Libby said. "We won't read anything into the fact that she's blushing like a woman who's been had, and her new boyfriend talks to her through the radio."

"Julian isn't my boyfriend."

"Well, I don't care if he is a celebrity," Rosemary said. "You should be careful."

Belinda forked in a bite of Caesar salad and chewed. That made two people who'd warned her about Julian. After a swallow and a drink of tea, she looked at Rosemary. "Do you know something about Julian that I should know?"

Rosemary shook her head but seemed overly preoccupied with her own greens. "At the risk of sounding like your mother, I just think young women should be more careful when they first meet men, especially in a city the size of Atlanta."

Libby huffed. "I say be careful even after you *marry* the man. How does the saying go—DON'T trust a man farther than you can throw him?"

"Or farther than you can blow him," Carole added with a grin.

"You have spinach in your braces," Rosemary said with a disapproving tone.

"Yes, Mother."

Rosemary scowled. "So what are we going to be subjected to at the spa tomorrow?"

Carole's eyes lit up. "We're all getting seaweed wraps, then Rosemary and Libby are going for facials, while Belinda and I do something a little more . . . adventurous."

Belinda choked down a hunk of romaine. "Adventurous?"

Carole smiled but thankfully hid it with her hand. "Have you ever had a Brazilian bikini wax?"

"Um, no."

"You're going to love it."

Belinda arched her eyebrow. "Isn't that supposed to be painful?"

"It's over, like, instantly. You won't feel a thing."

"Famous last words," Libby murmured.

"By the time Libby and Carole get through with you, Belinda," Rosemary said with a smirk, "you won't have any hair left at all."

Belinda smiled at the group of diverse women, feeling comfortable for the first time in recent memory. None of the women seemed to have anything in common other than working for Archer, and perhaps battling the traffic. Funny, but she had shied away from female relationships for that very reason—she hadn't seemed to have anything in common with most women she'd met. She'd been a loner her entire life.

And lonely.

But she was starting to realize that she didn't have to have obvious commonalities with friends—simply being female appeared to be a universally confusing condition. She was in good company.

They were pushing croutons around on their plates and coming down from their respective buzzes when Libby pointed to a television showing an aerial view of I-85. She sighed. "Darn, looks like traffic is breaking."

"It still won't be a picnic getting home," Rosemary said. "It'll be dark soon." She flagged the waitress for the check. "Belinda, are you okay to drive?"

Belinda nodded. "I'm a cheap date, but the effects seem to pass rather quickly."

They settled the bill and gingerly climbed down from their chairs, gathering purses and jackets. None of them, she realized, were anxious to hit the road, and all of them had different reasons for not wanting to go home. They moved through the noisy crowd toward the door, Belinda bringing up the rear.

But as she walked past the bar, Belinda did a double take—Lieutenant Alexander? In civilian clothes and from the side, she couldn't be sure. Dressed in jeans and a pale blue Atlanta Falcons T-shirt, he stood within arm's reach, talking to a small group of men, two of them in uniform. What was so unfamiliar about him was his smile—no, his *grin*—that transformed him from a solemn-faced cop into the mouthwatering neighbor boy that made a girl want to ride her bike up and down the street just to catch a glimpse. He lifted a bottle of beer to his mouth, but stopped when he caught sight of her. His dark eyebrows rose in recognition, and his friends turned to see what had captured his attention. She flushed, wishing she'd kept moving. But he stepped toward her, and for some foolish reason, her heart started pounding.

Association, she decided, wondering if she'd done anything she could be cited for.

"Hello," he said and offered a diluted version of that stomach-flipping grin.

"Hello," she said. "I'm beginning to think that Atlanta is a small city."

"It can be. Waiting out the traffic?"

She nodded. "You?"

He opened his mouth but was interrupted when a buddy of his, who'd apparently had much more to drink, stepped over and clamped a hand on his shoulder. "Buy this man a drink, pretty lady. We're celebrating Wade's return to single life."

She looked back to Wade, who was fidgeting with the label on his beer bottle. Compared to his friend, he seemed less jolly about the occasion. Her heart moved for the big man. "I was just leaving," she said. "But it was good to see you again, Lieutenant."

"I'll walk you to your car," he said, shoving his beer against his buddy's stomach with a glare.

"That's all right, it's parked at my office building."

"All the more reason."

"I'm with my friends," she said, pointing to the door where the women stood, craning for a look.

He looked at the women, then back to her. "Still."

Well, it was hard to argue with that. She conceded with a nod, then caught up with her friends. "Girls, you remember Lt. Wade Alexander."

"Wade," he said, nodding a greeting.

They chorused hello, but shot her quizzical looks.

"Um, Wade offered to walk us to our car."

More looks, which she ignored. Finally, Rosemary walked out, forcing Libby and Carole to follow and maintain a discreet lead.

He held open the door, and she walked out into the dusk. After the smoky interior of the bar, the fresh air felt good expanding her lungs, and the temperature had dropped with the sun. She lifted her jacket from her arm and responded with surprise when he took it from her and held it while she slid her arms inside. "Thank you."

"I'm sorry about my moron buddy back there. Believe it or not, he thought he was being a friend."

She resumed walking, ultra aware of his proximity. "No need to apologize. Friends don't always know what to do when . . . things like this happen. I'm sure he meant well."

They walked in silence. She longed for breezy conversation, but every encounter with this man so far had been fraught with awkwardness. "How long were you—"

"Six years," he cut in.

"Ah." So much for breezy conversation.

"The only good thing about my marriage was that we didn't have children."

Justification? She decided not to judge. "Divorce is hard on children."

"Do you—"

"No." She smiled. "I have a cat, and she's enough of a handful."

"I have a cat, too."

She laughed. "No offense, but you don't seem like a cat person."

"I'm not. The cat was . . . hers. But when she left, she didn't want it, and I didn't have the heart to take the poor thing to a shelter."

"Same for me," Belinda said with a sad smile. "Does your cat miss her—I mean, is it sulking?"

"He's shredding my furniture, if that's what you mean."

She winced. "At least Downey's not destructive. She just snubs me."

His laugh was a pleasing rumble. "They'll get over it."

"Think so?"

He looked at her directly for the first time, and she was struck by the full impact of his expressive gray eyes. "I'm counting on it."

She looked away first, and, alarmed by how far they'd fallen behind the women, increased her stride. When pedestrians approached, they were forced to walk closer together, and a couple of times, his hand hovered above her waist. An impulse of Southern manners, she was sure, like the ma'aming and the door-holding.

"Do you live around here?" she asked.

"Not too far from here. I have a small house in Ansley Park."

"I hear that's a nice area."

"It is. My place is a fixer-upper, but in the final stages, thank goodness."

"So you can do more with your hands than change a tire?" She wanted the words back as soon as they left her mouth.

He grinned. "Try me."

Belinda suddenly found it imperative to count the number of cracks in the sidewalk, and she hoped to find one large enough to fall into and disappear.

"So how do you like working at Archer?" he asked, probably to fill in the space.

"I'm getting acclimated."

"Did you make that important meeting Monday morning?"

She lifted her eyebrows in surprise.

He shrugged. "I remember your friend saying something about it at the time."

"No, unfortunately, I didn't make the meeting, and my boss was rather . . . perturbed with me."

"One of those, huh?"

She smiled. "Well, I try not to complain about her, but she can be a tyrant."

"So why stick around?"

"Greed. She brought me on to help take the company public."

"Works for me."

"At least you made *your* meeting. Not too late, I hope."

"Actually, it was a court date."

"Someone you ticketed?"

"Uh, no. Divorce settlement."

She winced. "And I almost made you miss it."

"I shouldn't have cut it so close."

"You looked as if you were just going off duty."

"A case I was working on ran late."

"All night?"

He nodded. "In hindsight, I don't think I was very nice to you."

"Under the circumstances, I thought you were incredibly nice. And now that I know everything, I can't imagine why you didn't shoot me."

He grinned, and she forgot to breathe.

"Listen," he said, his voice and expression changing. "How would you like to go to a Braves game sometime . . . with me?"

Thank goodness they were at the entrance to the parking garage, because she suddenly wanted to be away from him. Something about this man spooked her, reminded her of places she didn't want to go. Not yet, not so soon after her heart had been amputated, and his trampled as well. For now, she needed Julian's carefree smile and feel-good touches.

"Thank you for walking us back. This is far enough." She hadn't meant for the words to come out sounding so defensive, but there it was. Belinda stopped and signaled the girls, who were still ahead of them, to wait. "And I think I'll pass on the game."

He hesitated, then pursed his mouth. "Okay. You have my cell phone number in case anything . . . comes up."

"Yes." Her smile felt stiff. "Good luck with your cat."

"And you."

As Belinda turned to go, a sense of déjà vu settled over her. She was always hurrying away from this man. Later she realized she'd been so distracted by Wade Alexander's presence that she hadn't thought to tell him about the flying plant incident.

Chapter 13

Belinda opened her front door and contemplated her Saturday newspaper lying in the middle of her yard patch. She shot a glance toward Perry's driveway. The man himself wasn't in sight, but the lid to the coffin-sized stainless steel toolbox in the bed of his truck was ajar, so he was somewhere in the vicinity.

She slipped out the door as silently as possible and picked her way across the grass. Dew seeped through her thin house shoes, and the morning chill reminded her she wasn't wearing a bra. She leaned over to get the plastic-covered paper—almost there.

"Hey, Belinda!"

She winced, crossed her arms over her chest, and straightened. Perry walked toward her wearing a cutoff T-shirt and torn jeans that rode morbidly low. In one hand he held a coil of thick wire, in the other a wrench big enough to make her think about that road-safe weapon the girls had been hounding her to buy. "Hi, Perry."

He eyed the thin denim shirt she'd donned to do housework. "I saw you drive in last night—still don't have your car fixed?"

"Um, no. I'm supposed to get the estimate Monday."

"Want to go get a waffle?"

"Sorry—a friend is coming over."

"Boyfriend?"

She frowned. "No."

"Just askin'. Hey, I'll be down in your neck of the woods next week."

"Oh?"

"I got a work order for an elevator that's out of commission in your building."

That had taken long enough—Jeanie Lawford had been dead for six months. Of course, an investigation by the insurance company would have stalled the repairs.

He assumed as casual a pose as possible while holding a giant wrench. "So . . . what floor do you work on? Maybe I'll stop by."

"I don't think that's a good idea."

"I'll buy you lunch."

She took a deep breath. "Look, Perry, I'm not interested in us being more than neighbors and . . . friends."

He thought for a few seconds. "How good a friend?"

"Platonic."

He frowned. "Does that have anything to do with sex?"

"Yes. It means having none. Good-bye, Perry." She turned and started walking.

"A lot of women think I'm hot, you know!"

She closed the door behind her, heaved a sigh of relief, and carried the paper to the kitchen, where she poured a second cup of coffee. "Downey," she called. "Do you want to eat?"

Nothing.

She poured a scoop of dry cat food in the double-sided bowl for when the cat's stomach got the best of her pride. A yawn overtook Belinda. She covered her mouth with her hand and stretched high on her toes to send energy to her extremities. Last night she'd tossed and turned on her one pillow, plagued alternately by thoughts of her titillating encounter with Julian Hardeman and her unsettling encounter with Wade Alexander. The men evoked such opposite responses in her—just picturing Julian's face made her smile, and Wade's face . . . didn't.

His pain was too fresh, too familiar. She owed it to herself to spend time with a man who made her feel carefree. Sexy. Desirable.

On the kitchen table, Vince's envelope sat benignly, still propped against the yellow fruit bowl. She ignored it in favor of the *Atlanta Journal-Constitution*. Some local names and places were starting to become familiar. A good sign, but she still didn't feel connected to this big, sprawling city.

The best news came in the weather forecast: rain all weekend meant she might be able to pick up reception on her temperamental television and watch *The Single Files* tomorrow night. It was a petty thought, but she released it into the universe anyway.

She closed the paper and sipped her coffee. Vince's envelope taunted her, his precise cursive written, no doubt, with his favorite Mont Blanc pen. Return address: 137 Monarch Circle. It was to have been their address, their redbrick ranch with a sloping driveway, their front door with stained-glass inset. Instead, he lived there, and she lived—she glanced from corner to corner of her generic, rented town house—here.

Unbidden, tears pricked her eyes. She had wanted stainless steel appliances in the kitchen but had relented to his preference for white. She had coveted built-in bookshelves in the living room but had surrendered the space to a mammoth entertainment system. Had Vince been having reservations about their relationship even then? Had he planned all along to move into the house alone?

The phone rang, and Downey appeared from thin air.

"I think you're a shape-shifter," she accused the cat. "If you are, be a chocolate cake, would you?" She picked up the phone. "Hello?"

"Hi, dear, it's Mother."

She winced—she'd been so preoccupied when she'd

gotten home last night, she'd forgotten to call. "Hi, Mom, how are you?"

Long sigh. "Worried about you. Were you asleep?"

"No, I've been up for a while."

"You're not sleeping well?"

"I got up early to clean. A friend is coming over."

"Oh?"

"A *girl*friend."

"Oh."

"Guess what? I found my address book."

"Oh, good. The package is sitting right here in front of me."

She didn't doubt it. Belinda pulled up Suzanne's address and read it from the small screen of her organizer.

Her mother clucked. "I hope it isn't too late for Suzanne to return the candlesticks."

"If it is, she'll probably use them herself."

"Yes, her mother told me she and her husband have the most lovely home in Lexington." The envy in her mother's voice was palpable.

"Um, I bought a couch."

"You did? Oh, that's wonderful! What kind?"

"It's a sofa bed. Red."

"Did you say red?"

"Leather."

"Red *leather*?"

"It was on sale."

"Oh. Well, maybe you can cover it with a throw."

Sigh. "Are you and Dad ready for your trip?"

"Yes. Your father is out checking the tire pressure on the car. We're planning to leave first thing in the morning—your dad says the traffic will be light on Sunday."

"You'll have the best time."

"Of course we will. I'll call you often to check in." Then her mother cleared her throat. "Speaking of checking in, Belinda, have you heard from Vince?"

Her gaze bounced to the envelope on the table. "No. Why?"

"No reason. No reason at all, I didn't mean to upset you."

"You didn't."

"Well, I'd better go, dear. Mr. Finn will be here any minute to pick up this package."

"Okay, Mom. Give Dad my love." She hung up the phone and pursed her mouth. Her poor mother. Subjected to all the stress of a wedding, but cheated out of the aftermath of boasting to her friends how well her daughter and her new husband were getting along in their new home. Instead, Barbara Hennessey had been left with her penciled-in eyebrows raised in disbelief and no satisfactory explanation for the revoked wedding to pass on to shocked members of her Garden Club.

But she couldn't very well have told her mother that Vince might have changed his mind because she'd slept with him the night before the wedding and it had fallen short of earth shattering. (Okay, it had been a disaster.) Besides, he hadn't actually said that was the reason. Or said there was a reason at all.

She walked back to the table and sipped her coffee—now lukewarm—and squinted at the envelope. She could steam it open, and if the contents were innocuous, seal the flap and return to sender or toss the thing in the trash. And if the contents were completely objectionable, she could contaminate it with some hideous bacteria from the cheese in her refrigerator before sealing the flap and returning to sender.

Or she could rip it open and regardless of the contents, stomp on them, cut them up, and set them on fire. Or use the clippings to fashion a papier-mâché voodoo doll. Or to line Downey's litter box. Perhaps Martha Stewart should consider an episode on creative revenge. *Retribution—it's a good thing.*

On the counter sat the crumpled brown bag containing the embroidered pillow. Overcome by the urge to undo something, she pulled the pillow out of the bag and retrieved a pair of scissors. "Sorry, Aunt Edie," she murmured, then used the sharp end of the scissors to cut through the little stitches that formed the loving message. When she finished, frayed ends covered the pale blue surface, making her resent Vince all over again for the little injustices his behavior had foisted onto her family.

Downey had been studying her intently, and she realized the cat was captivated by the shiny sateen fabric. Belinda tossed the dainty pillow on the floor, and Downey pounced, then dragged it toward her food bowl.

"Go for it," Belinda muttered.

She sighed, thinking she should probably channel her anger toward straightening the town house before Libby arrived. She drained her cup and put it in the dishwasher, along with the few items that had accumulated over the week. She wiped counters and dusted, then ran the vacuum cleaner, which sent Downey into hiding. In the living room, Belinda maneuvered around the moving boxes that she had yet to confront.

But they weren't going anywhere.

She barely had time to finish, take a quick shower and dress before her doorbell rang. When she opened the door, a blue Volvo sedan was backing out of the driveway, and Libby stood on the stoop, her mouth tight and quivery.

"Everything okay?" Belinda asked, stepping aside to allow her entry.

Libby gritted her teeth. "Glen said I was going to have to get a part-time job to pay off my credit cards." She sniffed and bustled in, carrying a pink overnight case. She was dressed in cropped white pants that hugged her generous hips and showed off her tiny ankles. Her blouse was big and flowing, her hair poufy. She raised her hand, witness style. "I swear sometimes that man makes me so damn mad, a red haze just comes over me, and I think how nice it would be to just shut him up once and for all!"

The woman was shaking and her voice was so hysterical that Belinda had a vision of a news video showing a Bloomingdale's-dressed woman in handcuffs, with a reporter in the foreground saying, "The police are calling this murder a crime of passion."

Belinda spoke carefully. "Both of you are stressed, things will settle down."

"I told him about our book, and he *laughed* at me! He had a big old belly laugh at the idea of Libby Janes being an author!"

Belinda wet her lips. "Well, Libby, you have to admit the odds of getting the manuscript published are rather slim."

"This book is going to be *great*," Libby insisted, her eyes bulging. "I've been working on it at night. It's going to be more than just DOs and DON'Ts. I bought a book on getting published, and I tell you, the four of us could be like Margaret Mitchell."

Belinda lifted her eyebrow but kept her thoughts—that the idea of four carpooling office workers reaching the authorial status of Margaret Mitchell was indeed laughable—to herself. On the other hand, considering the amount of time they spent in traffic, the odds of them suffering a vehicular death like Margaret were pretty darn good. Instead she said, "Would you like something to drink?"

"Coke?"

"I have Diet Pepsi."

Libby sighed, then nodded, her anger spent. "Oh, I'm just in a mood. Keep your fingers crossed that I get that raise." Then she conjured up a big smile. "So, this is your place." She circled in the foyer, then followed Belinda into the kitchen. "It's really . . . bare."

"I haven't had time to do much decorating. I didn't have a lot of furniture, and my plants didn't survive the move."

"Still, it has potential," Libby said, tapping her finger against her chin. "Your couch will look great next to that bay window. And I've got enough stuff in my upstairs hall closet to decorate this whole place. You like dried flowers, don't you?"

"Well—"

"Oh, and you need a wallpaper border—I put a magnolia border in my foyer, and I have tons left over. It's removable, so your landlord won't have a conniption."

"Okay." Belinda opened the refrigerator and withdrew a can of soda.

Libby passed on a glass, cracked open the can, and chugged half of it on the spot. "Not bad," she said. "Although the way my nerves are acting up this morning, I don't need the caffeine."

No, she didn't, considering she would soon be brandishing shears. Belinda tapped her watch. "Carole and Rosemary will be here soon, so maybe we should get started."

"Okay, where do you want me to set up?"

"The bathroom upstairs is bigger than the one down here."

"Sounds good to me."

When they turned the corner, Downey sat on the bottom step like a sentry with a blue satin guard pillow by her side. The pillow looked worse for cat wear, already torn and stained.

Libby cooed. "I didn't know you had a kitty." She set down the overnight case and the soda, then scooped Downey into her arms.

"Careful, she's not very friend—"

Downey licked Libby's chin.

"—ly." Belinda frowned at the hairy little traitoress. Maybe she liked the taste of Aqua Net.

"What an adorable little fuzzy-wuzzy," Libby sang, pressing her nose against Downey's.

"She bites," Belinda offered.

"No, she's a pretty little kitty-witty. Yes, you are." Downey purred and rubbed her ear against Libby's cheek. "Too bad Glen is allergic," she said, setting down the satisfied feline. "Otherwise, I'd have a houseful. Have you had her long?"

Belinda climbed the stairs. "About a year. Vince adopted her from a humane society drive. I inherited her . . . afterward."

At the top of the stairs, Libby pointed to the room on the right. "Spare bedroom?"

Belinda nodded. "I was thinking I'd turn it into an office."

Libby made a face. "Forget that, you'll be working all the time."

Belinda smiled, walked across the landing, and pointed left. "My bedroom."

Libby stuck her head inside. "I wouldn't have thought you for leopard-print bed linens. Nice." Then she frowned. "Did you and your ex split up the pillows, too?"

"Hm? Oh, long story."

"I've got time," Libby said cheerfully. "I love to talk while I'm cutting hair."

Belinda arched an eyebrow—surprise, surprise. From her bedroom, she led Libby into the connected bathroom that was also accessible from the hall.

"It'll take me just a minute to set up," Libby said, humming with approval at the chair Belinda had placed in front of the vanity.

"Shall I get a towel?"

"No, I brought a poncho, just sit yourself down."

Belinda took a deep breath and did as she was told. In the wide mirror hanging over the vanity, the differences in their reflections were sobering. Libby, in her bright clothes and shiny makeup, was a neon sign, and she, with her J. Crew gear and scrubbed face, was a signpost. Maybe she *could* use a new look to go with her new outlook.

"Now," Libby said, fluffing Belinda's limp hair and peering over her shoulder into the mirror. "Do you have any last requests?"

Belinda swallowed hard. "Nothing startling."

Chapter 14

Belinda watched with morbid curiosity as Libby opened the overnight case, then removed a pink cotton smock for herself and a plastic poncho with a stand-up lip, which she settled around Belinda's shoulders.

The woman's preparations were a far cry from the piece of Scotch tape her mother used to put on her bangs for a trim with her sewing scissors.

Within a couple of minutes, the vanity was littered with colorful spray bottles, combs, and clips. Libby filled one of the spray bottles with water from the sink.

"So, do you ever hear from Vic?"

Belinda closed her eyes in preparation for being squirted—and for other reasons. "You mean Vince?"

Libby put her hand on Belinda's brow, then sprayed until water trickled behind Belinda's ears. "Vince, right. Look down for me. Do you ever hear from him?"

Belinda thought about the card sitting on the table downstairs and formed the words in her throat to tell her new friend about it—and about everything—before swallowing them. "No."

A comb sliced down the center of her head for a clean

part, then Libby circled, combing her hair straight down. "It was his idea to split, wasn't it?"

"Yes."

"Do you still love him?"

Belinda turned the question over in her heart. "Sometimes."

Libby picked up a pair of shears. "Was there another woman involved?"

Belinda's scalp tingled in anticipation of Libby's scissors touching down. "Not that I know of."

"Is he gay?"

"Not that I know of."

"Money problems?"

"No."

"Disagree on having kids?"

"No."

"So what was his reason for the breakup?"

Belinda shrugged carefully. "He honestly didn't say why he left."

Libby gaped at her in the mirror, scissors poised near her earlobe. "And you didn't ask?"

Belinda stared at the scissors. "At the time, I was too disoriented."

"I take it you didn't see it coming?"

"No."

Then, quick as a snake striking, Libby sliced a hank out of Belinda's hair. "Aw, honey, I'm sorry."

Belinda stared at the air where her hair had been. "That's okay. I guess I'll get used to it."

Libby squinted. "Hm? No, your hair is going to be fabulous. I mean I'm sorry you got your heart broken." She removed another hefty slice of hair, then smiled. "But Vince's loss was our gain."

"That's nice of you to say."

Libby kept cutting. "Between the traffic reporter and the cop, it doesn't look like you're going to be spending too many lonely nights."

Another careful shrug. "Julian is fun."

One last cut severed Belinda's tie to long hair. "What about Officer Goodbody?"

Belinda studied her new, less-hairy reflection. So far, so so. "He has too much baggage."

"I think you like him. You were all splotchy last night when we got in the car."

"Thanks for noticing, and what does that have to do with anything?"

"The man is under your skin."

"Maybe I'm allergic to his cologne."

"Whatever you say." Libby fluffed Belinda's hair again. "I'm thinking a few wispies, and some blunt tips so the ends will fly."

"I have no idea what you just said."

"It's the latest style, and it'll be marvelous, you'll see." Libby combed Belinda's overlong bangs in front of her eyes. "Carole and Rosemary will eat their words."

Belinda's nose tickled something fierce. "Those two seem very close."

"Oh, yeah. They argue constantly, but they're real protective of each other, sort of like mother and daughter."

"Carole seems like such a free spirit."

"She's a little kooky sometimes, but I think she grew up in a bad way, just because of things she says occasionally, like that crack she made about having been in the back of a cop car before." She made a rueful noise. "Which is probably why she falls for all that psychic mumbo jumbo and those green card grooms. But she's been good for Rosemary—they spend a lot of time together outside of work."

Chunks of hair were secured with biting clips. Then the shears started singing and snapping, and Belinda tried not to think about what was happening on the other side of her bangs. "Rosemary"—She spit out bits of hair—"doesn't have children?"

"No. Said she and her first husband tried, but couldn't. She was too old by the time she married her second husband—he died in his sleep. Stanley was her third husband, and since he died two years ago, she just hasn't been the same."

"That's understandable."

"Yeah, except to be honest, I never thought she was in love with the man."

"Maybe they were happy companions."

Libby grunted. "Between you and me and the fence post, I think she married him because he was loaded. Then his illness drained their finances—they had to file bankruptcy." She made a wry face. "That's why she's always after me about my spending habits. And I think the painkillers for her back cause mood swings. Some days she seems kind of out of it—and she was packing away the martinis the other night."

Belinda had noticed.

"I'm afraid something's wrong, health-wise. Since Stan died, every couple of weeks she bows out of the car pool for a day, and all she'll say is that she has an appointment after work that she can't miss." She sighed and loosened a clip. "And I worry about what might happen if Rosemary loses her job—she's right about Margo having it in for her. The worst part is that she's made an enemy out of Margo by taking up for the rest of us. Oh, dammit!"

"What did you do?" Belinda asked, visualizing a bald spot.

"There I go again, bad-mouthing Margo. I told myself that even though I hope that pygmy dies a slow, painful death, I won't drag you in the middle."

"Um, thanks." Belinda squeezed her eyes shut as the blades of the shears liberated her bangs.

"I mean, just because Margo makes working at Archer a living hell for the rest of us—"

"Libby."

"Right. Okay, I'm finished cutting. Let me clean you up a bit."

Belinda winced against the tickle of a soft-bristle brush.

"Do you have any mousse?"

Belinda opened her eyes. "I don't suppose you mean the chocolate kind?" Because she might need large amounts of it to get used to the new do.

Libby waved her hand and unzipped the hair-laden plastic poncho. "I brought some with me, just in case."

White airy balls of mousse went into the irregularly shaped mass, then Libby made Belinda hang her head upside down while she blew her hair dry. When Belinda was right side up again, she looked in the mirror and held on to the counter to keep from falling off the chair. "I'm a red-headed troll doll."

Libby laughed. "It's not done, pet. Drying it upside down gives you volume."

Belinda swallowed and watched with much trepidation as Libby manipulated her hair back down to a reasonable height, flipped up the ends, and arranged her abrupt bangs. A cloud of hairspray followed, then Libby stood back.

"Ta-da! What do you think?"

Belinda moved her head side to side, trying to absorb the style that made her look as if a perpetual fan were blowing in her face. A good look if she was on a modeling shoot, but a little forced, since she was sitting stock-still in her bathroom. She reached up to touch the crunchy ends. "I think it's, um—"

The doorbell rang, saving her from having to respond. "Thanks, Libby. It's great. Really."

Libby took a bow.

Belinda returned the best smile she could manage. It was only hair—it would grow back. Eventually. "That's probably Carole and Rosemary."

"You go ahead, I'll clean up in here."

Belinda stood and brushed herself off, then jogged down the stairs with Downey at her heels. Sure enough, the peephole revealed Carole, grinning. Belinda opened the door, and Carole's grin disappeared.

"Tell me that's a wig."

Belinda tried to ruffle her hair, but her fingers got caught. "No, it's all me. Libby says it's the latest style."

"Alrighty then."

Belinda waved past Carole to Rosemary, who was sitting in her gray four-door Chrysler in the driveway. The window came down halfway. "Did Libby do that to you?"

Belinda kept smiling, although her stomach had started to churn. "It's just going to take a little getting used to."

Rosemary looked doubtful and rolled the window back up.

Carole tore her gaze from Belinda's head. "Don't mind Rosemary, she's in a funk today." Then the young woman leaned forward with a conspiratorial brow wag. "Are you ready for your first Brazilian bikini wax? It'll change your life."

Belinda's smile slipped for a millisecond—she wasn't sure how many more life changes she could endure.

Hours later, Belinda unlocked her front door and turned to wave into the headlights of Rosemary's car. The twin beams spotlighted the light rain falling. She maintained her smile until the car pulled away, then her shoulders dropped. Every inch of her throbbed, stung, or itched, and she was stone tired. If she'd had a couch, she would have stumbled into the living room and fallen onto it facedown. The carpet would do.

"Downey, I'm home," she called as she closed the door behind her.

Nothing.

She locked the door, dropped her purse on the living room chair, and checked her phone machine for messages. The number 1 blinked. Her heart rate picked up as she sorted through the possible callers and pushed the button.

"Hello, dear, it's Mother."

Of course it was.

"I've been thinking about that red couch you bought."

Of course she had.

"I found a catalog of slipcovers that I'll drop in the mail before I leave town. I'll talk to you soon. Bye."

The beep sounded, and Belinda sighed. Some small part of her had hoped it was Julian, in Raleigh and thinking about her. Could they have dinner when he returned? Go to a movie? A ball game? Wade Alexander's invitation came to mind, but she pushed it away. The man's amazing grin notwithstanding, she didn't have the strength to help him over his heartache—she needed time and space to lick her own wounds.

She grabbed a pillow from the chair, tossed it on the floor and stretched out on the soft pile of the beige carpet where her wayward red couch would soon sit. A day of being girly was tougher than she'd imagined; after surviving Libby's shearing, she'd arrived at the spa to be bound like a mummy in slimy seaweed, then hosed off and whisked away to the only experience that rivaled the mortification of being abandoned after six hours of marriage: a Brazilian bikini wax.

Downey appeared and seemed to take the fact that Belinda was down on her level as some sort of concession. She sat down within arm's reach and blinked.

"A piece of advice, old girl," Belinda muttered, rubbing a knuckle between the cat's ears. "Any procedure described as 'Brazilian' means going places better left to a doctor or a thermometer."

Downey purred and bobbed her head against Belinda's hand, then bit her finger. Belinda yelped, and Downey vamoosed nice and slow, her tail high. The cat hadn't broken the skin, but she'd made her point—*I still don't like you.*

"He didn't want you," Belinda yelled after the cat. "He didn't want either one of us!"

She considered bouncing her cushion off Downey's retreating behind, but she was too tired to retrieve it afterward. Instead she clicked on the TV remote control and was rewarded with a semi-clear picture of *Mad About You* in syndication. It was the episode where Paul accidentally gave his and Jamie's bed to Goodwill. Turning on her side, she relaxed into the pillow. Reruns asked very little of the viewer. Reruns were comforting, predictable. Easy and familiar. The downside of starting over was that it left her with the unsettling feeling that her previous life was invalid. In the swirl of her new life, little bits of familiarity were balm to her soul.

From the next room, Vince's envelope called to her with the lure of reclaiming a piece of her former life, but exhaustion helped her resist. She smiled at the TV couple's banter and felt her eyelids growing heavy. Last night's missed sleep was catching up with her.

But what if Vince's card was a plea to forgive his foolhardiness and come back to live with him in the home they had selected together? Maybe he had ordered stainless steel appliances and installed bookshelves in the TV room. Maybe he realized that their pre-wedding consummation had simply been timing and excessive nerves and not a culmination of their relationship. She'd been sexy and lovable all along.

Her next conscious moment was being jolted awake by the telephone ringing. Downey had been curled against her stomach, but she went airborne with alarm. Belinda registered the fuzz on the TV and filtered daylight streaming in the bay window. The time on the VCR read 9:35 A.M. She pushed herself up, groaning when her back and shoulder muscles seized, and lumbered to the cordless phone. "Hello?"

"Belinda?" a woman's voice asked.

The voice was familiar, but she was still chasing the sleep from her brain. "Yes."

"Belinda, this is Margo. Did I wake you?"

Panic gripped her—had she somehow slept through Sunday and was, at this moment, supposed to be at work? "Um, no, you didn't wake me," she lied, her mind racing for an excuse as to why she wasn't at her desk.

"Good," Margo chirped. "Listen, I hate to bother you on Sunday morning, but I need for you to take a look at another set of Payton financials."

Weak with relief, Belinda shoved her hand into her hair—or at least tried to. It was an impenetrable mass on her head. "I thought the contracts were already signed."

"They are, they'll go out in the next couple of days."

Margo hesitated, or perhaps she was distracted. Belinda could hear another voice in the background—a male voice. The television? Suddenly all sound was muffled, as if Margo had covered the mouthpiece with her hand, then it cleared.

"These questions are for my own information," Margo said. "But I have to have the answers by tomorrow morning."

"Okay. Did you e-mail the documents?"

"No, I need for you to look at my notes in the margins—I'm having the papers couriered to your house. The messenger should be there within the hour."

Belinda glanced down. She'd slept in the clothes she'd worn to the spa, and they told the story. Downey sniffed her, then turned and walked away. "Okay, I'll be on the lookout. Should I call you if I have questions?"

"No, if we need to discuss anything, I'll schedule some time before your evaluation tomorrow."

Belinda swallowed. "Okay."

Margo hung up.

Chapter 15

Belinda looked at the phone, then disconnected her end of the call. "So much for a lazy Sunday," she murmured, then tore upstairs for a shower so she'd be presentable when the courier arrived.

One glance in the vanity mirror halted her in her tracks. Her hair was positively frightening, and the rest of her was only one step above. She turned on the showerhead, then peeled off her clothes and tossed them in a pile. When she removed her panties, the air hit her in places it hadn't since before puberty. She scrutinized her wax job with a critical eye—the little old lady who had painted on the hot wax, then ripped out the hair with equal levels of skill and detachment, had left a tiny landing strip on her privates but otherwise she'd been picked clean. The "gliding" feeling wasn't wholly unpleasant, but it would take some getting used to.

And the brilliant pain had lasted a bit longer than the "instant" Carole had promised.

She climbed into the shower and began the job of removing the gunk from her hair. Three shampoos later, she turned off the spray, squeezed the excess water from her hair, which felt disturbingly missing, then gave her body a brisk toweling. Her stomach growled—the quesadillas she'd eaten last night with the girls after they'd left the spa had run their course. She needed coffee and brain food—i.e., pancakes.

Since being fully clothed when the courier arrived was her first priority, she pulled on comfy jeans, T-shirt, and sandals. She brushed powder on her face and stroked on lip gloss, then tackled her hair—not a small task, considering she didn't know where to begin. To expedite matters, she turned the blow dryer on high, pointed it in the general direction of her head, and finger-combed the haphazard layers until they were dry. She looked in the mirror and squinted at the non-style, then experimented, finally tucking it behind her ears. While she scrubbed her teeth, she studied her new do from all angles and decided that the short bangs did highlight her brown eyes, and the extra detail around her face did bring out her cheekbones.

She had underestimated Libby—the woman knew hair.

The doorbell rang. She rinsed her mouth, then scooted out into the hall and down the stairs. She opened the door and smiled at the dark-haired lady holding a packet and a clipboard. A memory chord vibrated. "Hello."

"Belinda Hennessey?"

"That's right." Belinda took the clipboard and glanced at the woman's nametag. Tina Driver. "Tina, you look familiar. Do you work at Archer?"

"Not for Archer, for the management company at the Stratford Building, so you've probably seen me around. You're Carole Marchand's friend, aren't you?"

"Yes."

"I work with Carole in the mail room."

Belinda nodded. "We carpool together."

"I know—she talks about you. You're the one who tore Margo Campbell a new butt hole."

Belinda handed back the clipboard. "Well, I wouldn't put it that way."

"Everyone else does." The woman cackled and handed her the package. "Hope this isn't retribution."

Belinda gave her a tight smile. A sick feeling settled in

her stomach as she watched the woman climb into her van and pull away. Once a rumor sparked in the mail room, it spread like wildfire throughout the building via the mail employees of the individual companies. She'd have to watch what she said around Carole.

Of course, hadn't Carole expressed the same sentiment about her the other evening when they'd been having drinks?

She decided to let the incident slide. Maybe the story of the encounter had been an embellishment, but it hadn't been a lie. And hadn't she invited open commentary by choosing to play out the incident with Margo in a public place?

A distant rumble drew her attention to the dark clouds gathering on the horizon. A breeze had picked up, signaling imminent rain. Downey tried to make a run for daylight, but Belinda nabbed her, if inelegantly. By the time she closed the door behind them, the cat had nipped at her twice and left a long, bloody scratch down her arm. Belinda released the cat, and Downey bounded up the stairs.

"Run," Belinda yelled, surveying the gash. "I ought to have you de-clawed and those fangs of yours filed down!" She sighed, wondering which one of them would mortally wound the other first.

After washing up, she carried Margo's package to the kitchen. She began to read while she whipped up three pancakes, one of which she buttered and winged into Downey's bowl. "Come and get it," she shouted.

Nothing.

One of Margo's infamous neon orange notes had been plastered on the thick sheath of papers as a cover sheet.

B—

Please respond yes or no by item number on a separate sheet of paper to my handwritten notes.

M

But as far as she could see, the Payton financials were more of the same. And Margo's questions weren't nearly so urgent as she had made them seem.

Item #1—Yes or no, is this a reasonable figure for this type of expense?

On a separate sheet of paper, Belinda wrote:

Item #1—yes, this is a reasonable figure for this type of expense.
Item #2—Do you think this line item is something we should be concerned about?
Item #2—No, the line item represents standard industry procedure.

After two hours of scanning the pages for Margo's lightly penciled questions in the margins, her eyes were burning. Sometime while she was working, Downey's pancake had disappeared. Belinda shook her head and went back to work. An hour later, a clap of thunder shook the town house, and a black streak shot through the kitchen, ending at her leg.

"Fraidy cat," Belinda admonished. "Don't even try to suck up to me."

But Downey was in a repentant mood, winding around her legs. Belinda ignored her and pushed away from the table for another cup of coffee.

Margo confounded her, seeming alternately dismissive of and concerned about Payton's financials. Maybe the woman wasn't as confident as she wanted everyone to believe—not a stretch, Belinda decided, now that she knew Margo's background via Rosemary's story. And even as congenial as Margo had been the past few days, Belinda couldn't help but feel anxious about her evaluation.

The dark sky opened wide and sent the rain down in sheets, creating a cozy afternoon cocoon. She turned on the television in the other room for background noise and had almost finished wading through the financials when the phone rang. Probably her mother, she thought ruefully. Then, shot full of guilt, she answered.

"Hello?"

"Belinda? Hi, it's Julian."

An involuntary smile curved her mouth. "This is a nice surprise. I thought you were in Raleigh."

"I am, and it looks as if I will be for the night. The weather is horrendous."

"Here too. It's been raining for hours and doesn't seem to be letting up."

"Guess nobody will be flying in the morning." He sighed. "I wish you had been able to come with me."

"So do I," she said, and meant it. "But as it turned out, I had to work this afternoon anyway."

"On Sunday? Your boss must be some kind of slave driver."

"I work for Margo Campbell."

"Ooh. Did I get you in trouble Friday?"

She sighed. "I blame myself—I don't know what came over me to be so indiscreet at work."

His sexy laugh rumbled over the phone line. "I came over you."

Warmth flooded her thighs. She squirmed, managing a nervous laugh. She hadn't yet graduated to naughty banter. "I should thank you for your radio message Friday afternoon."

"What good is my eye in the sky if I can't help out a friend?"

"I took your advice and waited out the traffic." Wade Alexander's face materialized in her mind, but she blinked him away.

"Listen, I plan to be back in Atlanta by tomorrow evening. I was hoping we could get together again for lunch?"

Lunch, or foreplay? She shifted her weight and was reminded of her sexy new style down below—she needed to show it off sometime, didn't she? That exceptional pain had to come to some good. "I'm supposed to get an estimate for having my car repaired tomorrow, so I might be taking a day of vacation sometime this week. I'll have to play it by ear."

"Is this from your collision with Alexander?"

Him again. "Yes."

"I'll bet he wrote you a ticket, didn't he?"

"Three."

He guffawed. "The man's a real charmer. No wonder his wife was stepping out."

Sympathy for the officer barbed through her—no one deserved that kind of disregard. There were honorable ways to end a marriage.

Not that she could hold hers up as an example.

She pushed away from the counter where she'd been leaning, suddenly antsy. "Under the circumstances, I thought Lieutenant Alexander was generous." She managed a small laugh. "He even changed my tire."

"Yeah, I saw him. Must have felt guilty for fining you. Listen, I can make a couple of calls and have those tickets thrown out."

Although the idea appealed to her bank account, Julian's offer didn't feel right to her gut. "Thanks, but I'll take my medicine."

"Okay. If you change your mind, let me know. Meanwhile, I'll call you when I get back in town to check your schedule."

"Okay. Good-bye." Belinda disconnected the call slowly, contemplating her breezy relationship with Julian. A girl on the rebound could do worse than a handsome local celebrity. She looked back to her work spread over the kitchen table, then checked her watch. If she hurried, she could finish reviewing the financial statements before *The Single Files* came on.

Margo had flagged only two more areas, both as easily explained away as the others. Belinda perused the sheet of comments she'd made for her boss and shook her head. Maybe Margo was simply giving her busywork, testing her to see how responsive she would be on weekends. Margo's reference to her evaluation needled her, although she told herself she didn't have anything to worry about—Margo had already offered her the CFO position.

So why did she have the same prickly feeling of impending doom she'd had just before she'd rammed Wade Alexander's police cruiser?

The phone rang again, pulling her from her futile funk. She retrieved the phone from the counter. "Hello?"

"Belinda," said a bleary female voice. "This is Rosemary."

"Hi, Rosemary." She hesitated. "Is everything okay?"

"Actually, I need a favor. Would you mind driving the car pool tomorrow? I just remembered I have an appointment after work that I can't miss."

The mysterious appointments that Libby had mentioned. "Sure, I'll drive."

Rosemary made fretting noises. "If this weather keeps up, it's going to be a mess. I'd normally call Libby, but she won't get her SUV back until later in the week."

"It's no problem, really."

The older woman's sigh of relief seemed exaggerated, considering the issue. "Thank you, Belinda."

Was she drinking? Ill? "Rosemary, are you sure everything is okay?"

"Absolutely. I'll call Libby and Carole and tell them to look for your car. Everything will be fine. I'll see you sometime tomorrow."

"Yes. Goodnight." Belinda set down the phone, then frowned at the woman's phrasing. Everything *will be* fine?

Chapter 16

No one on the planet had the expertise or the right to complain about traffic, Belinda decided, until they'd driven in Atlanta during Monday morning rush hour in the driving rain.

An unending procession of steel machines crawled toward downtown, headlights on low-beam and wipers on high-speed against the gray downpour. Stalled cars were everywhere, and many traffic lights had malfunctioned. At every intersection, tempers were short and waits were long. In a word, it was misery.

"This is misery," Libby declared, looking around at the cars that hemmed them in on Peachtree Parkway. They were on their way to pick up Carole. "*Why* do we do this?"

"Because we aren't independently wealthy."

"Amen," Libby said with a sigh. "Lordy, I wish I would win the lottery. I'd hire your buddy Julian to pick me up and fly me to work."

Belinda gave her a wry smile. "*No one* is getting anywhere fast this morning."

The traffic reporters, all grounded by the soup, warned that road conditions were especially dangerous, since car fluids that had soaked into the asphalt were now slick puddles waiting for a bald tire. Belinda was glad Wade Alexander had badgered her into having her tire replaced right away. Operating with a broken headlight was enough of a hazard.

She wondered idly how the big man had spent his rainy weekend—trapped inside with his own temperamental cat, or pulling long shifts, since ugly weather usually meant overtime for public servants. She suspected he preferred working.

"Your hair looks great," Libby said.

Belinda smiled and stole a glance at her short auburn tresses in the rearview mirror. "Thanks to you."

"My hair, on the other hand, is going to look like crap."

Belinda eyed the pink sponge curlers, dreading the hairspray fumes, since they wouldn't be able to roll down the windows. "Maybe you should wait until we get to the parking garage to fix your hair."

"Okay," Libby mumbled, digging in a bag for her third doughnut. She had groused and fretted since climbing in Belinda's car, and Belinda suspected that the woman's evaluation weighed heavily on her mind.

She knew the feeling. How she wished for the distraction of Julian's voice.

After several long minutes of stop-and-go traffic, they pulled in to pick up Carole, who huddled beneath an awning of the apartment complex clubhouse.

She ran to the car, threw open the door, and fell inside. "Ugh, this weather! As if Monday isn't bad enough all by itself."

"I hate to think of Rosemary driving in this alone," Belinda said.

"I know," Carole said, removing her hat and pushing her black hair out of her eyes. "I tried to talk her out of it, but she insisted she couldn't miss her appointment."

"I think when she leaves the office this evening, we should follow her," Libby said matter-of-factly, handing the doughnut bag over the seat to Carole.

Belinda frowned as she eased the car through standing

water heading back toward the parkway. "I don't think that's a good idea."

"Wouldn't you want to know if Rosemary is sick?" Libby asked.

"Not if she doesn't want me to know."

Libby shook her head. "Did you have girlfriends in Cincinnati?"

Belinda blinked. "What do you mean?"

"Just what I said. Did you have any close girlfriends?"

She pushed her shoulders back. "I had a lot of friends." Was that her voice sounding so defensive?

"Anyone you've stayed in touch with since you moved?"

A flush warmed Belinda's face. "The split with Vince complicated matters."

"All your friends were his friends," Libby said bluntly.

Belinda balked. "That's not true." Was it?

Carole leaned forward. "What's with the inquisition, Libby?"

"I'm only saying that a woman is different with her own friends than she is with the girlfriends or wives of her husband's buddies." She took another bite from her doughnut. "If you had your own girlfriends, you'd know that sometimes sticking your nose into their business is part of what being a friend is all about."

"In this case," Carole said, "I agree with you. How can we help Rosemary if we don't know what kind of trouble she's in?"

Belinda squinted. "But why do you assume she's in trouble?"

"Because," Carole said, "if it were something good, she'd share it with us."

"That's how women are," Libby added, then she angled her head. "You don't like to take chances, do you, Belinda?"

She bristled. "I moved to Atlanta."

"On people, I mean. You don't like to take chances on people."

"Vince—"

"Vince broke your heart," Libby argued. "But that doesn't have anything to do with not having female friends in your life."

Belinda concentrated on the road through the furious blades of the wipers and kept her tone light. "I've always been a loner."

"I think you're afraid that if you stick your nose into Rosemary's business, someone will stick their nose into *your* business."

Belinda took a deep breath to stem the ridiculous tears that pressed at the backs of her eyes. "I think you're worried about your evaluation, and you're lashing out at me."

"She's right, Libby," Carole said. "Let Belinda drive."

"People who care about each other go out on a limb," Libby said. "Rosemary's gone out on a limb for us plenty of times. If she's in trouble, I want to be there for her."

Belinda met Carole's glance in the rearview mirror.

"I want to be there for her, too, Belinda."

Belinda looked back to the brake lights of the car in front of her. The truth was, she didn't want to get involved, especially with her own life still in restoration. Yet wasn't that Libby's point—that to be a friend, sometimes things got messy? And hadn't she promised herself that she *would* take chances, break a few of her self-imposed rules?

"Okay," she agreed. "But snooping makes me very uncomfortable."

Libby's smile was triumphant as she lifted her travel coffee mug. "We know."

Feeling absurdly as if she'd just passed some kind of initiation, Belinda turned her attention back to the road. Not that keeping her foot on the brake took much focus. They were going to be so late for work—as well as every OTP person who worked ITP. Margo would be supremely annoyed. She suddenly realized the women were whispering.

"Show her," Carole said. "We won't have time when we get to the office."

Belinda raised an eyebrow. "Show me what?"

Libby smiled. "Carole and I bought you something." Libby reached into a bag at her feet. "Belinda, meet your new best friend."

Belinda stared at the pink beribboned item Libby held up. "That's the biggest curling iron I've ever seen."

Libby laughed. "It's not a curling iron."

Belinda stared at the twenty-inch black wand. "That can*not* be a vibrator."

The two women looked at each other and fell out laughing. "No," Libby gasped. "It's your very own stun baton."

Belinda hit the brake a little too hard. "Stun baton? I . . . wow."

"To leave under your car seat," Libby said. "Five hundred thousand volts." She hit a button, and a crackling noise filled the air. "Three seconds on the end of this baby, and a man will be rehabilitated."

"Wow," Belinda repeated. "Is it, um, legal?"

"Good gravy, yes. You're in the South, girl. We'd arm ourselves with an alligator if we could get him in a holster."

"Ah. Right."

"We figured it was the least we could do for asking you to drive so much right off the bat," Libby said.

"Thanks. You. All." She started nodding and couldn't seem to stop.

"Rosemary will be jealous," Carole said, bouncing in her seat.

"Heck, *I'm* jealous of this Big Daddy," Libby said, sending another crackling jolt into the air, just for fun, Belinda assumed.

She, on the other hand, thought Big Daddy was downright terrifying, and she breathed much easier when Libby put him away. But it was the thought that counted, and she was touched that the girls were concerned for her safety. As soon as she received her raise, she planned to reinstate the service to her cellular phone.

After her account recovered from buying the evil couch. And after she bought a new television.

Which reminded her. "Hey, did anyone watch *The Single Files* last night?"

"Just the last half," Libby said. "It was a rerun, wasn't it?"

"Yeah, but one of the best episodes," Carole said. "Where Jill first met the locksmith."

"I love reruns," Belinda said.

Libby frowned. "I don't like reruns because I feel like I'm being manipulated into investing time in something that's long gone."

Belinda pursed her mouth. Something to consider.

"There's got to be a DO or a DON'T in there somewhere for our book," Carole said, then snapped her fingers. "I almost forgot to tell you—Ricky called me last night, and you'll never guess what he said."

Libby smirked. "If I guess, can I call myself a psychic and charge people for making outrageous predictions? Hey, maybe *that* can be my part-time job."

"Well, smarty-pants, it just so happens that he said he had a vision of my name on the front of a book."

That stopped Libby for a few seconds, then she scoffed. "You told him we were working on a book."

"No, I didn't."

Libby narrowed her eyes, as if she wanted to believe but couldn't bring herself. "That guy is ripping you off. Call-block him, and you wouldn't have to marry for money."

"But I trust Ricky," Carole said. "I believe he really has special powers."

"Girl, he's probably calling you from the basement of his parents' home."

"There's more."

"He's an alien?"

"No," Carole said, and the odd tone of her voice made Belinda look up.

"He said . . . that something bad was going to happen to someone I'm close to."

Libby made a disgusted noise in her throat. "Now

that's simply going too far. The man ought to be arrested." She looked at Belinda. "Why don't you put Lieutenant Goodbody on his tail?"

Belinda opened her mouth to protest, then realized there was nothing to protest—Libby was kidding. And Wade Alexander did have a good body.

Carole made a distressing noise. "Don't you see, Libby? I'm afraid Ricky's talking about Rosemary."

Libby's mouth tightened. "Enough about the psychic, okay? I'm worried about Rosemary, too, but not because *Ricky* announces that something *bad* is going to happen to someone *close* to you. Don't you see that his so-called prediction could apply to any person, any day of their life?"

Belinda's heart went out to the young woman who wanted so badly to believe in the ability to foretell the future. Lately, she could relate to that sentiment—it would be nice to know what was around the corner so that one could adequately prepare. Of course, if someone had told her that Vince would walk out on their wedding day, she wouldn't have believed them.

She merged onto I-85 at a roaring eleven miles per hour, and her stomach dipped at the gray sea of cars stretching in front of her. Without helicopters, the Department of Transportation and news stations had to rely on soggy cameras strategically mounted along the interstates and calls from drivers en route for traffic updates. Electronic marquees mounted above the interstates displayed delay information, although even those signs were difficult to read in the deluge.

"Oh, well, I'm in no hurry to get to work today anyway," Libby said.

"Me neither," Carole said. "Margo's had all weekend to work herself into a lather." Then she shot Belinda an apologetic look. "Sorry. I know you don't like to talk about Margo. I'm just nervous, I guess."

"I'm a little nervous myself," Belinda admitted.

"It's always the same," Libby said, sweeping her hand

as if she were directing a scene. "She starts out being nice as pie."

"How are you?" Carole mimicked. "Would you like a cup of coffee?"

"And then she goes for the jugular," Libby said. "Now then, let's *talk* about your *status* . . ."

". . . here at Archer," Margo said, her black-cherry-stained lips pulling back into a tight smile.

Belinda nodded, her stomach tangled. Margo had seemed satisfied with the page of last-minute responses to the Payton financials. But she'd seen Margo's personality swings. Despite their "agreement," would Margo turn on her again?

"This performance evaluation is a formality," Margo said, then flashed a full-fledged smile. "The contracts for the Payton acquisition are signed and ready to be mailed. You held up your end of our agreement, so I'll hold up mine."

Belinda waited.

"We'll make the announcement about the CFO position when I return from vacation. Until then, Juneau and I would appreciate it if you didn't say anything to anyone."

Pleasure bubbled in Belinda's chest. "Of course. Thank you." She rose and extended her hand.

Margo suddenly frowned and tapped a finger against her lips. "Which reminds me, with everything going on, I haven't given Brita my itinerary." She scribbled a few words on the orange From Margo notepad on her desk.

Belinda dropped her unshook hand and brushed imaginary lint from her skirt. "When are you leaving?"

Margo didn't look up. "Tonight. I'll be back in the office two weeks from today. I'll ask Brita to send any emergencies your way."

"Okay."

"Oh, and Belinda, since this is a performance evaluation, I would like to pass along one piece of constructive criticism."

Belinda held her breath—she didn't own any pink clothing, so it had to be something else.

"Your hair is too trendy." Margo waved her hand. "It's too cutesy."

A slow burn started in Belinda's stomach. Many people had told her how nice it looked. Was Margo threatened? "I just had it cut. I'm still experimenting."

Margo made a disapproving noise, still writing on the papers in front of her. "And lose the friends."

Belinda's neck tingled. "We've had this discussion before."

Margo finally looked up. "I know, and I'd hoped you would listen. Consorting with those women isn't good for your professional reputation."

"Consorting? We're carpooling."

"May I be frank?"

"Of course."

Margo sighed. "Rosemary Burchett has . . . mental problems. And Libby Janes was accused by a former coworker of stealing money. And that mail girl who gets her kicks from refugees is on administrative probation for opening confidential correspondence."

Belinda exhaled. "I . . . didn't know."

Margo looked back down to her paperwork. "That's why I'm telling you. Don't let them drag you down."

Belinda's brain resisted the urge to believe her boss's accusations, at the same time conceding their reasonableness. Rosemary could be . . . intense. And although Libby didn't seem like the type to steal, a person who was financially strapped could resort to desperate measures. And Carole . . . well, she herself had wondered if Carole was too free with the information she was privy to.

"I don't mean to be rude, Belinda, but I have to finish evaluations before five o'clock—"

The office door burst open. A balding man Belinda didn't recognize stood there, dressed in rumpled clothing, his face high in color, his eyes bulging. Brita was on his heels.

"I'm sorry, Ms. Campbell, I told him not to come in here."

Margo's mouth flattened into a thin line, but she was otherwise unruffled. "Brita, call security. Mr. Newberry will be needing an escort out of the building."

Belinda stared wide-eyed, unsure of what to do. This was the man whom Margo had fired, the company's previous CFO.

"Get out, Jim," Margo said. "Can't you see I'm having a meeting?"

"You conniving bitch," he said, taking two steps toward Margo's desk. "How could you do this to me?"

Margo gestured with her hand, indicating his appearance. "Look at yourself, Jim. You did this to yourself. You're the one with the drug problem."

"I don't do drugs. *You* set me up."

"I understand that addicts often blame others for their weaknesses."

He pointed a meaty finger. "You won't get away with this. I'll kill you first."

Belinda swallowed hard, but Margo only smiled. "No, you won't, Jim, because you're a spineless little insect. Now go away before I squash you for good."

Belinda's heart pounded, and gooseflesh rose on her arms. She wasn't sure she'd be able to move her feet if she had to.

The man's hands shook and his face turned scarlet, but just when she thought he was going to lunge for Margo, he burst into tears. Margo seemed even more irritated, rolling her eyes just as two security officers swept in.

"Get him out of here," she said, then went back to her writing as though nothing had happened.

Belinda watched a broken Jim Newberry being dragged out of Margo's office and down the hall. The commotion had attracted a crowd—people openly gawked at their former co-worker over the walls of their cubicles. Meanwhile, Belinda was trying to assimilate the scene that had just unfolded.

"Close the door on your way out, would you, Belinda?"

She looked back to her boss's bent head, and a chill settled over her. Either the woman was used to dealing with Jim Newberry, or she was calm beyond explanation. At a loss for words, Belinda walked out and pulled the door closed with a slippery palm. She ignored the curious stares as she made her way back to her own office. Her phone was ringing when she walked in—an internal call, she could tell from the double ring. She dropped into her chair, breathed in and out, then picked up the receiver. "Belinda Hennessey."

"It's me," Libby whispered. "Were you in Margo's office just now?"

"Yes."

"Is it true that Jim Newberry stormed in?"

Belinda looked over her shoulder and lowered her voice. "I can't talk about it."

"That turd has perfect timing—he went and got Margo all fired up right before my evaluation."

"I'd rather not—"

"How did *your* evaluation go?"

Belinda hesitated. "Fine. Good, even."

"I'll get the scoop later. Wish me luck."

"I do."

"Oh, I talked to Rosemary, and she said she'll be working until six, which tells me she's killing time until she leaves for her 'appointment.' I told Carole to meet us at the car at six sharp."

Margo's warning to find new friends sounded in her mind's ear. "You still want to go through with this?"

"Absolutely."

Belinda bit into her lower lip and went against her better judgment. "Okay."

Libby hung up, and Belinda returned the receiver slowly, light-headed from sensory overload. She had gone from elation over the promotion to awkwardness over Margo's comments about the girls to the explosive encounter with Jim Newberry in the space of ten minutes.

She needed a break. She swung around in her chair to remove her purse from a locked desk drawer, and in the process, she caught sight of the policies and procedures manual that Libby had loaned to her. A few pages were crimped where the woman had slammed the book shut Friday after looking up something in preparation for her evaluation. Belinda slid her finger into the spot and opened the binder.

Activities That Result in Immediate Dismissal

The subtitles were: lying on the job application or resume, insubordination (*yilk*), being convicted of a felony, possession of a firearm on the job, possession of an illegal substance on the job, breaching computer system security, and theft.

Belinda swallowed hard. Libby had been worried enough about the ramifications of one of those topics to look it up. Theft?

When the suspicions threatened to take flight in her imagination, Belinda closed the binder. She had too much on her mind right now to be adding fuel to the fire needlessly. Libby could take care of herself.

On the way to the stairwell, Belinda spotted Clancy hurrying in her direction. She braced herself for twenty questions about the Jim Newberry incident, but to her surprise, he was so lost in thought that he didn't even notice her. Probably fretting about his evaluation, like everyone else. She allowed herself a tiny smile when she thought about her own promotion and what it would mean to her career.

Not to mention her earning power.

She descended the stairs to the ground floor and made her way to the vending area of the food court, a wide but shallow room lined with soda and snack machines. A few grungy-looking young men sat around playing handheld video games or reading magazines. Belinda fished quarters out of her purse and held them to the mouth of the

Pepsi machine, then hesitated and considered the Coke machine a few steps away. Unbidden, Wade Alexander's roadside teasing came back to her.

"The Diet Pepsi will have to go. It's all Coke around here."

Well . . . when in Rome.

She walked to the Coke machine, dropped in her change, and a can of Diet Coke rolled out, so cold that condensation had formed. She popped the top and lifted it to her mouth for a drink. Not as sweet as Pepsi, but . . . good.

She fought a yawn and checked her watch—only 4:00. The interminable morning commute in the rain had set the tone for the day. At least the weather had cleared, so the journey home promised to be less perilous, but she dreaded the undercover caper that Libby and Carole had planned. Following Rosemary, spying on her. Libby called it friendship, but Belinda had another word for it: invasive.

And if what Margo had said about the girls was true, the last thing she needed to do was to get more involved in their lives.

She took another drink, then squinted. Something about a man on the fray of the foot traffic coming toward her seemed familiar. Saunter. Hard hat. Toolbox. *Yilk*—Perry. She'd forgotten he'd said he'd be working in the building today.

She ducked back in the vending room and darted behind the Coke machine. She peeked around the corner, praying the man wouldn't be assailed by a sudden thirst. At length, he walked by, whistling to himself, which made it easier to whistle when women walked by. The man was oblivious to his baseness.

"Hiding from someone?" a familiar male voice said behind her.

Chapter 17

Belinda jerked around, sloshing Coke, and almost fell into Wade Alexander, who leaned against the soda machine, arms crossed over his uniformed chest. "No. I . . ." She straightened. "Yes, if you must know, I'm hiding from my neighbor."

"Why?" He fought a smile, which made her feel ridiculous.

"Because . . . he's a kook." Unlike her, of course.

"Ah." He stepped out to look down the food court. "Which one is he?"

"Hard hat. Toolbox."

"Whistling at women?"

"That would be him."

"Want me to shoot him?"

She pushed her tongue into her cheek. "No, Lieutenant."

He scratched his temple. "I thought we'd graduated to first names."

Her neck itched, and Libby's comment about her getting splotchy around the man rang in her ears. "It's, um . . . the uniform," she said, indicating the snug-fitting, imposing attire that outlined his powerful physique to perfection. "It's hard for me to think of you as anything else when you're dressed." She coughed. "Like that."

"So if I wasn't dressed?" His smile widened. "Like this?"

She squinted. "What are you doing here?"

"Looking for you, actually."

"What did I do this time?"

"Nothing, I hope. A buddy of mine heads up security in this building. He called me to report an incident at Archer—some guy forced his way into a woman's office?"

She nodded. "I was there."

"Why am I not surprised?"

She smirked. "I was meeting with my boss, and the man interrupted us."

"Was he armed?"

"I didn't see a weapon."

"Was anyone hurt?"

"No. I thought he might attack her, but then he sort of broke down."

One dark eyebrow arched. "Crying?"

"My boss has that effect on people."

"The report said the guy was a former employee."

She nodded. "But he was let go before I came here. My boss alluded to him being fired for a drug problem."

"Was he high when you saw him?"

"I couldn't tell, but he was disheveled. And on edge."

"So what happened to our agreement?"

"Agreement?"

"That you would call me if anything unusual happened."

"Oh. I guess I . . . forgot." She frowned, and gestured around the vending room. "So how did you find me *here*?"

"I'm trained to spot suspicious-looking people. When I saw a woman hiding behind vending machines, then playing peekaboo, I thought I should investigate." He lifted his gaze to her head. "Especially when I saw the red hair. By the way, what happened to the rest of it?"

"I like my hair like this."

"Then so do I."

She nodded in a vague "away" direction. "I should be getting back to work."

"Me too. But you'll call me if anything else happens?"

Belinda angled her head. "Does your interest in Archer have anything to do with Jeanie Lawford's accident?"

He had a poker face. "An incident like that puts the company on the police radar."

"So you're just doing your job?"

"Yes, ma'am."

Belinda smiled. "Good-bye, Lieutenant." She turned to go.

"Hey."

She turned back.

"I see you're drinking the good stuff."

She glanced down at the Diet Coke can she held. A flush warmed her face. "The Pepsi machine wasn't working."

Next to him, a young man dropped coins into the Pepsi machine, pushed a button, and a can rolled out.

Wade looked back to her.

"Gotta go," she said and walked away as fast as she could. At the door to the stairwell, she looked back through the crowd and saw Lieutenant Good—er, Lieutenant Alexander still watching her. He was not smiling, and she was struck with the illogical desire to restore his cheerfulness. She lifted her can in a salute, then turned toward the stairs. The man was an enigma, and the last thing she needed in her life right now was more complications.

By the time she reached the eighth floor, she attributed her skittery mood to the events of the day, and her pounding pulse to the exertion. But the impromptu encounter with Wade Alexander had reminded her that she needed to call for the estimate on her car repairs. On the way back to her desk, she stopped by the ladies' room.

It was impossible for her to walk into the tiled room without remembering the episode between her and Margo only a week ago. It seemed as if much more time had passed, because so many things had happened in the space of seven days. She set her soda on the counter, then stopped at the sound of sniffling coming from the one closed stall door. She looked down and recognized Libby's red-and-black stiletto pumps.

Belinda shot a glance back to the entrance and considered giving the woman privacy. Chances were, whatever was wrong, she wouldn't be able to help anyway. But when another tearful snuffle sounded, her shoulders fell in defeat, and she walked over to the metal door. "Libby, it's Belinda. Are you okay?"

Libby emitted a tremulous exhale. "I decided to come in here, since my life is going down the crapper."

Biting back a smile, Belinda asked, "Do you want to talk about it?"

The door opened. Libby stood there, wiping her red nose with a tissue. "Come on in."

Belinda balked. "Well, I—"

Libby clasped her arm, hauled her inside the stall, and closed the door. Belinda squirmed at the proximity. The stall was roomy as far as bathroom stalls were concerned, but still. Libby blew her nose into a wad of toilet tissue, then dropped it in the commode with what looked like enough paper to do some serious pipe damage.

"My life is a disaster," she said, her eyes overflowing anew. "I'm in debt over my head, my husband is furious with me, my kids are belligerent, and Margo just told me that my performance over the past year 'doesn't warrant a raise.'" She blew her nose again. "Oooh! That woman makes me so furious. She didn't give Carole a raise either, and Rosemary's in there now."

Uncertain what to do, Belinda reached out and patted Libby's arm awkwardly. "Everything will work out."

Libby shook her head. "You know my friend in HR?"

"I remember you mentioning her."

"Well, she can't reveal any specifics, but she hinted that our personnel numbers were going to be reduced."

"And you think Rosemary is going to lose her job?"

Libby nodded tearfully. "And here I am, feeling guilty because I'm glad it wasn't me."

Belinda patted her again. "You shouldn't feel guilty for wanting to keep your job. And even if Rosemary is let go, she'll land on her feet."

Libby took a deep breath and nodded. "I just hate to think that she'd have to deal with unemployment if she's sick, too."

"You don't know that."

"I guess we'll find out this evening."

Belinda tried to smile. "Maybe Rosemary's seeing some dashing gentleman that she doesn't want anyone to know about."

Libby smiled. "Could be. I guess I'm not helping anything by standing in the john blubbering."

The door to the ladies' room opened and someone walked in. Belinda cringed, hoping the person wouldn't notice two sets of legs in the stall. Silence abounded. And either the person didn't notice and changed their mind about whatever they'd come in for, or they did notice and decided they didn't want to stick around. Quick footsteps sounded on the tile floor, then the door opened and closed.

Belinda and Libby looked at each other and started laughing. An alien sense of camaraderie flooded Belinda. She couldn't do anything to help Libby's situation except offer a sympathetic ear, but apparently, sometimes a sympathetic ear was enough. Funny, but she had always subscribed to the theory of not sharing her feelings with people unless they were part of a concrete solution. Now she wondered how many things she'd internalized over the years, when the simple act of unburdening herself might have been beneficial.

"At least *your* evaluation went well," Libby said, wiping her eyes. "And I suppose that Margo can't fire all of us. Oh—you have to tell me all about Jim Newberry!"

"Later, when we're playing private eye. Right now I need to get back to my desk."

"Me too." Libby reached forward and squeezed Belinda's hand. "Thanks, Belinda."

Startled, Belinda squeezed back after a half beat. "You're welcome. Now get out of here so I can relieve myself."

Libby laughed. "See you later."

Guilt plagued Belinda all the way back to her cubicle. While Libby and Carole had been denied even cost-of-living raises and Rosemary's job appeared to be in true jeopardy, she'd just been awarded the position and the salary of her dreams. Would the girls resent her when they found out?

The thought jarred her because it made her realize that she did care what the women thought of her, that she wanted to forge a real friendship with the motley crew, despite their idiosyncrasies and their faults. And hers. Margo was simply going to have to live with it. Belinda smoothed a strand of hair behind her ear. That, and her trendy do.

When she arrived back at her cubicle, she called the auto repair shop. Carole's husband's cousin recited a number that left her a bit breathless, but he promised to work her in the next day if she could bring the Honda in before lunch. She said she would, jotted a note to herself to ask Margo about taking the day off, and asked if he accepted credit cards.

She hung up, reminding herself that her raise would be forthcoming when Margo returned from Hawaii. The paperwork would probably take a couple of weeks, and then, heck, she might buy a *new* car.

But the idea didn't cheer her as much as it should have. In fact, the thought was a gut check because, she realized, lately all roads seemed to lead back to the deal she'd struck with Margo. She massaged her temples. And as much as she wanted to believe she could maintain her independence, and her friends, hadn't she simply given Margo more leverage to manipulate her?

What would the woman ask her to do next? Look the other way here, fudge a little there. Stretch, exaggerate, embellish. And to what end—personal wealth at the expense of personal worth?

She sat and mulled the big fat mess she'd gotten herself into. As the last hour of the workday clicked away on her digital clock, she felt as if the time was expiring on her integrity. Meanwhile, her blood pressure climbed higher and higher as the potential fallout of a bad deal unfolded in her mind. People's jobs were at stake, people who had more time and energy invested in the two companies than she. Her mind raced for a way out that would preserve the momentum of the deal. Margo had said the Payton contracts had been signed but not yet mailed. Belinda still had time to stop the process until everything could be analyzed more in-depth. She could offer to do the research while Margo was on vacation. The deal didn't have to be terminated, just postponed. And no one even had to know—the delay could simply be attributed to Margo's vacation.

She inhaled deeply, then puffed out her cheeks. Lesson learned—she was going to have to ease into this taking chances thing. Meanwhile, she would count herself lucky that she wasn't too late to make things right. She picked up the phone and dialed Margo's office. Brita answered.

"Is Margo available?" Belinda asked.

"Ms. Campbell is still here, but she asked not to be disturbed."

"I'll come over and wait until she's finished," Belinda said.

"That might be a while," Brita chirped.

Belinda pursed her mouth. "Still." Then she frowned—was she parroting Wade Alexander?

"Suit yourself." Then the woman hung up.

Belinda checked her watch—5:20. Libby and Carole would be expecting her to join them soon. She'd simply send them on with her car and find another way home. No way was she leaving before she got things straightened out with Margo. She was determined to sleep tonight.

Libby was packing up her desk when Belinda rapped on the outside panel.

The woman looked up and smiled. "Are you ready? It's early, but we have time to get a lottery ticket before we *you know*."

"Um, I've had a change of plans." She held up her keys and was mortified to see her hand shaking. "Would you mind driving Carole home and leaving my car at your place? I'll be over later to pick it up."

From the look on Libby's face, Belinda knew the woman thought she was pulling back, that she'd decided not to be involved in the messy details of friendship. "How will you get to my house?"

"I'll ride MARTA and take a taxi or . . . something. Libby, I wouldn't ask if this wasn't important."

"Okay," Libby said, still clearly confused. "I could stop back by and pick you up after the *you know*."

"You don't even know where you're going. And I don't know how long I'll be."

"Good gravy, what's wrong? You look . . . splotchy. Did Officer Goodbody drop by?"

"No—yes." Belinda stopped and issued a calming breath. "Never mind him. I need to see Margo about a couple of things."

"Yeah, well whack her once for me, will you?"

Belinda frowned. "I'll see you later."

Her heart thudded faster, but her steps were sure as she approached Margo's office. It was the right thing to do, the responsible thing to do. What kind of a CFO would she be if her first key decision was based on less than accurate financial information? She was astounded and dismayed with herself that she'd ever thought she could do anything less. She might have left her heart in Cincinnati, but thankfully, her scruples had tagged along.

Brita was sitting at her desk reading. She frowned at Belinda over her glasses. "She's on the telephone."

"I'll wait." Belinda set her purse, briefcase and raincoat on a credenza and took in the view of Midtown from the reception window. With a jolt, she realized this window was above the spot where the plant had nearly slain her. Cold fear gripped her, and she glanced around, looking for a telltale circle on the carpet where a plant might have been. Nada. But she had managed to gain Brita's attention.

"Nice plants," Belinda commented casually, gesturing to the intermittent foliage.

"We have a service," Brita said dryly.

Belinda pursed her mouth, then turned back to the view. Rush hour was in full swing, but police officers were stationed at strategic intersections to keep things moving. She wondered where Lieutenant Alexander was at this moment, but she willed her thoughts elsewhere lest she fall into the habit of thinking about the man. Instead, she passed the time flipping through furniture catalogs and thinking about her luscious leather couch.

Forty minutes later, Brita cleared her throat. "Ms. Campbell is off the phone, I'll tell her you're here." The woman punched a button on the phone. "Belinda is waiting to see you, Ms. Campbell." She set down the receiver and gave Belinda a bland smile while retrieving her own umbrella and purse. "She said she can't see you. Goodnight."

Belinda stood. "But I *have* to see her."

"No," Brita said sternly. "Ms. Campbell has been through enough today. Whatever it is, it'll have to wait until she returns from vacation."

"This can't wait." Belinda walked toward Margo's office door, sidestepping Brita's attempt to block her path with a red-and-white-striped umbrella. She rapped on the door, then opened it. "Excuse me, Margo. I need to talk to you before you leave."

"Ms. Campbell," Brita said. "I'm sorry—she insisted."

Margo sat at her desk, her hands on her computer keyboard. "You may go, Brita." When the door closed, she sighed. "Can't it wait, Belinda? I'm swamped here."

"No, I'm sorry, it can't." Belinda took a deep breath. "Margo, I'm still not comfortable with those questions on the Payton financials that I gave you the morning we presented to the board. Before the contracts are mailed, I'd like the chance to dig deeper into the numbers. Just to be sure."

Margo rubbed her forehead. "Belinda, we've been over this."

"But—"

Margo brought her hand down on her desk in an explosive smack. "We made a *deal*, remember?"

Belinda's stomach bottomed out. "Yes. B-but that was a mistake."

Margo's eyes narrowed. "I thought you were made of stronger stuff."

Belinda's skin tingled. The urge to buckle under the direct challenge was overwhelming. "My conscience demands that I revisit the figures."

A dry laugh escaped her boss. "In business, if you don't have a penis, you can't afford to have a conscience. The sooner you realize that, Belinda, the better."

Belinda inhaled and tried a different tack. "You hired me because I'm a top-notch numbers woman. Let me do my job."

Margo looked back to her keyboard and resumed typing. "You *did* your job. Now go home and celebrate with your roving reporter."

Belinda let the barb pass, then lifted her chin. "I won't change my mind."

Margo sat back in her seat and regarded Belinda with a level gaze. Her long black cherry nails tapped on her desk. *Plap, plap, plap.*

Belinda's mind flew ahead. If her boss refused to hold the contracts, then what? Was she prepared to contact Juneau Archer and jeopardize both their jobs, not to mention the entire acquisition? Her pulse thudded in her ears, and all moisture vanished from her mouth. The tension in the air whined.

"Okay," Margo said, lifting her hands. "I've waited long enough for this deal to fall into place, I guess another couple of weeks won't matter. But I want you to wait until I return, and we'll go over everything together."

Relief flooded her limbs. "Thank you, Margo."

One side of her boss's mouth slid back. "You're welcome. Now get out of here, I still have to go home and pack."

"Just one more thing. I'd like to take a day of vacation tomorrow to have my car repaired, if that's okay."

A small smile curved Margo's mouth. "One perk of being a senior manager is that you don't have to take vacation for a personal errand. Take as much time as you need." Margo's phone rang with the double bleep of an internal call, and she sighed. "It's a conspiracy."

Belinda smiled. "I'll let you go. Have a nice vacation."

Closing the door behind her, Belinda released a pent-up breath, glad beyond words that she had followed her instincts and talked to Margo.

The woman was a conundrum. Margo could come off as such a hardass, but she was genuinely looking out for the good of the company. So she didn't have the best bedside manner—if she were a man, her abruptness would be seen as a strength. And Belinda doubted that any man would have handled Jim Newberry with as cool a head as Margo had today.

Belinda gathered her belongings and retraced her steps down the hallway toward the back stairwell. The overhead lights were after-hours dim, the many cubicles sat vacant, and the air hummed with the distant drone of office equipment. At this time of day the department took on an almost eerie quality. A shiver traveled over her shoulders as she replayed the scene of Jim Newberry charging into Margo's office earlier, his eyes wild. How differently that encounter might have ended.

Violence in the workplace had always bewildered her, but lately she could see how someone who was having a personal crisis might construe a setback at work as the final straw. In hindsight, Lieutenant Alexander's concern today was well-founded, and she was grateful he'd thought of her safety.

Grateful and . . . *flattered.* But not swayed.

Her thoughts jumped to Rosemary, and she sent up a

little prayer that her friend had fared well in her evaluation. It was a shame that Rosemary and Margo had once been friends and were now at professional odds. A potential outcome, she supposed, when relationships got "messy."

She wondered if Libby and Carole had managed to follow Rosemary and uncover the root of her secret meetings. Yet Belinda's immediate concern was the best way to get to Libby's house to pick up her car. She pushed open the door to the stairwell, shifted her load, and began her descent down seven flights. What had begun as paranoia about the elevators had at least become a healthy habit.

A taxi from Midtown to Libby's house would cost roughly the same as the killer Gucci purse she dreamed of owning, so that was out. But she could catch the MARTA rail train at the Arts Center station and ride the northeast line to the end, then hail a taxi, and that would set her back only about the cost of a below-average pair of shoes.

One minute she was thinking about the pair of shoes she was sacrificing, and the next thing she knew, she was falling. She flung her arms out to catch herself, but momentum she blamed on those extra twelve pounds sent her skidding over the steps on her belly.

A wall stopped her. When she opened her eyes, pain was her instant realization—her head, her shoulder, her wrist. And a sense of having missed something more than a step . . . time? Had she passed out? She moaned and was gratified to hear her voice. She dreaded moving because she suspected the pain would get worse.

She was right.

The ache in her left wrist convinced her to use her right arm to push herself upright. Thank goodness no bones were protruding, but her wrist was swollen and she was going to have a knot on her head. Her cheek burned, and the knuckles on her right hand were skinned, but otherwise she felt lucky. And, being the pragmatic girl that she was, her immediate thought was if the ninety-day probation period on her medical benefits had passed.

A couple of minutes later, she felt well enough to stand and gather her wayward items. She'd managed to lose a shoe and become detached from her raincoat. Her purse and briefcase were intact and undamaged, so that was something. From the sign on the wall she'd collided with, she had made it to the second floor, so she decided to proceed to the ground level lounge for repairs.

She navigated the rest of the stairs carefully, then avoided eye contact with passersby until she crossed the threshold of the women's lounge near the entrance of the hotel lobby. Her navy jacket was filthy, torn, and minus one pewter-colored button. After removing the jacket, she pulled up the sleeve of her blouse and held her wrist under cold running water in one of the sinks.

A glimpse in the mirror revealed a bright patch of skin on her cheek. She'd probably have a bruise, but considering how hard she'd fallen, she was lucky she hadn't broken her preoccupied neck. She washed the blood from her knuckles and noted with relief that her wrist was already feeling better. A woman exited a stall and cast suspicious looks in Belinda's direction as she washed her hands. Belinda didn't blame her for staring—she looked as if she'd been in a barroom brawl.

After dabbing powder on her cheek and fluffing her hair, Belinda dusted off her jacket and slid into it with a grimace. She decided she'd rather wear the raincoat than carry it, which meant more contortions. Thoroughly exhausted, she gathered her briefcase and purse and left the lounge. Having tomorrow off was sounding better and better; at least she could sleep late. And it would be nice to have her car back in top working condition. She smirked—might as well get her Georgia driver's license while she was at it. Since she was going to be the new CFO of Archer Furniture Company, it looked as if she'd be staying a while.

At this time of day, most of the activity in the Stratford

Building surrounded the hotel and fitness center. Every time she thought about her brazen episode with Julian, she burned with embarrassment—and the teensiest bit of satisfaction that she had the potential to surprise herself. Then, as if she had imagined him into existence, across the enormous corridor she saw Julian walking into the gym carrying a black leather duffel bag, his shoulders rounded as if he were in deep thought.

Pleasure bubbled in her chest. "Julian!"

When he recognized her, he seemed surprised, then smiled.

She met him halfway. "Hi. I see you made it back."

He nodded, but seemed distracted—probably tired from the flight. "You cut your hair—nice."

"Thanks."

He shifted foot to foot. "What are you still doing here? Hasn't your car pool left?"

"Something came up that needed my attention, so I told the girls to go ahead. I was on my way to MARTA."

"MARTA? To Alpharetta?"

"Well, as far as I can go, then a taxi to Libby's house to pick up my car."

"I can take you."

She shook her head. "I don't want to keep you from your workout."

He hesitated, then smiled. "Nonsense, I'll take you. Maybe we can grab a bite to eat on the way."

She winced. "This sounds klutzy, but I fell in the stairwell and sprained my wrist, so I really need to get home and ice it down."

Julian shrugged. "Okay, I need to run an errand out that direction anyway."

"Thanks. I have to admit your offer sounds better than catching the train and a taxi."

He looked down at his bag. "Um, give me a minute to ditch this in a locker."

"Sure."

Julian waved to the cute girl at the desk, who motioned

him past the long check-in line. Local celebrity had its advantages, Belinda thought with a wry smile.

Then again, *fooling around* with a local celebrity had its advantages, too.

Chapter 18

Julian drove a navy blue Audi sedan with caramel-colored glove leather seats. Carole would have said it was a nice ride. So would she, Belinda decided, except she couldn't fully enjoy the experience because they were moving at seventy-eight miles an hour. Granted, it was a smooth seventy-eight miles an hour.

The man had a beautiful profile. Speed agreed with him—in fact, he seemed to get high on it. She had heard of driving gloves but had never known anyone who took driving so seriously as to actually own a pair. They were fingerless, with padded palms, and apparently were coated with some kind of substance that allowed him to control the steering wheel with as little contact as possible. He seemed giddy, his fingers drumming, his head moving to the beat on the radio.

"It's been a long time since I drove in rush hour instead of over it," he said with a laugh, oblivious to the fact that they were almost airborne. "Thankfully the worst of the traffic is over."

Thankfully. "You didn't arrive back from Raleigh in time to go up in the chopper?"

"Er . . . no. Tomorrow morning will be soon enough to

fly again, and hopefully conditions will be better than they were this morning."

"So you heard how bad it was?"

"Hm? Oh, yeah—I heard it was terrible."

"I missed hearing your voice."

He grinned. "You mean Talkin' Tom's voice."

"Now that I know the truth, I hear your voice in his."

He reached over to stroke her wrist with his thumb, sending little thrills up her arm, which might also have been terror because he was now driving with one hand. "So how did you fall?"

"Just carelessness," she said. "It's strange, but since I heard about Jeanie's accident, I've been taking the stairs. And then I almost break my neck on *them*."

His expression went still. "Guess it goes to show you that when your time is up, it's going to happen, regardless."

"That's a fatalistic outlook," she said softly. Especially for someone who considered the speed limit voluntary.

He shrugged, then gave her a little smile. "Pilots have to be fatalists, or we'd never climb into a cockpit."

She chose her words carefully. "Julian, how well did you know Jeanie?"

Another shrug. "Well enough. We biked together on weekends and competed in a couple of 10K runs together. We had fun. You remind me of her a little."

Hm. "Were you involved romantically?"

He pulled his hand away, and she missed it. "We were involved physically, but not romantically." Then he flashed a rueful smile. "Sorry, babe. You asked."

Babe? "No, it's fine," she said quickly, although her stomach felt swimmy—of course, it might have been carsickness. "The girls said Jeanie was jumpy, maybe even paranoid before she had the accident. Did you notice anything different?"

He shoved his hand into his hair, then shook his head. "No. I thought she was careful, just like any single woman should be."

"But not afraid of anything specific?"

"Not that I know of, other than that boss of yours."

Belinda frowned. "Margo?"

He gave a dry laugh. "Well, not literally, but she was always nervous about pleasing her, said the woman could make her life miserable. I don't know her very well, but you said yourself she could be a tyrant."

Belinda nodded, still warring with her feelings toward Margo. Many great leaders were misunderstood and were forced to make unpopular decisions. Margo couldn't be all bad—in fact, thanks to her, this starting over thing was starting to look like it might actually succeed. "Actually, I think Margo might have a little crush on you," she said with a grin.

"Yeah, she's come on to me in the gym before, but she's pretty severe."

Instead of being dragged into a discussion about her boss's attractiveness, Belinda decided to concentrate on hanging on for dear life. She hadn't realized that the distance between Midtown and Alpharetta could be traversed so quickly. "D-don't you worry about being pulled over?"

"Nah. I have friends in the APD. Alexander isn't one of them, by the way."

"I saw him today."

He scowled. "Where?"

"A guy Margo fired a few months ago barged into her office. No one was hurt, but Wade was following up."

"Wade?"

"Um, Lieutenant Alexander."

"He seems to have a knack for being everywhere," he said sarcastically.

She squinted. "What do you have against him?"

His jaw tightened, then he smiled. "I don't care enough for the man to have anything against him. How about lunch this week?"

"Maybe Wednesday? Tomorrow I'm having my car repaired."

"How much damage?"

"Headlight, dented fender, and a broken trunk latch. Oh, and the tire of course, but I already had it replaced."

"I meant how much is it going to cost you?"

She told him, and he whistled.

"The next time you need bodywork, let me know." Then he grinned and winked. "Not that you need bodywork."

She laughed at his friendly flirtation and marveled over her different reactions to the three men who had shown an interest in her. Perry sickened her. Julian incited her. And Wade . . . disconcerted her.

The clock on the dash read 7:35 P.M., and darkness was falling early due to cloud cover. Her wrist was beginning to throb, and her head was making itself known. She warned Julian of the upcoming turnoff to give him plenty of time to slow down. He did—some—then they were tearing through Libby's neighborhood in the semidarkness. She prayed that all children and pets were stashed away securely in their homes.

Considering the girls' Operation Nosy Friend and Julian's need for speed, Belinda worried they might arrive at Libby's before Libby, but when they roared up, the Honda sat in the Janeses' dark driveway.

He pulled alongside her car and shifted into park. "I'll wait for you."

"I might have to go in for a minute—I missed out on an after-work, um, project."

"Take your time."

She gave him a grateful smile, then closed the door and hurried up the sidewalk to Libby's house. Two sodden newspapers lay on the stoop, next to a pot of drowned geraniums. Belinda rang the doorbell and gathered her coat around her against the chill left in the storm's wake. The wind whipped her face, stinging the tender skin on her cheek, and she was thankful again that she hadn't injured herself worse. Her penchant for accidents lately would give a therapist pause.

An outside light came on and the door opened

abruptly. Libby, still in her work clothes, sans the shoes and panty hose, was in the middle of yelling at someone.

"—and I *mean* it!" She turned to Belinda and sighed. "Take my life . . . please. Come in if you dare."

Belinda laughed and stepped into a crammed foyer. The scent of fried chicken permeated the air, and two televisions blared from different directions. "I can only stay for a few minutes—a friend drove me over."

Libby's eyebrows climbed, and she peered out. "A friend?"

Belinda closed the door to circumvent Libby's curiosity. "I ran into Julian as I was leaving the building, and he offered to drive me."

Libby frowned. "Where did you get the shiner?"

"Oh." She touched her cheek gingerly. "I fell in the stairwell at work."

"Did Margo push you?" Libby asked sarcastically.

"*No.* I was alone, and it was an accident."

"What was so important that you had to stay over?"

"Just a matter on the Payton acquisition to clear up before Margo left for vacation." To change the subject and because her own curiosity was getting the best of her, she asked, "So, how did it go with Rosemary?"

Libby sighed. "Carole was late, so we missed her."

"Oh. Well, it was probably for the best."

"We'll be ready next time."

"Or you guys could simply tell her that you're concerned friends and see if she tells you of her own volition."

Libby shrugged. "Maybe."

Belinda shook her head. "I'm taking tomorrow off to have my car repaired and to get my driver's license changed—should I call Rosemary to let her know?"

"No, I'll tell her when she gets here in the morning. Are you sure you can't come in for a while?"

"Thanks, but I really need to get home."

Libby's head bobbed. "With Julian?"

"With an ice bag. I sprained my wrist."

"Oh. Well, feel better, and try to enjoy your day off. You'd better take something to read in that DMV line."

"Duly noted."

"In fact . . ." Libby disappeared into a darkened side room, then reappeared with a half-inch stack of pages and a huge grin. "You can be the first to read the opening to our DOs and DON'Ts manuscript."

Belinda hefted the pages in her good hand. "You're serious about this, aren't you?"

"Yes, ma'am. Especially if it means extra cash."

"Does this mean you're not getting a part-time job?"

Libby looked over her shoulder, as if she was afraid she'd be overheard. "I came into a little unexpected cash, so I'm okay."

Belinda really didn't want to know any details, so she pointed over her shoulder. "I'd better get going." She took the car keys Libby extended. "Thanks again for driving my car home."

Just as Libby opened the door for her, a huge crash sounded from another room in the house, and a wailing ensued.

"Libby!" a man roared.

Libby closed her eyes briefly. "One of these days, Belinda, I'm going to come unglued. Think of all the writing I could do in a nice, quiet prison cell."

Belinda gave her a pained smile and a quick wave, then vamoosed and closed the door behind her. Julian's car was still running. As she approached the driver's side, his window came down, and he leaned out. A sheen of perspiration glistened on his upper lip, and he seemed anxious to get going. Guilt stabbed her as she held up her keys. "I'm good to go."

"Are you sure?" he asked, his hand drumming.

"Absolutely. My place is only a couple of miles away."

"Maybe I can see it next time."

"Sure," she said, her chest warming at the prospect. "Thanks again."

He winked, then glanced at her car. "I can follow you home. Just to be safe."

"You're not safe."

His smile vanished. "What do you mean?"

Belinda laughed and leaned closer. "The first two times we met we literally ran into each other, then you set my mouth on fire with Thai food, then you seduced me in a public place, and now I discover that you drive as if you have a death wish."

His mouth curved into a sexy grin. "So I get a kick out of danger. Does that scare you?"

Electricity crackled in the air, reminding her of the Big Daddy stun baton the girls had given her. In the low lighting, he was handsome, frighteningly so. The hair raised on the back of her neck. "No," she lied.

His grin deepened. "Good."

"B-but really, there's no need to follow me home. I'll be fine."

"If you're sure."

"I am." She straightened and stepped away from the car.

"Okay—I'll call you." He flashed a killer grin, put the car into reverse and backed out onto the street, then sped away.

Belinda watched until his taillights disappeared, then walked to her car in the gloom of late dusk, plagued by the same creepy feeling she'd experienced leaving the office. After she slid into the driver's seat, the irrational feeling persisted while she stowed her briefcase and purse, the sense of someone bearing down, ready to pounce. At a rustling in the tall bushes, her heart lodged in her throat. She locked the doors, flicked on her headlights, and fumbled to start the car. When the engine roared to life, a bird flew away, and she chastised herself for letting her imagination get the best of her.

Perhaps witnessing the Jim Newberry episode had spooked her more than she realized. Or maybe it was Julian who had her spooked in an entirely different way.

Then she glanced down at the pages of the manuscript Libby had given her. She had one for the book:

DO assess the risk level of a relationship before you proceed.

Chapter 19

Being licked awake was not unto itself such a bad way to greet the day, but when the tongue belonged to a crotchety feline known for biting, it was less pleasant than alarming. Belinda turned her head into her pillow and pushed Downey off her chest. "I'm trying to sleep late."

Downey yowled, indicating that was not to be the case.

Belinda opened one eye and peered at the alarm clock. 6:20 A.M.—later than she'd slept any weekday since moving to Atlanta, but after tossing and turning all night from unreasonable fear she couldn't pinpoint, she felt far from rested. The daylight streaming through the miniblinds danced warm and comforting over her bed. Strange how one's anxieties could manifest, especially in the dark, and how unfounded they seemed by the light of day. She reached over to turn off the alarm that hadn't yet rung and was rewarded with a breath-stealing pain shooting up her left arm.

Gritting her teeth, she held up her compromised limb. The swelling had gone down, but her wrist had turned a purpley-cranberry color—nice for Kool-Aid, not so nice for flesh tone. Her cheek still felt puffy and tender beneath her fingers, so she dragged herself out of bed for a look in the mirror.

Yilk.

She would not make an attractive boxer. A brilliant blue bruise highlighted her cheekbone and the outer edge of her eye. Pancake makeup and sunglasses would be the order of the day.

Making the bed was a bit of a challenge with her tender wrist, but she managed to make it look slightly less rumpled in the event her mother put in a surprise appearance (or psychic phone call). The cold front that had settled over Atlanta had pervaded her bedroom, raising gooseflesh on her bare arms and legs. She shucked her nightshirt and stood under the showerhead emptying the hot water heater. When she stepped out, pleasantly magenta-hued from the rolling boil, she switched on the radio to dress by.

Julian's voice rolled out full-throated and sexy, hitting her in the glide. Last night . . . last night she wasn't sure what had happened to her, what had made her scramble away from Julian. Panic attack? Hormonal heebie-jeebies? Or was she simply afraid that Julian was going to nail her to the wall on this new impulse of hers to break a few rules?

He was in good form this morning as Talkin' Tom, diverting drivers around an accident at Jesus Junction (an intersection on Peachtree that boasted four sizable churches), and letting everyone know in thinly veiled code words that the police were patrolling the Alpharetta Autobahn (Georgia 400) southbound for speeders.

She wondered where the girls were in the melee, and what had happened in Rosemary's evaluation, and if Libby and Carole had managed to get out of her where she'd been going every couple of weeks. With a start Belinda realized she missed the morning conversation. Did they miss her?

And Julian's words about the speed trap made her think of Wade Alexander. She toweled off while replaying their conversation yesterday in the vending room, thinking what a buffoon she must have looked like, hiding from her neighbor behind the Coke machine. Come to think of it, the man had seen her during some of her most embarrassing moments. As if to remind her of one of those moments, Downey nosed open the door and dragged in the maimed satin pillow that had once proclaimed the joy of her and Vince's wedding day. Apparently the pillow had become Downey's imaginary friend.

And if that's how the cat chose to deal with Vince's rejection, then who was she to judge?

She pulled jeans out of a drawer and reached for a Cincinnati Reds sweatshirt, then remembered her last driver's license photo a la Mickey Mouse and switched to a lightweight lime green cardigan. Perhaps the loud color would distract everyone to the point of not noticing her black eye.

By the time she finished dressing, camouflaging her bruise, and feeding Downey and herself, it was nearly 9:00 A.M. Which was fine, because the nearest DMV office opened at 9:00 A.M. She'd be the first in line.

Apparently, six hundred other people had had the same good idea. Belinda had estimated she'd be an hour taking the computerized exam, tops. Two hours later, she was still waiting in line to be processed to be put in yet another line. After memorizing the exam booklet—thankfully, the traffic laws from Ohio to Georgia didn't differ that much—she was glad she had Libby's partial manuscript to pass the time.

She turned the cover page with no small amount of skepticism, but a couple of pages into the manuscript, she was laughing. Libby had taken their DOs and DON'Ts and expanded on them based on the conversations in their car pool. No one's privacy had been violated, but she could clearly see their individual tastes and attitudes emerging. She was impressed—Libby demonstrated a true knack for writing short humorous pieces. Finding a publisher for the manuscript would still be a long shot, but this project might provide Libby a more productive outlet than shopping.

Another hour later when she was still standing in the preliminary line, she began to weigh her need for a Georgia driver's license against the cost of the fine for not having one. Her wrist throbbed and she hadn't thought to bring painkillers with her—or lunch, as some people who were obviously more familiar with the system than she had thought to do. McDonald's bags prevailed, and many people sat on the floor, eating picnic style.

She was supposed to have her car to the auto body shop by noon, so she was already running late. But since she was nearing the front of the line, she hated to leave now. Her choice was made, though, when a stoic-faced processor informed her that to obtain a Georgia driver's license, she needed to produce two pieces of mail addressed to her current residence to prove that she was, indeed, a Georgia resident.

Vince's envelope flitted into her mind, although she had a feeling the state of Georgia expected something more official.

Belinda pushed her tongue into her cheek. "So I stood in line all morning for nothing?"

"Not for nothing," the man declared. "Now you know for next time."

She didn't trust herself to speak, so she simply turned and walked out. Across the street was a sandwich shop with a pay phone from which she called the auto body shop.

"We gave your appointment to someone else," a gum-snapping woman said.

"Do you have any appointments this afternoon?"

"No, but we'll call you if we have a cancellation."

That didn't sound promising, but what else could she do but go home and wait for a call?

She ordered a stromboli sandwich and a Diet Coke (a beverage choice she didn't want to analyze), then decided to call Margo's assistant while she waited for her order.

"Archer Furniture, Margo Campbell's office."

"Hi, Brita, this is Belinda Hennessey."

The woman sniffed an acknowledgment.

"I'm off today, but I thought I'd check in with you."

"Why?"

Belinda blinked. "Margo asked me to cover for her while she was on vacation."

"I take care of Ms. Campbell's affairs while she's gone."

"Okay. Well, has anything crossed her desk that would require my attention?"

"No. I'm processing the performance evaluations she left, and I just dropped the Payton contracts in the mail."

Belinda's heart stalled out. "Excuse me?"

"The Payton contracts, I just mailed them."

"Brita," Belinda said carefully, "when Margo and I talked last night, she agreed to hold those contracts until she returned from vacation."

"They were in my out box, so they went out."

Belinda inhaled to remain calm. "But I'm telling you, they shouldn't have. You have to get them back."

"I can't, and besides, I wouldn't, not without Ms. Campbell's say-so."

Belinda closed her eyes. "Is Mr. Archer in?"

"No."

"Okay, why don't you call Margo on her cell phone and ask her about the contracts yourself. Meanwhile, transfer me to the mailroom and I'll have them stopped."

"Mistake or no, it's a federal offense to impede the U.S. mail."

Belinda gritted her teeth. "I'll risk it."

The woman huffed, then Belinda heard the click of the phone being transferred. The implication of those contracts being mailed made her stomach cramp.

"Stratford mail room," a man's voice said.

"Carole Marchand, please."

The man yelled for her, and soon Carole's voice came on the line.

"Carole, it's Belinda."

"Hey, I thought you were taking the day off."

"I am, b-but I need a favor."

"Sure, if I can help."

"Margo decided last night to hold the Payton contracts until she returned from vacation, but Brita made a mistake and put them in the mail." She tried to keep the panic out of her voice. "This is urgent, Carole. Can you stop them from going out?"

"They were tagged to send via APS, and Hank made a pickup about twenty minutes ago."

Belinda groaned.

"Hang on, and I'll see if I can reach him on his cell phone."

Belinda shot up a fervent prayer, not wanting to think about what she'd have to do to circumvent those contracts if they'd already been mailed.

"Belinda?" Carole was back. "I got him, and you must have made an impression on the man because he said in your case, he'd make an exception."

Her breath whooshed out in relief. "Thank you!"

"No problem," Carole said. "What do you want Hunky Hank to do with them? I think he'd be *happy* to bring them to your house."

"That's not necessary. Just leave them on my desk."

"Will do."

"And Carole—keep this quiet, okay?"

"Okay," Carole said, her tone a bit defensive.

"I owe you one."

"That's what friends are for. See you tomorrow?"

A warm, fuzzy sensation filled Belinda's chest. "Yes." She hung up the phone, weak with relief. That was so damn close.

She picked up her order and, suddenly ravenous, ate the sandwich in the car—a mistake, because she dripped sauce on her sweater and smelled up the car with spicy meat. She half-listened to the radio, dwelling instead on her to-do list. The ringing of phones on seemingly endless cellular commercials reminded her she also needed to reinstate her wireless service. And maybe she would go television shopping this evening. By the time she arrived home, she was determined the day would not be a total loss. She parked in front of the garage door, optimistic that the auto body shop would call.

She took advantage of the free time to sort bills on the kitchen table and fill out change of address forms. Again. The credit card companies, alumni associations, and the federal government had probably not yet gotten around to processing her move from her former Cincinnati apartment to 137 Monarch Circle (aka Vince's address), and now she was remitting even more paperwork.

The thought of Vince receiving her mail made her ill, because it was further proof that she had so completely trusted him. She blinked back sudden tears, hating how they could sneak up on her. Picking up the envelope he'd sent, she marveled that the two of them used to share their days' events and now she couldn't count the people she'd met and the things she'd experienced that he would never know about.

That he had no interest in knowing about.

She ran her finger over the edges of the envelope twice before setting it back against the yellow fruit bowl. Like a smoker who had quit but kept a pack of cigarettes around as proof that they'd kicked the habit . . . and as a security blanket in the event they ever wanted to resume the bad habit.

She fished out a bill from the electric company and one from the phone company and set them aside for her next adventure at the DMV. She checked her watch and considered driving back there, but the thought of standing in that line again made her nauseous, and with her luck, she'd get to the front of the line just in time for the office to close.

Besides, Vince's envelope reminded her that she'd been putting off a chore for way too long. Since her sofa was being delivered tomorrow, she had extra incentive to clear the remaining packing boxes in the living room. After swapping her stained sweater for the Reds sweatshirt, she walked into the living room with Downey on her heels and a flutter in her chest, and studied the two boxes squatting in a corner.

MEMENTOS. KEEPSAKES.

With a sigh, she sank to her knees and opened the first and smallest box. Inside was Vince's infamous collection of cards that showed the progression of their relationship—*Let's get to know each other . . . I like you . . . I love you*—plus show ticket stubs, postcards from the places they'd visited together, and pictures.

She withdrew a 5×7 photograph that had sat on her desk in Cincinnati. She and Vince at a barbecue in her parents' backyard. They sat on opposite sides of the picnic table but had leaned together and turned to look at the camera. And she was sure that when the picture had been taken, they had pulled back to their respective sides. She pressed her lips together. Why had that detail escaped her until now?

The box was crammed with picture frames, stuffed animals, and other knickknacks he'd given to her. She had no idea what to do with the collection—she couldn't bring herself to throw it all away, but neither did she want to keep it.

Opening the second box required more fortitude—it contained all the leftovers from her defunct wedding day, packed by her mother and given to her the day she left Cincy. The simple white gown she'd loved wearing, the short veil, the satiny shoes. A pale blue garter, a dried white lily from her bouquet, a tiny satin sack of birdseed.

A lump lodged in her throat when she remembered how happy she'd been that day, so happy that she hadn't realized how preoccupied Vince had been. He had repeated his husbandly vows convincingly enough. If anyone—the groomsmen, Vince's parents, the minister—had known that something was amiss, no one had let on. Indeed, when the day was over and she was still single, everyone had seemed as equally shocked as she.

And if the episode itself hadn't been traumatic enough, the fact that Vince had declined to offer an explanation for his behavior had left her emotionally and physically inert, something she hated herself for even now. Oh, she'd wanted to wail and flail and demand that he account for himself, but since she'd had a good idea that his change of heart had had something to do with their uninspiring consummation, she had swallowed her indignation. And kept the accoutrements of the non-wedding because deep down she'd believed he would reconsider.

In hindsight, perhaps he'd been testing her, to see if she would fight for their relationship, if she would relinquish some of that "arrogant independence" he had accused her of possessing. But if Vince was willing to go to such lengths, to humiliate her to prove a point, then her love was wasted on him.

In truth? She suspected he'd been having second thoughts all along and had forced the issue of sex to either rationalize or allay those fears.

But regardless of Vince's motivation for canceling their life together, she wasn't obligated to preserve the reminders of that ghastly day—or of him at all. She took a deep breath and dumped all the wedding memorabilia back into the box, along with the stuffed animals and other bric-a-brac from the first box that someone, somewhere might find a use for. The photos, cards, and ticket stubs went into the trash. Then she collected empty boxes from her garage and went all around the town house gathering other items Vince had given her: clothing, books, CDs. All of it was going to Goodwill.

She hadn't felt this good since . . . since Vince.

She was finally putting him and her life in Cincy behind her. Moving to Atlanta was the best thing she'd ever done for herself. She carried the first box outside and filled her lungs with fresh suburban Atlanta air. Gratifying, liberating, invigorating. She was going to live a good life here.

She set down the box, ran the fingers of her right hand along the crooked seam of the trunk and tugged. She had a good job, and she was making good friends. Men did not seem to be repulsed by her. She tugged harder, thinking she might need to get her keys or a screwdriver to compensate for her one-handedness.

She, Belinda Hennessey, had done a very good job of not only getting her life back on track, but was on her way to making a name for herself.

The trunk popped open with enough force to send Belinda stumbling back. Good thing, too, since it put a tad more distance between her and the load that filled her trunk to capacity.

Margo.

Dead.

Belinda opened her mouth to scream, but she couldn't draw enough air into her lungs to make noise. Gasping, she acted out of sheer impulse to erase the unbelievable scene in front of her and slammed down the trunk lid. She sobbed into her hand, then wildly looked around to see if anyone had witnessed the fact that she'd found her boss's body in the trunk of her car.

But no, it was a lovely, quiet day in the Atlanta suburbs—birds sang and flowers bloomed. In a yard across the street and up a gentle rise, children jumped on a trampoline and screamed with laughter. She looked toward Perry's place, but the one time she might have called on the man, his truck was gone. He was at work, of course, like most everyone. And what could he do anyway?

What could anyone do? Blood rushed to her head, and she felt a faint coming on. She couldn't faint, she told herself—she had to summon help. She bent at the waist until the tingling in her brain subsided enough to stand. Walk. Run to her house. Margo was dead. And in her trunk.

How?

She skidded into the foyer. Hysteria pulled at her, and she pressed her fists against her eyes. This could not be happening. She was in the twilight zone. What to do first? Her mind raced, the people she knew spinning like a roulette wheel. Who to call?

The wheel slowed, and the ball settled on Wade Alexander. He would know what to do.

She frantically dumped the contents from her purse to find her organizer. The few seconds it took for her to call up his cell phone number seemed like an eternity. Her hands shook as she punched in his number, and she gulped for air. The phone rang once, twice. Her heart pounded in her ears.

"Alexander."

"Wade, this is Belinda Hennessey." She shook uncontrollably.

"What's wrong?"

"You t-told me to call you if anything unusual happened."

"Right."

"S-something unusual happened."

Chapter 20

"Belinda," Wade said, his voice fortified with concern. "Talk to me."

She gulped air, searching for appropriate words. Finding none, she blurted, "My b-boss is in the trunk of my car, dead."

Silence. Then, "*What?* Slow down, and say that again."

Belinda clung to the kitchen counter for support. "My boss, Margo Campbell. I just found her in the t-trunk of my car. She's dead. I d-don't know how she got there, and I'm on the v-verge of completely freaking out."

"Take a deep breath," he said in a soothing tone. "Are you at work?"

"No, I'm at home."

"You're at *home*? Where's your car?"

"Parked in my driveway."

"Are you sure you saw what you think you saw?"

"Yes."

"And how do you know she's dead?"

Belinda started bawling, and she never bawled. "The woman is crammed into my trunk—believe me, she's dead!"

"Easy now. Have you called 911?"

"N-no, I called you first."

"Give me your street address."

She couldn't remember, so she walked to the table, grabbed Vince's envelope, and read her own address aloud. Then she dropped into a chair, trembling all over. "I'm so scared, I don't know what to do."

"Don't do anything until the police get there. Except . . . do you have a lawyer?" His voice was erratic, as if he were on the move.

She hiccupped—she didn't even *know* a lawyer. "I have nothing to hide! I'll tell the police anything they want to know." She wet her lips. "Wade . . . will you come?"

"I'm on my way. Hold tight."

Belinda didn't want to hang up—the man's voice was like a lifeline. But she knew he had to take care of business. She disconnected the call and set down the phone with a hand that still vibrated. She sat frozen in place, trying to make sense of the awful scene she'd just witnessed.

Margo, still wearing her raincoat, curled up as if she were sleeping, although her chalky pallor told a different story. What had happened to her after Belinda had left her office, and how had she gotten into the trunk of the Civic?

Belinda swallowed and gagged—she'd been driving around with a body in the trunk of her car. Another stomach roll sent her running to the bathroom, where she heaved the remnants of the stromboli sandwich into the commode.

Afterward, she splashed cold water on her face until she was somewhat revived, then sank to the floor in the dark and pulled her knees under her quivering chin. Downey, who hadn't seen so much emotion commotion since . . . since Vince, yowled and rubbed against her legs frantically. Belinda reached out to stroke the cat's fur. It felt good to have another living thing nearby.

She'd never felt so alone in her life. She ached to reach out to someone who could make her feel better, but who would that be? She couldn't deliver a bomb like this to her parents. Sure, they'd cut short their cross-country trip and be here before she could say AARP, but to what end? Her mother was losing sleep over her daughter's unorthodox sofa purchase—a body in the car trunk would send Barbara Hennessey over the edge. And her dad would find a way to blame it on the fact that she drove a foreign car.

Libby was at work, and how traumatized would she be knowing she'd driven home last night with a body in the boot, even if Margo *was* the woman's nemesis. A crazy notion that Libby could be involved came into Belinda's mind and left just as quickly. Libby wasn't a murderer, but if Belinda called her, the news of Margo's demise would spread through Archer faster than the speed of sound, and that wouldn't help the police.

Vince? He would help her if he could, because he wasn't particularly mean-spirited, just chickenhearted. But she didn't relish the thought of calling to admit that her grand experiment of starting over had failed rather hugely.

Julian . . . now there was a thought. Since he worked for a news organization, he would probably hear about the incident as soon as it hit the police scanner airwaves. But she might have inadvertently involved him when she'd accepted his offer to drive her home last night—she didn't want to implicate him further by asking him to hold her hand through this unthinkable situation. He had a reputation to protect.

The faces of acquaintances from Cincinnati flashed through her mind. Lunch companions, yes—confidantes, no. Libby was right, she had no true friends of her own.

Because you are arrogantly independent. You've never wanted to need anyone, and now that you do, no one is there for you.

A wave of crushing panic loomed large. She felt herself begin to succumb when the phone rang. Belinda stared at the portable unit, then answered in case it was Lieutenant Alexander. "H-hello?"

"Belinda, it's Libby," the woman whispered loudly. "Girl, the shit has hit the fan here."

Belinda put her fist to her mouth—so they already knew.

"The police are in Margo's office, getting ready to question everyone. It's like a lockdown."

Her stomach dove.

"I bet Margo wishes she'd been here to see this. She'd probably fire anyone she remotely suspected."

Well, if anyone could reach back from death and issue pink slips for her own murder, it would be Margo.

"Personally," Libby whispered. "I think Clancy did it."

Belinda choked. "Clancy?"

"I never trusted that man. I wanted to warn you, because the police will probably want to talk to you since you're indirectly involved."

"Th-thanks."

"But don't worry, you'll still get your couch—the truck was already loaded and on its way before anyone found out."

Couch? Belinda squinted. "Libby . . . what are you talking about?"

"I didn't *tell* you? When Brita stopped by Clancy's desk to get the couch money to deposit, the bag was empty. Over five thousand bucks in cash, *gone*."

Belinda exhaled—no one knew about Margo. Yet.

"Clancy says someone stole it, but everyone thinks he took it and is trying to blame someone else. Brita called the police. You're missing out on all the excitement."

Belinda stood and walked into the living room. "Sounds like it." Stepping around the boxes she'd prepared for Goodwill, she peered out the bay window to the rear of her clover green car, where her boss lay in eternal repose.

"I heard they might strip-search everyone." Libby sighed dreamily. "Where's Officer Goodbody when you need him?"

Belinda was thinking the same thing. Panic licked at her neck. "Listen, Libby, I really need to go. I'm expecting . . . someone."

"Ooh, sounds mysterious. Well, you can tell me all

about it in the morning. Remember, Rosemary's driving the car pool. Don't be late."

"I won't," Belinda murmured absently, then disconnected the call.

A headache had landed behind her eyes, but she wasn't about to tempt her stomach with painkillers. Downey's insistent meowing and figure-eights, however, were dancing on her nerves. Belinda lured her into the bathroom, then closed the door in anticipation of the impending activity. The cat complained loudly.

Belinda was drawn to the bay window again, hoping that it was all some kind of macabre hoax, that the trunk would open and Margo would climb out yelling, "Gotcha!"

While Belinda stood staring at her car, a mail van pulled up. She chewed on her thumbnail, heart pounding, as the driver lowered the lid on her mailbox, shoved in her mail, closed the lid, then drove on. He would never realize how close he'd come to a dead body.

Who would want to kill Margo?

A lot of people, her mind whispered. But who would actually do it?

And frame *her*?

Her thoughts were derailed by the appearance of Wade's cruiser. He pulled alongside the curb, blue lights flashing, but without the siren, thank goodness.

She ran outside without bothering to close her front door. He was already out of the car, striding toward her. She couldn't help it—she threw herself into him, sobbing and pressing her cheek against the warm wall of his chest. His arms came around her, and he made shushing noises.

"Easy now, don't come apart on me. Tell me what happened."

She pulled away, embarrassed at her uncharacteristic collapse, and wiped her eyes. "I was going to t-take some things to Goodwill, and when I opened the t-trunk, there she was."

He frowned and put his hand under her chin. "What happened to your face?"

She touched her cheek—she'd forgotten about her black eye. "I fell in the stairwell last night when I left the office." She held up her left arm. "Sprained my wrist, too."

"Pretty wicked scratch."

"M-my cat did that."

He didn't seem to be in a hurry to move his hand, and he smoothed her hair back on the side of her bruise. "You're accident prone."

"Thank you for coming."

He finally dropped his hand. "You're welcome."

She bit her tongue and glanced toward her car. "I can't believe this is happening."

"Belinda." His voice held the timbre of a warning. "We'll get to the bottom of this, but you need to be strong. When the homicide detectives get here, they're going to have plenty of questions for you."

She sniffed and nodded. "Will you stay?"

He searched her eyes for a few seconds, then said, "I'm not going anywhere. Meanwhile, why don't you wait inside and let me take a look at your car."

"I'd rather be . . . here."

"All right, but give me some room."

Wade went to the trunk of his own car and removed a few items—namely, stakes and crime scene tape—which he used to block off her yard. The kids across the street had stopped jumping on their trampoline and were now staring, along with their mother. Wade made another trip, removed a tarp and a camera, then snapped on plastic gloves.

"Is the latch still broken?" he asked, stepping over the taped barrier he'd erected.

She nodded and inched closer, hugging herself.

He snapped several photos of the car and the surrounding area, including the box of items bound for Goodwill she'd abandoned on the driveway. Then he carefully lifted the trunk lid. From her vantage point, she could see Margo's gray face and dark hair. A shiver started at her neck and slid over her entire body.

Wade peered into the trunk but didn't touch anything, proceeding to take several pictures from different angles. Then he unfolded the tarp and draped it over the opening. He returned the camera to the cruiser, then withdrew a clipboard and walked her way, his expression grave. "I'll start a report. How do you know the deceased?" He was all business now.

The deceased. "Margo is—was—my boss at Archer."

"You didn't know her in any other capacity—as a friend?"

She shook her head.

"How long have you known her?"

"Almost three months."

"When was the last time you saw her alive?"

"Last night, I went by her office to discuss a work issue before—" Belinda stopped and collected herself. "Margo was leaving for vacation."

"What time were you in her office?"

"Around six o'clock, I believe."

"Do you know where she was planning to go on vacation?"

"Hawaii. For two weeks."

"Alone?"

"I don't know." The comments the girls had made about Margo flitting to exotic places with her "tadpoles" came to mind, but she didn't want to speculate.

"How long were you in her office?"

She squinted, trying to recall. "Ten minutes maybe."

"Did you argue?"

Belinda hesitated. "No."

He glanced up, then down again. "Was she acting strange? Upset?"

"No, just trying to get out of the office. Said she still had to pack for her trip."

"Did you leave together?"

"No. Her phone rang, so I went on."

"Do you know who called?"

"No." Belinda bit into her lip. "But I do remember it was an internal call—I could tell by the ring."

"Did you see anyone else in the area?"

"I can't say for sure, but I left by the back stairwell, and I didn't see anyone."

"That's when you fell?"

"Yes."

"Did anyone, um, see you fall?"

When he didn't look up, a finger of fear nudged her spine. "No. I was alone."

"And did you go straight to your car?"

"No. I stopped by the lounge on the first floor to clean up—my jacket was torn, and my hand was bleeding."

"Then you went to your car?"

"No." She pressed her lips together. "This is where things get complicated."

He looked up. "Complicated?"

She was prevented from answering by the arrival of two other cars, both unmarked, one with a red light flashing.

"Belinda," Wade said. "Are you sure you don't want to call an attorney?"

"I'm sure." Then her mouth went slack. "You don't think I had anything to do with this?"

He pursed his mouth and glanced toward the grim-faced entourage. "No, I don't. But it's not me you'll have to convince."

Chapter 21

Car doors opened. A man and a woman emerged from the first vehicle, their badges gleaming in the sun. A lone man climbed out of the second vehicle, armed with a camera and a medical bag. They all approached, staring at the tarp-covered trunk.

"How you doing, Lieutenant?" the woman asked, her teeth white against her mahogany skin. She was willowy, wearing chinos and a navy sport coat.

"I'm good, Salyers," Wade said. "Belinda Hennessey, this is Detective Salyers and Detective Truett."

Truett was a stocky fellow with a silvery crew cut and a paunch. "Hiya. This is Dr. Janney from the medical examiner's office."

Belinda swallowed hard and nodded a greeting.

"The victim's name is Margo Campbell," Wade offered. "Ms. Hennessey found the body."

Truett grunted. "Is this your car, Ms. Hennessey?"

"Yes."

"Did you move the body or touch anything?"

"No, nothing. I was so frightened, I slammed the lid back down."

"And can you tell us how this woman came to be in the trunk of your car?"

Belinda expelled a pent-up breath. "No, I can't."

"You took the call, Alexander?" Truett asked.

"Yes, sir. I'm acquainted with Ms. Hennessey."

The man's eyebrows climbed. "Oh?"

"We were involved in a fender bender earlier this week." He indicated her broken headlight and dented side panel.

"How many tickets did you write her, Lieutenant?"

Wade had the good grace to squirm. "Um, three, sir."

"What happened to you taking the detective's exam?" Truett asked, pulling gloves from his pocket and rolling them onto his fat hands.

Belinda watched as Wade's color heightened. "The exam isn't going anywhere."

"Neither are you until you take it," Truett said. The man clapped his gloved hands. "Now, let's see what we got here." He removed the tarp and winced. The M.E. set down his bag and started snapping photographs.

"The trunk was closed when I arrived," Wade said. "But I shot pictures before I opened it. The latch is broken," he said, pointing to the mechanism. "That happened during our collision—I remember checking myself."

"Didn't know you were a mechanic," Truett muttered.

"I had to access the trunk, sir, to change Ms. Hennessey's tire."

"I would have expected no less, Lieutenant."

Wade frowned. "What I'm getting at is that the trunk can be opened without a key. Anyone who had access to this car could have dumped the body inside."

"If they knew about the latch," Truett added. "We'll need prints lifted."

Detective Salyers circled to stand in front of Belinda. "What happened to your eye, Ms. Hennessey?"

"I fell down the stairs at work."

"Where do you work?"

"I started a report," Wade cut in, extending the clipboard. "Ms. Hennessey's employment information is there."

Detective Salyers looked back and forth between them, then took the report and began reading. "Lieutenant, why is Archer Furniture familiar to me?"

"An Archer employee fell down the elevator shaft of the Stratford Plaza building about six months ago."

"Yes, I remember now." She handed the clipboard back to him, then pulled out a notebook. "Ms. Hennessey, did anyone see you in the lounge at the Stratford Building, where you say you were cleaning up from your fall?"

"There was another woman in the lounge, but we didn't speak."

"The surveillance tapes will verify the time," Wade offered.

Salyers nodded. "Did you go straight to your car from the lounge?"

Belinda swallowed—the complicated part. "No. I'm in a car pool, and I drove yesterday. But at the end of the day I needed to discuss something with Margo—"

"The victim?"

"Um, yes. I asked one of the ladies I ride with to take my car, and told her I'd drop by her house later to pick it up."

"What are the names of the people you carpool with?"

"Libby Janes, Carole Marchand, and Rosemary Burchett—but Rosemary drove herself to work yesterday."

"Do all of these women work for Archer as well?"

She nodded.

"So why couldn't the two women have just waited for you?"

"I didn't know how long I'd be, and they had an errand to run."

"Which was?"

Belinda wet her lips. "Rosemary bows out of the car pool occasionally because of an appointment that she won't discuss. The other two women got it in their heads that she might be seriously ill, so they decided to . . . follow her." Belinda felt ridiculous.

"So you gave your car keys to whom?"

"Libby Janes."

"Where was your car parked?"

"In the Stratford parking garage, on the eighth floor."

"Every floor has a door to the parking garage," Wade explained.

"What floor is your company located on, Ms. Hennessey?"

"Eighth."

"Handy access."

Belinda decided not to mention that she'd felt pretty darn special to get a parking place so close yesterday morning, next to the spots reserved for handicapped drivers, delivery persons, the CEOs of respective companies, employees of the month, and expectant mothers.

"Do you know what time your two friends left the parking garage in your car?"

"No. When I talked to Libby later, she said that Carole had been late meeting her, so they weren't able to, um . . . follow Rosemary after all. Supposedly, Rosemary was leaving at six, so I assume it was after that when Libby and Carole left in my car."

Salyers squinted, as if she was trying to keep all the names straight. "How and when did you meet up with your car again?"

"I intended to take MARTA, then get a taxi, but on the way out, I ran into a friend who offered to drive me."

Wade's head came up.

Salyers noticed. "Does this friend have a name?"

"Julian Hardeman."

"Julian Hardeman, the traffic reporter?"

"Yes. He belongs to the gym in the Stratford Building."

"Uh-hm. So, Mr. Hardeman offered to drive you to your car, and you accepted."

"Yes."

"And where was he parked?"

"In the Stratford Building garage, on the ground level."

"What kind of car does he drive?"

"A dark blue Audi, I don't know the model or the year."

"Then what?"

"He drove me to Libby's, I got my keys and drove myself home."

"When you got to your friend's house, where was the car parked?"

"In her driveway."

"What time was that?"

Belinda shook her head. "Close to seven-thirty, maybe. I don't remember."

"We'll need this woman's address, of course."

"Did you come home alone?" Wade asked, his voice a tad sharp.

Belinda looked at him and knew Salyers was watching too. "Yes, Lieutenant."

He looked back to his notes, but his shoulders had eased a half-inch. Or maybe she imagined it.

"Did you stop anywhere on your way home?" Salyers asked.

"No."

"And when you arrived home, where did you park the car?"

"In the garage."

"Is it locked?"

"Yes, I have a remote control opener on my car visor, and there's one next to the door leading into the house."

The sound of a helicopter flying overhead interrupted them. It belonged to Julian's station, she could tell by the markings, although she couldn't be sure he was piloting. Foolishly, she wanted to wave to him, but even though he'd probably noticed the flashing lights, he couldn't know the police were at her address.

"Speak of the devil," Salyers said, watching the helicopter fly away.

Wade watched, too, his eyes narrow.

Salyers looked back to the Honda. "Ms. Hennessey, you said you parked your car in the garage, but it's sitting outside now."

"I drove to the DMV this morning to get my Georgia driver's license—"

"Where are you from?"

"I moved here from Cincinnati, Ohio, a couple of months ago."

"Go on."

"By the time I left the DMV, I'd missed an appointment to have my car repaired. I was hoping the garage would call with a cancellation, so I left my car sitting outside."

"Your car sat in the DMV parking lot for how long?"

"From nine in the morning to about twelve-thirty."

"Sounds par for the course," Salyers muttered. "Did you go anywhere when you left the DMV?"

"I walked to a sandwich shop, called the garage, and then I called the office."

"Who did you talk to at the office?" Wade asked, flipping to a new page.

"Brita Wheeling, Margo's assistant, and my friend Carole Marchand, who works in the mail room. Margo asked me to cover for her while she was on vacation, so I was checking in."

"And did her assistant say anything to indicate that Ms. Campbell was anywhere other than where she thought she'd be?" Salyers asked.

"No. In fact, her assistant was planning to call Margo on her cell phone to verify something." Belinda's stomach dipped—all those cellular phone rings she'd thought were coming from radio commercials had been coming from her trunk.

"Ms. Hennessey, did you like your boss?"

"We weren't friends, but I didn't dislike her."

"Did other people dislike her?"

"Tell Detective Salyers about the incident yesterday," Wade said.

Belinda gasped. "Jim Newberry—I'd forgotten."

"Who's this Jim Newberry?"

"I don't know him," Belinda said. "He worked for Margo before I came to Archer, and he was let go."

"Fired?"

"That's what I've heard, yes. I was in Margo's office yesterday afternoon, and he burst in, threatening her."

"What did he say?"

Belinda closed her eyes, replaying the scene in her head. "He called her a bitch and said he ought to kill her for what she'd done."

"Did he say what she had done?"

"He said something about Margo setting him up, but he wasn't specific."

"Did your boss seem to be afraid?"

"No. In fact, she was calm. She told him he'd brought it on himself and indicated that he had a drug problem."

"How did the incident end?"

"Security arrived, but by that time, he had backed down."

"I talked to the security guards yesterday," Wade said. "They said the guy didn't have a record, wasn't armed, and that he left peacefully around four o'clock."

Salyers's mouth puckered. "You seem to know a lot about this case, Lieutenant."

"Just doing my job, ma'am."

"And behaving very much like a detective, if I may say so." She turned back to Belinda. "Ms. Hennessey, was anything going on at work? Any scandals, layoffs?"

"No scandals that I know of, but perhaps you should talk with someone who's worked at Archer longer. As far as layoffs, there was a rumor about a staff cut. Margo had just finished performance evaluations—that's why I was in her office yesterday when Jim Newberry barged in."

Salyers angled her head. "And did she give you a good evaluation?"

"Yes. In fact, no one knows this yet, but Margo offered me the position of chief financial officer."

"Impressive. Why doesn't anyone know?"

Belinda gave a light shrug. "It was going to take a couple of weeks for the paperwork to be processed. Margo said she would make the announcement when she returned from vacation."

"Ms. Hennessey, do you have a police record?"

She blinked. "No. Lt. Alexander gave me my first traffic ticket."

"He was flirting with you," the woman said with a wry grin.

Wade looked as if he was going to say something to defend himself when Detective Truett called out.

"What did you find?" Salyers asked, walking over. Lt. Alexander was on her heels, but he positioned himself between Belinda and the trunk. Even so, she could see Margo's still face, frozen in a mask of death. Her black cherry lipstick was badly smeared, giving her a clownlike appearance. Belinda knew that expression would haunt her in her sleep.

Dr. Janney pointed to Margo's neck. "There was a struggle—she has a couple of scratches and bruises. Probably dead before she was put in the trunk, else she would have cuts and bruises on her hands from trying to get out."

Belinda winced.

"Any skin under the fingernails?" Wade asked.

The M.E. lifted a stiff hand into Belinda's view. The black cherry fingernail polish looked like drops of blood at the end of the woman's white fingers. "If there was any, it's probably gone. Her nails were clipped—see? They're white on the ends because the polished tips were cut away."

"Couldn't she have clipped them herself?"

"Sure, that too, although they look to have been hurriedly done."

A memory stirred in Belinda's brain, of Margo tapping her long fingernails on her desk while she decided how to handle the contracts. "Her fingernails were long yesterday when I saw her last."

Salyers made a note of it. "Can you tell how long she's been dead?" she asked the M.E.

He shook his head. "More than twelve hours—I won't know for sure until the autopsy. The van from the morgue should be here soon. Anyone notify the next of kin?"

Belinda started shaking—it sounded like something she might see on television . . . if her television were working.

"Her pocketbook is intact," Truett said. "But I didn't find any emergency contact names. I found credit cards, but no cash, so maybe robbery was the motive."

"If she was leaving town, chances are she'd have had a good deal of cash on her," Salyers agreed.

Which sparked another rather relevant memory in Belinda's brain. "A coworker called me a few minutes ago and told me money was missing at Archer—over five thousand dollars in cash. She said the police were there, questioning people in Margo's office."

The detectives exchanged appalled glances. Lt. Alexander withdrew his radio from his belt and directed someone to notify the officers on site at Archer to secure the area around Margo Campbell's office, then wait for further instructions.

"Wonder how many people have already been in there," Truett muttered, then glanced at Belinda and barked, "Why didn't you tell us sooner?"

She flinched. "Libby called after I talked to Lieutenant Alexander, and I guess I was—and still am—a little out of it."

"I told you not to talk to anyone until the police got here," Wade said, his eyebrows drawn together.

Her temper flared. "The phone rang—I thought it was you calling back. I didn't say anything about . . . this. I tried to act as normal as possible considering I had just discovered a dead body in the trunk of my car."

"Okay, time out," Salyers said. "What's done is done. At least we found out when we did." She looked back to the open trunk. "Do we know what killed her?"

"Janney says she was suffocated with a pillow," Truett said.

"I said *maybe* a pillow," the doctor corrected. "Whatever it was, it has her lipstick on it."

Detective Truett opened the doors of her Civic and peered inside. Belinda felt faint—for all she knew there could be another body in the backseat. Thank goodness he didn't find a body, but he did find Big Daddy.

"Planning to take down a horse, Ms. Hennessey?"

She stared, along with everyone else, at the colossal stun baton. "Um, that was a gift."

"A gift?"

"From the women I carpool with, for protection when I'm on the road."

He raised his eyebrows, then placed Big Daddy in a plastic evidence bag.

Across the street an impressive collection of neighbors had amassed to stare over the fence.

"What's in this?" Truett asked, pointing to the cardboard box she'd abandoned on the driveway.

"Some things I was going to take to Goodwill."

"What kinds of things?" He bent over to rummage.

"Just . . . things." A blush started at her knees, and by the time he pulled out her wedding gown, she felt splotchy all over.

"Recently divorced?" Truett asked.

"Yes," she murmured.

"Is that why you left Cincinnati?" Salyers asked.

She nodded.

"What's your ex's name?"

"I . . . how is that relevant?"

"You don't have to answer any question that makes you uncomfortable," Wade interjected, glaring at Salyers. "Right, Detective?"

"Right, Lieutenant," Salyers said with a friendly smile. "Ms. Hennessey, we'd like permission to look inside your house. It's just a formality."

"Well . . ." She looked to Wade, who seemed to want to say something but was holding back. "I guess that would be okay."

It wasn't as if they were going to find anything incriminating.

Chapter 22

"Nice place," Detective Salyers said, walking through the foyer. "A little bare."

"I haven't had time to decorate," Belinda murmured, holding open the door. Truett ambled by, scraping his heels on the parquet wood flooring with practiced carelessness. Wade brought up the rear, and she experienced a rush of intimacy that he was in her house—preposterous considering the circumstances, but there it was.

Her phone bleeped, but she ignored it. When the message recorder kicked on and a reporter identified himself, she turned off the machine.

From the bathroom, Downey was crying, as if someone were standing on her tail.

"My cat," she said to the questioning expressions. "She thinks she's human. And abused." Belinda opened the door and Downey streaked out, bounced around for a few seconds, then sat down to smooth her own ruffled feathers.

Meanwhile, Salyers and Truett had strolled off in different directions—Salyers into the living room, and Truett toward the kitchen.

"What are they looking for?" she whispered to Wade,

and watched while Salyers picked up the throw cushion in the chair and inspected it.

"Just following procedure," he assured her. "How are you holding up?"

"Fine," she said, although her head pounded. "Do they think *I* did this?"

"You've been very cooperative, and you don't have a motive."

"You didn't answer my question."

His mouth formed a flat line. "They need to eliminate obvious suspects first."

"Meaning me."

"Yes, since you found the body and you're acquainted with the victim."

The victim. Belinda puffed out her cheeks in an exhale. "What now?"

"We'll follow up on all the information you gave us. People, places, things."

"What do you think happened?"

His shoulders rose in a shrug. "Maybe the Newberry guy came back and they had another confrontation."

"But that doesn't explain how her body got into the trunk of my car."

"Was your car parked close to the stairwell?"

She nodded.

"Maybe he carried the body down the back stairs with the idea of putting her in his car. Maybe your trunk had sprung open, and he decided it was a better hiding place."

She brightened. "Aren't there cameras in the parking garage?"

He shook his head. "No, just on the outside of the building, directed toward the sidewalks. But we'll check the records of the parking garage booth—maybe Newberry kept his electronic badge and got in that way."

"But after five-thirty, the gates are open for public parking—anyone can get in and out with no badge."

He nodded. "Maybe we'll get lucky."

Salyers walked around them, her mouth curving into a

sly smile as she addressed Wade. "Is the bedroom upstairs?"

"I wouldn't know, Detective."

Belinda cleared her throat. "Yes, the bedrooms are upstairs. I'll show you." She climbed the stairs self-consciously, wondering why the woman would imagine she was involved with Lt. Alexander, and thinking about stupid things like what kind of mess she'd left the upstairs. Wade followed them, making her feel even more uncomfortable. She pointed to the right. "This is an extra room that I don't use."

Salyers walked in, peered inside the empty closet, then returned to the hall.

Belinda led them to the left. "This is my room." She saw the leopard-print comforter on her queen-size bed through the eyes of strangers and cringed inwardly.

Detective Salyers pointed to the bed. "May I?"

For all Belinda knew, the woman was going to take a nap, but she nodded.

Salyers pulled back the comforter to expose the one pillow in reverse animal print. "Where's your other pillow?"

"I only have one," Belinda said, feeling the splotchiness coming on.

"Why is that?"

"Because I only need one," she said, wondering if she could broadcast her singledom any louder.

Detective Salyers frowned. "Who has only one pillow on a bed this size?"

"Ms. Hennessey does," Wade said pointedly.

The woman pursed her mouth, then crouched down when something caught her eye. She pulled Downey's pale blue satin pillow from beneath the bed and held it up by the corner. "What's this?"

Belinda stared at the ripped-out threads and grew even warmer. First, Wade Alexander had hand-delivered the pillow to her, and now he was witness to the result of her juvenile rampage. She cut her gaze to him to see if he recognized the pillow.

He did.

"Um, that's my cat's, um, toy."

"What's this stain?" Salyers turned over the pillow and pointed to a dark reddish smudge.

Belinda shook her head. "Cat food? I'm not sure."

Salyers pulled an evidence bag from her pocket and sealed up the pillow.

It dawned on Belinda that the woman thought the stain might be Margo's black cherry lipstick. Her next thought was how contrary Downey was going to be when she couldn't find her satin sidekick.

The bathroom was free of embarrassing items, if Belinda didn't count the birth control pill pack on the vanity, and the little smiley face she'd drawn in the steam on the mirror that now stood out like a flare. Wade seemed to soak in every detail, down to the frumpy peach-colored robe hanging on the back of the door.

"Do you have a pair of nail clippers?" Salyers asked casually.

Belinda nodded and rummaged in her makeup bag until she came up with them. Salyers promptly bagged them. In the hallway laundry closet, the woman also seized the lime green cardigan sweater with the red sauce stain.

"Stromboli sandwich," Belinda explained, but it went into a bag anyway.

"Where are the clothes you were wearing when you fell in the stairwell?"

Belinda fished them out of a bag that was bound for the dry cleaner's. They went into evidence, along with the shoes she'd been wearing—her best pair, of course.

When Detective Salyers started downstairs, Belinda glanced at Wade. He gave her a reassuring wink, but his grim expression belied his offhand gesture. As she descended the stairs, her stomach began to roll, and she prayed she didn't get sick again.

Salyers was in the living room, rifling through the Goodwill boxes. She looked out the bay window. "Truett, the van from the morgue is here. Are you ready?"

"Yeah." Truett came strolling through the hall carrying the rolled-up DOs and DON'Ts manuscript. A dark reddish stain marred the back of the papers—she hadn't realized what a sloppy eater she was.

"I'd like to take this if you don't mind," he said, then dropped it into an evidence bag. He glanced at the pillow and clothing that Salyers held. They held a whispered conference. Belinda squirmed and looked to Wade for another reassuring wink. She didn't get one.

"Ms. Hennessey," Salyers said, "are you willing to take a polygraph test?"

"Yes, of course."

The detectives walked to the front door. Truett turned. "Lieutenant Alexander, will you keep Ms. Hennessey company for a little while?"

"Yes, sir."

The door closed behind them, and Belinda looked at Wade. "What?"

"They don't want an audience when the body is moved."

"Tell that to the people across the street."

He walked to the window and looked to the sky. "Or to Hardeman."

The faint *whop, whop* of the helicopter blades sounded overhead. She joined Wade at the window and looked up. "He doesn't know this is where I live."

"Are you sure?" he asked in a sharp tone.

She frowned. "Well, I suppose my address is a matter of public record, but to my knowledge, he hasn't been here."

"When Hardeman dropped you off last night at your friend's house, did he leave immediately?"

"No. I went inside to talk to Libby for a few minutes, and he waited."

"Near your car?"

She angled her head. "You aren't suggesting that Julian—"

"He had access to your car. Did he know about the trunk latch?"

She put her hand to her temple. "I mentioned having my car repaired today, but that would mean . . ." Then she sighed. "Look, Wade, I know there's no love lost between the two of you, but whatever problem you have with Julian—"

"He had an affair with my wife." He looked away. "I mean, with my ex-wife."

She blinked. "I'm sorry."

He waved off her sympathy. "It was a long time ago, and he didn't force Tania into anything. But the man's a player and I don't like him."

Tania. What was the woman like who had turned the head and heart of this man?

And she suddenly felt grubby for falling under Julian's charismatic spell. "Julian told me last night that he had been sleeping with Jeanie Lawford."

"I know. And I was never convinced that the woman's death was an accident."

She balked. "Do you think that Jeanie's death and Margo's could be related?"

He held up his hand. "I'm just saying that two deaths in six months at the same company is quite a coincidence."

"A serial murderer?"

"I didn't say that."

"But you think it."

He set his jaw. "I think you should be careful. Do you have a security alarm?"

"No."

"I can install sensors on your windows and doors—basic stuff, but it's better than nothing."

"You're scaring me."

"If that's what it takes to make you cautious, then I don't feel the least bit guilty."

She pursed her mouth, half irritated by his big macho Southern boy routine, half flattered that he cared what happened to her potentially endangered behind. Two news camera vans had arrived, and the bevy of neighbors had increased. She spotted Perry in the crowd and winced—the man would pester her ad nauseam for all the gory details.

Additional police officers had arrived to keep cars and foot traffic at bay. A gurney sat behind her car, draped with an unzipped black body bag. The body movers, Dr. Janney, and the two detectives used the tarp and their bodies to shield Margo's removal from prying eyes and camera lenses. Despite their best efforts, though, one of Margo's arms fell off the gurney and hung down. Cameras went off. Belinda stared at the lifeless hand, and the composure she'd managed to regain slipped. She turned her back to the scene and covered her mouth with her hand.

Next to her, Wade shifted from foot to foot, and she could feel that he wanted to comfort her. And she wanted him to, but right now she needed his objective expertise more than physical consolation, so she spared him the decision by walking to the kitchen to find aspirin for her pounding head. He followed her and leaned against the counter, watching, waiting, accessible.

"When will her name be released to the press?" Belinda asked softly.

"As soon as they notify her next of kin. Do you know who that might be?"

Belinda shook her head. "I honestly didn't know her that well." How sad to wind up in the trunk of someone who doesn't even know you that well. Insult added to injury. "When will *my* name be released to the press?"

"The reporters have had time to talk to your neighbors and your landlord. Don't be surprised to see it on the six o'clock news."

Belinda closed her eyes briefly, then tried to smile. "For once I'm thankful that my television is on the blink. When will the detectives question my coworkers?"

"They'll probably visit the women you carpool with tonight at their homes to question them separately, Newberry too. They'll talk to other employees as needed."

"Julian?"

His mouth tightened. "He's on the interview list."

"Will they tell everyone why they're being questioned?"

"Yes. Belinda, how well do you know the women you ride to work with?"

She shrugged. "I've only been riding with them for a little over a week. They seem nice."

"Did any of them have issues with the victim?"

"Well . . . Margo wasn't the most popular of bosses."

"You mentioned something about performance evaluations and jobs being cut."

She chewed on her tongue.

"Belinda?"

She sighed. "Rosemary was afraid for her job, and Libby and Carole were both denied raises, but the rumor was that almost everyone in the department was denied a raise."

"If you know anything else, tell me."

She closed her eyes and repeated the story that Rosemary had told them about how she and Margo had once been friends, and how the relationship had eroded. "Rosemary is the executive assistant to the CEO, who is rarely in the office. She thinks Margo was trying to take over the company."

"Is there a chance these women could have been in on this together?"

"You mean a *plot* to murder Margo?" Belinda shook her head. "No."

"If one of them had a confrontation with the woman that ended badly, would the other two cover for her?"

Belinda stopped. Libby and Carole were fiercely loyal to Rosemary—would their allegiance extend to covering the murder of a women they all detested, and framing her, the new girl? The day Libby had come to her house and suffered the mini breakdown came to mind. "I . . . don't know."

"How, um, close are you and Hardeman?"

Her pulse picked up. "Is that relevant to the investigation?"

"It could be."

The front door opened and closed. They looked up, and Detective Salyers appeared in the opening between the hall and the kitchen. Belinda straightened—the woman made her feel as if she had to account for her time with Lieutenant Alexander. Salyers stared, then pointed to the drinking glass Belinda had set on the counter.

"Did you use this glass?"

"Yes."

"May I take it with me for prints?"

Belinda swallowed and nodded. "But my prints are already on file."

The woman's eyebrows climbed. "Did you hold a government job?"

Belinda shook her head. "I've handled the financial aspects of mergers and acquisitions for public companies. When a person is privy to insider information—"

"The company and the SEC perform a background check, including fingerprints," Salyers finished.

"Right."

"Lieutenant," the detective said. "May I have a word with you?"

He nodded and pushed away from the counter, then followed Salyers to the far corner of the room where the table and chairs sat. Belinda walked back toward the front of the town house to give them more privacy to talk about her.

She stared out the bay window. The body movers slammed the back doors to the van, then climbed inside and drove away with no fanfare, just as if they were hauling furniture to the dump. Was death really so heartbreakingly mundane?

The police parted the crowd to make room for something large. As she watched, a tow truck came into view and expertly backed up to her car. She pressed her hand against the glass—*they were taking her car?*

Of course they were taking her car. It was a rolling crime scene.

A burly fellow jumped down and proceeded to reduce

her beloved Civic to an appendage of his wench. She watched the car—in perfect condition when it left Cincinnati, now battered and violated—be pulled by its ass from her driveway and down the street. She would probably never see it again.

The only saving grace in the entire predicament was that her parents were en route to the Grand Canyon and therefore less likely to hear how their daughter had made a name for herself in the big city of Atlanta.

And suddenly, the tears were there again.

"Ms. Hennessey," Detective Salyers said.

She turned, blinking furiously. "Yes?"

The woman sighed and put her hands on her hips. "I'm not going to lie to you—you're in serious trouble here. Ordinarily we would take you into custody until we sorted out your story, but Lieutenant Alexander has vouched for you and offered to stick around until we check out this Newberry fellow and run prints on the trunk. If that's agreeable to you, of course."

She looked past Salyers to Wade, who lifted his shoulders in a little shrug, as if to say it was her choice. Her heart cartwheeled with gratitude, but she didn't want Detective Salyers—or Lieutenant Alexander—to read anything into her response, so she affected a neutral expression and nodded. "That's agreeable, yes."

Salyers smirked. "Good. I need your car keys."

Belinda fetched them from her purse and handed them over.

The detective strode to the door, opened it, and cast a glance over her shoulder. "Remember, Lieutenant, you gave me your word."

"Yes, ma'am."

The woman walked out and closed the door behind her. Wade retraced her steps and turned the dead bolt, then walked around the first floor, checking window locks.

"Thank you for staying," Belinda said.

He nodded but seemed bent on putting as much space between them as possible as he moved around.

"On what did you give Detective Salyers your word?"

He stopped and looked at her. "That you and I aren't involved."

"Oh." She nodded. "Well . . . we aren't."

"I know." He wet his lips. "But I had to be honest and tell her it wasn't for lack of trying."

Her cheeks flamed, and she attempted nonchalance. "That was before you saw me with a black eye and pulling bodies out of my trunk."

His gaze swept her head to toe—she couldn't imagine how she must look after grubbing around all day, throwing up, washing off her makeup, and crying like a toddler.

"Speaking of which," he said, holding up his camera with an apologetic expression. "I was instructed to get pictures of your injuries."

She sighed. "Where do you want me to stand?"

"Against the wall in the living room will be fine."

She made the short walk and positioned herself against the wall painted with builder-grade off-white paint. "I think these photos just might surpass the one on my driver's license, which I'm still stuck with, by the way."

Beneath the camera lens, his mouth curved. "Can you pull your hair back from your face and turn your cheek toward me? Good." The shutter sounded twice. "Okay, now your wrist and arm."

She pulled up her sleeve and extended the bruised limb.

"Okay, now turn your arm over to show the scratch. Now your right hand."

Her knuckles were still red and tender.

"Did you sustain any other injuries when you fell?"

"A bruised rib, I think."

"Is there a visible bruise?"

She nodded.

"If you'd feel more comfortable with Salyers taking this photo—"

"No, this is fine," she said, then lifted the hem of her sweatshirt to the bottom of her bra. He set his jaw and took two quick shots.

"Is that all?" he asked.

"Yes."

He seemed relieved. "You got any coffee?"

She nodded and started for the kitchen.

"Just tell me where it is and I'll make it. You should sit."

She walked to the bar and sat on a stool so she could watch him clang around in her kitchen. Quite domestic.

"I didn't know that Southern men knew their way around a kitchen."

He laughed, and she was struck by how handsome he was when he smiled. "Coffee, eggs, and chili are the extent of my skills. And I tend to make my coffee strong."

"Sounds good to me."

He had the coffeemaker bubbling in no time. When he set a steaming cup in front of her, he made a rueful noise. "This isn't the way I'd hoped to get to know you."

She swept a hank of hair behind her ear. "Which brings up a point, Lieutenant. It was kind of you to vouch for me to the detective, but you really don't know me very well. How can you be sure I didn't have anything to do with this?"

"I can't," he said smoothly. "I'm going on my gut and hoping I don't regret it."

The air was suddenly thick with possibilities. She attributed the wholly inappropriate thoughts she was having about Wade Alexander to a diversion from the current state of affairs.

"It's strange," she said. "How I met you only a week ago and our paths have crossed so many times since."

"Fate, maybe," he said with a smile.

Fate really needed to brush up on its timing.

He reached for a notebook. "Unfortunately, Salyers didn't agree to let me stay just so that I could flirt with you. I need to know everything *you* know about your coworkers, especially the ones who might have known about your trunk latch."

The phone rang, and he shrugged. "Probably a reporter. Want me to scare them off?"

She nodded.

He picked up the receiver. "Hello . . . yes, this is the Hennessey residence—who's calling, please?" He covered the mouthpiece. "She says it's your mother."

Belinda closed her eyes.

Chapter 23

Her mother? Perfect timing. Belinda picked up the phone and used her most cheerful tone. “Hello, Mother.”

“Belinda, was that a man who answered your phone?”

She looked at Wade, who dwarfed the stool he sat on. “Um, yes it was.”

Her mother put her hand over the mouthpiece. “Franklin, she has a man there!” Then she uncovered the mouthpiece. “So your couch must have been delivered.”

She squinted at her mother’s jump in logic. “Hm?”

“I assume if you’re entertaining, you must have your couch.”

“Oh. No, not until tomorrow.”

“So who is this man who sits on the floor?”

She glanced at Wade and shook her head. “Um, he’s a friend, Mother. Where are you and Dad?”

“Iowa.”

“What’s in Iowa?”

“Lots of corn, dear. We’ve stopped at a Holiday Inn for the night in Dubuque.”

“That sounds . . . lovely.”

“So how are you?”

“Oh . . . fine.”

"Did you get your big promotion?"

"Um, not yet. But soon. I hope."

"Dad wants to know how your car is."

"Tell Dad the car is . . . fine."

"I worry about you—what if something happens and you need to get in touch with us? Your dad says we should have gotten one of those car phones."

She pressed her lips together. "Nothing's going to happen, Mom."

"I'd better go. I'm at a pay phone and I'm holding up the line."

"Okay, Mom." Belinda paused, suddenly loath to hang up. "I love you both."

"We love you, too. Good-bye, dear."

She slowly returned the phone to its cradle and, feeling Wade's gaze on her, tried to dissuade any comments by taking her time turning off the ringer.

It didn't work.

"I take it she hasn't heard about the murder?"

"No. She and Dad are on a cross-country trip they've been planning for years. I'm not about to ruin it for them when this thing could be over tomorrow."

"They sound nice, your folks."

She smiled fondly. "They're completely neurotic, but yes, they're great. I'd hate to cause them any more embarrassment." She sipped from her coffee, hoping he hadn't noticed the slip of her tongue.

But he had. "Any *more* embarrassment?"

"My mother had planned that by now I'd be happily settled into a grand home and working on grand*children*."

"A breakup can be hard on the entire family," he agreed.

"Do your parents live around here?"

"Birmingham, Alabama. That's about three hours away and where I grew up."

"Do you see them often?"

"Not as much as I should."

"Were they close to your ex-wife?"

"Not really. Tania wasn't the warm and fuzzy type."

So, in manspeak, Tania was exciting—the kind of woman who broke rules and got away with it. "But your parents were upset about the divorce?"

"Just disappointed. I hid all the problems from them, so to them our breakup seemed sudden. In reality, we'd been separated for two years." He cleared his throat. "But enough about me. I'm going to need a list of anyone who might have legitimately been around the trunk of your car."

The man was going to have to work on his interrogation segues. "Well, me of course. And any of the girls might have touched it getting in and out of the car. You. Then there was the guy at the auto shop who gave me an estimate for repairs—his name was Dave, I believe. And my neighbor, Perry."

"Was this the guy you were hiding from in the food court?"

She nodded. "He lives two doors down and can be a little pesky."

"I'll try to remember that you don't like pesky men."

A tingle passed over her shoulders, although she suspected Wade's teasing was a ploy to keep her mind off the matter at hand.

"When did your neighbor have an opportunity to be near the trunk?"

"A few nights ago he walked over to inspect the damage on my car."

"What's his last name?"

She guessed at the spelling, and he wrote it down.

He pursed his mouth. "This guy was at the Stratford Building yesterday."

"He told me he was going to repair the elevator—I assumed he meant the shaft that Jeanie Lawford fell down."

He made a few more notes, then asked for more information about her coworkers at Archer. She told him about Juneau Archer, Clancy Edmunds, Monica Tanner, and Tal Archer, plus the little she knew about each person.

"Clancy was the one who told me about Margo firing

Jim Newberry. He said that Jim had filed a lawsuit against the company. Clancy is also the person Libby said everyone suspected of stealing the money that was reported missing today."

"Juneau and Tal Archer—father and son?"

"Right. I've only met the son once. Juneau is rarely in the office."

"Any of these people have a beef with Margo?"

"Monica Tanner opposed an acquisition that we just signed with a company called Payton Manufacturing, but it didn't appear to be more than professional disagreement."

"Margo was pushing the acquisition?"

"Yes. In fact, I was brought on board specifically to facilitate and oversee the financial aspects of the deal."

"Did sealing the deal have anything to do with the promotion you were offered?"

Her neck itched. "Yes."

"What about the woman's assistant—" He read from his notes. "Brita Wheeling?"

"I don't know much about her either, although I gather she's loyal to Margo." Brita was willing to wield an umbrella on her boss's behalf.

"Okay, tell me more about the women in your car pool."

She hesitated. "I'd rather wait to see if Jim Newberry is found."

He put down his pen. "You don't want to talk about your friends?"

"Not if I don't have to."

"Are you afraid you'll get them into trouble?"

"I'm afraid that something I say will be misconstrued."

He steepled his hands and sighed. "You wouldn't want to appear as if you're covering up for them."

She bristled. "There's a difference between covering up for someone and protecting their privacy."

"Are you close to these women?"

"I've only known them for a short while, but I'd like to think I could be."

"What do you think they're telling the detectives about you right now?"

That she was aloof, standoffish, guarded, and maybe a little stuck up. She dropped her gaze to her hands. "I honestly couldn't say."

He was quiet for a long while, then asked, "Are you hungry?"

She shook her head, but her stomach growled.

He laughed. "How about I whip us up an omelet?"

"From my refrigerator? Good luck, Lieutenant."

"Just Wade," he said, rolling up the sleeves of his navy uniform shirt. "I went off duty a few minutes ago."

She finished her coffee. "If I hadn't seen you at Gypsy Joe's, I would have thought you never went off duty."

"See all the things you don't know about me," he said lightly.

"I'm learning." And rather liking it.

He opened the refrigerator. "While I'm doing miracles with condiments and bottled water, why don't you freshen up?"

She blinked. "That was subtle."

"Salyers and Truett will be back soon. I thought you might want to take a shower and maybe change clothes, you know, to recharge."

In case they arrested her, he meant. "Good idea," she said, sliding down from the stool. "I won't be long."

She dashed up the stairs and turned on the shower. While the water heated, she pulled clean, comfortable clothes from her closet, her mind spinning, still unable to fully grasp what had happened today and what was on the line. Her job, her reputation, her sanity, perhaps even her life, considering Georgia was a death-penalty state.

Wade's question about what Libby, Carole, and Rosemary would have to say about her dominated her thoughts. Would they think she was capable of committing such a heinous crime? Or was it possible that one of them had accidentally killed Margo, then conspired with the others to set her up?

She shook her head, resolved not to think about murder and mayhem for the duration of her shower. Even with the bathroom door secured, she felt strange undressing with Wade downstairs in her kitchen. She stepped under the showerhead and raised her face to allow the warm water to wash away as much of the day as possible, resisting the urge to stand there until she dissolved and washed down the drain.

As she ran a towel over her body, she wondered who would miss her if she had been the one murdered and stuffed into a trunk. Her parents, of course. And Vince would probably feel bad, but he would not be heartbroken. Her acquaintances and coworkers in Cincinnati would send flowers, and perhaps Rosemary would insist that Margo let people off to go to her memorial service. The girls would find a new carpooling buddy before long, and she would be relegated to a topic of conversation during long commutes and martini splurges.

She dressed quickly, then opened the bathroom door to the hall to help the steam dissipate from the mirrors. The delicious aroma of rosemary tickled her nostrils, and her stomach roared—no wonder, considering the fact that it was almost 7:30. The horrible day couldn't succumb to darkness fast enough, but she hoped that daylight didn't bring worse.

She used concealer to cover the bruise as well as possible, then she brushed powder over her shiny, clean skin. She skipped extras except for strawberry lip balm—her mouth was chapped from constantly licking her lips and from being dehydrated. The blow-dryer made short work of her hair, which she finger-combed and left as-is.

She sighed, dropped her wet towels in the laundry closet, then walked into the spare bedroom to peek through the blinds down at her bereft front yard. The dusk-to-dawn light flickered down on her narrow, empty driveway and little patch of yard, now trampled. The crowd was gone, but the stakes and yellow police tape remained, loose ends flapping in the light breeze.

Loose ends. A perfect analogy for her life.

"Soup's on," Wade called.

She released the mini-blinds to snap back, then left the room and walked downstairs, sniffing appreciably. "Wow, something smells good."

He glanced up, and his hands stilled. His look was so boldly admiring that she had an absurd blip of panic that she'd forgotten to put her clothes on. "Wow," he said. "I was about to say the same thing. That's some great perfume."

"Ivory soap."

"Like I said."

She was sure that no matter how pink she already was, she got pinker. He had found her radio and tuned it to a classic rock station. Fleetwood Mac's "You Make Lovin' Fun" made the small space seem even more cozy. To distract herself, Belinda gestured to the steaming omelets he'd served up on small plates at the breakfast bar. "Looks like you did work miracles."

He smiled—a look that was becoming alarmingly likable. "Don't give me too much credit. I just threw in a few spices and a little parmesan cheese."

"I hate to blow any image of my culinary skills you might have," she said, "but I only keep that stuff around to jazz up delivery pizza."

He was staring again, wiping his hands on a towel and shaking his head. "Lady, if it turns out that you're a cold-blooded murderer, I'm going to be mighty disappointed."

That made her smile. "I'll bet you've met all types of criminals, haven't you?"

He nodded and joined her on the other side of the bar. "Everyone has the capacity to do terrible things. Put someone in the right situation, then offer the right incentive or trigger the right emotion, and that person will choose wrong over right, even if it goes against their nature."

He might have been looking into her head, analyzing why a perennial good girl would suddenly compromise her integrity in exchange for outward signs of success that would prove she had made the right decision to move to Atlanta. Fudging to push through a merger wasn't as serious a transgression as taking a person's life, but it still led to unpleasant self-revelation.

"Aren't you going to eat?" he asked, pointing to her untouched plate.

She managed a smile. If he knew what she'd done, would he still be turning those amazing eyes in her direction? She cut into the fragrant omelet and delivered a forkful into her mouth. "Mm, wonderful."

He lifted his coffee cup to his mouth. "Says the starving woman."

They ate in companionable silence, listening to Sting and Heart, each lost in their own thoughts. Downey, having been ignored long enough, sauntered into the room, head held high.

"There she is, Miss America," Belinda murmured.

Wade leaned over and gently scooped the cat into his lap.

"Careful—she bites."

But Downey lay on her back over his knee and gave him full access to her underbelly, the little hussy.

Belinda sighed. "I guess she bites only me."

He scratched the cat's stomach for a few minutes, then set her down. She prowled every corner.

"She's looking for that pillow the detective took."

"Attached to it, huh?"

"She hasn't exactly acclimated to the move."

"What about you?" he asked quietly. "Does this incident make you want to go back to Cincinnati?"

She studied her coffee. "Yes."

"It looked to me from the items you were taking to Goodwill, that you were ready to put all of that behind you."

"Ironic, huh?"

"So are you going to tell me what happened to you and Vince?"

She lifted an eyebrow.

"I remember his name from the pillow."

Of course. Belinda took a deep breath. "It's simple, really—"

The doorbell rang, and she gratefully bailed to answer it. Wade followed. He walked into the living room and looked out the bay window. "It's Salyers and Truett."

The omelet was subjected to another flip in her stomach as she opened the door. The man and woman weren't smiling and didn't wait for an invitation to enter. Salyers took in the music, the plates. "Hope we weren't interrupting anything."

"What did you find out?" Wade asked, his tone impatient.

Truett grunted. "Jim Newberry is AWOL—his wife hasn't seen him since he left their home earlier today. She gave us something with his prints on it, though, so we'll be able to run them against the ones lifted from the trunk lid." Then he looked at Belinda. "And those carpooling friends of yours are a closemouthed bunch."

She swallowed hard—Rosemary, yes, but the only thing that could keep Libby and Carole from talking was a mouthful of Krispy Kreme doughnut. Or guilt?

"But right now," Salyers said, "it looks as if Newberry is our man. His wife confirmed that he hated the Campbell woman and made threats against her life. We have a three-state APB out on him, though, so we'll find him."

"Meanwhile," Belinda said, "what about me?"

"For now, go on about your business," Salyers said. "Ride the car pool to work tomorrow, follow your normal routine."

"What do I tell my coworkers about the murder?"

"As little as possible. Everyone will be talking plenty, but pay special attention to anyone who seems overly interested. Sometimes the perp will be eager for details."

Chapter 24

"*I have* to know every last detail," Libby insisted, her eyes as large as eggs.

"Let the poor woman get in the car," Rosemary said from the driver's seat.

Belinda slid into the seat behind Rosemary and pulled the door closed, wincing at the twinge in her wrist. "I'm not supposed to talk about it."

Libby's shoulders fell. "You *can't* not talk about it."

"I don't have the strength to rehash it, Libby."

"You do look pooped," Carole offered.

The young woman was being kind. In all, Belinda might have slept thirty minutes. Sitting up. With the lights on. An image of Margo's face was branded on the insides of her eyelids.

After Detectives Salyers and Truett had left, Lieutenant Alexander had gone outside to remove the stakes and tape from her yard. When he'd come back, they'd been as awkward as teenagers entangled in a murder investigation. She had offered him another cup of coffee, and he'd declined. Then he'd offered to stay—on the couch. She had reminded him she didn't have a couch, and for some reason had felt the need to repeat the fact that she had only one pillow. More awkwardness had ensued until he'd finally saluted and left.

That exchange alone would have kept her awake, but with the other demons on her back, sleep had been nowhere to be found.

"You should have come over to spend the night at my house," Libby said.

Belinda smiled. "It was nice of you to offer, but I truly thought I'd sleep better in my own bed." And considering how nosy Libby had been in a three-minute conversation on the phone last night, she knew the woman would ply her for particulars about the murder until the wee hours.

"It was on the eleven o'clock news," Carole said, turning around in her seat. "They showed Margo's picture and Jim Newberry's."

"Was my name mentioned?"

"Oh, yeah. And they showed your car being towed away."

Great. Libby offered her a doughnut, but she shook her head—her stomach was still a little on the puny side.

"When the police showed up at my door last night," Libby said, talking even faster than usual, "I thought it was about the missing money. I couldn't believe it when they told me Margo was dead, and that you had found the body in your trunk. Now I feel kind of bad about how many times I slammed on the brake while I was driving your car—she was probably bouncing around back there like a sack of potatoes."

"Libby," Rosemary chided.

"I'm just saying what everyone else is thinking." She turned to look at Belinda. "Good gravy, when you opened the trunk, did you freak plumb out?"

"You could say that."

"Those two detectives were pretty sneaky," Libby said. "They tried to get me to say I thought you did it."

"Me, too," Carole said.

"Same here," Rosemary added. The pinch between her eyebrows had become a distinct furrow.

Belinda wet her lips. "What did you guys say?"

"Well," Libby said, her voice higher than normal, "I told them about the disagreement you had with Margo last week—but that was no secret."

Belinda's stomach began to gurgle.

"And they asked if I heard Jim Newberry threaten Margo, but I told them you were the only one. Even Brita said she couldn't hear anything from her desk."

Her stomach bucked, but it was, fortunately, empty. So she was the only person who had heard Jim Newberry threaten to kill Margo, and the woman had been found in her car. There had to be a word to describe that kind of coincidence, but all she could think of at the moment was *unlucky.*

"But that was all I said," Libby declared.

"I didn't tell them anything," Carole declared. "I don't trust the police."

Belinda glanced at Rosemary, who shook her head. "I told them they'd be better off looking for Jim Newberry than asking questions about you. I'm surprised you're going to work today."

Belinda stifled a yawn. "I thought it was better than sitting at home." Although now she was rethinking that thought.

"Well, I doubt if anyone gets much done today," Libby said. "Do you know if Mr. Archer is coming in, Rosemary?"

"I doubt it. The news really hit him hard."

Belinda worried the inside of her lip with her teeth. Since Margo probably hadn't had a chance to talk to anyone about stalling the acquisition before she'd *departed*, approaching Juneau Archer and confessing the truth about the Payton financials would be the only responsible thing to do. The CEO would probably fire her on the spot, but at least she would have a clearer conscience. And she could relinquish some of this crushing guilt that the bad kismet she had put out into the universe had somehow set into motion this series of terrible events.

She leaned her head back and strained to hear Julian's voice on the radio. His sexy voice never failed to soften her, but his cheer seemed forced this morning, his accent more exaggerated, his comments about careless drivers more biting. Regret overwhelmed her for involving him in this mess. The police had most certainly already talked to him about the murder, so she would be surprised if she ever heard from him again. On the other hand, considering what Wade had told her about Julian's womanizing, she wasn't so sure that was such a bad thing. Of course she hadn't objected when she was the woman being *ized*.

The morning sun slanting through the window felt so comforting on her face, almost maternal. She closed her eyes. It was heaven not to have to drive.

"Belinda, don't go to sleep!" Libby said. "Tell us *something*."

She fought another yawn and lost. "I read the DOs and DON'Ts manuscript, and I thought it was great."

"Really?"

"Really. And I have another one for you—'DON'T forget that men are unnecessary.' "

"Let her sleep," Rosemary said. "She's been through hell, and a person can only take so much."

"Yeah, well, we're proof of that."

"Be quiet, Libby. Do your hair."

Belinda heard them through a haze as she sank deeper into the seat. The steady rhythm of the tires on pavement and the gentle sway of the car was . . . so . . .

Sexy. Like Wade Alexander's smile, when he let himself . . . his ex-wife had taken his smile with her . . . taken his smile and left a cat . . . like Vince . . . Red Rover, Red Rover, make Belinda start over . . .

A murmur of voices came to her . . . Libby . . . Carole . . . Rosemary . . . drinking martinis . . . poor Jeanie in the wrong place, wrong time . . . Margo had gotten what she deserved . . . what goes around comes around . . . as long as everyone keeps their mouth shut . . . everything will be fine . . .

She was crossing the street with a man . . . Julian . . . from around the curve came a speeding car . . . she couldn't move . . . she didn't want to move . . . exhilarating terror gripped her just before impact—

She started awake. Fear drained from her slowly, like a bathtub full of cold water, drawing off to leave a person even colder. She shivered and tried to focus on the passing scenery. She felt as if she'd closed her eyes for only a few seconds, but they were nearing the Stratford Building. She wet her lips and tasted Aqua Net. Gradually she tuned in to the conversation around her.

". . . maybe Margo was the person Ricky was referring to when he said something bad was going to happen to someone I'm close to," Carole was saying.

"You and Margo weren't close," Rosemary said.

"We were close in proximity."

"When?"

"Whenever I delivered her confidential envelopes."

"That's a stretch," Libby said. "Hey, sleeping beauty, are you awake?"

Belinda sat up and rubbed her eyes. "Sorry about that."

"Feeling better?" Carole asked.

Belinda nodded, but the remnants of her troubling dreams still hunkered in the corners of her mind. Had she imagined the conversation between the women? It had seemed so real . . . but then so had the car racing toward her. It must have been how Margaret Mitchell had felt, paralyzed with fear, marveling over the sheer absurdity of her life ending in such a trivial fashion.

Here lies Belinda Hennessey. She was caught off guard.

Rosemary slowed to turn into the parking garage, then buzzed down her window and swiped her employee badge to trigger the steel arm to raise. As they drove up and around, eyes peeled for an empty parking space, Belinda fought a rising sense of panic. Everything about the building had taken on an eerie quality—dark corners and shadowy twists and turns.

The entire eighth floor of the garage had been cordoned off, no stretch of the imagination as to why. Belinda's heart rate speeded up. They climbed to the twelfth floor before they found an empty spot. Rosemary parked, and they all took their time rolling out. Belinda looked around nervously, expecting to see Jim Newberry jump out from behind every concrete column.

"This ought to be an interesting day," Libby said as they walked toward the elevator bays. "Well, what do you know, they finally got the sixth elevator fixed."

Belinda stared at the clean spot across the doors, where the Out of Order sticker had been, and she started to perspire. She wasn't normally a touchy-feely person, but this building seemed to vibrate with bad karma. "I'm taking the stairs."

"Are you okay?" Libby asked.

Belinda nodded, pushed open the door to the stairwell, and exhaled. Perhaps, she thought as she gripped the handrail and descended at a child's pace, she *should* have stayed home today. It was ludicrous to think that she or anyone at Archer could simply go on about their business. Margo was still too alive in her memory to be dead. By the time Belinda reached the eighth floor, she was imagining she could smell the woman's overpowering perfume.

Too many elements in her life were spinning out of control. She longed for the unexciting existence she'd enjoyed before moving to Atlanta, with her future mapped out in tedious detail. Tears of frustration pricked at her eyelids, but she blinked them away. So many things were out of kilter, could she ever set them right?

As Belinda walked through the Archer reception area, conversations halted and people stared. She strode to her cubicle, her skin prickling from their unabashed fascination. Her head felt light—the lack of sleep and the stress of the previous day were catching up to her. When she entered her cube, she dropped into one of her mismatched chairs and breathed deeply until the stars subsided. Fatigue pulled at her shoulders, tears threatened. Her phone rang, startling her—an external call. She inhaled and picked up the receiver, determined to sound normal.

"Belinda Hennessey."

"Belinda, it's Julian."

Her pulse jumped. "Julian . . . hello."

"God, I heard about everything." From the background noise, she could tell he was calling from a cell phone. His voice rose and fell as if he were walking. "I tried to call you last night, but I couldn't get through."

"I stopped answering the phone," she murmured. "Reporters, you know." Then she caught her gaff. "I'm sorry, I didn't mean—"

"My colleagues can be annoying, I know. How are you holding up?"

"I'm okay, considering."

"I'm surprised to find you at work today."

"The police encouraged me to maintain my routine. I assume they've talked to you, too?"

"Yes, they questioned me about taking you home Monday night."

"I'm so sorry to have gotten you involved."

"It isn't your fault." His breathing was labored. "I can't imagine what you've been going through. Have the police been bullying you? Alexander?"

"Um, no." Her thoughts flicked to what Wade had said about Julian and his ex-wife, and she thought it best to change the subject. "Everyone will be much happier when Jim Newberry is found."

"He's the man who threatened your boss?"

"Yes."

"He has to turn up sooner or later."

"Where are you calling from? I heard you on the radio only a few minutes ago."

"I just landed. But I'm headed to Chattanooga for a couple of days of flight training. I wanted to check on you before I left."

Her first thought was that they were supposed to have had lunch this week. Her second thought was that she really didn't mind them not. Still, he had called. "That's very kind of you, Julian."

A shadow fell over her desk. When she looked up, her

mouth parted slightly at the sight of Wade Alexander in uniform standing in the opening of her cubicle. He looked . . . good. And irritated.

"If the police badger you about my involvement," Julian said, "let me know, and my boss will have it stopped."

"Um, no," she said hurriedly, holding up her finger to indicate to Wade that she'd be off the phone in one minute. "That won't be necessary."

"Just don't let them push you around, okay? I'll call you soon."

"Okay. Good-bye." She hung up and manufactured a smile for Wade. "Hello."

A vein had popped out in his temple. "Hardeman?"

"Yes. He was checking on me."

"That makes two of us. Did you get any rest last night?"

"No." And from the shadows under his eyes, she suspected he hadn't fared much better. "Has Jim Newberry been found?"

"No." He pushed his hand into his hair. "I hate to hit you with this first thing, but can you come back to Ms. Campbell's office? We want to go over a few details."

Belinda nodded and pushed to her feet—too quickly. The blood rushed to her head, and she swayed. Wade was there with a big steadying arm. "Easy. Have you had anything to eat this morning?"

She shook her head.

"Have a seat—I'll be back with some food and coffee."

She nodded gratefully. When he disappeared, she took a deep breath, picked up the phone, and dialed Juneau Archer's office. Rosemary answered.

"Rosemary, it's Belinda. Did Mr. Archer make it in?"

"No. He's not feeling well, probably because of the news. He said he'd try to be in tomorrow. I guess you'll want to talk to him about divvying up Margo's duties."

"Among other things."

"I'll make sure he knows."

"Thanks, Rosemary."

"Belinda." Rosemary's voice held an odd note. "I'm sorry all of this happened . . . to you. It wasn't supposed to be this way."

Alarm filtered through her chest. "Rosemary, what do you mean?"

"I . . . I know you came to Atlanta to start a new life. I'm sorry it's turning out so badly. You don't deserve this."

"Thank you, Rosemary." Belinda swallowed. "Your concern means a lot to me." She hung up, part of her relieved to be able to delay the discussion with Mr. Archer, part of her desperate to get it over with, all of her perplexed by Rosemary's behavior. Why did she have the feeling that the girls knew something she didn't know?

A rap sounded on her cubicle wall. Clancy Edmunds stood there, wide-eyed and twitchy. "Hi, Belinda."

"Hi, Clancy. I heard about the money—did it turn up?"

He shook his head. "I collected your payment last. I don't suppose you saw me drop it as I was leaving?"

"No."

He looked forlorn. "Oh, well, I guess the money is pretty small potatoes considering everything else that's going on. Listen, Belinda—" His face reddened. "All those things I said about Margo . . . you know I was just kidding, right?"

Ah. "Everyone says things they don't mean."

He leaned forward. "Do the police think that Jim Newberry came back to off Margo and stuff her in your trunk?"

"Um, I believe that's the general consensus."

"Do you know who's going to take over for Margo?"

"No. I'm going to meet with Mr. Archer as soon as he comes in to talk about transitioning things."

He tugged at his psychedelic tie. "Do you know if Margo had a chance to sign the performance evaluations before she . . . checked out?"

Belinda's eyebrows rose. "No, I don't."

His expression was sheepish. "Well, I thought maybe you could suggest to Mr. Archer that evaluations be, um, revisited."

"I can't make any promises, but I'll mention it to Mr. Archer."

Wade appeared with a brown paper bag and two coffees, and Clancy perked up.

She bit back a smile. "Clancy Edmunds, this is Lieutenant Alexander."

Wade inclined his head. "Mr. Edmunds."

Clancy crossed his fidgety arms. "Will the police be here all day?"

"Looks like it, sir. We'll be getting prints from everyone. And between the theft and the murder, the CEO has requested that all employees submit to a polygraph exam."

"A l-lie detector test?"

Wade nodded. "Considering that two employees have died, we agree that it's a good idea. Examiners are setting up in the conference room."

Belinda's throat constricted. Would pervasive ethical guilt skew the results?

"That's against my civil rights," Clancy sputtered, then he squinted. "Isn't it?"

Wade gave a little shrug. "No one can force you to take the test, sir."

"Ah-hah—but if I don't, I'll look guilty!"

The man's melodrama might have been comical if Belinda hadn't been thinking the same thoughts.

Wade set the coffees and the food on Belinda's desk. "I suppose an unwillingness to take the polygraph could be perceived as having something to hide. The money that's missing—wasn't it stolen from your desk?"

Clancy's Adam's apple bobbed. "Yes."

"Was it common knowledge that you kept cash there?"

He shrugged. "If there was something going on, a pool, or a collection for flowers, I typically took care of it."

"Would Jim Newberry know there was money in your desk?"

"I suppose so."

"We'll need a list of people who had access to the drawer where you kept the money bag to match against the prints that were lifted yesterday."

"That's easy—I have a key, Brita Wheeling, and Carole Marchand."

Belinda frowned. "Carole?"

"In case she has checks or anything valuable to deliver and no one is here to take it."

Wade withdrew a notebook and made notes. "The money bag was taken?"

"No, just the cash. I told all of this to another officer yesterday. Tom, I think was his name—blond, nice eyes."

Wade looked up, then returned the notebook to his pocket. "I'll get with Tom for all the details."

"Anything else, Officer?"

"Not now."

Clancy started to turn, then snapped his fingers. "Belinda, I came by to remind you that your sofa will be delivered this evening. Sorry about the timing, but the truck gets loaded for a week's worth of deliveries. Will you be home?"

"I plan to be."

"Good. I need to check with Rosemary, too." The man gave Wade an appreciative once-over, waved toodle-loo, then disappeared around the corner.

She smiled at Wade. "I think he likes you."

One dark eyebrow went up. "He's not my type."

The words "but you are" hung in the air between them. Her smile froze.

"Your eye looks better," he said.

"Thanks, it feels better."

He opened the bag and withdrew a bagel. "Cream cheese okay?"

She reached for the food. "Perfect. Thank you."

He sat in her pea green visitor's chair, pulled a lid off the other coffee, and drank from the steaming cup. His big frame took up most of the available space in the cubicle, pressing on her breathing room. His gray eyes were clear and alert, framed with dark lashes and expressive eyebrows. His profile was jutting and imperfect, his skin ruddy from razor burn. The man emanated a physical intensity that set her on edge. He seemed unbridled and . . . hazardous.

Hazardous in a "reorder a woman's life" kind of way.

"You okay?" he asked. "You look like you just had a scary thought."

She blinked. "Any updates on Jim Newberry?"

"No. But he has family in Columbus, Georgia, and Gainesville, Florida, so we have a lot of places to look."

She bit into the bagel and chewed slowly. Her jaws ached at first, reminding her how long it had been since she'd eaten anything solid. The women's magazines were missing out on the Find-a-Dead-Body diet. "What now, Lieutenant?"

"Now the investigation keeps moving forward. It'll take a long time to question everyone, and even longer to assimilate all the information. By the way, I had a chat with your neighbor last night."

"Perry?"

"Yeah. I can see now why you were hiding from him. You said he pestered you, but did you ever feel threatened?"

"No, but I've only talked to the man in the yard in broad daylight."

"He has a record."

She stopped mid-chew. "For what?"

"One count of Peeping Tom a year ago. He got off with a fine. You should consider blinds for the bay window in your living room."

She laughed. "The most racy thing he's likely to see is my cat cleaning herself."

One eyebrow lifted. "Really?"

Belinda swallowed carefully to keep from drowning on her mouthful of coffee. "You said I was needed back at Margo's office?"

He checked his watch and stood. "Actually, I should

leave to look into some other matters. Detectives Salyers and Truett are back there, they'll handle everything."

A foul day was suddenly looking even less palatable. "You're leaving?"

He nodded, then a casual smile curved his mouth. "Actually, since you're going to be home tonight, I thought I'd stop by to install a security alarm."

The day improved a smidgen. "Do you think that's necessary?"

"Humor me," he said.

Who was she to withhold humor from a man who so rarely smiled? Belinda pursed her mouth and nodded. "I suppose that would be acceptable."

Chapter 25

"How do they expect us to get this ink off our fingers?" Libby asked, frowning at her ruined manicure as she slid into the backseat.

"I don't think they care," Rosemary offered from the driver's seat.

"Well," Carole said, turning in her seat, "after being fingerprinted and being given a lie detector test, I'll never complain again about going to the gynecologist."

Belinda fastened her seat belt in silence. She had been spared the fingerprinting, but the polygraph exam had been plenty unnerving. Nearly every question they'd asked her, she could have answered, "It depends." Throughout, the examiner had prompted her many times to reply with a simple yes or no. She was relatively sure she had failed even the part where they had asked for her name.

Detectives Salyers and Truett had made her walk through her last meeting with Margo in excruciating detail, exchanging cop looks when she'd admitted she had pushed her way past Brita, although she was sure the woman had already informed them of her insistence. But she'd stubbornly refused to discuss the details of their meeting until she could talk to Mr. Archer in private—she owed the man that much. "It's confidential company business," she'd told them. "For now, I can only promise you it has nothing to do with Margo's murder."

Their expressions had been dubious and dubiouser.

Meanwhile, coworkers had cast suspicious glances her way and whispered behind her back. Some people had actually appeared to be frightened of her. When she'd gone to the copier room to make duplicates of quarterly corporate tax forms (she was attempting to get *some* work done), Martin Derlinger would look only as high as her elbows.

The presence of the police had set everyone on edge. Employees had stood in clusters around their cubicles, making predictions about their jobs, the murder, the theft. Wild rumors had surfaced—the most bizarre being that Margo had been dismembered in her office and transported to Belinda's car trunk limb by limb.

Yilk.

It was surreal, and the frenzied atmosphere in the office had reached a fever pitch by quitting time. If ever Mr. Archer needed to step up to resume the leadership role, it was now. In his father's absence, Tal Archer had made the rounds, presumably to calm fears about the future of the company, but his green pallor and skittish body language had only served to push concerns higher. Belinda figured his behavior had had something to do with what Rosemary had said about his drug use and the proximity of so many uniforms.

The tense mood, Belinda noted, seemed to have followed them from the office to the car. They all kept to their respective corners. Nail nibbling and sigh heaving prevailed. She herself had chewed her thumbnail down to the nub after Carole had called that afternoon to tell her the Payton contracts were missing.

"How can they be missing?" she'd asked.

"Hank doesn't know where they are, but he's pretty sure they weren't delivered."

"Pretty sure? I'm from Ohio, Carole—how sure is 'pretty sure'?"

"You don't have to get testy."

"I'm sorry. If Hank says they weren't delivered, I'll take his word for it. But does he have any idea where the envelope could be?"

"Um, no. But he's working on it," Carole had assured her cheerfully, then she'd lowered her voice. "Is this still top secret?"

"Yes."

Belinda now closed her eyes. Not only did she have to confess her unethical behavior to Mr. Archer but she also might have to explain the absence of the contracts.

"The memorial service for Margo will be held Friday," Rosemary said, breaking the silence.

"Who on earth arranged it?" Libby asked.

"I did." Rosemary shifted in her seat but kept her gaze on the traffic ahead.

Libby glanced sideways at Belinda and raised her eyebrows.

"Did the police find her relatives?" Belinda asked.

"There's only an ex-husband in Alaska, who didn't want anything to do with the burial, and a great-niece in New Mexico who's never met her."

"An ex-husband?" Carole asked. "Wow, Margo was married once."

"Briefly, when she was young," Rosemary said.

"Are you all going to the memorial service?" Carole asked over her shoulder.

A guilty silence descended.

"Margo didn't go to Jeanie's service," Libby muttered.

"I'll bet Margo would've been more generous with time off for Jeanie's memorial service if she'd known the next one would be hers," Carole said matter-of-factly.

Sympathy barbed through Belinda for her boss, who seemed to have been alone in the world. She swallowed—was it a glimpse into her own future? Margo alienated people with her abrasive personality. According to Vince and Libby, *she* alienated people through detachment. If loneliness was the end, wasn't the means insignificant?

They were a morose lot during the remainder of the ride home. There was no mention of the book, of Rosemary's secret appointments, of Libby's shopping withdrawal, or of Carole's psychic. Everyone seemed to turn inward with their own thoughts and problems. Belinda certainly had ample torment for the long drive. By the time they pulled up to her town house, she was battling a thumping headache and a hearty cry. She said good-bye and climbed out. When she lifted her hand for a wave, she frowned at their turned heads. Was it her paranoia, or had the women engaged in conversation the minute her door closed?

Her thoughts were diverted by the slamming of a car door across the street. A well-dressed woman jogged in her direction. "Ms. Hennessey—Joann Cameron, *Atlanta Journal-Constitution*. I'd like to talk to you about the murder of Margo Campbell."

"Please leave," Belinda said, then turned to stride toward her front door. This she did not need.

The woman galloped up beside her. "Ms. Hennessey, is it true that local traffic reporter Julian Hardeman is your boyfriend?"

Belinda gritted her teeth. "No, it isn't true. Julian and I are mere acquaintances."

"A source tells me that you and he and your boss were involved in a love triangle."

She stared, agape. "Your source is spinning outrageous lies. Julian is not involved in this situation."

"My source tells me his car"—she pulled a notebook out of her purse and ran her finger down a page of notes—"a 2002 dark blue Audi was spotted at the home of the deceased the night before she was killed."

Belinda squinted. "Sunday night?"

"Yes."

Belinda scoffed. "That's impossible. Julian was stranded in Raleigh that night because of the storm. He didn't return to Atlanta until Monday afternoon."

"I checked the flight records myself," the woman said. "Mr. Hardeman left for Raleigh Saturday morning and returned later that same day."

Belinda shook her head. "The records are inaccurate. Mr. Hardeman called me from Raleigh Sunday afternoon."

"Do you know for a fact he was calling from Raleigh?"

Belinda's breath caught in her chest. "I asked you to leave." She fumbled in her purse for her door key.

"Ms. Hennessey, I'm trying to help. Don't you want to see the murderer caught?"

Belinda found the key and shoved it into the lock. "Need I remind you that the police are still looking for the prime suspect?"

"Prime suspect, or convenient scapegoat?"

"This interview is over. Good-bye." Belinda pushed open the door and closed it behind her as quickly as possible. With her back pressed against the door in the dimly lit foyer, she took great calming breaths, replaying the woman's words in her head.

Was it possible that Julian was involved with Margo? She scoured her mind for details. Margo's phone call Sunday morning . . . it *had* sounded as if someone was in the background. Margo Campbell was definitely the kind of woman who would have gotten a thrill out of putting her subordinate to work for the day while trouncing with the man she was pseudo-involved with.

And Julian? Well, she hadn't deluded herself that Julian had fallen head over heels in love with her—indeed, it was his cavalier attitude about sex that had drawn her to him. He certainly could have been calling her from his cell phone that Sunday. In fact, when he'd driven her home Monday night, he'd made a comment about that morning's traffic that had seemed like firsthand knowledge.

Cold fear washed over her. What if Margo's last-minute office call had been Julian? He could have gone to her boss's office while she'd been tripping down the back stairwell. What if he and Margo had argued and he'd killed her? He could have carried the body to his car trunk to dispose of later. A recollection made her gasp—the black gym bag he had been carrying and had left at the gym—had it contained incriminating evidence? Maybe whatever he'd used to smother Margo?

Her throat convulsed as more pieces tumbled into place. The errand he'd said he'd had in the general direction of her town house—had it been to dump Margo's body? Alpharetta was known for pockets of woods and sporadic open fields between dense subdivisions. He had insisted on waiting while she'd gone inside to talk to Libby. The driveway had been dark—had he transferred the body from his trunk to hers while she and Libby had chatted?

She covered her mouth with her hand—was it possible that she had been riding with a killer? That he had set her up?

Belinda dropped her briefcase and purse on the parquet flooring and gulped for air. That lady reporter seemed to know a lot about Julian. Had she already left? Belinda hurried to the living room to look out the bay window, and came face to face with . . . a man's face.

She opened her mouth and screamed loud enough to make the man scream back. When oxygen reached her brain, she realized the man was Perry, and her vital signs slowly returned to normal, only to skyrocket again with anger.

"Perry!" she shouted. "What are you doing?"

"Are you okay?" he yelled back. "Why did you scream?"

"I—" Why was she standing here yelling to the man through the glass? She stalked to the door and threw it open. The Cameron woman's car was nowhere in sight.

Perry turned toward her, his hands palm up. "What?"

She gritted her teeth. "*What* are you doing looking in my window?"

"I was just seeing if you were home."

"Have you ever heard of a doorbell?"

"I didn't think you'd answer."

She narrowed her eyes at him. "Go home, Perry."

"I just wanted to say I'm sorry about that little boss lady of yours winding up in your trunk. Do you need anything? My cousin Leonard is a fancy-pants lawyer."

"No thanks, Perry."

"Are you sure I can't do anything for you?"

"There is one thing," she said with her hand on the doorknob.

He looked hopeful. "What?"

"Stop looking in my *window*!" She glared at him, then opened her door, walked inside, and locked the dead bolt behind her. She exhaled slowly until some of the tension drained from her shoulders and she was able to think more clearly. She had probably overreacted to the reporter's information about Julian. Jim Newberry would be in custody soon, and his arrest would no doubt close the investigation. For all she knew, the woman could be a rival reporter with ulterior motives for implicating Julian.

"Downey, I'm home," she called.

Nothing.

Deciding that her day and outlook would improve dramatically with the removal of her panty hose, Belinda climbed the stairs to exchange her slacks and jacket for jeans and a button-up shirt. She told herself she had selected the yellow shirt because it was in the front of her closet, not because it was a flattering color for her skin and hair. She wasn't doing anything special in anticipation of Wade Alexander's arrival. After all, the man was coming to work, not to . . . play.

At the last minute, she traded the yellow shirt for a white T-shirt with a small coffee stain. There.

She walked down the stairs, retrieved her briefcase and purse from the floor, and carried them to the kitchen counter. There were six messages on her machine, five of them from reporters, and one from the auto body shop saying they could work her in tomorrow if she could bring in her car before noon.

A nostalgic sigh for her beloved clover green Civic escaped her, but the call reminded her of a chore she'd been putting off. She dragged out the phone book and called a car rental place that would bring the vehicle to her. She arranged to rent the cheapest thing available with four wheels and a standard transmission, and to have it delivered tomorrow evening after 6:30.

She had barely hung up the phone when her doorbell rang. Downey materialized and beat her there, ears piqued as if she were expecting a tuna to come calling. Belinda checked the peephole to find Wade standing expectantly. She attributed the increase of her pulse to the fact that she would have to relay the details surrounding Julian, no matter how unfounded they might be.

When she opened the door, he looked distressingly good in faded jeans and a gray Atlanta PD T-shirt. He smiled and held up a white plastic bag emitting superb odors. "Hope you like fish sandwiches."

She looked down to see Downey's whiskers convulsing.

"We do," Belinda said. "Come on in."

In the other hand he carried a six-pack of bottled beer, no doubt in deference to her empty refrigerator. The man thought of everything. He wiped his feet on the tiny rug in the entryway (her mom would love him), then walked to the kitchen to deposit everything on the table. She foraged for plates, utensils and a bottle opener, rebelling against the implication of sharing another meal and possibly enjoying it.

"Something wrong?" he asked.

She walked back to the table and set down the plates. "A reporter was waiting for me when I got home."

He bent over to offer a wedge of deep-fried fish to Downey. The cat snagged it and carried it off to devour. "Were you able to get rid of them?" he asked.

She sat down and spread a paper napkin on her lap. "Yes. But not before the woman implied that Julian and Margo were . . . involved."

He pulled out the chair adjacent to hers and sat. "Sleeping together?"

She shrugged. "She said Julian spent Sunday night at Margo's."

He opened two bottles of beer, then lifted one to his mouth. "I can't say I'm surprised, but it appears that you are."

Belinda drank from the bottle and swallowed. She hadn't drunk beer in ages. Vince preferred mixed drinks, and she wasn't a connoisseur of any kind of alcohol. "I'm not surprised that he would be involved with someone else—I mean, with someone." She took another drink to cover the slip. "But if it's true, then he lied to me, and I'm not sure why he would think that was necessary."

"Maybe to cover his ass when the woman turned up dead."

She closed her eyes.

"Belinda, this is serious. Two women are dead, and both of them were involved with Hardeman. Tell me what you're not telling me."

She opened her eyes and told him everything she recalled about the night Julian had driven her home. "I wasn't holding back any details before, I just didn't have a reason to remember them, or to think they were relevant."

Wade's face grew more grave. "You don't know what was in the gym bag?"

"No, it could have been workout gear."

"Do you remember seeing any scratches on his face or hands?"

"No, but he was wearing driving gloves."

"When Hardeman called you at work this morning, did he say anything out of the ordinary?"

"He was concerned that the police were hassling me . . . because of him. He implied that, um, you might try to make something of his driving me home that night." She took another drink from the bottle and swallowed slowly.

"Anything else?"

"He said he was going to be in Chattanooga for a couple of days of flight training. But the trip must have been last-minute, because when we talked on Sunday he asked me if we could have lunch sometime this week."

A muscle worked in Wade's jaw as he stood. "I need to make a phone call."

"Are you going to sic the detectives on him?"

He frowned. "Yes."

"Don't you think you should wait to see if Jim Newberry is found?"

There was that muscle again. "Why don't you go ahead and eat. I'll just be a few minutes."

"I'll wait."

He nodded, then walked down the hall and, she presumed, into the living room. The sound of his lowered voice reached her, but she couldn't make out what he was saying. She sipped the beer, which had begun to taste rather good, then caught sight of Vince's envelope propped against the fruit bowl.

Open me. I could be a letter begging you to come back, where there are no dead bodies or missing contracts or endless commutes.

She picked up the envelope, but when she heard Wade's returning footsteps, she turned it facedown on the table.

Wade gave her a too-cheerful smile. "Okay, let's eat."

The fish sandwiches were good, and she was ravenous. In fact, she and Downey both made pigs out of themselves, although Wade still managed to outpace them. She told him about taking the polygraph exam and the general mood around the office.

"No offense, but it seems like a fairly crazy place to work. Do you like it?"

"I was looking forward to the challenge of growing the company to the point of taking it public."

"And now?"

She shrugged. "I've decided to take things one day at a time."

"Good plan."

"So what about you?"

"What about me?"

"Truett and Salyers were riding you hard about taking some kind of exam."

He shifted in the seat. "The detective's exam."

"You're not interested?"

"Not right now." He drained his second beer, then stood. "Guess I'd better get that security alarm installed."

Belinda blinked at the sudden change in subject, then began to clear their meal. Downey followed Wade through the hallway like . . . like she used to trail Vince. Belinda smirked. Fickle feline. Feelings didn't evaporate just like that, not if they had been true to begin with. She glanced at the facedown envelope and bit into her lip.

"Belinda," Wade called from the door. "I believe your couch is here."

She hurriedly dumped the trash, then went outside to guide the delivery men. Despite everything else, she allowed herself to be a tiny bit excited about finally having a new piece of furniture. Two burly men removed the sofa from a truck and carried it inside. She signed for it, then pulled away the plastic, revealing the deep red leather.

Wade was attaching some kind of sensor thingy to the bay window. He wore a tool belt, and nicely. Downey wound between his feet, rubbing her head against his legs and purring like a vibrator.

Shameless pussy.

Wade nodded toward the sofa. "Nice."

"Thank you."

"Looks comfortable. Does it unfold to make a bed?"

She coughed—probably cat hair in the air—then nodded.

"I'll be needing some new furniture soon," he said. "The renovations to my den are almost finished."

"What did you do to it?"

"The big jobs were refinishing the wood floors and replacing the crown molding."

"Wow. When do you have time for that?"

He looked up from what he was doing and shrugged, then looked back down, and she understood—it was what he had thrown himself into when his marriage had dissolved. She had done the same thing with Kraft macaroni and cheese dinners.

"What are you doing to my window?"

"Since these don't open, I'm installing a glass shattering sensor. If the glass is broken, an alarm will sound there." He pointed up to a white box the size of a deck of cards sitting on the landing of her stairs, against the wall. "I'll put motion sensors on the two windows in the kitchen."

"I think you're overreacting."

He leveled his gray gaze on her. "I hope so."

There was that Southern I'll-take-care-of-you attitude again. She tried to rally her feminist defenses, but they were cowering behind her ovaries. To be honest, it felt kind of good to be fussed over. "What am I supposed to do if the alarm sounds?"

"Lock yourself in your bathroom and call 9-1-1. Do you have anything to protect yourself with?"

"The detectives took Big Daddy."

"Oh, right." He grinned. "The gift from your girlfriends."

"What would you suggest?"

"A big dog that barks."

She pointed to his feet. "How about a little cat that bites?"

"It's not quite the same."

Belinda made a rueful noise. "You're going to hurt Downey's feelings. She thinks you like her." She lowered herself to the couch for a trial sit, and sighed as the leather cushions hugged her.

"I do like her," he said, but he wasn't looking at the cat.

She squirmed farther down into the cushions, thinking what a great spot this would be if her television were working. And if Margo were alive.

"You really should cover this window," he said. "It's like a huge glass door. Anyone can see in."

"I know, I had to scare Perry off when I got home."

He frowned. "You should have let me shoot him in the food court."

"He was just curious about all the commotion. I think he's harmless."

"If you see him lurking around again, call the police and file a report."

"Yes, sir."

Wade gave the sensor a final inspection, then walked over to the couch and, after removing his tool belt, sat down on the couch next to her. He draped both arms along the back and made a satisfied noise as he settled into the creaky cushions. He turned his head and smiled. "Very nice."

With his leg pressed against hers, she could only nod and smile. Downey sought to join them, but Belinda shooed her away. "No," she said in her best master voice. "You'll scratch the leather."

"Aluminum foil," Wade said.

"Hm?" He was so close that she could feel his breath against her temple.

"Put aluminum foil on the couch when you're not using it. Cats hate the way it feels and sounds, so when she jumps on it, she'll get a bad association with the couch."

"Oh," she murmured, looking up to meet his gaze. "You know a lot about . . . cats."

"Not so much," he said, and she could tell by the set of his jaw that he was feeling the same prickly awareness that she was feeling. Maybe the smell of new leather was an aphrodisiac.

She swallowed audibly. "So . . . where do we go from here?"

He turned and leaned in close. Her breath caught as he cupped his hand under her jaw and made his approach. In a split second, she registered so many details about his face—smoky gray eyes, shadowy square jaw, determined mouth. She managed to inhale just before his lips touched hers. The pressure was light at first, but within a couple of seconds, the kiss ignited, and soon they were going at it like a couple of teenagers. She kept waiting for the wrongness to set in, for the unfamiliarity of his touch to disturb her, but the overriding thought in her brain was that this man knew how to kiss. And his intensity alone hinted at other skills in his repertoire.

She had mentally settled in for a nice long session of necking on the couch when he suddenly pulled away. While she recovered, he stood and pulled his hand down his face. "I'm sorry about that."

He was? She touched her tender mouth.

"If I don't behave myself," he said in a thick voice, "Detective Salyers will yank me from this case. So, for now, we can't 'go' anywhere."

She pressed her bruised lips together. "I meant . . . where does the *investigation* go from here?"

His color rose. "Oh."

The phone rang, thank God. She jumped up from her couch to answer, hoping it wasn't another reporter with disturbing details. "Hello?" She stared at the large impression her behind had left in the couch and willed it to fill in quickly.

"Hello, dear, it's Mother."

Of course it was. "Hi, Mom."

"Are you alone, or is your friend there?"

She glanced at Wade and wet her lips. "What friend would that be, Mom?"

"You know, your *man* friend."

"Oh, *him*." She watched as Wade reattached his tool belt. "Yes, he's here doing . . . handiwork."

Wade arched his eyebrow.

Her mother partially covered the mouthpiece. "Franklin, he's *handy*." She came back on the line. "Your father wants to know if he knows anything about cars."

Wade walked away from her toward the kitchen. "Tell Dad I don't know. Where are you calling from?"

"North Platte, Nebraska. The scenery is absolutely lovely."

"Are you taking a lot of pictures?" Her mother was a notoriously bad photographer.

Barbara Hennessey sighed. "Yes, but I just discovered that somehow the camera lens cover has been on from Indianapolis to Omaha."

Somehow.

"Did your sofa arrive, dear?"

"Yes, just a few minutes ago, in fact."

"Is it still red?"

"Um, yes."

Another sigh sounded. "I suppose there are worse things that could happen."

If her mother only knew.

"I'd better let you get back to your guest. I'll call you in another couple of days."

"Okay. Give my love to Dad. Talk to you soon." Belinda hung up the phone and shook her head. Her poor dad had probably heard enough about her red couch to make him want to drive the Buick off a bridge.

"Finished," Wade said, walking back through the hallway, wiping his hands on the tail of his T-shirt.

She dragged her gaze from the glimpses of his planed stomach. "That was quick."

"They're contact sensors, so don't forget and accidentally open your windows."

"I won't." She followed him to the door, almost tripping over Downey, who was trying to get there first.

At the door he turned. "Call me if . . . anything."

"Okay." She nodded. "Thanks for the kiss—I mean *fish*. Thanks for the fish. Sandwiches. And the beer. And the security alarm." She couldn't shut up.

"No problem," he said with a little smile. "I'll most likely see you tomorrow—about the investigation."

"Of course."

He left, and she closed the door before Downey could escape. The cat meowed and circled in place. Belinda sighed, scooped the forlorn feline into her arms, and carried her, wriggling, to the couch. "Don't get your hopes up, old girl," she murmured, stroking her pet's dark fur to calm both of them. "We humans call it 'being on the rebound.' And when both humans are on the rebound, there's another word for it: *doomed*."

Chapter 26

Belinda descended the stairs to the eighth floor alone, relieved to be free of the women's company after a tense morning car pool. Terse exchanges and rueful glances convinced her that something was going on between Libby and Carole and Rosemary that excluded her, probably something to do with Rosemary's secret appointments. But frankly, she didn't want to ask questions on the chance that she might be expected to answer some of her own, and she didn't have the strength.

Wade's kiss and her reaction to it had dominated her concentration for most of the evening. Then her thoughts had switched to Julian and his possible involvement in the murder, and if there was a connection between Jeanie's death and Margo's. Around midnight she had begun to obsess over her part in the Payton acquisition. She needed to talk to Mr. Archer, but she planned to stall, hoping the missing contracts would turn up.

Around 2:00 A.M., all the events of the past few days had gathered to press upon her mind like a vise. Hoping a cup of herbal tea would help her sleep, she had tied on her robe and walked downstairs by the illumination of strategic night-lights (for Downey's sake, she'd told herself when she'd bought them).

The sheet that she'd hung over the bay window had fallen onto the floor, allowing light from the dusk-to-dawn streetlamp to stream in. As she had walked by, the hair had stood up on her arms—she could have sworn someone had been at the window, peering in. Perry? She blinked, and whatever she'd thought she'd seen was gone. She'd laughed at herself and rehung the sheet. Instead of preparing tea, though, she'd curled up on the new couch that she'd covered with two quilts in deference to Downey's claws until she could buy a couple of rolls of aluminum foil. She hadn't worried about oversleeping because she hadn't thought she'd be able to sleep.

When Downey had licked her awake, the alarm on her clock upstairs had been sounding, her brain had been gummy, and her limbs leaden. The urge to lie there until Christmas had been appealing, but the sensation had been so similar to the way she'd felt the days following the wedding that it had frightened her into mobility. That, and the knowledge that the car pool was coming.

By simply showing up, the girls had saved her from slipping into that murky place where she could wallow in the futility of Why me?, so at first she hadn't minded the quiet in the car. But after an hour of listening to their prickly silence and a stand-in traffic reporter on the radio, she was ready to implode.

Hopefully today they would find Jim Newberry, and the nightmare would end.

Well, one of the nightmares—there was still the little matter of the missing contracts.

She opened the stairwell door, strode into the reception area, and blinked at the welcoming party—Detectives Salyers and Truett, and a dour-faced woman she didn't know. Wade Alexander stood in the wings, his expression regrettable, not unlike after he'd kissed her.

"Good morning, Ms. Hennessey," Truett said.

"Good . . . morning."

"Where are your carpooling buddies?"

She shifted her briefcase to her other hand. "They rode the elevator. Why?"

"We found Jim Newberry."

Her pulse raced. "And?"

"And he has an alibi for his whereabouts after leaving here Monday afternoon."

Dread washed over her just as the elevator doors opened and the women alighted. They came up short and stood expectantly.

"And since Jim Newberry didn't kill Margo Campbell," he said to all of them, "we need to have a little pow-wow with your car pool and clear up a few *inconsistencies*."

She glanced at her friends, and the expressions on their pale faces sent a rock to her stomach. What was it Libby had once said about lies?

"Lies are the glue that holds relationships together. We lie to our spouses, to our kids, to our ministers, and to ourselves."

Belinda swallowed. And to our friends?

"Let's get started," Truett said, pulling a swivel chair to the end of the boardroom table. Libby sat to his right, and Rosemary to his left. Next to Rosemary sat Carole, then Detective Salyers. Across from Salyers sat Lieutenant Alexander. Belinda was wedged between him and Libby. The unknown woman sat away from the group, near the other end of the table. Everyone looked as if they wanted to be elsewhere.

"I'd like to introduce Ms. Greer, Fulton County assistant district attorney. Ms. Greer is here as an observer."

Ms. Greer nodded solemnly.

Belinda was quivering in her Aerosoles. A D.A.'s presence could not be a good thing. She had convinced herself that Jim Newberry had murdered Margo . . . eliminating him as a suspect tore the lid off an entire barrel of worms.

"Lieutenant Alexander has been on the case from the beginning, so we asked him to be here out of professional courtesy."

Detective Salyers's tiny smirk didn't go unnoticed by Belinda. The comfort she took from Wade's dominating presence next to her was negated by the fact that he was privy to so many nooks and crannies of her life—and before this interview ended, was likely to discover more.

Truett slurped coffee from a Styrofoam cup and pushed a button on a tape recorder at his elbow. He recited the date and time and those present. "First, let me say that you ladies are here voluntarily and are not under arrest. You may refuse to answer questions at any time, and you may request an attorney at any time."

An attorney? How about her mommy?

"Ladies, I got a dead woman in a trunk, and not a whole hell of a lot of answers." Truett gave them a tight smile. "And the polygraph exams indicate that all of you are hiding something about the circumstances surrounding the murder."

Belinda's heart pounded in her ears.

"Since all of you had access to the car where the body was found, I thought it would be best if we sat down and talked through Monday's events again, nice and slow like." He glanced all around, pausing a few seconds on each of them. "Now, then—Ms. Hennessey, you drove the car pool Monday, with Ms. Janes and Ms. Marchand."

"Yes."

"Ms. Burchett, you drove separately."

"That's correct."

"We'll get back to that later."

Rosemary blanched but remained silent.

"Ms. Hennessey, you said you parked your car on the eighth floor. Did you move your car during the course of the day?"

"No."

"I understand that in the afternoon, you were called to Margo Campbell's office for a performance evaluation."

"Yes."

"And your evaluation went well. You had been offered the CFO position?"

When the other women looked her way, she squirmed. "Yes. Margo said she would make the announcement when she returned from vacation."

"But before you left her office, Jim Newberry forced his way in."

"Yes."

"After Newberry was taken away, then what?"

Belinda shrugged. "I left Margo's office, made a few phone calls."

"Did you run into Libby Janes in the ladies' room?"

Her memory clicked. "Yes."

He looked at his notes. "A witness said she went into the ladies' room around 4:00 and that you and Ms. Janes were in the same stall. She recognized your shoes."

She looked at Libby, her cheeks flaming. Libby's were pinker than usual, too.

"I was upset about something," Libby said, "and Belinda was being a friend."

"What were you upset about?" Detective Salyers asked.

"My husband and I had been arguing about finances," Libby said quickly.

Belinda bit into her lower lip. From what she remembered, Libby had been upset about her evaluation, but she supposed it all led back to the fact that her husband was leaning on her about bringing in more money.

Truett turned to her. "Ms. Hennessey, tell us again what happened at the end of the day."

"I wanted to talk to Margo about something before she left for vacation, so I asked Libby if she would drive home and let me pick up my car later, and she agreed."

He looked down at his notes. "Ms. Janes, you stated that Ms. Hennessey seemed 'flustered' at the time."

"I wasn't flustered," Belinda said with a frown.

"You were shaking like a dog's hind leg," Libby declared softly.

That was vivid.

Truett cocked an eyebrow. "It's time to tell us, Ms. Hennessey, what was so important that you had to talk to Ms. Campbell."

Belinda squirmed. "It's confidential. I must discuss it with Mr. Archer first."

His eyes narrowed. "As long as we can sit in."

"F-fine."

"So skip to the part where you were getting ready to leave. You said Ms. Campbell received a phone call. An internal call, you could tell by the ring."

"That's right, although I don't know who it was. I walked out of her office and left by the back stairs, and fell. I went to the lounge to clean up, and you know what happened from there."

"You ran into Julian Hardeman."

"Yes."

"We talked to Julian Hardeman before he left town," Detective Salyers said. "He said you were agitated when he saw you."

Surprise and anger barbed through her that Julian would say something to implicate her further—although she'd done a good job of implicating herself all by her lonesome. "I had just taken a bad spill, so perhaps I was jittery."

"What is the nature of your relationship with Mr. Hardeman?"

Not here. "I told you—we're acquaintances."

"That's not what he said."

Next to her, Wade shifted in his chair. Belinda set her jaw. "We had lunch twice."

"And a sexual encounter in the sauna in the bottom floor of this building."

This could only be better if her mother were here. "I don't see what any of this has to do with the murder."

"Because you told your friends here that Ms. Campbell might have been jealous over your relationship with Julian."

She glanced around the table. "I didn't say that."

"What Belinda said," piped in Carole in a squeaky voice, "was that Margo saw her in the gym with Julian and made a snide remark."

"Regarding Julian Hardeman's taste in women?"

Carole nodded.

Salyers tapped her pen on the notepad in front of her. "Didn't that make you angry, Ms. Hennessey?"

"No, because I knew it was Margo's nature to be cutting and because I wasn't as involved with Julian Hardeman as she assumed."

Truett grunted. "Ms. Campbell wasn't a very nice person, was she?"

Belinda decided to let that one go unanswered.

"Ms. Janes," he said, turning in his chair, "let's get back to you. Why didn't you and Ms. Marchand simply wait Monday afternoon until Ms. Hennessey had finished her discussion with Ms. Campbell so you could all ride home together?"

Libby splayed her manicured hands. "Belinda said she needed to meet with Margo and told us to go on. I assumed it was going to take a while."

"And you had something planned that you wanted to do?"

Libby looked at Belinda with a flash of accusation. "Yes."

"What was it, exactly?"

Libby's mouth tightened. "Carole and I were concerned about Rosemary." She gave Rosemary an apologetic look. "We were afraid you were sick and not telling us, so . . . we were going to follow you to your appointment."

Rosemary's eyes widened. "Follow me?"

"But we didn't get the chance. Carole was late getting to the car—"

"I was only a little late," Carole interjected, wagging her finger. "But the car wasn't where it had been parked. I waited there for maybe twenty minutes, then Libby drives up, saying she'd been waiting for me on the bottom floor."

Truett leveled his gaze on Libby. "Is that true, Ms. Janes?"

Libby fidgeted. "I figured I had time to drive to Bloomingdale's for a quick look around. They're having a big sale," she added in her defense.

"Did you buy anything?"

She didn't answer.

"We're going to check, Ms. Janes."

"A pillow," she whispered. "Goose down, thirty percent off."

Belinda's mouth went dry.

"Why buy only one pillow?" Salyers asked. "Why not a set?"

"It was for a daybed in our bonus room."

"And I assume you can produce that pillow?"

Libby wrung her hands. "I promised my husband I would stop spending so much money. I was so ashamed of myself, I threw the pillow in a Dumpster at the mall before I came back to pick up Carole."

The detectives exchanged disbelieving glances.

"When you returned to the parking garage," Truett said, "Ms. Burchett had already left?"

Libby nodded.

"Ms. Burchett, what time did you leave the parking garage?"

"Around 6:00."

"Where did you go?"

She pursed her mouth, as if she were physically trapping the words.

"Does it have anything to do with your probation?"

Belinda's gut clenched. Libby and Carole looked shocked.

"Ms. Burchett?" he repeated.

"Yes," she said softly.

"For everyone's information, Ms. Burchett here is on probation for a count of involuntary manslaughter for killing her husband, Stanley Burchett."

"I didn't kill him," she murmured, her eyes shimmering.

"The M.E.'s report says he was smothered with a pillow."

"He rolled over and was too weak to lift his head," Rosemary said. "It was a blessing."

"You were supposed to be watching him."

"I left the room to prepare a bath for him. When I came back, he was already gone."

"You accepted probation."

"To relieve some of my own guilt for not being there," she whispered. "And I've done everything I've been asked to do, including seeing a therapist every few weeks."

Carole reached over to squeeze the older woman's hand. "Why didn't you tell us?"

"There was no point," she said.

"Maybe you didn't tell anyone because you were afraid you'd lose your job," Truett said.

Rosemary's mouth tightened, but she remained silent.

"Did Ms. Campbell know about the probation, Ms. Burchett?"

Rosemary hesitated, then nodded.

"When did she find out?"

"I . . . don't know."

"When did she first bring it to your attention that she knew?"

"Monday, during my performance evaluation."

Belinda's breath caught.

"Did she fire you?" Truett pressed.

"No." Rosemary spoke through clenched teeth. "That would have been too quick for Margo, too easy. Better to keep me around to hold it over my head."

"Blackmail?"

"Not per se."

"Ms. Burchett, Ms. Marchard mentioned that you use a lumbar cushion when you ride in a car."

Rosemary cut her gaze to Carole, then back. "That's correct."

"Where is that cushion?"

"Monday morning, when it was raining, I dropped it in

the mud. It seemed easier to buy a new one than to try to save it, so I threw it away."

"Monday, the day Ms. Campbell was smothered, possibly with a pillow or some other soft object."

Rosemary's tongue flicked out to moisten her lips. "Coincidence."

Truett emitted a humorless laugh and angled his coffee cup in Carole's direction. "While we're on coincidences, Ms. Marchand, how's married life?"

Carole's chin dipped. "Fine."

"Your husband, Gustav Marchand, he's just a couple of months away from receiving his green card, isn't he?"

Carole nodded.

"Ms. Marchand, we checked Ms. Campbell's phone records, and guess what we found."

The blood drained from Carole's cheeks. "I don't know."

"Don't you? Margo Campbell called the INS office last Friday and had a conversation with a Mr. Penley. Do you know the topic of that conversation?"

Carole was silent.

Truett expelled a long-suffering sigh. "Mr. Penley told me that Ms. Campbell informed him that your marriage to Mr. Marchand was a farce, that you had done this twice before. Mr. Penley said he planned to talk to Ms. Campbell when she returned from vacation."

Carole had apparently been struck mute. Belinda's mind reeled at the revelations.

"And you know what else?" Truett leaned forward to rest his elbows on the edge of the table. "We were able to trace that call Ms. Hennessey told us Ms. Campbell received just before she left—it came from the mailroom."

Belinda's heart clenched.

Carole seemed to sway, then she recovered. "I . . . did call Margo, because I had a confidential envelope for her. She told me to bring it up, that's one of the reasons I was late getting to the parking garage."

"Ms. Campbell was in her office when you delivered the envelope?"

"No. But her briefcase was on her desk, so I assumed she was still in the building, perhaps in the ladies' room."

"You didn't see her at all?"

"No."

"Did you touch anything in Ms. Campbell's office?"

"No." But Carole answered much too quickly; even Belinda could see that.

Truett held up his fat index finger. "Careful, Ms. Marchand. I'll ask you again. Are you sure you didn't touch anything in Ms. Campbell's office, didn't take anything with you?"

Carole was completely white now, and trembling. She glanced at Libby and Rosemary, who were darn near colorless themselves.

Truett set down his coffee and opened one of the thick folders in front of him. "Ladies, I have here some sort of manuscript that the four of you were working on."

"That's private," Libby said, shooting an angry look in Belinda's direction.

She could only return a remorseful expression and lament her sloppy eating habits that had left the suspicious red stain on the back page.

Truett flipped to one of several pages marked with a colored tab. "I'd like to read a few items." He cleared his throat. " 'DO have the courage to cut harmful people out of your life.' The passage that follows suggests that a person 'get rid of' the people in their life that are keeping them from achieving their goals."

"You're taking it out of context," Belinda said.

"Right," Libby said. "This is a book about men, not murder."

Truett pursed his thick lips. "Here's another one: 'If a relationship isn't working, DO kill it quickly.' Sounds like some kind of code to me."

"It is," Libby said dryly. "It's written for *women*."

He almost smiled. "Okay what about this one: 'DO develop a system for keeping your lies straight.' The passage that follows explains how to master the art of telling a good lie and covering your tracks." He closed the manuscript with a smack and looked back to Carole.

"Ms. Marchand, I'm asking you one more time—did you touch anything in Ms. Campbell's office?"

Carole teared up and nodded.

Belinda sucked in a breath and held it.

"What?" he asked.

"Evaluation forms," Carole said miserably. "I took mine and Libby's and Rosemary's."

He withdrew forms from the folder in front of him. Belinda recognized them as the final evaluation sheets. "Why?"

"B-because Margo gave us all bad evaluations—we each got a five."

"On a scale of one to five, five being the lowest."

Carole nodded. "A five means you don't even get a cost-of-living increase."

"What did you do to the forms?"

She swallowed. "I altered them. I changed the fives to fours so we would all get a tiny raise." She sniffed. "We deserved it—Margo had it in for all of us."

Belinda cringed inwardly—the young woman was only giving the detective more ammunition. But at least now she knew what the women had been keeping from her.

On second thought, they'd been keeping lots of things from her.

"But Libby and Rosemary didn't have anything to do with it," Carole said tearfully. "I did it all on my own and told them later."

"She meant well," Libby said softly. "Changing our reviews from a five to a four wasn't going to give anyone a promotion or a huge jump in salary. To Archer, the dollars would have been negligible. No one would have known."

"What made you think Ms. Campbell wouldn't notice that you'd altered the papers?"

"She had already signed them," Carole said. "I knew they would go to HR next. I used correction fluid to change the forms, then took them to the copy room and made a duplicate of the corrected forms. Those are the copies I put back in the folder. I took the originals with me and shredded them."

Truett nodded. "Didn't you think that Martin Derlinger would remember you had been there and would tell us?"

Carole shrugged. "I'm in the copy room all the time—it wasn't anything out of the ordinary."

"Except it was around the time that Ms. Campbell was murdered."

"I didn't see her," Carole said, shaking her head. "I swear. I took the duplicated forms back to her office and left."

"Was her briefcase still there when you went back?" Detective Salyers asked.

Carole squinted. "I can't remember—I was in a hurry."

"I have another question, Ms. Marchand," Truett said. "Why didn't you change Ms. Hennessey's evaluation? Isn't she a friend, too?"

Belinda's skin tingled—how was she supposed to feel about being excluded from a cheating sisterhood?

Carole looked at her across the table. "Of course Belinda is a friend. But Libby told me on the phone that Belinda said her evaluation went well. I didn't even look for her form."

"Then why is it missing?"

Belinda frowned. *Missing?*

"I don't know," Carole said, wide-eyed. "I didn't touch it."

"Maybe you don't regard Ms. Hennessey as a friend at all. Maybe the three of you conspired to kill Ms. Campbell and frame Ms. Hennessey."

Belinda sat back in her chair, while the other women leaned forward.

"That's not true!"

"That's absurd!"

"That's just plain crazy!"

Truett leveled his gaze on her. "Or maybe Ms. Hennessey did it knowing the rest of you had issues with Ms.

Campbell that would shift the blame—maybe she set up the rest of you."

Belinda felt all eyes turn in her direction. Her chest felt as if it might explode from the air she couldn't seem to exhale. Starbursts went off behind her eyes. "Th-that simply isn't true. I had no reason to want Margo dead."

"Maybe, maybe not," Truett said with a shrug. "Maybe you didn't get the good evaluation you told us you did. Maybe the woman simply insulted you, and you snapped. A person doesn't need a good reason to commit a crime of passion."

"I didn't kill her," Belinda murmured. "And I have no idea where my evaluation form is. I didn't see it, and I didn't take it."

"But you haven't been completely truthful with everyone, have you?"

"What do you mean?"

"I mean you told everyone you were divorced, but when we checked, we found no record of a divorce, and no record of a marriage."

She held on to the edge of the table, mortification rolling over her in waves. The women were giving her suspicious looks. Her entire right side burned from Wade's scrutiny.

"I can explain," she murmured.

"Please do," Truett said.

She swallowed and looked for her voice. "I had a wedding April 5 of this year in Cincinnati. But after the ceremony, the m-man I married . . ."

"Yes," Detective Salyers prompted.

"Refused to sign the marriage certificate." There. There it was, laid out for everyone to snicker at: Belinda Hennessey, the laughingstock. A dress, a cake, a ceremony, and nothing to show for her trouble.

"So why did you tell us you were divorced?" Libby asked.

"It seemed . . . easier." And less humiliating.

"So you've never been married?" Carole asked.

Belinda shook her head.

Wade broke his silence by suddenly shifting forward. "What does all this have to do with murder? Especially when Hardeman—"

"That's enough, Lieutenant," Detective Salyers said with a stern look. "We'll discuss that outside of this meeting."

"Right," Truett said, adding his own warning look. "My point is that Ms. Hennessey moved to Atlanta to start her life over. Maybe she was a little desperate for things to work out."

This was worse than being naked in public—this was being naked in public and wearing a polka-dot neck scarf.

"Maybe she clashed with her boss one too many times," Truett continued, now looking at her. "On top of the anger she was already feeling over the derailed marriage, maybe it was too much."

What could she say? Hadn't she practically ripped a little innocent embroidered pillow to shreds? Tossed out the photos and cards Vince had given her? Been on the verge of chucking her wedding gown? "I was angry and hurt over my breakup," she admitted carefully. "And it is the reason I moved to Atlanta. But I didn't kill my boss. Call me crazy, but the state penitentiary is not my idea of starting over."

Truett nodded. "Ms. Hennessey, do you watch a show called"—He consulted his notes—"*The Single Files*?"

"Occasionally," she said, puzzled.

"We all watch that show," Carole offered.

"I don't," Rosemary said. "Not regularly."

"You do, too," Libby insisted.

"Wasn't there a recent episode where a woman was locked in a trunk?"

Belinda could see where this was leading, and it wasn't a happy place.

"Yes," Carole said. "It's one of our favorite episodes." When she realized what she'd said, she balked. "But on the show, the lady in the trunk isn't dead. She locked herself in . . . by accident." Her voice petered out, but the damage was done.

Truett drained his coffee cup and wadded it up in his hand. "I swear to God, I ought to arrest all four of you right now. All of your fingerprints are on the trunk or somewhere on the car, all of you have pillows freaking galore, all of you have motive." He shook his head. "Jesus, what a big damn mess."

Assistant District Attorney Greer stood. "I think that's enough for now, Detective. Ladies, search warrants have been issued for your desks, your homes, and your vehicles. If any of you have something to say, now's the time."

Belinda was sure everyone in the room could hear her heart slamming in her chest as she scoured the faces of the women who had befriended her. How well did she really know them? And from the revelations made in the last few minutes, how well did they really know each other? Rosemary seemed composed, but pale. Carole twirled her hair nervously. Libby hovered near tears.

She would have been disappointed, but not wholly shocked, if any one of the three had jumped to her feet and admitted to smothering Margo in a moment of blind rage. Hadn't Wade said that anyone was capable of doing something terrible?

No one said anything for a full minute. Belinda started to feel light-headed. At last, Greer lifted her hands. "Okay. I strongly suggest that no one leave town. Meanwhile, whoever comes forward first will receive the lightest treatment. Think about it, ladies—friendship isn't worth sacrificing your life for."

The woman and the detectives gathered their things and left the conference room. Wade leaned close enough to murmur, "I'll be in touch."

In touch—ironic word choice. She nodded absently and watched him leave, resisting the urge to run and wrap her arms around his leg. What must he think of her, the pathetic little bride whose groom had reneged while the

Macarena was still playing at the reception, who was now immersed in this drama?

Belinda sat at the table, waiting for one of the women to say something, but everyone seemed preoccupied with their own thoughts.

Finally, Carole moaned and looked all around. "What are we going to do?"

Rosemary stood. "If they had enough evidence to arrest us, they would have," she said in a low tone. "I suggest we get back to work. And act normal."

Belinda resisted the urge to laugh hysterically. Act normal? Acting *ab*normal had landed her in this mess. Normal seemed like a long time ago, and a place she might never get to go back to.

Here lies Belinda Hennessey. She got caught.

Chapter 27

Margo's memorial service the next morning was an awkward affair, with a small wad of attendees. It was, Libby had told her, the same place the memorial service for Jeanie Lawford had been held. Belinda wasn't sure it was such a good thing that a company had established a standard procedure for memorializing employees.

The four of them had agreed to go for reasons ranging from obligation to keeping up appearances, and they had walked the five blocks to a small chapel in jerky silence. It seemed to Belinda that silence now defined the relationship between the women, along with wounded looks and betrayed glances. The commute home last night and to the office this morning had been interminable. She considered suggesting that they call off the car pool arrangement, but Carole didn't have a car, and Libby hadn't yet recovered her repossessed SUV. She herself was the proud renter of an egg-yolk-yellow Ford Focus, aka the largest Matchbox car ever produced, and she didn't relish going bumper to bumper with eighteen-wheelers through Spaghetti Junction.

Plus she had a theory that this pervasive sense of distrust was actually holding them together—it was as if they were afraid to let each other out of their sight.

"We are gathered today," a robed minister announced, "to remember the life and the death of Margo Eleanor Campbell."

Belinda sat with hands folded, listening to the generic words offered up on behalf of Margo's soul, trying to fold them into her heart. No matter what her faults, Margo hadn't deserved to die so tragically. But in truth, Belinda wasn't able to reach past the buffer of numbness she'd acquired and work up sentiment for the recently departed. It was self-preservation, she recognized, an anesthetized fog of denial to keep her moving through her days as if she weren't a murder suspect.

"But let this be a happy occasion," the minister said, "for death is the beginning of a life with God."

Apparently no one had enlightened him on the particulars of Margo's send-off.

Julian hadn't called, although she knew he was back from Chattanooga because he had resumed his regular chopper reporting. It was difficult to reconcile the man of the mellow voice with the man who might have murdered Margo, yet she couldn't dismiss his proximity or his strange behavior the night of the murder.

"Margo Campbell made her home in Atlanta for twelve years. For most of that time, she was a valued employee of Archer Furniture Company."

She hadn't spoken to Wade. When she'd arrived home last night, he had left a short message on her machine saying that considering the turn of events, it was better if they didn't speak directly. (He apparently had made his call after her place had been searched, because the message was one of the few things that had appeared untouched.) He'd warned her to keep her doors locked and the security alarm activated. "And if Hardeman contacts you, call me." Wade suspected that Julian had murdered not only Margo but Jeanie Lawford as well. But she had to wonder how much of Wade's belief of Julian's guilt was rooted in the fact that he wanted the man to be guilty.

"Let us pray for Margo's soul, and for our own souls. If you are carrying a heavy burden on your conscience, let this be the time to confess your sins."

Was it her imagination, or was everyone in the chapel glancing in her direction? Actually, there was one sin she wanted to confess, but Juneau Archer was still ill and not expected in the office until Monday morning. She wasn't entirely disappointed, though, because she had yet to track down those damned—er, *darned* contracts. She made a mental note to call about the packet again when she returned to the office, then forced her attention back to the remainder of the service. The minister struggled for words to describe a woman he didn't know, but Belinda wondered if anyone had really known Margo Eleanor Campbell.

A lesson for the arrogantly independent souls left behind.

"Amen," the minister said finally. "Go in peace."

Everyone stood to file out with the proper solemnity. Since they had arrived early and had sat in the front, Belinda had a chance, while they waited to exit their pew, to study the crowd.

Clancy Edmunds, sporting his signature bright colors and, bizarrely, sunglasses. Monica Tanner, impeccably dressed, talking to a short man that Belinda recognized as one of the board of directors. The buff trainer from the gym, and a couple of women she vaguely recognized, perhaps from the locker room, although it was hard to tell, since they were fully clothed. She scanned the group and noticed that Tal Archer was missing. Not surprising, but supremely bad form, considering the fact that his father couldn't attend. Libby's friend from HR had come, and stood to the side, presumably waiting for Libby. Tina Driver, the courier who had delivered the papers Sunday, waved to Carole and waited for her near the entrance. A man sitting in the far corner, away from everyone else, caught Belinda's attention. He lifted his hand.

Julian.

Wade's warning sounded in her ears. Perspiration

broke above her upper lip. The girls were already ahead of her, so they didn't notice when she slowed. He stood and made his way toward her, his steps unhurried, his shoulders down. He was minus the bomber jacket, plus a tie, his handsome face grave, his green eyes lined with fatigue.

When he stopped, she was glad to have the pew between them. Everything about the man she had once found appealing now seemed to repel her because she had been so blindly charmed. She had done what every parent feared most for their daughter: Moved to a big city and started dating a potential serial killer.

"I'm surprised to find you here," she said.

"I came to see you. I wanted to see for myself how you were holding up."

"I'm . . . fine."

He made a rueful noise, then gestured vaguely to the pulpit in the front of the chapel. "And I suppose I wanted to assuage some of my own guilt."

She chose her words carefully. "What do you mean?"

"I lied to you."

Her pulse raced. "Oh? When?"

"When I told you that Jeanie Lawford and I weren't romantically involved. To be honest, I was crazy in love with her."

She was struck silent. Julian didn't seem like the kind of person who could be crazy in love, but perhaps that judgment wasn't fair to Jeanie.

He gave her a sad smile. "I did, I loved Jeanie."

"And . . . did she feel the same way about you?"

He shook his head. "No, Jeanie was so independent. She had no intention of settling down. At least not with me."

His expression looked pained, and for a split second, scary. Had he been stalking Jeanie—was that why she had been acting skittish before her death? Individual hairs raised on Belinda's neck.

"This is where her memorial service was held," he said wistfully.

"I know."

He pushed his hand into his hair. "The police have been questioning me about my relationship with Margo."

She nodded calmly. "Were you involved with her as well?"

"Yes. But it's not what you're thinking."

"What am I thinking?"

He averted his gaze, then looked back. "That I killed Margo, that I might have killed Jeanie, too."

Just hearing him say the words put ice in her veins. Was he taunting her? She'd heard that some killers liked to talk about what they'd done, work it into dinner conversation. "That's not what I was thinking," she managed to get out.

"That's what the cops think," he said. "Especially Alexander."

"You're wrong," she said, taking an inadvertent step back.

"The radio station grounded me until the investigation is over."

"I'm sorry, Julian."

"Yeah," he said, nodding. "Me too."

"My friends are waiting. I need to get back to the office."

He leaned closer, putting his knee in the bench seat and gripping the back of the pew. "Just be careful, okay? I don't want to see anyone else get hurt."

His eyes looked moist and glassy. She nodded and stumbled back, then race-walked to the entrance of the chapel with as much composure as she could summon. She pushed on the door and practically fell out into the June sunshine. Yet she couldn't completely dispel the chill that had permeated her.

Libby, Carole, and Rosemary stood at the bottom of the stone steps, waiting for her. "Saying your last respects?" Libby asked, squinting up at her.

"Something like that," Belinda said. "Thanks for waiting. It was a nice service, wasn't it?" She made her feet move as fast as her mouth.

"Everyone is spooked," Carole said, falling into stride beside her. "Someone's brother's friend works in the police department and said that a serial killer might be on the loose in our building."

Julian's glazed eyes came to her, and she swallowed hard. "I'm sure that's an exaggeration."

"My friend in the mailroom—Tina—she said that someone broke into her apartment, but nothing was stolen."

"That's weird," Belinda said, but she remembered the figure she thought she'd imagined outside her bay window.

"Even weirder, Monica Tanner said the same thing," Libby added. "That someone had entered her condo through a window while she was at work yesterday, but didn't take anything."

Rosemary quirked an eyebrow. "All this talk about a serial killer has shifted the attention away from the money that was stolen."

Belinda happened to be looking at Libby when Rosemary made the remark, and she didn't miss the flush that stained the blond woman's face. Did Libby know something about the missing money? A forgotten remark came back to her from the night she'd picked up her car.

"I came into a little unexpected cash."

"Clancy broke down after the polygraph and admitted he might have left the drawer unlocked," Carole said. "He called and told me, said he felt guilty that the police might think either Brita or I took it since we both had keys."

"So," Libby said in a falsetto voice, "everyone thinks whoever murdered Margo also stole the money?"

Carole nodded.

Belinda worried the end of her tongue with her teeth during the walk back to the office building, pondering Libby's reaction, and still too shaken by her encounter with Julian to converse easily. She certainly didn't want to start a wild rumor about Julian being a potential stalker/killer. But at least the ice had been broken between the women, and they were talking again, if haltingly. Perhaps Margo's memorial service had reminded them all that life could be a lonely business without friends.

Belinda was certainly starting to get the picture.

When they arrived back at the office, they were greeted in the reception area by an armed guard. Clancy waved them by and let them know they would need to carry their identification badges with them at all times until further notice.

The mood of the department had taken on a pronounced gloom. Voices were lowered, and people were openly discussing self-defense classes and the purchase of weapons. Belinda fought the panic bubbling in her chest and escaped to her cubicle. She rummaged for one of the packets of aspirin she kept in her desk—the police search had displaced nearly everything in her office. She found the painkiller wedged between a stapler and a hole punch, and she swallowed the pills dry.

Her first call was to Hank Baxter's cell phone, a number that she'd practically memorized.

"This is Hank."

"Hi, Hank. This is Belinda Hennessey. Again."

"Hi, Belinda," he said cheerfully. "I might have a line on that lost package."

She straightened. "Really?"

"Yeah. I removed the label so it wouldn't be processed, and I realized that the package might have been sent to the undeliverable department. I'm going to the terminal this weekend to look for it myself."

She heaved a tremendous sigh. "Oh, Hank, that is great news. Keep me posted?"

"Sure thing, glad to help."

She hung up, feeling lighter than she had in days. At least when she went in Monday to talk to Juneau Archer and explain her actions, maybe she could hand him the contracts in question.

Her next call was to Wade Alexander's cell phone—also memorized . . . hm.

"Alexander," he barked.

She gripped the phone, trying to touch his big, grumbly voice. "Wade, this is Belinda."

"What's wrong?"

"I saw Julian. He came to Margo's memorial service."

"Did he touch you? Threaten you?"

Why did she have the feeling that he was standing now? "No. He did say some weird things, though. He told me he was in love with Jeanie Lawford, but that she didn't love him."

"Slow down, I'm making notes. . . . Okay, what else?"

"He admitted to being involved with Margo, although he told me it wasn't what I thought. He asked me to trust him."

"Yeah, right."

"He said the station had grounded him."

"That's standard procedure when a pilot is being investigated."

"He said he knew you thought he killed Margo and Jeanie. He told me to be careful, that he didn't want anyone else to get hurt."

A thump sounded in the background—a fist meeting the top of a desk? "*Stay* away from him."

She blinked. "I . . . am."

"Do you have someone you can stay with tonight?"

"I . . . probably."

"Do that." He slammed down the phone.

She frowned at the receiver. The man was good at telling people what to do. On the other hand, he wiped his feet before he came in.

What was a woman to make of that?

Her wrist was well enough to go to the gym with Rosemary, but she didn't want to risk running into Julian again, so she opted for lunch at her desk, getting so caught up on paperwork that she spent the afternoon moving things around on her desk and trying to assimilate just how her life had gone in the toilet. It was, she decided, the traffic.

A hellish morning commute had led to the accident,

which had left her with 1) Disabled Car and 2) Furious Boss. Confrontation with Furious Boss had led to subsequent Shameful Bathroom Deal, which had led to her regretting Shameful Bathroom Deal and confronting Furious Boss again, this time mere minutes before Furious Boss had been murdered. While she'd been tumbling down the back stairs, someone had been stuffing Furious Boss into trunk of Disabled Car, which wouldn't have been possible if she hadn't had the accident in the first place.

Yes, all the bad things that had happened to her since she'd arrived in Atlanta she could attribute to the traffic.

Tal Archer came over the intercom around 3:30 and told everyone that in light of the week's disturbing events, he and his father wanted everyone to go home, spend time with their families, and come back refreshed on Monday. "Until further notice, please wear your employee badge at all times, and report any suspicious individuals to the armed security guard posted by the department entrance. Have a nice weekend."

Not the most comforting of parting remarks, but she was arguably more relieved than anyone to end this dreadful workweek. She cleared her desk and joined the mass exodus, thinking at least they'd get a jump on the traffic, then she once again pondered the influence that traffic had on the lives of Atlantans. (Atlantanians? Atlanti?)

"Well, I'm shocked at the man's generosity," Libby murmured a few minutes later as they climbed into Rosemary's car.

"Me, too," Carole said. "But grateful."

Rosemary rolled her eyes as she turned over the ignition. "It was my idea. I found Tal asleep at his desk and suggested that he let everyone go home. No one was getting any work done, and being cooped up just fosters gossip."

Next to Belinda, Libby sighed. "A serial killer at Archer. I'm going to have a hell of a time putting a good spin on this in the annual report."

Rosemary gave her a pointed look in the rearview mirror. "You'd better hope the company survives to *have* an annual report."

"What do you mean?"

Rosemary backed out of the parking place. "What I mean is that I'm not sure Juneau is prepared to come back and run the business." She made a rueful noise in her throat. "And we all know that Tal isn't CEO material. The company lost Jeanie, then Jim Newberry, and now Margo. It might fall to you, Belinda, to hold things together—especially in terms of the Payton acquisition—until senior management is restored."

Yilk. Belinda saw Carole's head turn slightly in her direction, but she willed the young woman to keep quiet about the missing contracts.

She did.

Rosemary eased into the light traffic on Peachtree Street. "I heard that Jeanie's accident is being reopened as a possible murder."

Libby frowned. "Her family is probably just getting settled—I'd hate to see this all dredged up again if the police aren't sure of a connection."

Belinda kept her thoughts to herself—that the connection was Julian.

"But if Jeanie was killed," Carole said, "her family would want to see the person punished. And so would I."

Libby huffed. "You think I don't?"

"Girls," Rosemary chided.

"No, wait a minute," Libby said, chopping the air with her hand. "What Carole doesn't seem to realize after our little interview yesterday is that the police are trying to pin Margo's murder on *us*, and if they reopen Jeanie's case, they might try to pin her death on us, too. I have children to think of, Carole. I can't be pulled any deeper into this mess that you—" Libby stopped.

Carole turned around. "That I what?"

Belinda looked from woman to woman, her stomach tight. A confrontation had been hovering beneath the surface for two days, and it appeared to be coming to a boil. She moved closer to the window—this could get messy.

Libby's mouth tightened. "Why didn't you tell us that Margo had called the INS?"

The young woman's eyes popped. "You don't think I offed her because she was threatening to tell about me and Gustav?" She covered her mouth. "You *do*—you think I killed Margo."

Libby held up her hand. "All I'm saying is that it looks bad. And since you changed my evaluation and Rosemary's, it looks bad on us, too."

"I was trying to do you a favor."

"Yeah? Well next time, don't!"

Carole's mouth opened and closed. "Well, maybe you can tell me how Margo found out about me and Gustav in the first place?"

"Not from *me*. Good gravy, you've told everyone and their kin—you told Belinda as soon as she joined the car pool."

Carole sent a curious glance in Belinda's direction before she looked back to Libby. "If the police think you're involved in Margo's murder, it's because of that pillow you bought and supposedly threw in the Dumpster."

"Supposedly?"

"Everyone knows how much you hated Margo."

Libby wagged her finger. "I didn't lie about anything, unlike everyone else in this car."

Belinda's neck warmed.

Rosemary braked. "I didn't lie about Stanley."

"You didn't tell the truth," Carole countered.

"You can't believe I killed him."

"I don't," Libby said. "But even if you let him die, I wouldn't hold it against you. You could have told us."

Rosemary shook her head. "The detectives were right—my job was on the line. I knew that Margo would use my probation as an excuse to fire me. I couldn't risk it."

"You thought we would tell?" Carole asked.

"Please. Neither one of you are the model of discretion."

"I take offense to that," Libby said.

"Well, I take offense to your hairspray," Rosemary declared. "Why don't you fix your hair at home instead of subjecting us to your satanic ritual every morning?"

"Why don't you take another painkiller?"

Rosemary clenched her jaw. "I take those pills for my back."

"And for your front, and for your sides," Libby said sarcastically.

"What's the matter, Libby—Glen didn't give you lunch money today?"

Libby's face turned red.

Carole turned around, her eyes narrowed. "Speaking of money, Libby, it seems pretty coincidental that you're so hard up for cash and suddenly all that money is missing from Clancy's desk."

"I'm *not* a thief," Libby sputtered.

"So, are you a murderer?" Rosemary asked lightly.

Libby crossed her arms. "I won't even answer that. Besides, the police think it's a conspiracy, remember?" She looked at Belinda. "Because you gave him our manuscript."

Belinda shook her head. "Detective Truett took it—he thought the stain on the back was Margo's lipstick or blood or something."

"So you say." Libby angled her head. "You know, you look more guilty than the rest of us. You arrive in town, snuggle up to Margo, have it out with her in public, and a week later, the woman is snoozing in your trunk. Now we find out you've been lying to us all along about being married."

"I . . . told you why I lied."

"Because you were *embarrassed*?" Libby harrumphed. "You must have led a charmed life, girl, if you think you're exempt from being embarrassed. Life doesn't work that way."

Belinda pulled air into her lungs to counter the sting of the woman's words. "I'm a private person."

"But we hardly know anything about you," Carole

said, then gave her a knowing look. "Except that you like secrets."

Belinda felt the women's distrust descend over her like a blanket. She bit the end of her tongue and turned her head to look out the window. She couldn't blame them—she hardly knew anything about herself these days. Lying to coworkers, making shady deals, entertaining the attention of two men, and now suspicious of everyone she came in contact with. "I think it's time I left the car pool."

"I think it's time we all found our own way," Rosemary said.

"Fine," Carole said. "I'll go this weekend to buy my Thunderbird."

"Fine," Libby said. "I'll have my SUV back by Monday."

"Fine," Rosemary said.

"Fine," Carole said.

"Fine," Libby said.

Fine, Belinda thought. She could go back to relying on herself, the only person she could truly depend on. Arrogant? Maybe. Safe? Absolutely.

Here lies Belinda Hennessey. She was insulated.

Chapter 28

In the midst of the disagreement with Libby, Rosemary, and Carole, Belinda forgot about the promise she'd made to Wade to spend the night elsewhere—until she was tucked in bed staring at the fluted globe on her ceiling. At least it explained why he hadn't called—he didn't think she was home. Not that she'd expected him to call. The man was out fighting crime, after all, which included investigating Margo's murder. He had more important things on his mind than her need to be comforted at a particularly low point in her life.

But reporters were still calling; Joann Cameron in particular had left more than one message. Had Belinda seen Julian Hardeman, or did she know of his whereabouts? Belinda didn't return the call and had, in fact, decided that if she tried to process one more question through her overtaxed brain, she'd probably combust right there on her animal print bed-in-a-bag.

And then who would take care of Downey?

Belinda finally sighed and turned on the lamp next to her bed to resume reading one of the novels she'd bought for the long honeymoon flight to Paris that hadn't happened. When her mind threatened to wander back to the drama unfolding in her own life, she forced herself to concentrate on the words on the page until she was drawn into the story. At length her eyelids grew heavy and she was close enough to sleep to fall there quickly after she extinguished the light. Still, she dreamed of shadowy figures climbing through the windows and of being all alone when danger encroached. She started awake predawn and hovered in that blissfully unaware state for a full five seconds before her memory klunked in and the week's events flooded back with crushing clarity.

She was overwhelmed with the urge to burrow deeper into the covers, but she made herself get up and face the day, reminding herself that Jeanie Lawford and Margo would never have the chance to face another day, bleak or otherwise.

Her place was a wreck from the police search, so she spent the day straightening every room of the town house, boxing more items for Goodwill to add to the ones she'd planned to take earlier in the week. If she lost her job and had to live in her Civic, she was determined that all of her belongings would fit.

Assuming someday her beloved Civic would be returned and she wouldn't have to rent an egg-yolk-yellow Ford Focus for the rest of her natural life.

In the late afternoon, she nudged aside the bed sheet covering the bay window to make sure no reporters were loitering before she attempted to raise the garage door. No reporter, but she was disturbed to see large handprints on her window, made from the outside. Perry's, no doubt, from the other day when they had practically scared each other to death.

She gathered glass cleaner and a roll of paper towels, then raised the garage door and carried the first box to the back of the rental car. She paused a moment before opening the tiny trunk. It was ridiculous to think she'd find another body, if only due to sheer size constraints, but she still breathed a sigh of relief when she lifted the lid and found the space empty. From this point on, she would probably always hesitate a split second before opening the trunk of a car.

"Hey, Belinda!"

Perry. She winced, then turned. He was shirtless, and barefoot. It was hot, but still. "Hi, Perry."

"Need some help?"

"No, thanks. I got it."

"Where you headed?"

"To Goodwill."

He looked interested. "Can I go through the stuff first?"

"It's women's clothes and things, nothing you'd want."

He still looked interested, then recovered. "New car?"

"It's a rental until I get my Honda back."

"Oh. Right. Have the police figured out who murdered your boss?"

"Not yet."

He scratched his nipple. "Want to go get a burger?"

"No, thank you."

"You got anything else you want hauled off?" He jerked a thumb toward his truck. "My truck will hold a shitload, and I'll drive you wherever you need to go."

She gave his truck a dutifully admiring glance. "Thank you, Perry, but I'll manage."

"You don't like me, do you?"

At the sudden change in his tone, she looked up, her heart skipping a beat. He cracked his knuckles one at a time, and she had a feeling he could be mean when he wanted. Wade's observation that Perry had been at the Stratford Building on the day of the murder came back to her, stealing her breath.

Suddenly he looked contrite. "I shouldn't have said that. I came over to apologize."

She swallowed. "For what?"

"For looking in your window the other day—that was wrong, and I'm sorry I scared you."

He seemed sincere, and honestly, too simpleminded to pull off what she'd been thinking. "Okay," she said.

"And I want you to know that I won't bother you anymore. But if you need anything, just holler."

His words were so heartfelt that she couldn't help but feel a rush of sympathy for the man. "Thank you, Perry. And you *can* do something for me."

If he had been a puppy, his tail would have wagged. "What?"

She handed him the glass cleaner and the paper towels. "Clean your handprints off my window."

His face fell, but he took the supplies and trudged to the window. She loaded the box, then went inside to retrieve another one. When she returned, Perry was scratching his head. An itchy man. "I don't mind cleaning your window," he said, "but these ain't my handprints."

She frowned and walked over. He held his hand next to the prominent print on the glass. Indeed, his hand was three-quarters the size.

Had Wade left it when he'd worked on the alarm? The police, when they'd searched her town house? A reporter? She swallowed hard. Julian? Had he come over to spy on her? She had a slightly different view of his large hands now than when he had applied them to her in the sauna.

"You can wipe them off," she murmured. "There have been so many reporters around." Of course, now that she thought about it, if a serial murderer was on the loose, having reporters around at all hours was darn good security.

"Gotcha a security system, I see," he said, pointing to the imposing sticker Wade had affixed to the window and the front door. Similar stickers were on the windows in the back, too.

It was, she'd learned, a secret of the security business—big honking stickers to warn would-be intruders that if they breached the house, a siren would sound on the roof and a dragnet would fall over the perimeter.

"Just a precaution," she said.

"You need a big-ass dog, like a Rottweiler. 'Course it'd eat your kitty."

She frowned, then pursed her mouth that the thought

actually bothered her. Was it possible she was becoming attached to the hellcat?

Perry finished and loped back to his own yard, presumably before she asked him to do some other kind of women's work.

The Goodwill drop-off was a tad painful, and rather anticlimactic. While a man wrote a receipt for her items, she watched the box containing her wedding gown being handed down an assembly line of people who were moving donations from the delivery area to be sorted. Near the end of the line, someone dumped the box onto a table and quickly sifted through the items. The gown and veil were separated and handed to a woman who added them to a clothing rack on wheels. The heavily laden rack was then pushed from the loading area through an open doorway and disappeared. A lump rose in her throat over the realization that the dress had once symbolized so much.

"Ma'am?"

Belinda blinked and looked at the man who was holding her receipt for taxes. She thanked him and stepped aside to make way for the people in line behind her who were all shedding pieces of their former lives.

On the way home she blinked back a few achy tears, then stopped to rent two movies and buy a couple of rolls of aluminum foil to cat-proof her couch—she was tired of having her one good piece of furniture covered with old quilts.

At home she checked her phone messages, hoping for word from Hank Baxter on the missing contracts, or an invitation from Libby or Rosemary or Carole that signaled a truce, or a call from Wade Alexander about a break in the case, or a call from Vince about why she hadn't answered his card, or a call from her mother about the cleanest rest areas in Colorado. But the only call was from the car rental place hoping she was enjoying her "zippy" Ford Focus. If she was interested in keeping it, they could arrange for financing, even if her credit was "murky."

So, apparently even the lady reporter had stopped calling.

The best part of being arrogantly independent, she decided, was having the entire evening to do whatever she wanted to do.

So she ordered a pizza with extra mushrooms (Vince hated mushrooms) and watched a double feature of independent films she'd missed. She gave Downey a reprieve and allowed the cat to join her on the quilt-covered couch. All in all, not a bad evening, and she even allowed herself to think that someday her life would return to some version of normal. She was innocent, and the police would catch the bad guy. That's the way it was in the movies, and in life.

Probably.

The mushrooms gave her dreadful nightmares about Vince, and Sunday morning she opened the door to find the street in front of her town house chock full of reporters. She managed to wrap the raggedy peach robe around herself and snatch the *Atlanta Journal-Constitution* from her doorstep before darting back inside to find the Archer Furniture Company Serial Murders story on page three. By Joann Cameron. Which explained the new round of reporters.

Thank God the piece was short. The Cameron woman had quoted a lot of unnamed sources, but she'd managed to work in the fact that Julian Hardeman, local traffic celebrity, had been linked romantically to both of the victims and to the Hennessey woman in whose trunk the body had been found. Also, Julian had apparently ditched a scheduled polygraph exam and skipped town. His picture was printed next to the article, plus Jeanie's, Margo's, and—

She yanked the paper closer. *How* had they gotten her Ohio driver's license photo? The only good thing about the dreadful picture of her in the Mickey Mouse sweatshirt was that she was practically unrecognizable.

But Julian. She covered her mouth with her hand, trying to digest the idea of him committing such an appalling crime. It seemed inconceivable.

Her judgment in men was now officially abysmal.

The doorbell rang incessantly, but she didn't answer it. Instead, she carried her laptop to the kitchen table and booted up. Signing onto the Internet served two purposes—it tied up the phone line and it gave her a diversion for the afternoon. She checked e-mail, frowning at all the junk and porn spam. No personal messages, which wasn't a surprise. She hadn't exactly stayed in touch with anyone in Cincy, and anyone who might have been inclined to contact her was probably still too stumped over the reneged wedding to know what to say. And the way she'd left town, everyone most likely thought she wanted to put everything about that part of her life behind her.

Her relationships there had been tenuous, but were they completely disposable?

She pushed the troubling question from her mind and decided to surf a few sites she'd always wanted to check out but had never gotten around to. Since Downey hadn't yet run away, she really should research how to care properly for the poor rejected puss.

There was a *lot* of cat stuff on the Net. Too much, in fact, to read even if one had nine lives. Instead, Belinda browsed and still learned oodles. Like that she probably shouldn't have fed Downey the pizza with extra mushrooms, and she might need to check far corners for cat upchuck.

She made a very passable dinner out of Triscuit crackers, salsa, and cheddar cheese for herself, then a la one of the cat discussion boards, beat up a raw egg as a treat for Downey. At some advanced hour, she tired of shopping sites, news sites, and computer games, and searched for mentions of Archer Furniture Company. The search engine returned little beyond product information, but there was a mention of a couple of industry awards, one for a just-in-time inventory system, and one for a specialized shipping container . . . both developed by James Newberry, CFO. Belinda pursed her mouth. Not too shabby. At some point, the man must have been good at his job.

At the sound of fabric tearing and a subsequent stream of noise that could only be described as cat cursing, Belinda jumped to her feet, rushed to the living room, and flipped on the light. Downey had either pulled down the sheet covering the bay window, or had just happened to be lying beneath it when it fell. Regardless, she was trying her darnedest and loudest to free herself from its folds.

Belinda saved her, and the cat streaked upstairs, no doubt to find solace under the bed. Belinda signed off the Internet, then rummaged in the kitchen junk drawer for safety pins to rehang the sheet over the window until she could afford to have blinds installed, or maybe someday before her mother visited, hang real live curtains.

It seemed she had managed to waste the entire day. It was dark outside, save for the dusk to dawn light. As she climbed onto a chair to pin up the sheet, it occurred to her that she was visible to anyone who cared to look toward the window—if a reporter lingered, they'd be able to get a photo for a mediocre headline: "Murder Suspect Can't Afford Window Treatments."

She stretched high to rehang the sheet but stopped cold when she noticed the set of large handprints and smudges on the outside of the window. Her heart skipped and took its sweet time finding a rhythm again. Had the same person left the prints? Out of the corner of her eye, she saw a shadow move in her yard. A reporter, or worse? Belinda grabbed the empty curtain rod to keep from falling off the chair and almost tore the entire contraption off the wall. When she realized the shadow was only a bush moving, she finished pinning the sheet and climbed down, shaking.

The tears came then, the ones she'd been holding at bay all day, all week. Great heaving, hiccupping sobs that tore the air out of her lungs but couldn't alleviate the primal fear that had taken root in her stomach. Worse than the fear of someone coming to get her was the fear that her lifelong philosophy of strength and independence had backfired. The joke was on her, to be in a situation that had spun out of her control, and forced to face it alone. The worst of it . . . she was even *more* afraid of changing, of letting down her defenses. She had let Vince in as much as she'd dared, and look what he'd done to her.

She wasn't sure she could take that kind of emotional hit again.

The phone rang, and she waited for it to roll over to the machine.

"Belinda, it's Wade. If you're there, pick up."

She picked up. "I'm here."

"Are you okay? You sound funny."

"I'm fine." She sniffed.

"Did you have the phone off the hook? I was about to drive up there."

He was? "You were?"

"Yeah." He cleared his throat. "I need to talk to you about the case."

The case. Of course. "I'm listening."

He expelled a noisy sigh. "I guess you saw the piece in the paper today?"

"Yes. Reporters have been here all day."

"That's because things are starting to heat up. The D.A. is being pressured by the mayor to make an arrest. Having a serial killer on the loose isn't good for convention business."

She swallowed. "And?"

"And . . . they're considering charging you and your three friends with conspiracy to commit murder in the hope of forcing someone to confess."

Her mouth moved, but no sound came out for a few seconds. "But we didn't do it," she finally sputtered.

"*You* didn't do it, but are you sure they didn't?"

Her mind spun as she tried to sort the varied images of the women with whom she'd been sharing a commute. "I can't imagine it. Kill each other, maybe, but kill Margo . . . it would've had to have been an accident."

"If it was an accident, and the person comes forward now, the D.A. would probably cut them a deal, perhaps take murder one off the table."

She shivered. "You don't think my friends did it, do you?"

"I'm following other avenues. But you should talk to them."

"Everyone argued on the way home Friday, and we disbanded the car pool. They're not talking to each other, or to me."

"Then where have you been staying?"

"Um, see, here's the thing—"

"You've been staying at your place?"

"Yes."

His sigh vibrated with frustration. "I haven't been worried about you because you were supposed to be with one of your girlfriends."

He was worried about her? "I told you, the girls and I argued."

His silence crackled over the line. "You're taking a chance with your safety because you're *pouting*?"

"I—" She frowned. "I'm not pouting, but I can't hide out indefinitely. You installed an alarm, and reporters are here all the time. And don't forget my ferocious biting cat."

"Belinda, this isn't funny."

She sighed. "I know."

"You need to talk to your friends, let them know what's on the line."

"I'll try." She hung up slowly, knowing she'd have to think of some way to get them all talking again, for their sakes and for hers. Considering the fact that she was the least photogenic person on the planet, she couldn't imagine how bad her mug shot might be.

Chapter 29

Libby walked into the ladies' room and crossed her arms. "What did you want to talk to me about?"

Belinda glanced at her watch, trying to stall. "Um, how was your ride in?"

Libby barked a laugh. "Terrible. Yours?"

"Same." An understatement, considering she'd spent most of the hour-plus drive hemmed in on all sides by vehicles exponentially larger than the Ford. The hassles of a solitary commute seemed to symbolize all the tie-ups in her life. Alone and racing toward . . . *something*, feeling as though she could be crushed at any moment.

Libby averted her eyes. "Listen, I'm expecting a really important phone call, and I don't want to be away from my desk for long—"

The door opened and Rosemary came in. "You wanted to talk to me, Belinda?"

Rosemary frowned at Libby, who frowned back, but before either one could speak, Carole walked in and added her frown to the mix. "What's this all about?"

"I think we've been had," Libby said, eyeing Belinda.

Belinda walked over and leaned her back against the

door to prevent interruptions (and exits). "We all need to talk."

"I thought we did a pretty good job of talking Friday," Libby said, shooting daggers around the room.

Belinda inhaled—this wasn't going to be easy. "Lieutenant Alexander called me last night and told me the D.A. is being pressured to make an arrest in Margo's murder to quiet things down."

"They know who did it?" Carole asked, her eyes bulging.

"They think it's one of us," Belinda said, then waited for that sobering tidbit to sink in. Carole and Libby both sent panicked looks toward Rosemary. Were they gravitating to her quiet wisdom, or was their fear a product of something else entirely?

Rosemary leaned into the vanity. "Which one of us?"

"Wade said they were considering charging us all with conspiracy."

"Hoping someone will confess," Rosemary murmured.

Belinda nodded.

"Can they do that?" Carole asked in a choked voice.

"They can do whatever they want," Libby said. "We all had motive to kill her."

"Along with practically everyone else the woman came into contact with," Rosemary said.

"But the four of us had easy access to Belinda's car," Libby said.

"And none of us were completely forthright with the police," Rosemary added, wearing the pinched look that had become her permanent expression lately.

Carole fluttered her hands. "What are we going to do?"

"We're going to relax," Rosemary said sternly. "And we're going to stick together. Didn't you see the paper yesterday?" She glanced toward Belinda. "Is it true that Julian was involved with you *and* Margo?"

Belinda flushed. "There was just one encounter between me and Julian. It meant nothing, it was stupid. And I don't think he was involved with Margo then." Because she felt sure Margo would have let her know after she'd spotted her coming out of the sauna. "But apparently Julian spent the night at Margo's the day before she died."

"The man certainly makes the rounds," Libby observed dryly.

"He was at the memorial service Friday," Belinda said. "That's why I was late coming out. He told me he had been in love with Jeanie, but that she hadn't loved him back." She wet her lips. "Wade thinks Julian might have killed Jeanie *and* Margo."

"But Jeanie's death was an accident."

"Wade said he has never thought it was an accident."

"Someone pushed Jeanie?" Carole's eyes swam with tears. "That's horrible."

"The newspaper said that Julian skipped town," Rosemary said. "Has he?"

Belinda lifted her shoulders in a helpless shrug. "All I know is what the paper said. He hasn't contacted me since Friday."

"Well, there you go," Rosemary said, lifting her hands. "How can the D.A. arrest us when they suspect Julian Hardeman?"

Belinda hesitated. "I'm not so sure the detectives and the D.A. share Wade's opinion that Julian is involved."

Rosemary gave her a pointed gaze. "Let me get this straight—your boyfriend suspects Julian, but he told you the detectives and the D.A. suspect one of us?"

Belinda swallowed. "He's not my boyfriend."

"For all we know, you could be feeding us this conspiracy theory to make things look better for you."

Belinda shook her head. "Wade asked me to talk to all of you." She closed her eyes. "He said that if Margo's death was an accident, the D.A. would take murder one off the table, but the person would have to come forward soon."

"So you're doing us a favor?" Rosemary asked with a little smile.

Belinda wiped wet palms on her slacks. "I know that if

any one of you had k-killed Margo, it would've been an accident."

"Really?" Rosemary asked, her eyes narrowed slightly. "What about you, Belinda? You look more guilty than the rest of us."

"And we don't know anything about you," Carole said, "not really."

"You lied about being married," Libby added. "Who knows what else you could be lying about?"

The weight of their collective disapproval and suspicion struck her hard, flattening her against the door. This, she realized, was why she'd never fostered friendships with women—the emotional intensity was too demanding. Women knew best how to hurt other women, knew the soft tissue points.

The drip in the sink hadn't yet been fixed, she realized in the ensuing silence. The water plopped into the sink like a ticking clock.

Belinda searched their faces and realized that if she expected them to believe in her innocence, she needed to take the same leap, to trust her instincts that these women were good people despite the fact that her instincts had let her down before.

"You don't know me well enough to believe anything I say," Belinda agreed, then bit down on her tongue to quell the sudden swell of emotion in her throat. "And that's my fault, because the three of you have been nothing but kind to me since I arrived." She swallowed. "But I didn't kill Margo, and for what it's worth, I don't believe that any one of you did, either."

Shoulders eased and mouths softened.

"Do you think it was Julian?" Libby asked finally.

"Possibly. But his fingerprints weren't on my car." Belinda shook her head. "I just don't know." She straightened and gestured between the women. "But one thing I do know is that the three of you were friends long before I came on the scene. Don't let me or anything that's happened because of me come between you." She gave them the best smile she could summon. "*Y'all* are going to need each other's support to get through this." She turned and put her hand on the doorknob.

"Belinda . . . wait," Rosemary said.

She turned back.

The three women exchanged contrite glances. Rosemary looked up and returned a shaky smile. "All *four* of us are going to need each other's support to get through this. I . . . don't think it's over."

The surge of warmth Belinda experienced was tempered by the woman's ominous last words. "What do you mean?"

"I believe someone was in my apartment over the weekend."

Carole gasped. "Was anything stolen?"

"That's the strange part—I don't think so. Sunday afternoon when I came back from shopping, I just had the feeling that someone had been there."

"Just like Monica Tanner reported," Libby said. "And my friend."

Belinda's heart pounded. "Why do you think someone was in your apartment?"

"There was a scent in the air . . . maybe cologne. And I found grass clippings on the living room rug, as if someone had tracked them in."

"Could the police have done it when they searched your place?"

"It's possible," she conceded. "They left the place a mess, but I cleaned top to bottom when I got home Friday."

"How would a burglar have gotten in?"

Rosemary sighed. "I burned something in the oven, so I left my kitchen windows open to air it out. I was gone for only a little while."

"Did you call the police?" Belinda asked.

"I couldn't prove anything, and since nothing was stolen, it seemed silly." She rubbed at the furrow between her eyebrows. "I shouldn't have mentioned it."

"No," Belinda said. "In fact, I've been thinking that if

we put our heads together, we might be able to help the police instead of spending all our time defending ourselves."

"How?" Libby asked. "We've already told them everything we know."

Belinda put her ragged thumbnail between her teeth. "But have we told each other everything? There must be some detail we're overlooking. Did you ever notice anyone around my car? Even if it looked innocent."

They each thought for a few seconds, then shook their heads.

Belinda put her hand over her mouth as her mind spun in numerous directions, sifting all the bits of information. The door bumped into her from behind.

"Give us a few minutes," Libby yelled, irritated. Then she leaned in conspiratorially. "Belinda's right—I'll bet we can figure this out, girls, we're just missing something. Let's meet for lunch downstairs at the burrito place to hash it out."

"How about the salad bar?" Rosemary said with an arched eyebrow.

Libby opened her mouth to argue, then a magnanimous smile encompassed her face. "Okay. I'll even treat."

Despite much hashing and thrashing of the facts, though, the women left the food court with no new theories or leads. They did, however, cheerfully bury their respective hatchets and agree to reinstate the car pool. And Libby offered to drive the following day since she had indeed retrieved her repossessed SUV.

The news reminded Belinda of the conversation she'd had with Libby about coming into sudden cash the very day that the money had disappeared from Clancy's desk. She pushed away the nagging questions, however, because she had a more pressing matter on her mind: the discussion she needed to have with Mr. Archer about the Payton acquisition, which she had postponed until his return, hoping the contracts would show up.

They hadn't.

And she'd decided she simply couldn't carry the burden on her conscience any longer. According to Rosemary, Juneau Archer had arrived midmorning and would see Belinda at 1:30. As she climbed the stairs, she shot a prayer to the heavens that the contracts miraculously would be lying on her desk when she got back to her cubicle.

They weren't.

Might as well get it over with, she decided as she practiced deep breathing techniques to calm her nerves. On the way to the CEO's office, she passed Margo's eerily empty office, and a chill passed over her. Brita paused to look over the top of her glasses, then looked away. The woman had a frantic, lost look about her. Belinda experienced a pang of sympathy for the giantess—she had probably cared for her boss in some . . . *unexplainable* way. She walked over to the woman's desk. "Brita."

The woman typed for a few more seconds, then stopped and looked up with wounded eyes. "What do you want?"

"To tell you that I'm sorry for your loss. You were probably closer to Margo than anyone, you must have known she wasn't as severe as everyone thought she was."

Brita blinked, and her thin lips parted slightly. "Oh. Well, I suppose I did understand Ms. Campbell better than most."

"I'm on my way to speak to Mr. Archer. One of the things I want to discuss with him is how to transition Margo's workload until her position is filled. I was hoping I could tell him that you'd be willing to help me with that task."

High spots of color stained Brita's cheeks. "I . . . think that would be fine."

Belinda smiled. "Good. I'll let you know what he says."

The tall woman seemed flustered, but she managed a small smile in return.

Down the hallway and to the right, Rosemary sat adjacent to Juneau Archer's office in her own work area, identical to the Margo/Brita setup. Rosemary nodded to Belinda with wide, bright eyes and seemed to be telegraphing something to her, but when the door opened and Mr. Archer stuck his head out, Rosemary busied herself with the filing cabinet behind her. Trying not to read anything into the behavior, Belinda offered Mr. Archer a smile. "Hello, sir."

He didn't smile. "Come in, Ms. Hennessey."

Not a promising start. She gulped air, walked through the door he held open, then balked. Detectives Salyers and Truett sat in the matching visitor chairs. Wade stood in the back of the room, arms crossed, looking at the floor. Another bad sign.

"Mr. Archer," Belinda said, "I was hoping we could speak in private."

He settled into a chair behind a massive desk. "Have a seat, Ms. Hennessey."

So much for privacy. An odd chair had been set out—pea green, in her honor. She sat.

Mr. Archer clasped his long hands together on his desk. "Ms. Hennessey, the detectives and I want to talk to you about something."

She folded her hands to keep them from shaking. "I'll answer whatever questions I can."

Truett shifted in his chair. "We want to know why you went back to Ms. Campbell's office last Monday."

Belinda cleared her throat. "Mr. Archer, this is what I wanted to talk to you about." Her voice sounded hollow in her ears. "I went back to Margo's office to talk to her about some concerns I had with the Payton acquisition."

Juneau Archer's gray eyebrows met in a frown. "But the previous week you told me and the other board of directors that everything was in good shape."

Belinda wet her lips. "To be honest, sir, I was concerned all along that Payton might be hiding debt in its capital expenditures. When I pointed out those discrepancies to Margo, she, um, convinced me to overlook the problems to accelerate the acquisition."

His eyebrows shot up. "Convinced?"

"You mean bribed?" Salyers prompted.

"Y-yes." Belinda exhaled. Her face was on fire. "In return for not raising questions that would stall the deal, she offered me the position of CFO." Her back prickled from Wade's gaze. What must he think of her?

Mr. Archer's face turned a mottled shade of red, and all she could think was that if he stroked out, she'd have two deaths on her hands.

"I'm not proud of what I did," she added quickly, "and I regretted it. I knew the contracts were signed and on the verge of being executed, so I went to Margo's office late Monday to tell her that I'd changed my mind."

"You argued?" Truett said.

"No." Belinda shook her head. "At first she wasn't happy that I was reneging on our deal, but I persuaded her that we could postpone the deal long enough for me to dig into the numbers. If things were on the up and up, then we would go forward with the acquisition as planned."

"So she agreed to hold the contracts?" Salyers said.

"Yes. She said we'd revisit the Payton financials when she returned."

"Where are the contracts?" Juneau Archer asked.

Yilk. "I'm sorry to say, sir, that they're . . . lost."

"Lost?"

"When I called in Tuesday to see if anything needed my attention in Margo's absence, I talked to Brita, and she said that the contracts had been mailed by mistake. I called APS and had the packet intercepted."

"And?"

Her intestines twisted. "And the contracts seem to have gotten . . . waylaid . . . in the delivery system."

Mr. Archer dropped his head in his hands.

Her career was over. *Here lies Belinda Hennessey. She was incompetent.*

Salyers leaned forward in her chair. "So you're saying that when you told Ms. Campbell you had changed your mind, she just caved? That sounds out of character from everything else we've heard about the woman."

Belinda lifted her shoulders. "I guess she knew it was the right thing to do."

"But you must have expected a confrontation when you went to her office?"

"I knew she'd be angry with me, but it was something I had to do."

Truett narrowed his eyes. "Why the sudden change of heart, Ms. Hennessey?"

Belinda lifted her chin. "It was a change *back* to the real me, Detective. I got caught up in the promise of success, but then I realized that I couldn't lie, not when so many people's jobs were involved."

"Even if reneging on the deal with Ms. Campbell jeopardized your own job?"

She nodded.

"Mighty noble of you," Truett said dryly, and she realized with a sinking heart that he didn't believe a word she'd said. "Show her the memo, Mr. Archer."

Her nerves fluttered. "Memo?"

Mr. Archer stood and extended a sheet of paper across the desk. "We've been going through the files on Margo's computer, and we came across this memo. It was created Monday afternoon but went undelivered. Apparently, she was having some misgivings about your credibility, Ms. Hennessey."

Bewildered, Belinda took the memo. It was addressed to Mr. Archer. In one short paragraph Margo explained that she had raised last-minute issues with items on the Payton financials and had been concerned about Belinda's pat response to those questions. The memo went on to say that the exercise, while not reason enough to halt the acquisition, had shaken her faith in Belinda's abilities and she would, in Margo's opinion, have to be let go.

A lump lodged in Belinda's throat, and her hand holding the memo started shaking. "I think I know what she's referring to here." She told them about Margo couriering over a set of financials for her to review on the previous Sunday, and her opinion that the items Margo questioned had seemed self-explanatory.

"This set of financials?" Mr. Archer asked, pushing forward a set of papers held by the red rubber band Belinda had put around them when she'd finished.

"Yes." She flipped through the pages and frowned. "No. These aren't the questions Margo had for me—these are the questions I had for *her* early on."

But the generic way Margo had asked her to respond to inquiries by item number had allowed Margo to change the source document so that Belinda's answers seemingly corresponded to different questions. Her mind raced—Margo had covered her bases in the event the Payton financials would come back to haunt her. Betrayal hit Belinda like a slap in the face. Tears pressed behind her eyes. Moisture left her mouth. How stupid could she have been not to have seen she was being used?

"Ms. Hennessey," Mr. Archer said, steepling his fingers, "I'm not as involved in the day-to-day activities as I used to be, but Margo certainly would have had to obtain my approval before offering you the CFO position of my company, and I assure you, the subject never came up."

Confusion flooded over Belinda, and her chest heaved. "I don't . . . understand. She told me you had already agreed."

Juneau Archer pursed his mouth, looked at the detectives, and shook his head no.

Belinda blinked, trying to grasp the ramifications of what Margo had done to her.

"Let me sketch a scenario," Truett said to her, leaning forward. "During your performance evaluation Monday afternoon, Ms. Campbell alludes to the fact that she's going to reveal the discrepancies in your recommendation. You go back later and, according to her assistant, practically force your way into her office. The two of you argue, one thing leads to another, and she winds up dead. You think you can blame it on Jim Newberry because you were there when he burst into Ms. Campbell's office. The problem is, no one else heard Newberry threaten to kill her."

"Th-that's ridiculous," Belinda whispered, forcing air past her parched throat. "And besides, Margo gave me an outstanding evaluation." As soon as the words left her mouth, she remembered the evaluation was missing.

Truett must have read her mind. "We found a copy of the evaluation, too. Let's just say it reflected her wish to fire you. Did you destroy the original?"

"No." Belinda gripped the arms of the chair. "Don't you see? Margo tricked me. She . . . set me up."

"Isn't that what you told us Jim Newberry said?" Truett asked with a sad little smile. "Ms. Hennessey, you'd better hope that we find Julian Hardeman and that he makes a complete confession."

The crushing revelation of Margo's treachery was bulldozed by another more formidable realization: She now had a concrete motive for murdering her boss.

Chapter 30

Belinda didn't make eye contact with Wade as he and the detectives left Mr. Archer's office. She didn't want to see the censure in his eyes, although no one could possibly think as little of her as she thought of herself at the moment.

From behind his desk, Mr. Archer radiated disapproval. "Ms. Hennessey, you have put my company in a precarious situation."

Feeling as if she had little to lose, Belinda stood and pulled her shoulders back. "I accept full responsibility for my behavior, but it seems to me that you, sir, are the one who has put your company in a precarious situation by turning the reins over to a tyrant like Margo Campbell."

His mouth opened in outrage.

"I've heard that Archer was a great place to work before Margo was given carte blanche around the office. Pardon my boldness, sir, but this company needs a strong leader right now, and everyone wants you to come back full time, at least until a new senior management team can be put into place. Meanwhile, I'm willing to stay until you can find a replacement for me, or as long as you need me, sir, to facilitate the transition. Although I would understand if you wanted me to . . . go." She swallowed hard, waiting.

He sat back in his chair and studied her until she squirmed. She had a vision of him ten, twenty, thirty years younger and suspected he once had been a rock of strength for the people around him. It would be a shame if everything he'd built fell apart.

"Ms. Hennessey," he said finally, "I expect you to stay long enough to straighten out this holy mess with Payton. Then we'll see."

She exhaled. "Brita agreed to help me put together a report on Margo's outstanding projects."

"That would be helpful," he said in a tone that suggested he realized that without Jeanie Lawford, Jim Newberry, Margo, or the interest of his own son, the ranks were growing slim and business still needed to be conducted. "Meanwhile, *find* those contracts."

She exited on taffylike legs and glanced at Rosemary, who was possibly as pale as she felt.

"I heard," Rosemary murmured, pointing to a small vent in the wall between Mr. Archer's office and her work area. "What are you going to do?"

Belinda shuffled closer and lifted her hands—they were numb, like the rest of her. "I'm going to do my job. Everything else is out of my control, unless the four of us can think of something to help the case."

Rosemary sighed. "So Margo set you up?"

Belinda nodded. "She was going to use me to cover her tracks on the Payton financials. She told me she was going to hold the contracts, but she'd planned to mail them all along. By the time she returned from vacation, the deal would be done, then I would be fired."

"And no one would be around to ask questions?"

"Right."

Rosemary's mouth tightened. "Makes me wonder if she was setting up Jeanie, too. Maybe pressuring her to do something, and when she wouldn't . . ."

It was a terrible thought, but Margo had proved her ruthlessness.

"Are you going to hire an attorney?" Rosemary asked.

"I don't want to. Anytime I hear about someone hiring a lawyer, I think they must be guilty."

"Me, too," Rosemary admitted. "But maybe Julian will turn up soon. You have to admit it's pretty suspicious that he wouldn't take a lie detector test."

"Although maybe the radio station advised him not to."

Rosemary angled her chin. "You don't think he's guilty, do you?"

Why was it so hard for her to accept that Julian was somehow involved? Because she didn't want to be wrong again? "I don't know what to think anymore."

Belinda returned to her desk, feeling disembodied. She was moving and walking, but it was almost as if an energy field separated her from the people she passed in the aisles. Perhaps it was a physical manifestation of that "arrogant independence" Vince had accused her of using to shield herself from others. Maybe so, but the auto-defense part of her psyche realized the nice, hazy buffer was keeping her from falling completely apart.

In desperation, she dialed Hank Baxter's cell phone number. When his voice message kicked on, she spoke with as much calm as she could muster. "Hank, this is Belinda Hennessey, checking again on the lost Archer package. I'm assuming you didn't find it over the weekend, but please call me as soon as possible and let me know."

She returned the receiver and sat quietly, trying to wrap her mind around events that had occurred at Archer—Jeanie's death, Margo's murder, the stolen money, the random break-ins. Were they arbitrary events or somehow connected?

And how pathetically ironic that the first time in her life she had done something unethical, she had incriminated herself so thoroughly into a murder investigation. Note to self: She wasn't good at being bad, and if she got out of this mess with her sanity and freedom, she would never break another rule, not even remove a mattress tag.

Her phone rang, and she yanked it up, hoping for news of the missing package. "Belinda Hennessey."

"Belinda," a man's voice said, "this is Perry."

She pulled back and stared at the receiver.

"Hello?"

"Um, sorry, Perry, I'm just surprised to hear from you. Is something wrong?"

"I thought you'd want to know that when I came home, I saw somebody sneaking around your place."

She swallowed hard. "Was it a man?"

"I guess so—now that you mention it, I'm not sure. By the time I parked my truck, they'd run off."

"They were on foot?"

He hesitated, and she pictured him scratching. "I didn't see a car, but it might have been parked on another street. I figured it was some kind of reporter, and in case they left handprints on your window, I didn't want you to think I'd been peekin'."

"Thanks, Perry. You were right to call me."

"Well," his voice swelled with pride, "I figured you must be spooked, since that cop kept watch all night."

She squinted. "Excuse me?"

"Did you burp?"

She closed her eyes. "No, Perry, I meant, what are you talking about?"

"A cop sat in a cruiser in your driveway all night. That big fellow who came around asking me questions."

A warm tingle found its way through the nice, hazy buffer. *Wade.* He must have driven up after his shift to keep an eye on things after he found out she wasn't staying with a friend. She frowned—why hadn't he rung her doorbell?

Because he was afraid he would wind up ringing her doorbell?

Or because he already knew what the detectives had just revealed?

A pecking noise sounded in her ear. "Belinda? Are you there?"

"I'm here, Perry. Thanks for calling. If you see anyone else snooping around, call the police and ask for Lt. Alexander."

"Sure thing. This is some kind of exciting."

She murmured something appropriate and hung up slowly, thinking it was highly unlikely that Julian would be looking for her at the town house during the day—unless he'd lost his grip on reality. More likely, it was a reporter poking around. Or maybe the creeper who'd supposedly been breaking into employees' homes?

On a hunch, she walked around the corner and down to Libby's cubicle. She found the woman staring into space with a private little smile on her face. "Libby?"

Libby blinked and looked up. "Yes?"

"I'm glad to see someone smiling. Would you like to share?"

"Not yet . . . but soon. How'd it go with Mr. Archer?"

"I'll tell you about it later. Would you do me a favor?"

"If I can."

"Would you call your friend in HR and ask her if anyone in the office is out sick today?"

Libby dialed the number, had a brief conversation with her friend, then hung up. "Tal Archer called in sick, but my friend said that was nothing new. Diane Bailey in IT is having knee surgery today. And Clancy called in sick."

"Clancy?"

"Said he has a stomach virus."

Belinda nodded slowly.

"Is there a problem?"

"Too many to count, but thanks for the info." She walked back to her desk, mulling Clancy's possible involvement, or even Tal's, although the Archer heir seemed so uncomfortable with his role since Margo had died that she couldn't imagine him getting rid of the woman who had made his life easier. And the man's sexual orientation contradicted a scorned lover/stalker theory. Clancy's too.

And why either man would be breaking into Archer

employees' homes for no apparent reason, she couldn't fathom.

Her phone was ringing when she walked back into her cubicle. At the sound of Hank Baxter's cheerful voice, her hopes rose.

"Ms. Hennessey, I just got a call that a package matching the description of yours has been located."

Her shoulders fell in relief. "Thank God. Where is it?"

"Tulsa."

"As in, Oklahoma?"

He laughed. "Yeah. But I'm having it overnighted to me, so hopefully, it's the one we're looking for."

Hopefully—the catchphrase of her life. *Here lies Belinda Hennessey. Hopefully.*

"Thank you, Hank, for all your trouble. Keep me posted."

"Will do."

She hung up and considered calling Wade. She even picked up the receiver, but she changed her mind. What would she say—I'm not a bad person, I just did a bad thing? Was there really a difference once a person passed their tenth birthday?

Right now, she wanted to push thoughts of the investigation as far from her mind as possible. Armed with a legal pad and two pens, she headed toward Brita's work area to begin portioning out Margo's mail and reports. She took a shortcut through the hall that passed in front of the elevators and passed Martin Derlinger as he alighted. He was an oddly shaped person who wore cartoon ties to work and colored Puma tennis shoes. And he was sweating profusely, as if he'd just come in from the outside temperatures. He made brief eye contact, then looked down and headed toward his copy room cubbyhole and his menagerie of tiny stuffed animals. Wade was right—Archer was populated by a fairly exotic group of individuals.

She and Brita were awkward together at first, both skittish in view of the No Entry—APD Crime Scene sticker on Margo's office door, but soon the projects and memos engrossed them past the point of unease. Brita, Belinda discovered, was clever and organized, which, in hindsight, made perfect sense; if nothing else, Margo had been a perfectionist. Belinda was glad for the distraction from the investigation, which hung over her like a black cloud. And for some relief from her guilt over abusing Mr. Archer's trust, when he'd agreed to hire her.

She sent Brita home at 5:30 and carried a stack of memos on a new consumer financing plan back to her cubicle for take-home reading. She needed to stay late but conceded that she didn't want to hang around after hours in a place where dead bodies tended to turn up, armed guard or no. Being a suspect was still significantly better than being a victim. She waved at Libby on the way out, but the woman seemed to be in a fog, albeit a happy fog.

"What's up with Libby?" she asked Rosemary as they headed toward the exit.

Rosemary shook her head. "Maybe the hairspray has finally killed one too many brain cells. If she's still like that when she picks me up in the morning, I won't let her drive." She touched Belinda's arm. "Do you want to stay at my place tonight? I have a sleeper sofa now."

A surge of warmth filled Belinda's chest, but she shook her head. "Thanks, but I have a cat to look after, and . . . I'm fine."

"Okay. See you in the morning."

That evening's commute was pure torture. The traffic was no worse than normal, but without Julian's friendly voice in the sky, or companionship to pass the time, Belinda felt as if she'd aged a year by the time she steered the little yellow Ford into her garage. She expected Perry to be waiting for her, but thank goodness, his truck was gone and there were no reporters in sight. She checked her mailbox, and at the sight of an envelope from the Atlanta Police Department, her heart tripped double-time. When she tore it open, though, she frowned wryly—notice of a court date to pay her fines and/or produce proof of a valid Georgia driver's license. She was a murderer *and* a bad driver.

She walked to the bay window to check the effectiveness of the sheet she'd hung—not bad. The only thing a Peeping Tom would see was the brand of bed linens she preferred. But at the sight of more smudged palm and fingerprints—large ones—she froze. The same person who'd left them before? The person Perry had seen skulking around today? It seemed likely. She swallowed hard and unlocked the front door, carefully turning the dead bolt behind her.

"Downey, I'm home."

Nothing.

She looked to the left into the living room and knew instantly why the cat was in hiding—because she knew one of her nine lives was about to expire.

Torn sheets of aluminum foil were scattered about the living room, the apparent casualties of a war declared by Downey when she'd found her new favorite sleeping spot covered with the offensive stuff. And the feline must have worked herself up into a frenzy, because she'd also exorcised her hostilities on the red leather couch.

Belinda stared at the countless claw scratches, rips and tears in the soft leather. Ruined. Destroyed. Non-repairable.

She burst into tears. Her life was a disaster. She stood, leaning on the doorjamb, bawling like a newborn calf. Was this a sign for her to give up? To go back to Cincinnati with her tail tucked between her legs? That is, of course, if she wasn't locked up in a holding cell by the end of the week.

At a brush against her legs, she sucked in enough air to hiccup. Downey looked up at her with big innocent green eyes, then rubbed her head against Belinda's shin and purred like a clothes dryer. Belinda sighed and squatted down to address the cat, puss to puss. "You were very naughty today."

Downey rubbed herself against Belinda's chin like a contrite child, effectively neutralizing her master's anger.

Even more pathetic, Belinda's heart went out to the cat. "I know how you feel," she said, scooping the recalcitrant animal into her arms. "I wanted to tear Vince apart, too. But it's better to let go of the unhealthy people in your life and move on. We're stuck with each other, and we're going to make it."

She carried the cat to the kitchen and held her with one hand while opening a can of cat food with the other hand. Downey seemed content to snuggle, as if she realized they had come to an understanding. Belinda dumped the meaty food onto a saucer, then stuck it in the microwave for a few seconds. She tested it with her finger for appropriate warmness, then set it on the floor for Downey. The cat's tail fairly shuddered with pleasure at the first warm bite.

Now, Belinda realized, they were friends.

But she had one more thing to do. She retrieved Vince's card from the table, now smudged and wallowed, and reeking faintly of fish and French fries. She ran her finger over his name for old time's sake, telling herself she would remember the fond moments together. With a purple felt-tip marker (Vince thought felt-tip markers were the scourge of all writing instruments), she wrote RETURN TO SENDER across the envelope in neat capital letters. Then she walked the envelope out to her mailbox, placed it inside, and raised the red metal flag so the mailman would pick it up tomorrow.

She made a mental note to weigh herself soon, because she suddenly felt as if those added pounds had evaporated. Yet she knew the scales wouldn't reflect the fact that she'd shed the old Belinda Hennessey and the old Belinda Hennessey ways of needing for every day, every hour, every minute of her life to be planned. Life was an adventure, and the most she could wish for were that the good days outnumbered the bad. And along the way, hopefully she would meet people who cared about her, and she would be brave enough to let them in.

The warm summer day was passing through dusk on its slide toward night. The smell of freshly cut grass permeated the still air, and crickets chanted their evening song, mocking the idea that anything could be wrong with the world. At the sound of a car behind her, she turned to see a set of headlights heading toward her. Her heart jumped wildly, but her feet wouldn't move. When she recognized a police cruiser, relief flooded her, but her heart continued to do funny things. Wade slowed, pulled into her driveway, and zoomed down the window. His face was alarmingly comforting.

She walked over and leaned down. "I hear you're doubling as a night watchman."

He reached out to finger a hank of hair that had fallen onto her cheek. "You would be safer inside," he said. "What are you doing out here?"

She glanced toward the mailbox, then back. "Doing something I should have done a long time ago."

He stared at her for a few seconds, then smiled. "Always good for the soul." Then he pressed his lips together. "Truett and Salyers were a little hard on you today."

She shook her head. "They were doing their jobs. I'm so ashamed of that deal I made with Margo, it's just a relief for it to be out in the open. Remember what you said about everyone having the capacity to do something terrible?"

He nodded.

"I didn't think I had that capacity. I guess I didn't know myself very well."

"So this secret deal you made with your boss is why you failed the polygraph."

"I suppose."

He gave her a little smile. "You know only a truly *good* person could be such a bad liar."

She smiled back. "Thanks. I don't suppose you've heard anything from Julian?"

"No, but the general consensus is he's still in town somewhere. We'll find him."

"So, in light of my revelation about the Payton deal, has the D.A. dropped the conspiracy theory in favor of me doing away with Margo all by myself?"

He shook his head. "I don't think the D.A. is sure of

anything, but I've convinced her to hold off until we find Hardeman." He wet his lips. "I just hope Hardeman doesn't find you first."

Her gaze locked with his, and she couldn't look away. "You don't have to be my bodyguard, you know."

"I know."

She waved vaguely toward the house. "Why don't you come in?"

He looked away and shifted in his seat. "I don't think that would be a good idea."

Was he remembering their kiss? Or was he thinking of what he'd heard her confess today? She straightened slowly. "Oh. Okay. Well, I appreciate you coming by, but you really don't have to stay."

"Still," he said, in that inarguable one-word way of his.

"Goodnight, then," she said with a little wave and a little jerk of her heart. When she closed the door behind her, she sighed. It was for the best. She was recovering, he was recovering. She was in a bind, and he was trained to come to her rescue. After the commotion passed, he, too, would pass.

She'd taken one step away from the door when the doorbell rang. Thinking he'd gotten word of a new development, she opened the door. His frame filled the opening. His dark hair fell over his forehead, into his eyes. "I changed my mind."

The sexual energy bouncing between them put enough static in the air to lift Downey's fur. Belinda wavered, knowing it wasn't the smartest thing to do, that if she were planning her life, this attraction was leading nowhere. But she wasn't planning her life anymore, and who knew how many more nights of freedom she might have?

She stepped aside to allow him to enter, and they were kissing before the door closed. When he folded her into his arms, she went loose all over, reveling in the sensation of having so much man around her. His maleness overwhelmed her and she had the ridiculous urge to submit to him, to let him take her where he wanted them to go. He lifted her off the ground and pulled her against his—arousal? Radio? Gun?

"Are you still on duty?" she murmured against his mouth.

"No," he managed between hard breaths.

"Then can we lose the uniform?"

He laughed, and she'd never heard a more sexy sound in her life.

The clothes were coming off before they could make it to the living room. Her jacket fell in the foyer, as well as his button-up shirt. Her shoes were next, then his belt. He made a rueful noise when he saw the couch.

"The aluminum foil didn't work," she said, pulling her blouse over her head. "My couch is ruined."

"How about the floor?" His gaze devoured her as he unzipped his pants.

"The floor seems to be in good shape," she agreed, tearing off her panty hose. They were both on the carpet before their underwear landed.

He appeared to be fascinated with her breasts but not the least bit intimidated. Two tweaks in, she knew she was in the hands of a man who knew how to make things happen. Her body was one long, living nerve. He seemed to be everywhere at once, his mouth, his hands, his . . . well, the significance of having a large man make love to her was starting to sink in . . . literally.

Her knees parted like the Red Sea to bring him closer, but a couple of inches in, he set his jaw to restrain himself. "Whatever you got going on down there," he said through clenched teeth, "it's making me crazy."

She was thinking likewise. So maybe the Brazilians were on to something with this inside and out wax job. Pain? What pain?

He groaned into her mouth as he drove inside her, and her eyes rolled back. This . . . this had to be breaking some rule, it felt too good.

He held himself above her, giving them both a few seconds to take each other in before falling into a delicious glide. She had never been so swept away on pure physical pleasure. He talked in her ear, asking if this felt good and if that felt good. Too soon and not soon enough, she came on a this and he came on a that. He rolled over, pulling her on top to recover. She lay with her head on his chest, listening to his heartbeat, filled with feminine satisfaction that their bodies had interacted so supernaturally.

"Could you be suspended for this?" she asked against his nipple.

"Hell, yes."

"Will you stay anyway?"

"Hell, yes."

A few minutes later, they roused long enough to make omelets and drink the beer that was left. She marveled at the ease between them and resisted thinking past tonight. It was a good thing she had adopted that "men are unnecessary" rule, because Wade Alexander, with his omelet pan and his this and that, would be easy to fall for. But she wasn't going there again. Not yet. Not for a long while.

They took a shower in the dark and made love again on her bed-in-a-bag animal print sheets, then settled down to share one pillow—not an easy feat, considering his size.

Belinda was quiet, studying the white fluted globe over her bed, trying to squash the panic fluttering in her chest beneath his warm hand. This was feeling dangerously good. Nothing this good could last—it would burn itself out. Wade would chalk it up to his rebound fling and move on. She wasn't ready for another relationship either, but her heart was still needy and might not recognize a rebound fling. Might instead mistake the rebound fling for the real thing and incite her to crazy thoughts like picturing her furniture in his house. Or worrying that all those omelets weren't good for his cholesterol.

"What are you thinking about?" he asked.

"Hm?"

"You're sighing."

"How many eggs do you eat in a week?"

"Huh?"

"I was thinking maybe . . . maybe you shouldn't stay."

Silence, then he swung his legs over the side and reached for his shirt. "Okay, I'll leave."

She closed her eyes. "I don't want you to get in trouble."

"I'm a big boy. But it could mean trouble for you if things . . . get worse. You're right, I shouldn't stay."

She lay still, feeling miserable as she watched him dress. "Do you think things will get worse—for me, I mean? Should I get a lawyer, tell my parents?"

"Hardeman will turn up soon. Then you should be off the hook." He gave her a flat smile. "For everything."

"But—" She bit her tongue.

"But what?"

"What if he didn't do it? Is there something you aren't telling me? Do you have proof?"

"Not definitive proof," he said, then expelled a sigh. "Are you still hung up on the guy?"

She sat up and pulled the covers to her neck. "What? Of course not."

"You seem more concerned about his innocence than your own."

She wanted to say she hoped Julian was innocent to prove her judgment wasn't so off-base, that she wouldn't just crawl into a dry sauna with a serial killer, but she didn't think it would come out sounding very elegant. And then a thunderbolt hit her.

"I'm your revenge," she said quietly.

He turned his head. "What?"

"I'm your revenge on Julian." She touched her temples. "He slept with your wife, you thought Julian was hung up on me, so you slept with me."

"That's not true," he said, shaking his head.

"Get out." She set her jaw, reeling from her own gullibility.

"Belinda—"

"Get out *now*." She looked away until she heard his footsteps on the stairs, in the foyer, the door open and close, then she slipped on her robe to go down and turn the dead bolt. She sat on the bottom step for a good half hour, rocking to stave off the lake of tears behind her eyes. Downey came to keep her company, settling next to her with little mewling noises.

Their lovemaking hadn't meant anything, so why should his betrayal hurt? She wasn't looking for a relationship, and now she didn't have one.

Fine. Everything was just fine.

Oh, except for the murder rap and the missing contracts and the unemployment line she was likely to be facing soon. She opened her mouth for enough air to fuel a marathon crying jag, and the doorbell rang.

She gulped back a sob, wondering what Wade could possibly have to say, hating herself for wanting to see him again. Already. Pathetic.

Belinda inhaled and exhaled deeply, then turned the dead bolt and opened the door. Moonlight streamed in around his head—she couldn't see his face.

"Hello, Belinda."

Her heart stood still. "Julian."

Chapter 31

Her throat convulsed. "Wh-what are you doing here, Julian?"

"I need to talk to you. Can I come in?"

She could smell the alcohol on his breath. "It's late, Julian. Why don't you call me tomorrow, or come by my office?" She started to close the door.

"No," he said, blocking the doorframe with his body and forcing his way into the foyer. The light fell on his gaunt face, highlighting beard stubble and his glassy green eyes. "I have to talk to you now."

Primal fear seized her. She had to get to the bathroom, lock herself in. She whirled to run up the stairs. Julian grabbed the back of her robe. She screamed, then fell hard on her chin. Despite the stars in her head, she kicked at him and clawed at the stairs.

"Be still!" he bellowed. "I just want to talk to you. You remind me so much of Jeanie. I loved her." He covered her body with his, pinning her facedown on the rough carpet. The steps jabbed her painfully. His breathing rasped in her ear, his wet mouth sliding on her cheek. She felt faint and gasped for breath under his considerable weight.

"I just want to tell you something," he wheezed. "I was in Margo's office the day she died. I went to see that bitch because she killed Jeanie, I just know it. I went to confront her, to make her conf—unhhh!"

His weight was suddenly gone. She gulped air into her aching lungs, then collapsed in a fit of coughing and flopped over on her back. The door stood open and she realized that someone had Julian facedown in the foyer. Wade.

"Are you okay?" he shouted.

"Yes," she managed, then dragged herself up and pawed for the light switch. She blinked against the sudden illumination that showed Julian struggling beneath Wade's knee in his back. Wade was reading him his rights, placing him under arrest for assault. He cuffed Julian and left him on the floor, then turned back to her, his jaw set, his eyes grave. "Did he . . . hurt you?"

"No," she said. "I'm fine, just a couple of bruises." She jammed her fingers into her hair and choked back a sob. "He told me he was in Margo's office the day she died. He said he went there to confront her about Jeanie."

"That bitch killed my Jeanie," Julian shouted.

"Shut up, Hardeman," Wade yelled. "You'll have your chance to tell your story."

He looked back to Belinda. "I need to take him in. Will you be okay?"

She pressed her lips together, then nodded.

Wade looked as if he wanted to say something, wanted to do something. "I should have been here to protect you."

"You were."

"Still, I'm sorry for . . . everything."

"Me too."

"Try to get some sleep. Someone will find you tomorrow to get a statement."

Someone. She nodded, then watched him drag Julian to his feet and lead him to the cruiser. He put the man in the backseat, then stood outside the car, talking on his radio for a few minutes before climbing in and driving away.

Belinda was so limp with relief and exhaustion that she could barely pull herself back up the stairs. Her clock read 2:20 A.M. The nightmare was over for her, just beginning for Julian. Three lives wasted—Jeanie's, Margo's, and now his. Swallowing against the nausea in her stomach, she acknowledged with knee-bending gravity that she might have been next. She collapsed into the bed and Downey yowled, then tunneled her way out from under the bedclothes to lick Belinda's face. It was a kind gesture, meant to soothe, but she lay there for an hour with adrenaline coursing through her body before turning her well-groomed face into the pillow to drift asleep. The pillow smelled like Wade.

Belinda jogged down the stairs, poking in earrings. She was going to be late for the car pool again, but she suspected the girls wouldn't mind sitting in the driveway for a few minutes, considering the news she had for them about Julian being apprehended.

It was a beautiful day. She was anxious to get to the office and start repairing the damage to her credibility. If Mr. Archer would give her a chance, she'd make the Payton acquisition work. Chances were, if the company had problems, Archer would be able to buy it at a much cheaper price. Either Margo had been getting a kickback from someone at Payton to push through the deal, or she had simply been dead set on getting it done in her own timeframe.

Belinda was in such a good mood, she was determined that not even last night's lapse—lapses? lapsi?—with Wade was going to pull her down.

The doorbell rang as she grabbed a Slim-Fast drink from the fridge. Still in her stocking feet and mascara-less, she swung open the door. And just like that, her day got better.

Hank Baxter stood on her doorstep, grinning and holding the envelope of Payton contracts.

Belinda squealed with delight. "Thank you, Hank! But you didn't have to drive all the way out here."

"I was scheduled to be in this area already," he said, "and I thought you'd want them right away."

She grinned back. "You're right. You made my day."

"I'm glad."

She held up a finger. "In fact, hang on—lunch is on me."

He waved. "That's not necessary."

"Yes, it is. Come on in. I'll be right back." She laid the envelope on the stairs, then walked upstairs to get her purse, unable to believe her good luck. Mr. Archer would be relieved. They could start all over with Payton. She stepped into her pumps and stole a few seconds to put on her mascara. On the way back downstairs, she rifled through her wallet, withdrawing a twenty-dollar bill. It was the least she could do for badgering the poor man for the past week.

"Here you go," she said at the bottom of the stairs, then stopped.

Hank was in her living room, trying to fold the mattress of the shredded sofa bed back into place. The leather seat cushions were at his feet.

Alarm boomeranged through Belinda. "What are you doing?"

He looked up, then his handsome face rearranged into a scowl. "Dammit, Belinda, couldn't you have stayed upstairs another twenty seconds?"

"What are you talking about?" Then her gaze landed on a glove dangling from his large hand. A padded glove with the APS logo. Stained with the godawful black cherry lipstick that Margo used to wear.

Terror paralyzed her. "Y-you killed her?"

He pulled his hand down his face, then he sighed. "Yeah, but the bitch had it coming." He put his hands on his hips and shook his head. "She killed Jeanie Lawford, you know. I saw her."

"You s-saw her?"

"Yeah. It was late and I had a—" He laughed and put his hand over his chest. "Shall we say a *special* delivery for Margo? I came out of the stairwell just as she shoved Jeanie down the elevator shaft."

Belinda's throat convulsed. "But why would she . . . do that?"

"Margo said the company would be able to collect 'key executive' insurance on Jeanie—two million bucks. She promised to make me a rich man if I kept my mouth shut, but she didn't pay me enough, thought she could keep me quiet with sex."

Belinda's stomach rolled. *Run*, her mind screamed, but her feet were rooted to the floor.

"I wanted to go with her to Hawaii," he said, walking closer. He laughed. "Can you believe she said no? I called her that night before she was supposed to leave, and she said she'd meet me in the boardroom for a quickie." He gestured to the couch. "These couches were a godsend. We got it on in there all the time." He shrugged. "I didn't mean to kill her, but when I told her I needed more money, she laughed at me, called me a 'delivery boy.' I showed her."

Keep him talking. The girls were on their way. Hopefully they'd know something was wrong. "But how . . . why did you put the body in the trunk of my car?"

He made a rueful noise. "I'm real sorry about that. But when I carried her down the back stairs, your car was sitting right there. I remembered the trunk latch was broken because I helped you carry that crate of books to your office."

A bell rung in her memory. Of course.

"Seemed like the best thing to do under the circumstances. I hope you understand."

She nodded as if she meant it. "The glove."

"Hm? Oh, yeah, well, later I realized I'd lost my glove in the couch. I found out the couches were sold to employees, but I couldn't find out who had which one."

Monica Tanner, Libby's friend, Rosemary—the phantom break-ins.

"I finally narrowed it down to you, but your place was

like some kind of freaking fortress with an alarm system and reporters and that cop friend and that neighbor who looks like Charles Manson."

Her phone rang and Belinda lunged for it. Hank beat her to it and ripped the phone cord out of the wall. The phone upstairs kept ringing. His face was blood red. "No one else had to get hurt, if only you'd stayed upstairs another *lousy twenty seconds*."

She started backing up. "You'll never get away with this."

"Oh, yes, I will." He pulled a box cutter from his gear belt. "You're going to write a nice little letter about how you killed Margo and just couldn't live with the guilt anymore."

She shook her head. "Why would I do that?"

"To live a few minutes longer." He smiled. "I might even let you call your folks—do you have folks back wherever you came from?"

She nodded and blinked back tears. Her parents were probably astride burros, lurching their way down into the Grand Canyon.

"Okay, then—where's a sheet of paper?"

"In the kitchen."

"Let's go together."

He grabbed her upper arm with the strength of a vise, then shepherded her to the drawer she indicated. Her mind raced, trying to think of anything she could use as a weapon on his muscular frame. Big Daddy would come in handy right about now.

"Write it," he commanded. "Write 'I killed Margo Campbell and I can't live with myself anymore.' "

She put the paper on the counter and wrote as slowly as she could. Suddenly her doorbell rang, and her spirits soared. But when she moved in that direction, he yanked her back. "Write it now, write it fast. I guess I'll have to say I found you."

Damn the sheet she'd hung over the window—without it, someone would be able to see through the living room and the hallway to where they were standing. She bore down on the pencil as hard as she could, snapping the lead.

Someone was pounding on the door. "Belinda," Carole yelled. "Are you in there? We're late!"

"Dammit," he yelled in her ear. "Get an ink pen and write *fast*." He leaned down and came up with Downey by the scruff of her neck. The cat cried in pain and clawed at the air.

Belinda's heart twisted.

"Do it, or I'll slit your cat's throat right now."

"You'll m-mess it up for yourself," she stammered. "People would know I'd never kill my cat."

He sneered. "Maybe people don't know you as well as they thought."

True enough, she thought sadly. She hadn't let them.

More pounding on the door sounded. "Belinda, are you in there?"

She opened her mouth to scream, but he clamped his hand over her mouth. Except to do that, he had to let go of Downey. The cat landed on the counter, then sank her teeth into Hank's arm. He screamed with pain, and Downey went flying. Belinda wrenched away and ran through the hallway. "Help! Help me!" she screamed at the top of her lungs. "Please, help me!" But before she could get to the door, he tackled her from behind.

They both went down in the hallway, with his crushing weight landing on top of her. Her forehead bounced twice against the parquet floor. Hank rolled off, then dragged her to her feet. Through a haze of semiconsciousness, she realized the pounding on the door had stopped. The car pool had left without her. She was a goner.

Then a horrific crash rent the air, shaking the town house on its foundation. Hank fell to the ground and covered his head. The wail of an approaching siren registered in Belinda's mind as she sank to her knees against the stairway. She opened her eyes and stared into the living room at a glorious sight: The front end of Libby's SUV sitting where the bay window used to be. And Libby, pink rollers and all, climbing over the hood of the SUV, heedless of the glass and falling debris. She hefted a tire iron and glared at Hank. "Stay on the floor, you sonofabitch, or I'll spill your brains."

They were the sweetest words Belinda had ever heard.

Chapter 32

The details that Belinda couldn't remember immediately after the crash, the girls gave her while she recuperated in a hospital bed—a one-night's stay for observation, she was informed, in case she had a concussion. Since being observed meant lying in a bed surrounded by flowers from coworkers and having food carried to her on a tray, she went along.

"We brought you the newspaper," Carole said, spreading the *Atlanta Journal-Constitution* on the bed. "I'll bet it would have made the front page if that commuter plane hadn't landed on Interstate 75 and backed up traffic to Chattanooga."

Perfect—upstaged by traffic.

"Isn't it a great picture?" Libby asked, preening. "I'm a mini-celebrity in my neighborhood."

Belinda stared at the picture taken from the foyer of her town house, showing the nose of the white SUV sitting in her living room. It still gave her chills. *"Sometimes, friendships get messy,"* Libby had once said. Belinda was incredulous and humbled at the risk the woman had taken. "You're my savior, Libby. What made you think of it?"

"Well, we had to get in there some way. When you didn't answer the doorbell or the phone, we thought you'd driven on by yourself. We circled around and saw the APS truck on the street. Carole knew it was Hank's truck from the number, then she remembered hearing you say that Hank had helped you carry something up from your car, so we thought he might have known about the latch on your trunk. We got suspicious and came back. That time Carole heard you inside yelling. I called Lieutenant Goodbody, but I was afraid he wasn't going to get there fast enough." She shrugged. "The window was the only way in."

Carole made a rueful noise. "Who would have thought someone who looked as good as Hank could be so evil?"

"Did you know he told the police that he saw Margo push Jeanie down the elevator shaft?" Libby asked.

Belinda nodded sadly. "He told me, too. I'm sorry, girls."

"At least now her family knows the truth. And Margo got hers." Libby sighed and turned in her chair. "I wonder what happened to Rosemary? She was right behind us."

The door opened, and Rosemary tiptoed in, carrying a large canvas bag. She smiled at Belinda. "I thought you could use a pick-me-up." She set the bag on the bed, and a black head emerged.

"Downey!"

"Shh, the nurses will have my hide if they see her in here."

Belinda snuggled the cat to her face and received a good licking in return. "I hope she isn't being too much trouble."

"Not at all," Rosemary said. "I like the company. Libby, did you tell Belinda your news?"

Libby grinned. "Not yet."

"What? Tell me."

"We won the Southern Lotto!"

"You and Glen won the lottery?"

"Not me and Glen—everyone who works for Archer."

"Huh?"

Libby squirmed. "Well, everyone else knows, so I might as well tell you." She wet her lips. "I found the money that Hank stole from Clancy's desk—he dropped it in the parking lot. I know I should have turned it in, but with the number of people in and out of that parking lot, well, how could I even be sure it would get back to the rightful owner?"

"You still should have turned it in," Rosemary chided.

"All right, I should have. But when I found out the next day that the money was stolen from Clancy's desk, I'd already bought lottery tickets for Saturday's drawing."

Belinda gaped. "You bought over five-thousand dollars' worth of lottery tickets?"

"Yeah. But I decided that if I won, I'd share it with everyone in the office."

"And if you didn't?" Rosemary asked.

"I was going to cross that bridge when I got there," Libby huffed. "Why are you complaining? It's going to good use."

Rosemary smiled. "I know."

"What was the jackpot?" Belinda asked.

"Four million, give or take a couple hundred thousand."

Belinda inhaled sharply. "Oh my God."

"I know, I was ready to *pop* not telling you all yesterday at work, but I had to wait for confirmation before I could say anything. I took the cash option on all the tickets, so it's more like two and a half million. But since Mr. Archer is going to pay back the two million in insurance proceeds from Jeanie's death, we all decided to take it out of the lottery money. That leaves us five hundred thousand divided by forty-eight employees, and that's about ten thousand bucks each."

Belinda's jaw dropped. "You're kidding."

"Nope," Libby said with a squeal. "I'm the most popular woman at the office."

"I'm going to pay off my Thunderbird," Carole said.

"Are you staying with Gustav?" Belinda asked.

"Oh, good gravy, don't get her started."

Carole grinned sheepishly. "I finally slept with him,

and it was just . . . magical. I think Gustav is the person Ricky was talking about when he said the love of my life was right under my nose."

Belinda sighed. "Martin Derlinger is going to be heartbroken." She cleared her throat mildly, then asked, "So . . . how are things at the office?"

"You'll be happy to know," Libby said, "that Brita found your missing evaluation form in the crack between Margo's desk and her printer stand. It was simply lost—how ironic is that?"

"Mr. Archer is like his old self again," Rosemary said, her cheeks glowing. "He's coming back to work full-time, for a year at least. And he sent Tal off to rehab."

"Did you give Mr. Archer the Payton contracts?"

"Yes, but he said he's turning it all over to you when you return."

Belinda exhaled. Employed—whew.

"He feels terrible about what you've been through, Belinda. I think he's hoping you'll be willing to take over Margo's position."

"Me?"

"And he said he was going to talk to Jim Newberry about coming back."

More good news.

"Are any of these flowers from Vince?" Carole asked, looking around the room.

Belinda stroked Downey's fur and shook her head. "No one back there knows anything about all this, not even my folks."

"How have you kept it from them?"

"My folks are on a cross-country trip, and I . . . haven't really made an effort to stay in touch with anyone in Cincy." She looked at Libby and gave her a little smile. "But I'm going to."

"You once told me," Carole said, "to ask you on another day what Vince was like."

Belinda nodded and lay her head back on the pillow. "Vince was . . ." Memories crowded her, already more distant than just yesterday. "Vince was a rerun."

The girls smiled, and Libby snapped her fingers. "I'm going to use that in the book!"

"Oh, not the book again," Rosemary said, rolling her eyes.

A rap on the door sounded. They scrambled to get Downey back in the bag, then Belinda called, "Come in."

Wade Alexander stuck his head in. "Maybe I should come back later?"

"No," Rosemary said quickly. "We were just leaving."

Libby frowned. "But—"

"Come on, Libby." Rosemary winked at Belinda and reached forward to squeeze her hand. "I have one for *your* book, Belinda."

"What?"

"DO hold out for your happy ending."

Belinda squeezed back. "Someday, Rosemary. Thank you."

The girls shuffled out, smuggling Downey with them. Wade waited until they were clear of the door before he entered. He was off-duty, wearing dark jeans and a pale blue dress shirt, carrying a sheath of wildflowers.

She was sure she looked like two kinds of hell and vacillated between wanting to touch him and wanting to become invisible.

"Hi," he said.

"Hello." She played with the hem of the sheet. "I don't know how I can thank you for . . . everything."

"I was just—"

"Doing your job," she finished. "I know. But you helped me through this nightmare, and saved my life at least twice, so let me say thank you."

He nodded. "You're welcome." He looked at the flowers around her. "I brought you these, but it doesn't look like you need them."

She reached for them and inhaled their light scent. "They're lovely. Will you sit for a few minutes? But I warn you, it's ten minutes until Jell-O, and I never miss Jell-O."

He gave her a little smile and sat on the edge of the chair next to her bed. "You're feeling okay?"

"I'm fine, everything is going to be . . . fine. Really."

"Where will you be staying?"

She shrugged. "I was thinking about getting a place ITP if I can afford it, cut down on the commute."

"Inside the perimeter, huh? By the way, you should have your car back in about a week."

"Great."

"Yeah."

She sighed and he shifted, and the silence was sticky.

"I came to apologize," he said finally.

"For what?"

"For the way things . . . ended."

Ended. "No reason to apologize."

"You were partially right," he said, clasping his hands together. "I was convinced Hardeman was guilty. I let my prejudice get in the way."

"You had good reason to believe he was guilty."

He inhaled. "But you were wrong about the reason I . . . *stayed* last night."

She toyed with the flowers. "It's okay, Wade. I'm not looking for a relationship, and neither are you. I'm still trying to . . . acclimate. We got caught up in the moment, and it was fun. End of story."

"End of story?"

She angled her head. "Don't make this any more awkward than it has to be. We're both adults. Let's just chalk it up to the drama and part as friends."

He pursed his mouth. "Okay."

"Okay."

He stood. "Okay then."

"Okay."

"Stay out of trouble."

She smiled. "I'm reformed."

He smiled back, then walked to the door and looked back. "Call me if . . . anything."

"I will." She smiled until the door closed behind him, then turned over and snuggled against her pillow. Things were good . . . considering.

Chapter 33

"It's a great day in Hot-lanta, folks—unless you're drivin'. The connector is backed up due to a wreck in the center lane and it's causin' fits for the HERO units. I-285 eastbound is a parkin' lot because a water main break at the Ashford-Dunwoody exit left about six inches of water standin' on the road. The two leftmost lanes of southbound I-75 are closed for repavin' from Windy Hill all the way to North Avenue—whew, it's ugly out there. This is Talkin' Tom Trainer for MIXX 100 FM traffic."

Belinda turned down the volume on her headphones and smiled as the MARTA train slowed at her stop. Julian was in good form today after being off the air for eight weeks. And he sounded rejuvenated—she hoped he had put his demons to rest. It seemed that no one, not even a smooth-talking celebrity, was immune to the torture of unrequited love.

When the train doors slid open, she exited onto the platform along with dozens of other in-town commuters and set off walking toward the city hall building, where she would pay the fines for her tickets and put that part of her life behind her.

Her driving life, that is. Oh, she had obtained her Georgia driver's license for emergencies (with requisite dreadful picture), but when her Civic had been returned to her, she'd realized she didn't want to drive around the car that had once held her boss's body. So she'd sold the car through the want ads and bought a scooter. Very chic. Very in-town. Very slow.

And perfect for her twelve-block commute to Archer on the days she didn't walk or ride MARTA. She missed the car pool companionship, but her one-bedroom apartment in Midtown provided a walking lifestyle that made her feel much more connected to the city. (Once a week she stopped at the corner of Peachtree and 13th Street and left a flower in the memory of a wonderfully creative writer and her untimely end.) And besides seeing the girls every day at the office, they all met for lunch at least twice a week to dish about life in general and to work on the book.

Her cell phone rang. At this time of day, it could only be a wrong number or an emergency. She withdrew the phone from her bag and answered, "Hello?"

"Belinda, dear, it's Mother."

Or her mother. "Hi, Mom."

"I called your office, but your assistant Brita said you had taken the morning off."

She smiled. "I had to run some errands. Is something wrong?"

Her mother made fretting noises. "Well, I just heard something very upsetting. Mrs. Lakes in my garden club—you remember her, she used to teach Sunday school."

"Yes," Belinda said, wondering where this was going.

"Well, Mrs. Lakes has a nephew in Atlanta who was here to attend a Reds game—he's a pharmaceutical sales rep—and he said he saw something in the Atlanta paper a few weeks ago about a woman named Belinda Hennessey being mixed up with two murders, and said it had something to do with a furniture company, too. Isn't that strange?"

Belinda swallowed hard. "Yes, that's very strange."

"Well, I told Mrs. Lakes that it simply couldn't be you . . . could it?"

Dredging up all the terrible things that had happened would serve no useful purpose, and it would only give her mother nightmares. Besides, she didn't even feel like the same person who had come to Atlanta in the spring, afraid of herself and emotionally inaccessible.

"Atlanta is a big city, Mom. It must have been a different Belinda Hennessey."

Barbara Hennessey emitted a musical sigh of relief. "Of course it was. I'll call Mrs. Lakes and let her know. Are you looking forward to Suzanne's visit?"

"Yes, I have all kinds of things planned for us to do." She was pleased that Suzanne had responded so warmly to her e-mail messages and phone calls. The women had developed a stronger bond through correspondence than they'd had when they had both lived and worked in Cincy. Suzanne promised she was bringing the silver candlesticks as a housewarming gift for Belinda's new place.

"Have you seen that handyman lately?"

Belinda's heart strummed. "Um, no, Mom, I haven't. We were just . . . friends."

"I could give your number to Mrs. Lakes to pass along to her nephew."

"Um, no, Mom, thanks anyway."

"Okay, well, I'll let you get to your errands. Your father says hello."

"Give him my love. I'll talk to you soon."

Belinda hung up and heaved a sigh of relief. That was close. At least the phone call had taken her nearly to the steps of City Hall. A few minutes later, she entered the double doors and stopped at the information desk for directions to the courtroom where she was scheduled to appear. It was more like a classroom, the woman explained to her, nothing to be nervous about. She would show her driver's license and pay her fines and would once again be in good standing with the city of Atlanta.

Belinda couldn't very well explain she wasn't nervous because of the courtroom, she was nervous because the ticket resurrected memories she didn't want to revisit. Wade Alexander had certainly forgotten all about her, had moved on to other damsels in distress. The reason she still thought about him at night wasn't that she had fallen for him, but that she was so grateful for all he had done for her.

And to her.

Because it was nice to know that she had the capacity to evoke and experience that kind of passion with a man. But if she allowed herself to be lulled into the belief that it could happen only with Wade Alexander, well, then she would be, as Libby would say, "in a bad way."

She found the courtroom, where she sat on a folding chair with dozens of other traffic violators. She had come armed with reading material, though—the first complete draft of the DOs and DON'Ts manuscript that Libby had finished. And it was actually very good—entertaining, insightful, hopeful. Libby had begrudgingly conceded to Rosemary's traditional outlook by devoting the last chapter to "DO hold out for your happy ending."

Almost two hours later, her name was called. As she approached the podium and the tiny microphone, she remembered Julian's offer to have the tickets taken care of, and for a split second, she wished she had taken him up on it. At the podium, she stood while the lady judge read the violations.

"Is the ticketing officer in the room?" the judge asked. "A Lieutenant Alexander?"

Belinda's heart jumped to her throat—she hadn't realized he would be here. She glanced surreptitiously to the left and right but didn't see him.

Apparently, the judge didn't see him either. "No?"

A sharp pain stabbed her chest. He hadn't wanted to see her.

"Do we have a written statement from the lieutenant? No? Ms. Hennessey, do you now have a valid Georgia driver's license?"

Belinda presented her license to the bailiff, who then nodded at the judge.

"Then the ticket for driving without a valid state operating license is hereby voided, and I'm going to throw out the other two tickets because the officer didn't bother to do the paperwork." The woman smiled at Belinda. "It's your lucky day, Ms. Hennessey."

Belinda conjured up a smile and left the courtroom. It was nearly noon, so she was in good shape to get to Archer by 1:00 for the board of directors presentation. A new and improved deal to acquire Payton Manufacturing, this one reflecting the lower purchase price indicative of the financial problems she and Jim Newberry had uncovered. She didn't want to be late for this meeting. Not again.

She had exited the building and was walking down the ancient stone steps to the sidewalk when something made her look up.

Yilk.

Wade Alexander stood at the bottom of the steps, dressed in slacks and a dress shirt. He looked like someone she wanted to let in.

If he wanted in.

"Hello," she said, pulse thumping.

"Hi."

"The judge was upset because you didn't submit any paperwork."

He smiled. "I figured you'd been through enough. Besides, I was distracted that day you hit—I mean, the day *we* hit. It could have been partly my fault."

"Thank you." She indicated his clothing. "You're not working today?"

"As a matter of fact, I am. This is what detectives have to wear."

She grinned. "Congratulations."

He grinned back, and her heart caved. Wow, she had it bad for this man.

"You didn't call," he said.

"Hm?"

"I asked you to call me if—"

"If anything. I remember."

He moved his mountainous shoulders with a little shrug. "So I guess I should give up on the . . . anything? I mean, I know you don't like pesky guys, but I thought I'd check."

Her heart jerked sideways. He did want in.

He cleared his throat and looked adorably unsure of himself. "I was hoping I could take you to lunch."

She pursed her mouth and considered his invitation for long seconds, then shook her head. "I'm sorry, I can't do that."

Disappointment flashed in his eyes, but he recovered. "Oh. Okay."

A perfect, perfect joy filled her heart. She tapped her watch. "I have a meeting in a few minutes. I only have time for a Coke." A smile curved her mouth.

He laughed and pulled her hand between both of his, then kissed her fingers. "I've missed you."

"I've missed you," she murmured, easing into him. Belinda realized she was going to have to renege on her promise to herself and break one more rule—that pesky "men are unnecessary" rule.

Here lies Belinda Hennessey. She was imperfect. And happy.

ROMANCE HEADLINES

LOVE! PASSION! SEDUCTION!

Everything you need to know about Avon's Romance Superleaders

Amazing Authors
Unforgettable Books
And a lot of great sex

MOTHER OF THE BRIDE KEEPS SANITY BUT LOSES HEART TO EX-SPOUSE IN WEDDING GONE AWRY

Once Upon a Wedding
by Kathleen Eagle
September 2003

[Minneapolis, MN] What was Camille thinking? Her determination to make her daughter's wedding a day to remember has gone completely out of control. It's simply too much for one woman to handle! And to make matters somehow worse, Camille's ex-husband, Creed, returns to town, suddenly longing to make up for lost time. Not only does he want to do "the father thing," he's ready, willing, and able to tempt her back into his arms.

"What are you doing here?"

She regretted the words as soon as they came out of her mouth. It was a rude way to greet the man, even though he had no business messing in her kitchen anymore.

He didn't appear to take offense. He went right on putting cream and sugar in her old "Favorite Teacher" mug. But he'd always taken his coffee straight.

"You haven't had your coffee yet this morning, have you? You still buy the best. I still make the best." He handed her coffee with that same old sloe-eyed, sleepy morning smile. "My daughter lives here."

"Is that how you got in?"

He sipped his own coffee. "She says she's getting married. She's not old enough, is she?"

"How old should she be?"

"Older than my little girl." He boosted himself up the

few inches that it took him to seat himself on the counter. His long legs dangled nearly to the floor. "I always liked Jamie. I thought he was really going to make something of himself. Pick up a couple of instruments, put a band together. He couldn't sing, but he had a good ear."

She let the "make something of himself" jibe sail past her ear.

"How did you get here? I didn't see a strange vehicle in the driveway."

"And you don't see a strange man in your kitchen. You know us both. I'm still driving the same pickup, the one I left here with."

"How old is that thing now?"

"I've lost track. But she had zero miles on her when I got her." He gave his signature wink. "Just like you."

"What a flattering comparison."

"More than you know. That pickup is the only thing I have left that I don't share, but Jordan needed it to haul some stuff." His eyes went soft, as though resting them on her felt good to him. "How've you been?"

"Fine."

"Your mom?"

"Not so fine." She tried to remember what had been going on in her life when she'd last heard from him. "You know she has cancer."

"No, I didn't know. I'm sorry." He wagged his head sadly. "Jordan said she'd moved back, but she didn't say why. How's she doing with it?"

"Jordan, or my mother? Coping, both of them." She took her mothering stance, arms folded. "You haven't given me one straight answer so far. Why are you here, Creed?"

"Jordan called to tell me she was getting married. Actually, she left a message on my new answering machine." He grinned proudly. "I can call from anywhere and check in. So I got this message from her saying she had some news. I was coming into town anyway, so I . . ."

Her undeniable curiosity must have shown, because he was quick to explain. "I've got a gig. Haven't had one here in a long time." His smile seemed almost apologetic. "Yeah, I'm still at it. And, yeah, I still work construction to pay the bills."

"So why are you here," she repeated with exaggerated patience, "in *this house?*"

"Like I said, Jordan called. Talked to her last night. She called again this morning, wanting to use the pickup. She said you were gone with the van."

"That's right," Camille recalled. "She told me she needed it today."

"Said you'd been gone all night." He shrugged diffidently. " 'Course, we weren't worried."

"I left—"

"I haven't seen the boy yet. What's he like now? Still smart? Still . . ." A trace of the worry he'd disclaimed appeared in his eyes. "I know he's not a boy, and I know I missed my chance to send the bad ones packing and give the good ones fair warning. I left it all to you. He'll treat her right, won't he?"

"I hope so," she said with a sigh. "What am I saying? If he doesn't, she's outta there." Another double take. "*What am I saying?* They'll treat each other right."

"Like partners?"

"They'll make it, Creed."

"They haven't yet?" He gave a nervous laugh. "Just kidding. I don't want to know. I'd have to break his neck, and I don't think that would look too good. A neck brace with a tux." Hunkering down, he propped his elbows on his knees and cradled his coffee between his hands. "She's got her heart set on a fancy wedding, huh?"

"Fancier than ours was, I guess."

"A ten-dollar chapel in Vegas with an Elvis impersonator would be fancier than ours was." His eyes smiled for hers, hauling her into their private memory. "But the wedding night was a different story, wasn't it?"

"It wasn't fancy."

"Neither is heaven."

"Oh?" She raised her brow. "When were *you* last there?"

CURSE MAKES VISCOUNT THE MOST UNMARRIAGEABLE MAN IN ENGLAND

Who Will Take This Man?
by Jacquie D'Alessandro
October 2003

[London, England] Word is out! Philip Ravensly, Viscount Greybourne, is the victim of a curse, making him completely unmarriageable. Despite all attempts by Meredith Chilton-Grizedale, the Matchmaker of Mayfair, to find him a suitable bride, he remains unwed. Then the viscount begins viewing *her* as a potential mate . . .

Lord Greybourne stepped in front of her. His brown eyes simmered with anger, although there was no mistaking his concern. Reaching out, he gently grasped her shoulders. "I'm sorry you were subjected to such inexcusable rudeness and crude innuendo. Are you all right?"

Meredith simply stared at him for several seconds. Clearly he believed she was distraught due to the duke's remark, which cast aspersions upon Lord Greybourne's . . . manliness. Little did Lord Greybourne know that, thanks to her past, very little shocked Meredith. And as for the validity of the duke's claim, she could not fathom that anyone could so much as look at Lord Greybourne and have a doubt regarding his masculinity.

Lowering her hands from her mouth, she swallowed to find her voice. "I'm fine."

"Well, I'm not. I'd have to place myself firmly in the category of 'vastly annoyed.' " His gaze roamed over her face and his hands tightened on her shoulders. "You're not going to faint again, are you?"

"Certainly not." She stepped back, and his hands lowered to his sides. The warm imprint from his palms seeped through her gown, shooting tingles down her arms. "You may place me firmly in the category of 'females who do not succumb to vapors.' "

He cocked a brow. "I happen to know that is not precisely true."

"The episode at St. Paul's was an aberration, I assure you."

While he did not appear entirely convinced, he said, "Glad to hear it."

Clearing her throat, she said, "You came to my defense in a very gentlemanly way. Thank you."

A wry smile lifted one corner of his mouth. "I'm certain you don't mean to sound so surprised."

Indeed, she was surprised—stunned actually—although she had not meant to sound as if she were. But she'd have to reflect upon that later. Right now there were other, bigger issues to contemplate.

Unable to stand still, Meredith paced in front of him. "Unfortunately, with the duke's news, we must now recategorize our situation from 'bad' to 'utterly disastrous.' Your bride is well and truly lost, thus doing away with our plan for you to marry on the twenty-second, and my reputation as a matchmaker is in tatters. And with your father's ill health, time is short." Her mind raced. "There must be a way to somehow turn this situation around. But how?"

"I'm open to suggestions. Even if we are successful in finding the missing piece of stone, my marrying is out of the question without a bride." He shook his head and a humorless sound escaped him. "Between this curse hanging over me, the unflattering story in the newspaper, and the gossip Lord Hedington alluded to circulating about my ability to . . . perform, it seems that the answer to the question posed in today's issue of *The Times* is yes—the cursed viscount *is* the most unmarriageable man in England."

Unmarriageable. The word echoed through Meredith's mind. Damnation, there must be a way—

She abruptly halted her pacing and swung around to

face him. "Unmarriageable," she repeated, her drawn out pronunciation of the word in direct contrast to her runaway thoughts. She stroked her jaw and slowly nodded. "Yes, one might very well christen you The Most Unmarriageable Man in England."

He inclined his head in a mock bow. "A title of dubious honor. And one I'm surprised you sound so . . . enthusiastic about. Perhaps you'd care to share your thoughts?"

"Actually I was thinking you exhibited a moment of brilliance, my lord."

He walked toward her, his gaze never wavering from hers, not stopping until only two feet separated them. Awareness skittered down her spine, and she forced herself to stand her ground when everything inside her urged her to retreat.

"A *moment* of brilliance? In sharp contrast to all my other moments, I suppose. A lovely compliment, although your stunned tone when uttering it took off a bit of the shine. And brilliant though I may be—albeit only for a moment—I'm afraid I'm in the dark as to what I said to inspire you so."

"I think we can agree that Lady Sarah marrying Lord Weycroft places us both in an awkward situation." At his nod, she continued, "Well then, if you are The Most Unmarriageable Man in England, and it seems quite clear you are, the matchmaker who could marry you off would score an incredible coup." She lifted her brows. "If I were successful in such an undertaking, you would gain a wife, and my reputation would be reinstated."

He adjusted his spectacles, clearly pondering her words. "My moment of brilliance clearly remains upon me as I'm following your thought process, and what you've described is a good plan. However, I cannot marry unless I am able to break the curse."

"Which a brilliant man such as yourself will certainly be able to do."

"*If* we are able to locate the missing piece of the Stone of Tears. Assuming we are successful, whom did you have in mind that I would marry?"

Meredith's brow puckered, and she once again commenced pacing. "Hmm. Yes, that is problematic. Yet surely in all of London there must be one unsuperstitious woman willing to be courted by a cursed, gossip-ridden viscount of questionable masculinity who will most likely fill their homes with ancient relics."

"I beg you to cease before all these complimentary words swell my head."

She ignored his dust-dry tone and continued pacing. "Of course, in order to ensure the reinstatement of my reputation, I must match you with just the perfect woman. Not just any woman will do."

"Well, thank goodness for that."

"But who?" She paced, puzzling it over in her mind, then halted and snapped her fingers. "Of course! The perfect woman for The Most Unmarriageable Man in England is The Most Unmarriageable Woman in England!"

"Ah. Yes, she sounds delightful."

Again she ignored him. "I can see the Society pages now—England's Most Unmarriageable Man Weds England's Most Unmarriageable Woman—and praise to Meredith Chilton-Grizedale, the acclaimed Matchmaker of Mayfair, for bringing them together." She pursed her lips and tapped her index finger against her chin. "But who is this Most Unmarriageable Woman?"

He cleared his throat. "Actually, I believe I know."

Meredith halted and turned toward him eagerly. "Excellent. Who?"

"You, Miss Chilton-Grizedale. By the time Society reads tomorrow's edition of *The Times, you* will be the Most Unmarriageable Woman in England."

WOMAN MARRIED FOR JUST SIX DISASTROUS HOURS STUNS CITY WITH MURDER CASE INVOLVEMENT

Kill the Competition
by Stephanie Bond
November 2003

[Atlanta, GA] Belinda Hennessey moves to Atlanta to escape all memories of her six-hour marriage. Her new friends are a hoot—they pass time spent in traffic writing an advice book on marriage and men. But the new job is *murder*—literally. When a dead body turns up at the office, Belinda fears for her life. Luckily, she's already acquainted with Officer Wade Alexander . . .

The police cruiser's blue light came on, bathing Belinda's cheeks with condemning heat each time it passed over her face. The officer was male—that she could tell from the span of his shoulders. And he wasn't happy—that she could tell from the way he banged his hand against the steering wheel. Since the cruiser sat at an angle and since her left bumper was imbedded in his right rear fender and since his right signal light still blinked, he apparently had been attempting to change lanes when she'd nailed him.

The officer gestured for her to pull over to the right. When traffic yielded, he pulled away first, eliciting another sickening scrape as their cars disengaged. She followed like a disobedient child, and despite the odd skew of her car and an ominous noise that sounded like *potato potato potato* (probably because she was hungry), managed to pull onto the narrow shoulder behind him. The driver side door of the squad car swung open, and long uniform-clad legs emerged. Belinda swallowed hard.

"Whip up some tears," Libby said.

"What?"

"Hurry, before he gets back here."

"I can't—owww!" She rubbed her fingers over the tender skin on the back of her arm where Libby had pinched the heck out of her. Tears sprang to her eyes, partly from the pain and partly from the awfulness of the situation. She tried to blink away the moisture but wound up overflowing. She was wiping at her eyes when a sharp rap sounded on her window.

"Uh-oh," Carole whispered. "He looks pissed."

An understatement. The officer was scowling, his dark hair hand-ruffled, his shadowed jaw clenched. Belinda zoomed down the window and waited.

"Is everyone okay?" he barked. Bloodshot eyes—maybe gray, maybe blue—blazed from a rocky face.

"Y-yes."

"Then save the tears."

She blinked. "I beg your pardon?"

Libby leaned forward. "My friend is late for an important meeting, Officer."

He eyed Belinda without sympathy. "That makes two of us. I need your driver's license, registration, and proof of insurance, ma'am."

Belinda reached for her purse, which had landed at her feet. "I'm sorry, Officer. I didn't see you."

"Yes, ma'am, these big white cars with sirens really blend."

He glanced at her license, then back at her.

"It's me," she mumbled. The worst driver's license photograph in history—she'd been suffering from the flu, and for some reason, wearing a Mickey Mouse sweatshirt had seemed like a good idea. She was relatively certain that a copy of the humiliating photograph was posted on bulletin boards in DMV break rooms across the state of Ohio.

"I'll be right back."

He circled around to record the numbers on her license plate, then returned to his car, every footfall proclaiming his frustration for inexperienced, un-photogenic female drivers. He used his radio presumably to report her vitals. She'd never been in trouble in her life, but her gut clenched with the absurd notion that some computer glitch might finger her as a lawless fugitive—kidnapper, forger, murderer.

The crunch of gravel signaled the officer's approach. She opened her eyes, but the flat line of his mouth caused the Berry Bonanza with calcium to roil in her stomach.

"Do you live in Cincinnati, Ms. Hennessey?"

"No, I moved here two months ago."

A muscle worked in his jaw as he scribbled on a ticket pad. "I need your address, please."

She recited it as he wrote.

"You were supposed to obtain a Georgia driver's license within thirty days of moving here."

His tone pushed her pulse higher. "I didn't know."

He tore off one, two, three tickets, then thrust them into her hand. "Now you do." He unbuttoned his cuff and began rolling up his sleeve. "I need for you ladies to move to my car, please."

Belinda gaped. "You're hauling us in?"

The officer looked heavenward, then back. "No, ma'am. You have a flat tire and at this time of day, it'll take forever for your road service to get here."

She pressed her lips together, thinking this probably wasn't the best time to say she didn't have a road service. Or a cell phone to *call* a road service.

He nodded toward the cruiser. "You'll be safer in my car than standing on the side of the road."

"I . . . thank you."

He didn't look up. "Yes, ma'am. Will you pop the trunk?"

While the women scrambled out of the car, Belinda released the trunk latch, but the resulting *click* didn't sound right. She opened her door a few inches, then slid out, bracing herself against the traffic wind that threatened to suck her into the path of oncoming cars. The toes of her shoes brushed the uneven edge of the blacktop, and she almost tripped. Her dress clung to her thighs, and her hair whipped her cheeks. The rush of danger was strangely exhilarating, strangely . . . *alluring*.

Then a large hand clamped onto her shoulder, guiding her to the back of the car and comparative safety. "That's a good way to become a statistic," he shouted over the road noise.

She tilted her head to look into reproachful eyes, and pain flickered in the back of her neck. Tomorrow she'd be stiff. "This is very nice of you," she yelled, gesturing as if she were playing charades.

He simply shrugged, as if to say he would've done the same for anyone. Dark stubble stained his jaw, and for the first time she noticed his navy uniform was a bit rumpled. He frowned and jerked a thumb toward the cruiser. "You should join your friends, ma'am."

At best, he probably thought she was an airhead. At worst, a flirt. She pointed. "The trunk release didn't sound right."

He wedged his fingers into the seam that outlined the trunk lid, and gave a tug. "I think it's just stuck." Indeed, on the next tug, the lid sprang open. He twisted to inspect the latch as he worked the mechanism with his fingers. "The latch is bent but fixable." He raised the trunk lid and winced. "I assume the spare tire is underneath all this stuff."

A sheepish flush crawled over her as she surveyed the brimming contents. "I'll empty it."

He checked his watch. "I'll help. Anything personal in here?"

She shook her head in defeat. Nothing that she could think of, and what did it matter anyway?

But her degradation climbed as he removed item after item that, in his hands, seemed mundane to the point of intimate—a ten-pound bag of kitty litter, a twelve-pack of Diet Pepsi, a pair of old running shoes with curled toes, an orange Frisbee, a grungy Cincinnati Reds windbreaker, a *Love Songs of the '90s* CD, two empty Pringles Potato Chips canisters (she'd heard a person could do all kinds of crafty things with them), and two gray plastic crates of reference books she'd been conveying to her cubicle one armload at a time.

Her gaze landed on a tiny blue pillow wedged between the crates, and she cringed. Unwilling to share that particular souvenir of her life, she reached in while he was bent away from her and stuffed it into her shoulder bag.

"I'll get the rest of it," he said.

She nodded and scooted out of the way. "Can I help with—"

"No." He looked up at her, then massaged the bridge of his nose. "No, ma'am. Please."

Glad for the escape, Belinda retreated to the cruiser, picking her way through gravel and mud, steeling herself against the gusts of wind. The girls had crowded into the backseat, so she opened the front passenger door and slid inside, then shut it behind her. The console of the police car was guy-heaven—buttons and lights and gizmos galore. The radio emitted bursts of static. No one said anything for a full thirty seconds.

"How much are the fines?" Carole asked.

She gave up on her hopeless hair and pulled out the three citations signed by—she squinted at the scrawl—Lt. W. Alexander. After adding the numbers in her head, she laid her head back on the headrest. "Two hundred and twenty-five dollars."

"Ooo," they chorused.

Ooo was right.

CLASS REUNION REUNITES "PERFECT" COUPLE CAN LOVE SURVIVE BAD '80s COVER BAND MUSIC?

Where Is He Now?
by Jennifer Greene
December 2003

[Michigan] Teen toasts of the town reunite! Man Most Likely to Succeed Nick Donneli and Most Popular Jeanne Cassiday brace themselves for their class reunion. It's time to discover who still has bad hair, to see who *really* became a doctor . . . and to figure out if they can have another chance at love. It's true that sometimes maturity isn't all it's cracked up to be . . . but sometimes love really is better the second time around . . .

"Boots."

The sudden masculine voice shocked her like a gunshot . . . but that voice wrapped around her old nickname—the nickname only one man had ever called her—punched her right in the heart and squeezed tight.

It took only a second for her to turn around, but in that second, she saw the round clock with the white face on the far wall. The photographs of old cars—so many they filled one wall like wallpaper. The red leather couch, the red stone counter—furnishings that seemed crazy for a garage, but then, what the Sam Hill did she know about mechanics and garages? She also saw the pearl-choking Martha drop her aggressive stance in a blink when it finally became obvious that Nick Donneli really did know her.

"Mr. Donneli," Martha said swiftly and sincerely, "I'm terribly sorry if I misunderstood this situation. I was trying to protect you from—"

"I know you were, Martha, and you're a wonderful protector. But the lady thinks she's looking for my father instead of me. That's what the source of the confusion is."

"I see." Martha obviously didn't.

Jeanne didn't either. She was pretty sure she'd get what was going on in a second. Or ten. But she needed a minute to breathe, to gulp in some poise, to lock onto some sense somehow.

Only damn. Temporarily her heart still felt sucker punched. Her pulse started galloping and refused to calm down.

He looked just like he always did. More mature, of course. But those dark, sexy eyes were just as wicked, could still make a girl think, *Oh, yes, please take my virginity; please do anything you want, I don't care*. He still had the cocky, defensive, bad-boy chin. The dark hair, with the one shock on his temple that wouldn't stay brushed. The thin mouth and strong jaw, and shoulders so square you'd think they were huge, when he wasn't that huge. He just had so damn much personality that he seemed big.

He was. So handsome. So in-your-face male. So take-on-all-comers wolf.

And double damn, but he'd called her Boots.

She hadn't heard the nickname in all these years. Hadn't and didn't want to. But the fact that he even remembered it completely threw her. For God's sake, she'd been over her head, over her heart, over her life in love with him, and believed he'd felt the same way about her. Then suddenly he'd sent that cold note from Princeton: *Life's changed for me. Everything's different. I'm moving on. I don't want to hurt you, but this relationship isn't going any further. You go on with your life, find someone else. I'm never coming back.*

Those weren't the exact words. She didn't remember

the exact words, because it wasn't the words themselves that had devastated her. It was going from one day when she'd believed herself loved, when she'd loved him more than her life, believed she knew him, believed he was The One. Her Prince. The Only Man For her.

To being hurled out of his life after a semester in college because he'd "moved on"—as if that were some kind of explanation. As if real love could die as easily as a mood change.

She'd been stunned. So stunned, she realized now, that it wasn't as simple as being hurt. It rocked her world. And it was from that instant, that time when she'd been knocked flat and crushed, that she'd started down a different road. She'd started making choices she'd never wanted to make. She'd started doing what other people wanted her to do.

It was that letter. His rejection. His dropping her the way he had. That was the catalyst for her losing Jeanne Claire Cassiday. And she'd never found herself since then.

And whatever she'd meant to say, on seeing him again, what came out was "Damn it, Stretch!"